HEARTS INN

HEARTS INN

Lily R. Mason

SAPPHIRE BOOKS

SALINAS, CALIFORNIA

Editor - Tara Young
Book Design - LJ Reynolds
Cover Design - Treehouse Studio

Sapphire Books Publishing, LLC
P.O. Box 8142
Salinas, CA 93912
www.sapphirebooks.com

Printed in the United States of America
First Edition – November 2018

This and other Sapphire Books titles can be found at
www.sapphirebooks.com

Dedication

For anyone who ever found themselves in an unexpected desert.

Acknowledgments

This book would not be what it is without the dozens of people who helped me write it: first and foremost, my longtime collaborator and friend Muriel, who challenges me to make my stories thirty-three percent angstier; the team of beta readers who gave me feedback that made the story so much better; the people who read my previous work and assured me I could be signed by a publisher; the corners of the internet that aren't horrible; my parents, who took me to New Mexico as a child; my writing group friends Lynn and Autumn who offered enthusiasm and companionship during the writing process; my editor Tara with her sharp eye and cheerful notes; and Chris, whose faith in me and made this process smooth and easy to navigate. Thank you all!

Chapter One

Vacancy

Rosalie Campbell didn't know what she'd expected to accomplish before her thirtieth birthday, but it certainly didn't include becoming the manager of a shitty motel in the middle of nowhere. Behind the counter in the lobby of the once-beautiful Hearth Inn, she picked at her nail polish, listening to the drone of the antique air conditioner as it battled with the New Mexico heat. It had been two weeks since Gran had died and one week since Rosalie had arrived to deal with the estate.

A guest came into the lobby, ruddy complexion highlighted by how sweaty she was. She was round to the point that it looked like someone had inflated her torso and it extended out to her fingers. She spoke to Rosalie in rapid Spanish, the strange and familiar cadence of mumbled couplets and triplets sending Rosalie into a panic.

Rosalie hated when this happened. It rarely did back home in Philadelphia, but here in Ashhawk, New Mexico, it had happened a dozen times already. A practiced shame flowed through her, heating her face and making her hands fidget. She felt like an interloper: a girl who looked Latina but didn't speak a word of Spanish.

"Um, sorry," she said. "I don't speak Spanish."

She hoped the woman wouldn't look at her strangely or laugh at her.

"Oh, uh…" The woman fought giving her a judgmental expression. "We need more towels."

"What room?"

"Six," the woman said. "Some might say *seis*."

Rosalie looked down at the counter. "I'll bring some right over."

The woman left, and Rosalie paused a moment before following her out of the drab lobby, heat overwhelming her as she walked in front of the hotel. The hotel stood two stories high with little balconies on the top level, and its crumbling exterior was an eyesore. She noted the obvious areas for upgrades: paint the exterior, derust the window frames, replace the dilapidated chairs outside the rooms where guests sat smoking cigarettes and drinking beer near the parking lot. The faded sign of the Hearth Inn that was peeling and sorry for the wear. Several letters were so faint the sign looked like it read *Heat In*. It was apropos; the heat was the only constant in the town aside from the trickle of truckers and the plodding of time. Below the sign was a small sign reading *Vacancy*, with a hook in front of it where she would hang the part of the sign reading *No* if she were to sell out the rooms. The rusted hook hadn't been used in years.

As she opened the door to the housekeeping room, Rosalie was met with more dry heat and the choking smell of fabric softener, chemicals, and lint. She held her breath as she found a stack of haphazardly folded towels. The room was filthy, the corners almost obscured by dirt and lint, while the rest of the floor had a layer of fine desert dust spread across it, such that it crunched under her shoes. The shelves opposite the washer and dryer were unorganized and full of empty bottles and rags worn to threads. As she turned to go, she almost tripped over a bottle of bleach that sat uncapped on the floor next to the door.

Rosalie slammed the towels down on top of the dryer and looked around for the cap. Had the housekeeper really left an open bottle of bleach right there where someone could trip over it?

Rosalie looked all over for the cap and was about to give up hope of finding it when she spotted it tucked in the corner behind the door, cozying up to a large insect Rosalie didn't recognize, belly-up, legs curled.

Rosalie couldn't hold in a noise of disgust as she gingerly reached for the cap with two fingers, lifting it out of the dust away from the insect and screwing the cap on the bottle. She slung the bottle onto the lowest shelf and grabbed the towels, eager to leave the room.

When she'd arrived at the hotel for the first time in fifteen years, she realized her childhood memories of the place had been rosy; snapshots of splashing in the pool while Gran watched, roasting marshmallows behind the building, and walking down the street to get pizza every summer were miles away from the rundown building that stood in the same spot. Rosalie only intended to stay in Ashhawk for as long as it took to sell the place and get back to her life in Philadelphia. She couldn't imagine living here for longer than a few weeks. How Gran had lived here for forty years baffled her.

Rosalie knocked on the door of room six, bracing herself with an obligatory customer service smile. When the door opened, she held the towels forward. The woman grabbed them without a word of thanks, then said, "You know, our bathroom isn't very clean."

Rosalie tried to maintain her professional smile, though her will to do so vanished.

"I'll get someone to come clean it." Rosalie gritted her teeth to avoid snapping at the woman. She wished she could tell her she was no happier with the accommodations herself, that she'd been saddled with this shitty hotel and had no more desire to run it than she wanted to clean the woman's bathroom.

Rosalie went back to the housekeeping room, tied up her long, dark hair, and put on a housekeeping apron. She bit her lip the entire time she scrubbed the bathroom, mouth pulled together tight to avoid cursing at the guests. When she finished, she went back into the lobby, relishing the coolness but choking on the Freon-thickness of the air. She opened a rickety file cabinet, flipped to the sparse personnel files, and opened the record of the single other employee currently working at Hearth Inn, an old woman named Susan who couldn't see six inches in front of her face.

When Rosalie had seen the poor state of things, her first impulse had been to fire Susan. But there weren't enough hours in the day for Rosalie to do all the housekeeping herself, and Susan had worked at Hearth for thirty-five years. Rosalie didn't want to fire her without an immediate replacement and plan for her retirement. Rosalie was there temporarily, and Susan appeared to be related to one of the local Native tribes.

Rosalie sat back down behind the counter, trying to make sense of a business she knew nothing about. Having a degree in accounting, Rosalie had foolishly thought she should know how to run the business until she could sell it. It couldn't be too hard, so long as the rooms were clean and there were no bedbugs. She could manage the books and the payroll and, if worse came to worse, call law enforcement to ask some of the less savory guests to leave. But the job was proving more difficult than she imagined, which made her miss the predictability of her nine-to-five office job in a clean, well-maintained building in Philadelphia terribly.

The lobby was more spacious than it needed to be. A worn carpet bearing the brands of local ranchers stretched from the tired wooden counter across the large room to a stone fireplace that hadn't seen a flame in decades. There was a single sagging couch set against the window opposite the door, and light strained in through dusty blinds. A weary plant drooped in the corner. The walls and furniture were too dark, all wood and forest greens and browns. At twenty-nine years old, with her pink blouse and lively brown eyes, Rosalie was the youngest thing in the room. But listening to the drone of the air conditioner drown out her computer speakers as the Internet struggled to load even the simplest pages, Rosalie felt herself aging.

As she flipped through a file reading REV MGMT 07, the air conditioner in the window sputtered and coughed. Used to the constant drone, Rosalie looked up. The lights flickered. She held her breath, hoping it was a blip. The lights came back on, then flickered off again, remaining off as the air conditioner whined to a halt, leaving Rosalie in a silent panic.

She turned to her computer, determined to call a handyman to come fix whatever had gone wrong, but realized the Internet wouldn't work without power. Her cellphone got some data service in this part of the state, though it was unreliable. Rosalie figured it was her bad luck when no signal came up and even a basic search yielded a blank page.

A large man in a denim shirt with the sleeves pulled off opened the door, letting the bells clang against the glass. He was a regular who came to stay when he and his "lady friend" were on the outs.

"Power's out," he said.

"Sorry about that. I'm working on it."

The man nodded and turned his burly body back toward the outside of the hotel.

"You wouldn't happen to know any reputable electricians in town, would you?" Rosalie asked.

"Check the fuse box first. No use paying for an electrician to come flip a switch for you."

Rosalie bit her lip and nodded, feeling foolish. She was a numbers and lines girl, not someone useful with her hands. She debated asking the man if he knew where the fuse box was but didn't want to embarrass herself.

Rosalie left the fading chill of the office and wandered around the building. She had no idea where the circuit breaker might be, but looking for it was better than doing nothing. She walked around the building, finding nothing resembling a utility box, though she did locate the gas meter. Then she remembered the maintenance shed out back where there had once been a fire pit for roasting marshmallows.

The land at the back of the hotel sat crisping in the sun, the cracked earth and scraggly, dry shrubbery appearing exactly as they had fifteen years ago. A pile of bricks lay forgotten where the fire pit used to be. The land stretched on and on out into the desert, and Rosalie wasn't sure where the property line was. In the distance were sage-colored hills, appearing motionless by day but alive with the sound of coyotes at night.

Daring to enter the rundown shed with its clutter

of old tools and cobwebs, Rosalie saw a promising lead—a metal box against the wall. Grateful it wasn't locked or too far inside the hazardous shed, she opened it, squinting to see one of the main breakers was flipped in the wrong direction. Faintly proud of herself, she reached forward. But before her hand met the switch, anxiety took hold of her. What if there was something wrong with the electrical system? What if she got shocked or electrocuted? Glad the soles of her shoes were rubber, she lifted the hem of her blouse, feeling it pull tight around her waist, and used the material to flip the switch from off to on. She heard a few air conditioning units shake back on toward the hotel, but nothing else happened. She let her shirt fall back against her body and tiptoed out of the shed, careful not to let her foot catch on a wayward shovel.

Back in the office, the lights were on, the printer was making a faint buzzing sound, and nothing was on fire. But after the door closed behind her and the bells clanged, she realized her air conditioner hadn't come back to life. She approached it, frowning at the ancient monstrosity. She turned the dials and pressed all the buttons, but nothing happened. She unplugged it and plugged it in again, hoping it just needed a reboot. Still nothing happened.

Fed up with the crumbling building, Rosalie let out an exasperated sigh. Living in New Mexico was bad enough *with* air conditioning. She debated retreating to her room to lose herself in a book but knew she needed to work if she was to ever escape Ashhawk.

She plopped down in her swiveling chair, twisting her hair into a bun that unraveled down her back as soon as she leaned forward. She Googled *HVAC Ashhawk*, hoping for a few seconds as the Internet chugged along that a decent result would appear. But the closest HVAC service was in Albuquerque. Rosalie couldn't live without the AC, so she packed up her laptop, locked the front door, taped up a sign with her cellphone number on it, and got into Gran's vintage Oldsmobile parked outside. The diner down the street would have air conditioning, Internet, and most importantly, coffee.

Rosalie drove down the street, taking in the sleepy buildings and faded signs of the storefronts. When she'd arrived back in Ashhawk, she was struck by how rundown it was from baking in the Southwest sun for so long. It was as though time had left it behind, and the residents who hadn't left limped along its pothole-ridden streets in beat-up cars and rattly old trucks. Freight truckers came through on occasion but not at the rate they had before the mega truck stop had been built one town up. The town wanted for everything but heat and sky.

Ashhawk's inhabitants were half rednecks with beer guts and nicotine stains on their teeth and half granola-eating hippies who had wandered away from Santa Fe. Rosalie wasn't sure whom she wanted to steer clear of more—the men who ogled her from under their sweat-stained baseball caps or the women with straggly braided hair asking her what her sun sign was. On both sides were descendants of Hispanic settlers and several Native American tribes forced to relocate or assimilate countless times in the last two hundred years. It was an odd combination of people to run into at the gas station or drugstore.

A few well-meaning townspeople had come to visit Rosalie during her first week in town. A woman wearing a ghastly teal blouse, her cheeks ruddy and her gut spilling over her jeans, came bearing a sausage casserole, saying she hoped to see Rosalie at the next Catholic service. Another woman came sliding into the hotel lobby on silent sandals, wearing a hemp skirt, bearing a vegan lasagna. She invited Rosalie to a yoga and meditation group and made a few unsolicited suggestions for effective aromatherapy. Not wanting to engage with either side of town, Rosalie had kept to herself. Cleaning up after Susan and organizing the last twenty years of files kept her busy enough.

Rosalie pulled into the parking lot of the diner and slipped inside, eager for the relief of cool air and caffeine. The waitress working the afternoon shift was young and attractive, with blond hair and pale pink skin that stuck out among the tan-skinned masses of Ashhawk. Rosalie studied her painted nails, simple jewelry, and a figure that didn't stretch or pull her white-cuffed diner uniform. She didn't wear a name tag, and Rosalie couldn't discern anything about her other than she wasn't a redneck or a hippie. Without a topic of conversation, she retreated to a table with her laptop.

Since the last time she'd been in Ashhawk, Rosalie had busied herself with school, work, and a few relationships. The latest girl, Tara, had crept along the boundary of Rosalie's comfort zone while Rosalie debated how far to let her in. She adored Tara's company, and she knew the ease with which they conversed was rare. But she found herself needling through Tara's personality for flaws, looking for a reason to avoid entanglement. She hadn't found any but had kept Tara at a distance that was perhaps unnecessary.

Just when she'd decided to step into their relationship with both feet, Rosalie had gotten the news she was now the owner of a shoddy hotel in the middle of nowhere, and they had agreed to reassess where they were when Rosalie returned. They'd talked on the phone once since Rosalie had arrived in Ashhawk, but the conversation had been superficial. Rosalie didn't know if she should be relieved or sad about it.

Rosalie decided to look through pictures of her friends on Facebook to remind herself of home. A picture of Tara and some of her friends popped up first thing. Looking at her didn't bring on the sadness or guilt she'd expected. She missed Tara, but only in the way she missed many things about Philadelphia. Tara was familiar, while everything in Ashhawk was not. She felt only a dull ache paired with a familiar comfort.

She tried not to miss anything too hard, as she didn't think of herself as a sentimental person. With any luck, she'd be out of Ashhawk and back to her accounting job soon. Her employer had given her a generous six weeks off with guaranteed job security. She tried to think of her life as being on an uncomfortable pause for a few weeks. It was easier to endure that way.

When the waitress brought over her coffee, Rosalie looked up, clicking out of Facebook and murmuring her thanks. She thought for a moment she should try to strike up a conversation but couldn't find the energy or a topic. She figured it wasn't worth putting forth effort to make new friends anyway. She was only here until she figured out how to manage the hotel from afar or sell it for more than pennies.

After ordering coffee, she busied herself with actual work. Her task for the day was to explore how much it would cost to set up a functioning website for the inn that included a booking agent. If she could increase occupancy, it would be more attractive to potential buyers, but building a website was time-consuming and slow. She thought back to the lobby and figured she ought to do something about the air conditioner.

Rosalie stood and walked to the counter.

"Is your coffee okay?" the waitress asked, looking up.

"Yeah, yeah. Hey, you wouldn't happen to know a handyman around town, would you?"

The waitress looked as though she was surprised to be asked about something besides coffee. "Like someone to build and fix stuff?"

Rosalie nodded. "I just took over the Hearth Inn for Estelle Campbell. I need a little help with maintenance."

"Ohhh," the waitress said. "Umm..." She glanced around the register before reaching for an old receipt. "There's this guy Ralph lots of people call. He can fix anything." She scribbled a name on the receipt, then paused, scrunching up her nose in apology. "I don't know his number."

Someone at the counter piped up. "You looking for Ralph Ecker?"

The waitress turned her head toward the man. "Yeah."

"I got his number." The man shifted in his seat to take out his phone. It was a silver flip phone, something Rosalie hadn't seen in years. He opened it, sliding it along the counter toward Rosalie with a grin Rosalie couldn't decide was friendly or predatory.

Rosalie tried not to touch the phone as she copied down the number and slid the receipt into her purse, noticing the man's body odor and stained hat.

"Thanks."

Rosalie retreated to her table again. All too soon, her phone rang, and she had to return to the hotel where a disgruntled guest was looking for her to unclog his toilet. If the trucker who had clogged it couldn't figure out the problem, Rosalie sure as hell couldn't. Rosalie tried to conceal her disgust as she called a plumber. Then she retreated to her room and found the receipt with Ralph's number on it.

By the sound of his voice, Ralph was an older man, his voice etched with years of smoke and breathing in desert dust. Rosalie pictured him with a bushy mustache and paunch, though not as unkempt as some of the other local men.

"Hi, I'm at Hearth Inn, and I've got an AC unit that just quit on me. Any chance you'd be able to help me out?"

"'Fraid I'm tied up at the drugstore helping them with their refrigerator unit this afternoon. I might be able to come by tomorrow. Where'd you say you were?"

"I just took over the Hearth Inn for Estelle Campbell. I'm her granddaughter."

"Oh! Why didn't you say so? Let me send my kid Alex your way. Twenty minutes okay?"

Rosalie exhaled in relief. "Sounds great."

"No problem," Ralph said. "Take care now."

Rosalie hung up and lay back on her bed, relieved to have figured at least one thing out for the day.

She decided to rest for the twenty minutes she had before the handyman arrived. She stared at the popcorn ceiling. It was probably filled with asbestos. She ought to have it inspected. The thought of how much its removal would cost gave her a sick feeling in her stomach.

Rosalie hadn't brought many of her own belongings, so everything in the room from the appliances to the bedspread to the wall decorations was Gran's. There was nothing, save for Rosalie's computer and phone, indicating it was the twenty-first century. The same could be said for the rest of the hotel. Rosalie did intend to address the décor problem to make the hotel more attractive to buyers but had no idea where to start. The tacky gold-framed stock art? The faded polyester bedspreads? The textured wallpaper? The cracking lampshades? Rosalie wondered if it might be less work to raze the building and start from scratch or burn it down for the insurance.

It didn't feel like twenty minutes before Rosalie heard a knock on her door. She jolted up, feeling guilty to have been caught daydreaming. She rushed toward the door, expecting to be greeted by a younger but just as heat-toughened man as Ralph had sounded.

But instead she found a woman—perhaps five years older than herself—with warm, tan skin, light brown eyes, and curly chestnut hair pulled back into a low ponytail. She had a stoic look to her face, a long nose, and a small, serious mouth. Her shoulders were square and strong, her stance androgynous, though her long eyelashes and curly hair offset any confusion about whether she was female. She wore a plain black tank top, straight-cut jeans, and work boots, without a stitch of makeup or jewelry.

"Uh…hi," Rosalie greeted. "Can I help you?"

"My dad said your AC went out." Her voice was sturdy, neither too high nor too low for her body.

"Oh! You're Alex. Yeah, in the lobby."

Rosalie stepped out of her room and shut the door so Alex wouldn't see how shabby her accommodations were.

Rosalie walked the short distance to the lobby door, unlocking it and leading Alex inside. The temperature of the room had already risen to an uncomfortable swelter.

"How'd you know which room was mine?" Rosalie asked.

"I lived here for a few months while I was doing some repairs for Estelle."

"What did you repair?"

As soon as she said it, Rosalie realized she sounded critical. The hotel was in such disarray, it was hard to imagine Gran had done any maintenance at all. She'd made it sound as though Alex was responsible.

Alex stared at Rosalie, unsmiling. "Other air conditioners."

Rosalie felt herself warm with embarrassment. "This one's the same," she said, pointing to the machine that had sighed its last breath of cool air hours before.

Alex moved toward the rusting old machine, crouching in front of it before giving a stiff nod. "No problem," she said. "I'll get my tools."

Rosalie gave a grateful nod, hoping Alex would forgive her tactless comment. She retrieved her laptop from her room and sat in the sweltering office for the next hour while Alex worked.

Frustrated with trying to set up the website, Rosalie began browsing commercial real estate agents. She couldn't find any in the area with a decent website, which didn't bolster any confidence. She didn't know who to trust for guidance.

The office phone rang just as Rosalie was about to give up her search for the day. Hoping it was someone calling to book a room, she picked up with her usual response:

"Hearth Inn, this is Rosalie speaking. How may I help you?"

"May I speak to Estelle Campbell, please?"

It was awkward to respond to people asking for Gran. "She's deceased. I'm her granddaughter."

"Oh...I'm so sorry," the man said. "Hmm, well, do you know who I might get in touch with about her estate?"

"Her estate has been settled," Rosalie said, wary. "I was the sole beneficiary."

"Oh, then you're the person I want to talk to. My name is George Tackett, and I'm with Shaylin Development Inc. I'm calling in regard to a piece of property in Ashhawk. We're interested in buying and wondered if there might be a time to set up a meeting."

Dumbfounded an opportunity to sell the hotel had fallen into her lap, Rosalie sputtered. "Uh, yeah. Sure. I'm free any time."

"Wonderful," George said. "I'll be out your way next week. Does Tuesday afternoon work?"

"Absolutely," Rosalie said, relief spilling over her as though the air conditioner was working again.

"Where would be the best place for you to meet?"

"Right here on the property. It's hard for me to get away."

There was a pause, and Rosalie wondered if their connection had been disrupted.

Then George spoke. "We are talking about the property at 578 Cocheta Way, correct?"

Rosalie frowned. "The address here is 682 Mohan Drive."

"Oh, I'm sorry. Are you also the beneficiary of the property on Cocheta Way?"

Rosalie thought back to the many phone calls and meetings she'd had with Gran's lawyer. Not once had another piece of property been mentioned.

"I'm not aware of any such property."

George hummed. "Would you be able to give me the name and number of the late Mrs. Campbell's counsel?"

Recalling the nervous twitching and fragmented way Gran's lawyer spoke, Rosalie didn't think it was a good idea to give his name out to an opportunistic business developer like George Tackett.

"I'm sorry, I can't. I'd be more than happy to speak with you about the property on Mohan Drive, though." Her mind hopped to the next step—getting a real estate lawyer and consulting with anyone who might help her get the best deal out of the property.

"Unfortunately, our client is only interested in the Cocheta property," George said.

Rosalie sank into her chair. She had been so hopeful. "I'm sorry to hear that. Please let me know if you ever need accommodations in Ashhawk."

"Will do. Good day, Miss Campbell."

She hung up, feeling the heat of the room overtake her.

Alex kept her back to Rosalie, her attention focused on the air conditioner. Though she'd given no indication she was listening to Rosalie's half of the conversation, she spoke.

"You trying to sell this place?"

Rosalie looked up, feeling a surprising flicker of guilt. "Maybe."

Alex was quiet for a moment before she said, "Probably a tough sell these days."

"Yeah." Rosalie sank lower in her chair at the

suggestion she might be doomed to stay in Ashhawk longer than she intended.

Alex said nothing as she worked on the heavy white machine, her arms and back flexing in her tank top. Her skin was smooth and taut over her muscles. A sheen of sweat made her even more of a distraction. Rosalie caught herself staring and felt her own brow prickle with sweat. She wiped it away and got up to fill a cup with water. But as she tried the tab on the water cooler, she found the cooler was empty. Of course it was; nothing in this stupid hotel worked.

Rather than disrupt Alex's work by asking if she might be able to help heave a giant water cooler jug up onto the stand, Rosalie walked across the street to the convenience store and bought two bottles of ice cold water. She brought them back into the lobby, offering one to Alex, who accepted it with a stiff smile.

After another twenty minutes of tinkering, Alex stood and wiped her hands on her jeans. She pressed a button and the machine jerked on, vibrating the whole wall before it found its rhythm. Rosalie felt a cool breeze on her damp face.

"Fixed," Alex said, as though it was unclear.

"You're a lifesaver," Rosalie said, hoping to make up for her snide comment earlier.

Alex looked at her, expressionless. "Just a handywoman."

Rosalie asked how much she owed Alex for her services. She pulled out a checkbook and was in the middle of writing a check when Alex strode out the door. Rosalie was bewildered until Alex walked back into the lobby with two huge water cooler jugs on her shoulders.

Rosalie bounded up from the desk, not knowing

how to help with the heavy load.

"Careful," she warned.

Alex walked over to the cooler and plopped a jug in, sighing as it gurgled and glugged into place, air bubbles blasting through it until it settled.

"Thank you," Rosalie said.

"No problem."

"I'll call you if I need anything else fixed." Rosalie smiled genuinely this time.

"Please do." Alex gave a faint smile as she rested her hands on her hips. "I'd hate to see this place fall apart."

Rosalie held a check for Alex's hourly rate plus tip forward, and Alex took it before collecting her tools and leaving without ceremony.

No sooner had Alex's truck rumbled out of the parking lot, a guest came into the lobby reporting yet another clogged toilet. Disheartened, Rosalie called the plumber again.

The hotel was not going to let her go without a fight.

⁂

As she tried to fall asleep that night, Rosalie heard coyote pups howling in the distance, their calls pinched into whiny yips. Rosalie thought of Gran and how she'd loved those coyote calls. She hoped wherever Gran was now she could hear the coyote calls, too.

Chapter Two

Short-term Guest

Rosalie was sound asleep when her phone rang. She answered, sleepy panic seizing her, hoping something hadn't happened to her parents.

"Morning, sweetie!" Marisol chirped. Her tone indicated nothing was amiss.

Rosalie squinted in the dim light of her room, eyes crusty with sleep and desert dust. "*Mom*, it's six thirty in the morning," she grumbled.

"Oh, sorry, I forgot the time difference." Marisol giggled. "Well, I've woken you up anyway. How is it there?"

Rosalie sat up in bed, feeling her back seize and whine from the crappy old mattress she had to sleep on. She felt where her sleep shirt was sticking to her body. "It's okay."

"Tell me all about it," Marisol said. Rosalie could hear shuffling, as though Marisol were out shopping or walking briskly down the street.

"It's so freaking *hot* here, Mom," Rosalie said, letting her morning creakiness seep into her voice. "I don't remember it being this hot when I was younger."

"Yeah, I heard you're having quite a heat wave. You've got the pool, though, right?"

Rosalie pictured the crumbling pool outside without a drop of water in it. "It's not filled right now."

"Are you joking? Fill it up, silly! You've got to keep your guests happy."

"They're not *my* guests," Rosalie said, trying not to sound grumpy. "I'm just running the place for now."

"Well, you're doing great, sweetie."

Rosalie had the sneaking suspicion Marisol was already distracted. On the rare occasions she had her mother's attention, she was eager to hold on to it.

"How are you? Is everything good with Dad? And Ahbie?"

Ahbie was Marisol's mother, whom Rosalie had named Ahbie as a child in lieu of calling her *Abuela*. If Ahbie hadn't been so enamored with her only grandchild, she might have lectured Marisol about what a disgrace it was that Rosalie didn't speak a word of Spanish.

"Yeah, yeah, they're good," Marisol said. "Dad's got some new book he's reading about owls. He was going on and on about it the other night."

It was quiet as Rosalie pictured her father, Frank, cradling an open book in one large hand, gesturing with it with as much enthusiasm as he ever had about anything, which wasn't much. He was gentle and warm like Gran, hardworking and soft spoken like his father had been. As he spoke, Marisol would nod in circles and give him a blank smile, all the while planning an outfit for some activity he wasn't involved in. Perhaps the most unfortunate thing about being in Ashhawk was leaving her father to grieve the sudden loss of his mother alone. He'd seemed as steady as ever at the funeral, but he was quick to leave town when it was over. He hadn't even stayed the night in the hotel. Like Rosalie, he kept his emotions carefully guarded.

Rosalie felt sorry for her dad and made a note to

call him and ask him which owls were indigenous to New Mexico.

"Sorry, sweetie, I've just run into Carla, and I have to ask her how the twins are doing. Give my love to Gran!" Marisol chirped before making kissy noises and hanging up.

Rosalie sat there, not sure if she should be more stunned by her mother's sudden hang-up or the fact Marisol had forgotten her mother-in-law was dead. Gran being dead was the entire reason Rosalie was there.

It was possible Marisol had meant Rosalie was to *metaphorically* give Marisol's love to Gran as an underhanded way of encouraging Rosalie to be more assertive with the way she managed the hotel, but Rosalie couldn't be sure.

She put her face in her hands, wishing she'd had a calmer start to her day.

Rosalie didn't begrudge her mother her zeal for life. If anything, she wished she had it for herself. But when it did bother her, it had more to do with how little space Rosalie felt she took up in her mother's life. She sometimes felt no different from Marisol's bridge club or softball team or Thai cooking class or whatever her latest hobby was. Perhaps motherhood had been another whim of hers, one which she tired of and decided to move on from. Marisol was never cold or deliberately neglectful of Rosalie. She simply had a great appetite for life, and being a doting parent was too inconvenient for most of the adventures Marisol craved.

Rosalie and her father had often been left to their own devices for dinner and on weekends. They got along well, with little need for superficial conversation.

They watched the news and talked about books and played chess. The household was always calm until Marisol came crashing in late at night.

Sighing and wishing again she was anywhere but Ashhawk, Rosalie looked around the room. Gran's suite was dingy and dated. The bed was not too far from a counter, a small stove, mini-fridge, and microwave. On the other side of the bed was a wall with a door leading to an adjoining room currently set up for occupancy. In front of Rosalie was a card table with two folding chairs and a TV hanging over it.

Gran's ashes sat in a wooden box on the table. At first, Rosalie had thought it was creepy to have the remains of her Gran sitting there, but she'd grown accustomed to them.

When she'd first picked up the ashes from the cremation center, she'd set them on the table without thinking; she'd noticed later that she'd set them next to the framed photograph of herself Gran had kept by the door to show anyone who came to visit.

Rosalie had put the photo away, trying to tamp down the swell of guilt she felt for not visiting in almost fifteen years.

The ashes didn't feel entirely dead yet, and Rosalie wasn't sure what to do with them. She knew it would sound ridiculous if she said it out loud, but sometimes, she felt there was some spirit or energy around the ashes Rosalie couldn't name. She didn't think she was alone when she had the box in her sight. Or at least she wanted to believe she wasn't. Gran's presence had always been soothing.

Through a small doorway to the left of the table was a closet and a large bathroom. Drooping off all the walls were small framed pictures of cats or faded still-life paintings that gave the room anything but life. Taking it all in, Rosalie wished she could go back to sleep and pretend she wasn't stuck in New Mexico. But knowing things didn't get done unless she did them, Rosalie took a shower, made coffee, and went outside to survey the building. Perhaps if she stared long enough, she'd figure out what to do with it.

Thinking of her conversation with her mother, she walked over to examine the pool, long since dried out, tiles crumbling and laying on the bottom of the basin with a few empty beer cans in the faded blue basin some seven feet deep. It wasn't a large pool in diameter, but it was deep enough for a slide. A metal fence enclosed the area, its gate locked in a halfhearted effort to prevent local teens from daring each other to jump into it with their skateboards. The fence was rusty and needed to be repainted.

Rosalie decided she'd make a list of all the things needing repair to make the property more attractive to buyers. She finished her coffee and found a yellow legal pad, walking around as she surveyed the exterior. The list she made was long; everything needed to be painted, reinforced, cleaned, or replaced. After completing a preliminary list, she went back into the office, overwhelmed and dreading another hot day.

After examining Gran's financial records from previous years for the fifth time to calm herself and make sure she wasn't missing anything, Rosalie began drafting a new operating budget. With the current occupancy, there wasn't much to work with, but the situation wasn't dire. She'd have to be strategic in what she worked on. Thinking a functioning pool would be a singular perk to having to live in Ashhawk, Rosalie decided to get a quote for its repair first.

When the Internet failed her again in finding someone who could help her, she called Ralph. Ralph answered in his scruffy voice, sounding busy before she'd even said a word. When she inquired if Ralph knew anyone who could come look at her pool, he responded, "You call Alex? I bet she'd give you a good estimate."

"Oh, really?" Rosalie didn't think air conditioner repair and pool repair were related, but apparently, Alex Ecker was a woman of many talents. "Can I get her number?"

Cheerful but brief, Ralph gave Rosalie Alex's number and hung up.

Rosalie wrote the number in purple pen on a yellow Post-It. It wasn't a pretty color combination. She wished she'd used black or blue ink. But her numbers were neat and looped, and there was something pleasing to the way the numbers were centered in the square. She pressed the Post-It on the wall of the counter beside her computer but didn't pick up the phone. She wasn't sure why. She only knew Alex made her feel like a useless city girl.

Instead, she went to the diner for lunch, figuring it would be a nice change from a microwave meal. She brought her computer, intent on using the fast Wi-Fi to do some more work on the website and booking engine. The waitress from the day before was there, and Rosalie found herself watching her, admiring the efficient movement of her hips as she navigated tables and worked behind the counter. Her uniform was neat and pressed, the powder blue complementing her pale skin and straw-blond hair. Her ponytail was smooth and shiny, her eyebrows perfectly arched. Her skin had a few blemishes, which she'd covered with industrial-strength concealer. She smiled halfheartedly at diners, wearily revealing crooked teeth. She was pretty, and Rosalie hoped she wasn't staring at her too much.

Rosalie liked the waitress' posture. It was an odd thing to find attractive, she knew, but Tara had told Rosalie a few months ago her posture was soothing. Rosalie had found it an unlikely compliment but had accepted it as it was meant to be: a gesture of grace and goodwill from someone she found attractive, as well. Their whole relationship had been small gestures of goodwill and companionship, but not once had fireworks gone off. Rosalie supposed it was childish to want such things; only teenage girls wanted the drama of grand gestures. She hadn't earned a grand gesture, either, with the uncertain way she kept Tara at arm's length.

Feeling guilty, Rosalie pulled up Tara's Facebook page. She was greeted by the same profile picture Tara had had of herself at the Grand Canyon since Rosalie had known her. Aside from a picture a friend had uploaded, there was nothing new on Tara's page. Since Rosalie and Tara had never put their relationship on Facebook, there was no change in status to be concerned about.

Rosalie felt the urge to text Tara. She needed Tara to be an option when she got home and started putting her life back together. She pulled out her phone, wondering what she might say to indicate she was thinking about her without seeming desperate for reassurance. She settled for snapping a picture of her sandwich, sending it to Tara with the caption, *It's nowhere near as good as Zippy's*, with a sad face emoji. She didn't hear back, but Tara was probably busy at work.

When Rosalie finished her sandwich, the waitress came over to give her the bill and clear her place. She hovered by the table as Rosalie concentrated on the website.

"Hey, um, you said you're running the Hearth Inn now, right?"

Rosalie looked up, surprised the waitress had initiated conversation with her. "Yeah."

The waitress shifted on her feet, looking uncomfortable. "Do you need any help? Like, cleaning or working the desk or anything?"

Rosalie thought of the dirty housekeeping closet Susan maintained and the sorry state of the rooms. She thought of the endless hours she spent cooped up in the too-big lobby with nothing but the drone of the air conditioner to listen to. She would have loved some company—especially such attractive company as the waitress—but knew she couldn't afford a full-time salary on what Hearth was bringing in.

"Actually, yeah. I could use someone at the desk here and there. I have some meetings in the next few weeks, and I need someone to cover for me."

The waitress' face lit up. She was even prettier when she smiled genuinely.

"Come by when you get off," Rosalie said. "I'm there…almost always."

The waitress nodded, extending a shaky hand. "I'm Shelley, by the way."

"Rosalie."

Rosalie took Shelley's hand before Shelley reached for Rosalie's plate, doing an awkward shuffle before moving to take it behind the counter. Rosalie watched her. It would be nice to have Shelley around a few hours a week.

When Rosalie grew restless in the almost-empty diner, she headed back to the hotel. She pulled into her parking spot, and the pool caught her eye again. Telling herself it was foolish not to fix things, she found Alex's number and called her. The exchange was brief, and before she knew it, Alex's truck rattled into the parking lot.

Alex frowned into the dry blue pit and nodded. "Four hundred," Alex said, then walked off behind the building. Rosalie didn't know what she was doing until Alex reappeared with a ladder. Rosalie took a few steps toward her, offering to help lower the ladder into the pit as a way of accepting Alex's bid, but Alex glanced at her as though to say her offer was appreciated but ultimately unhelpful.

Rosalie felt her presence was annoying to Alex. She had no brawn or practical knowledge Alex would find useful, so she retreated into the office, moving her chair so she could see the pool through the glass doors. She wondered why Alex was so quiet. Was it because Rosalie was an outsider? Or was she this way with everyone? Whatever the reason, Rosalie felt awkward around her.

As she plodded her way through finishing up the homepage of the website, she watched as Alex disappeared around the building again, reappearing with a large, dark bundle she began unfolding. Rosalie frowned until she realized Alex had retrieved a collapsible canopy from the storage shed. She recalled Alex saying she'd done work at the hotel before and wondered if perhaps Alex was better acquainted with the property than Rosalie herself.

Having secured some flimsy shade, Alex lowered herself into the empty pool, disappearing from sight.

Rosalie craned her neck over the desk, curious what Alex was doing but not wanting to be a nuisance.

The people of Ashhawk were a mystery to Rosalie. They seemed content to stay in their depressed town, their bodies sluggish and their faces tired. Without office jobs to attend or concerts to go to or trendy bars to frequent, Rosalie wondered what they did all day and night while she was stuck in the Freon-chilled lobby or curled on her uncomfortable bed reading or watching reruns of *The Office*.

She wondered what Alex did when she wasn't working odd jobs. Did she go to bars? Watch TV? Spend time with family? Despite having been to Ashhawk many times as a child, Rosalie had no idea what small-town life was like.

After half an hour, Rosalie realized Alex didn't have access to the cooler down in the pool. She filled a cup with chilled water that sweated through the glass. She ventured into the heat, feeling Alex needed water more than anyone else in Ashhawk.

Down in the pool, Alex was filling several large cracks with some type of plaster or putty. She scraped it on with a tool, smoothing it so once it dried, the pool could be painted and filled and look like new. Despite the weak shade covering the section of the pool where Alex was working, Rosalie could see Alex was sweating. She felt guilty for not calling Alex first thing in the morning before the heat got too bad.

Rosalie cleared her throat, alerting Alex to her presence. Alex looked up, squinting at the bright light where Rosalie stood before her, straightening up to reach for the glass with a weary "thank you."

Rosalie had to crouch to hand it to her. As she did, she felt heat radiate up from the painted plaster of the pool walls.

"If it gets too hot, you can take a break," Rosalie encouraged. "You're welcome to work on it in the evenings or early mornings when it's cooler. As long as it gets done in the next week or two."

Alex gave a stiff nod, looking back at her work.

"Should take me three days, long as I can find tiles like these." She pointed to the crumbling row of decorative tiles around the edge, and Rosalie wondered where someone might find such tiles in a town like this.

Not having any knowledge or other conversation topics, Rosalie stood there awkwardly. She didn't want to sit alone in the office any longer than she had to. She hoped Alex would say something or initiate conversation to help pass some time or at least make her feel welcome, but Alex was focused on her work. Rosalie gave up and slunk back to the office.

At the end of the day, Alex packed up the canopy and returned the ladder to the shed. Rosalie thought she would come into the lobby to say goodbye, but she got into her truck and started the engine. Rosalie walked to the door, watching as Alex pulled out of the parking lot.

Ten minutes later, Shelley came in, looking around. Rosalie welcomed her and explained how she might be able to help her. She asked Shelley about her work experience and was stunned to hear Shelley had been working at the diner since she was sixteen and had never had another job. Shelley had to be at least twenty-five now. Rosalie couldn't imagine doing the same mundane jobs she'd had as a teen into her twenties.

Rosalie went over the check-in process and showed Shelley where all the keys were kept.

"As you can see, we're still in the Dark Ages and use actual keys." Rosalie had been surprised Gran hadn't updated to keycard entry, but the entire town felt like it was lagging twenty years behind the rest of the country, so it wasn't too shocking.

"Have you ever seen one of the rooms?" Rosalie asked.

"Yeah, my boyfriend and I sometimes came here for a night or two before he moved in with me."

Rosalie tried not to deflate at the mention of Shelley's boyfriend. She hadn't been hoping for anything romantic with Shelley; she was still dating Tara, and she didn't plan to stay in Ashhawk longer than necessary. But it would have been nice to meet one other girl who liked girls. She was beginning to wonder if she was the only lesbian in New Mexico.

Rosalie had never hired anyone before, and the whole exchange felt unorganized and informal. But knowing Shelley was there to help if Rosalie needed to meet with a real estate agent or go searching for pool tiles was a relief.

When she'd exhausted every possible business matter Shelley might need to know, Rosalie felt the urge to keep her there. She didn't have any friends in town, so she extended an invitation.

"Do you want a hard cider or something?"

"Oh, no, thanks. I don't drink," Shelley said.

Rosalie was surprised. Shelley would have fit in at pretty much any sorority at Rosalie's college, with her bright blond hair and exact makeup. Rosalie had pegged her as a party girl.

"I have ginger ale," Rosalie offered.

When Shelley looked uncertain, Rosalie explained herself. "I haven't talked to anyone our age since I got here two weeks ago, but I understand if you need to get home."

Shelley smiled. "How old are you?"

"I'm twenty-nine."

Shelley's smile grew. "I'm twenty-five. Ginger ale sounds good."

Rosalie smiled in relief and ducked into the back room to retrieve two ginger ales.

"You're welcome to have hard cider," Shelley said. "I don't mind."

"I'm fine with this," Rosalie said, examining the ginger ale can. "Probably better for me anyway."

Shelley nodded, and there was an awkward silence. Rosalie gestured toward the couch. They walked across the lobby and sat down, the silence following them.

"I'm fine with people drinking around me. I choose not to drink because of my dad," Shelley said. "I figure if he's got a problem, I'm probably wired for it, too, so I'd rather not risk anything, you know?"

Rosalie nodded, surprised at how forthcoming Shelley was. People in Ashhawk were strikingly honest. Rosalie had discovered her complexion and affiliation with Gran went far; people were willing to talk to her.

"Sounds smart."

Shelley shrugged, as though to refute Rosalie's assertion. "I just want a better life for me and Bobby."

Rosalie tried to make polite conversation. "How long have you been together?"

"Since sophomore year."

"Where'd you go to college?"

There was a loaded pause during which Rosalie realized Shelley had meant sophomore year of high school.

Rosalie didn't know anyone who had stayed with a high school sweetheart. She hadn't even had a high school sweetheart; her straight best friend whom she hadn't spoken to in a few years didn't count.

"I don't know anyone our age who's been with someone that long."

Shelley smiled. "He's pretty great. I want to get married, but he's been out of work for a while, so not anytime soon. He might have to move to Albuquerque if he doesn't find something here soon."

Rosalie nodded, not knowing what to say.

"Most of the young people around here move away for work anyway." Shelley sounded sad, as though she'd slowly been deserted by all her friends.

"Would you go with him?"

Shelley gave an uncomfortable shrug. "Someone has to take care of my dad," she said after a moment. "We live with him."

Rosalie felt herself sink. She felt bad for Shelley. No twenty-five-year-old deserved to be stuck at home taking care of her parent.

"What does your dad do?"

"Drink," Shelley said. "He's been out of work for a while, too."

Rosalie felt herself sink lower. Driving through the rundown town and seeing how depressed the buildings were was hard enough. Hearing how the people in the town Gran loved so much were suffering too was worse.

"I wish there was something I could do," Rosalie said.

Shelley shrugged, sitting up straighter, as though realizing she was being a downer. "Letting me work here once in a while is plenty."

Thinking of how much responsibility Shelley had compared to the responsibilities Rosalie had had at her age, Rosalie felt generous.

"Would you like to do some cleaning here, too?"

Shelley's face lit up but backed down with hesitation. "I could use the money," she said. "But don't feel like you have to offer me work because I told you my sad story. Plenty of people have it worse."

"I know," Rosalie said, realizing she'd turned her pity into money. "But I could use the help."

"Okay." Shelley took a sip of her ginger ale. "So do you have a boyfriend back home?"

Rosalie gave an amused half-laugh. She usually corrected people's assumption she liked men in certain contexts, but here in Ashhawk where people probably believed they had never met a gay person, Rosalie was out of her element.

"Eh...my relationship is kind of up in the air right now."

"Well, it's a good thing you're not totally single. Most guys our age here are unemployed or drink too much."

Rosalie bit her lip and lifted her eyebrows as she nodded in amused agreement. She realized being the loneliest lesbian in the Southwest had its drawbacks, but being a single straight girl wouldn't be much better.

Shelley left a few minutes later after expressing appreciation for whatever work Rosalie had for her. Despite her initial friendliness, Rosalie could tell she was eager to go home to her boyfriend. Rosalie was sad her efforts to make a friend hadn't worked.

After heating up her Lean Cuisine, Rosalie debated watching reruns of *The Office*, as had become her routine. But sitting alone in Gran's sad little room wasn't something she wanted to do. Instead, she picked up one of the chairs from outside her room and walked along the building with it.

Facing the street from the front of the hotel, the sky was vermillion and fuchsia and gold, as though all the colors the sun sucked from the earth during the day were concentrated and projected into the sky for one glorious hour, saturated past their previous glory.

But Rosalie took her chair behind the hotel, into the shade, staring out at the dusty shrubs and the skyline where the sky was faded lavender and ashy gray. The desert stretched out before her, completely still, almost lifeless save for the occasional flicker of a lizard. Rosalie felt small and fragile in her chair, balancing the flimsy microwave meal on her lap.

A few feet away, Rosalie saw a pile of bricks that had once been the fire pit she and Gran had loved to sit around after dark, telling stories and roasting hot dogs and making s'mores. The fire pit had crumbled since the last time she'd visited, like so many other things in town. Rosalie wondered if Gran had ever come out here by herself and contemplated the vast, unmoving desert or if Gran had been as lonely in Ashhawk as she was.

Wanting to reassure herself her stay in Ashhawk was temporary, Rosalie took out her phone and called Tara. She grew nervous as she waited for her to pick up, wondering what they'd have to say to each other. Tara answered, her sweet, low voice soothing despite their state of limbo.

"Hello?"

"Hi," Rosalie said, hoping she didn't sound too sad.

"Hi," Tara said. "How's it going?"

Rosalie looked down at her sad little meal, balanced on her pinched knees. "Okay, I guess."

There was a moment of quiet.

"How are you?" Rosalie asked.

The question felt jerky and obligatory, a building block in a contrived conversation. She didn't know what she would say after they'd greeted each other. She only wanted to fill a few minutes of time.

"I'm okay," Tara said. "I'm headed out to meet Ashley and Missy."

Ashley and Missy were a couple they'd hung out with together a few times in recent months. It was odd to think of Tara spending time with them without Rosalie, but Rosalie didn't say so. "Say hi to them for me. Where are you guys going?"

"To Zippy's."

Rosalie was quiet for a minute. Tara going to their favorite restaurant without her made the desert feel even more oppressive.

"Can you send me a sandwich?" Rosalie asked, trying to keep the conversation light.

"Sure," Tara said. Rosalie could hear her smile. "I'd ask you to send us some cooler weather in return, but I know you don't have any to send."

"No kidding," Rosalie grumbled. "Although I'm outside right now, and it's not awful. It gets cold at night."

"Huh," Tara said. "Where are you?"

"Sitting behind the hotel." Rosalie glanced around her at the dry shrubs and bricks. "I wanted a change of scenery from the office."

"I bet," Tara said.

It was quiet, and Rosalie cringed. She needed to be reassured her life was still waiting for her in

Philadelphia, but having a forced conversation with Tara was not helpful in the least.

"I miss you," Rosalie said, desperate for some kind of affirmation.

"I miss you, too," Tara said. Her words felt rote and rife with obligation.

"Hopefully, I'll be heading back soon."

"Hopefully," Tara said.

It was quiet again. It pained Rosalie to have so little to say.

"Well...say hi to Ashley and Missy for me," she offered. "Call me if you want to chat. I'm pretty much always bored."

"Okay," Tara said. "I will."

It was quiet again, and Rosalie knew Tara's promise was empty.

"Talk to you later."

"Later," Tara echoed.

Hanging up, Rosalie had even less of an idea of where they stood.

Rosalie felt her muscles tighten and weight push down on her shoulders until she felt she would break. Tears pushed up her throat and she curled forward, putting her face in her hands as she cried.

As foolish as it was, Rosalie wanted a firework. She wanted a grand gesture or declaration or passionate embrace. She wanted someone to come rescue her from this terrible place or to help her overhaul it for sale or to at least keep her company while she fixed the clogged toilets and crumbling pool and broken air conditioners. If nothing else, she wanted some sense of purpose in what she was doing. She wanted there to be some meaning to why she'd had to leave her life and come to this strange, depressed town.

For a fleeting moment, she wanted a fiery blooming of her relationship with Tara to be the reason. But she knew it wouldn't happen. Even if it had, Tara's presence in Ashhawk would be more uncomfortable than her absence. They were nowhere near the level of commitment or romance that would justify Tara coming to Ashhawk. Like the desert stretched before Rosalie, their relationship had been quiet and still.

At first, Rosalie thought she was missing someone or someplace or something. But thoughts of home and Tara and her job didn't comfort her. The feeling pressing down on her with unrelenting force wasn't missing something, it was the feeling of being utterly lost. She was stranded in an unfamiliar place, orphaned and abandoned, and she had no idea how long she'd be held captive.

She felt so heavy she worried she wouldn't be able to stand if she sat in her chair much longer. She was about to shuffle back to her room when something moved in the corner of her vision. Looking over, she saw a small gray cat slinking toward her.

She sat still, not wanting to scare it. It was thin and didn't have a collar. It didn't appear to have anyone looking after it.

Hesitantly, the cat slunk toward Rosalie, as though gauging whether or not she was safe. Rosalie let her hand drift down to the cat's level, offering it for the cat to sniff. The cat approached, growing bolder, and pressed its wet nose to Rosalie's hand before rubbing its brow against Rosalie's hand.

"Hey, buddy," Rosalie cooed, keeping her voice low. "Are you lost, too?"

The cat head-butted her hand with more force, a hint of a purr vibrating through it.

"Yeah, I don't have anyone taking care of me, either," Rosalie murmured.

She studied the thin frame of the cat. It wasn't starving, but it probably had to work hard for its meals. Birds and small prey camouflaged well in the desert.

"Are you hungry?" Rosalie asked.

The cat kept nuzzling Rosalie's hand, then slunk toward her legs, weaving around them, pressing its side into her shins as its purrs grew louder.

"What a sweet little thing you are."

She felt silly talking to a cat, but the cat was bringing her more comfort than Tara had.

The cat took a few steps away, and Rosalie wondered if she had offended it. Then the cat leapt up, knocking Rosalie's plastic dinner tray off her lap and sending her fork flying, rubbing against her stomach as it made itself comfortable.

She felt a smile overtake her face for the first time in hours, her heavy skin growing lighter.

"Hi," Rosalie said.

The cat continued purring, settling into her lap.

"Are you hungry?" Rosalie asked again. She ran her hand down the cat's back, feeling its vertebrae beneath its fur.

The cat looked around the desert with disinterest.

Rosalie sat rooted to her chair for a minute before she decided to get some food for the cat. She didn't have any on hand, but she knew the convenience store across the street sold cans. Carefully, she picked up the cat and stood. The cat didn't respond, only adjusted as Rosalie held it. If she hadn't been starved for companionship, Rosalie might have set the cat down to go buy food, but she didn't want the cat to wander away as she retrieved her purse and walked across the street. Her feet crunched on the asphalt of the parking lot and road as she crossed, feeling its heat radiate into her.

The air inside the store was stale and hinted at sugar, gasoline, and industrial cleaner. The row of refrigerators hummed, the beer and soda the freshest items in stock. The sound of indistinct Reggaeton radio followed Rosalie as she looked for cat food. The clerk, a Latino boy with reddish-brown, pocked skin and over-gelled hair, said nothing of her bringing an animal into the store. Rosalie wondered if he'd even looked up long enough to see what she was holding. The cat turned its head to watch its surroundings as Rosalie paid and left the store but otherwise remained inexpressive until Rosalie returned to the hotel.

Rosalie set the cat down in front of her room, sitting in one of the battered old chairs as she peeled the lid off the can of food.

"Here you go," Rosalie said in a baby voice. "Dinner."

The cat looked up at Rosalie before lowering its nose to sniff the food and began to eat enthusiastically, its jaw hinging as it tried to gobble down large chunks of wet food. Rosalie was glad she had made the cat happy. Helping Shelley and now this cat were the only good feelings she'd had since arriving in Ashhawk.

After the cat ate its dinner and licked the tin clean, pushing it along the cement a few inches, it hopped up on Rosalie's lap again, its tail swishing as it settled and cleaned its face and paws. Rosalie stroked its fur, appreciating the warm weight in her lap as the night chill of the desert set in. The dim, eerie glow of the exterior lights was soon the only light by which she could see, making everything ghostly and pale. When a hard shiver took her, she knew she needed to go inside.

"I gotta go inside now, buddy."

She lifted the objecting cat from her lap, setting it on the ground. When she opened her door, the cat tried to follow her inside.

"No, no," Rosalie said with pout. She realized she shouldn't have fed the cat if she didn't want it to attach to her. "I don't have a bed or litter box for you. I'm only here for a little while." The cat stared up at her, ears pointed up. "Come back tomorrow, and I'll give you some dinner again."

She knew it was silly to negotiate with a cat, but she had no one else to talk to. She closed her door and got in bed, trying not to think about the cat outside.

The next morning, Rosalie was surprised to see Alex's truck already in the parking lot as she made her way to the lobby to start her long day of hoping someone would buy the hotel. Looking down into the pool, she saw Alex had finished filling the cracks and was set up to start replacing the decorative tiles.

"You found the tiles," Rosalie said, glad to have a conversation topic.

Alex looked up. "Yeah, they weren't too hard to track down." She looked proud for a moment before she refocused on the task of chipping the old, broken tiles out so they could be replaced.

"Do you want anything?" Rosalie offered. "Coffee? Tea?"

"I'm okay for now," Alex said. "Maybe in a bit."

"Come in the lobby whenever you're ready for a break," Rosalie offered. She hovered by the edge of the pool for a minute until she was certain Alex wasn't going to say anything.

Rosalie considered that perhaps Alex resented

her for trying to sell the inn. The people of Ashhawk were distrustful of outsiders, and while Rosalie had been afforded familiarity on account of her relation to Gran, whoever purchased the hotel wouldn't receive the same courtesy. Seeing as no one in town could afford the hotel, Rosalie wondered if perhaps Alex begrudged her willingness to let strangers take over a local business.

Rosalie watched the pool area from the office for a few hours, venturing out as often as she could justify to bring Alex water and try to start a conversation. The row of tiles around the edge of the pool filled in. Rosalie found Alex's work ethic remarkable; she didn't know anyone else who could concentrate on such a mundane task for so long.

Around noon, Alex went across the street to buy food, and Rosalie felt guilty, as though she should have thought to offer Alex lunch. It was the least she could do. Rosalie would have invited Alex to eat in the lobby, but by the time she walked out, Alex had scarfed her food down and was back to work. Rosalie retreated, not wanting to be a nuisance.

Alex appeared in the lobby an hour later, sweat shimmering off her skin, collecting in small beads she wiped off her upper lip. She took her cup over to the cooler and filled it.

"How's it going out there?"

"Done for the day. Gotta let the plaster dry before I paint the basin."

"Cool."

The door of the lobby opened with a startling clang, and Rosalie looked up to see one of the residential guests of the hotel, a stocky middle-aged man named Jorge, walk in.

"The sink in my room is leaking everywhere," Jorge said, jerking his thumb back toward his room.

"Oh, gosh, I'm so sorry about that."

Rosalie's gaze darted up to Alex, pleading.

"I can take care of it," Alex offered, setting her glass on the counter.

"Thank you," Rosalie said, grateful. She wouldn't have known who to call.

"Show me what's happening," Alex said to Jorge, heading toward the door.

"Water started coming out from the cabinet under the sink..." Jorge said as he led Alex outside. The door shut behind them, and Rosalie was left in the quiet office.

Wanting a mental escape from the worries of Hearth, Rosalie pulled up her Facebook feed. As she scrolled, she came across a picture of Perene. Though they hadn't spoken in years, the pang that had dulled to a ping still pulsed in Rosalie's chest. It rang of affection, loss, and shame, now whittled down to manageable bites. Perene had brought forth the fear Rosalie had tamped down since her pubescence. Rosalie's fascination with changing bodies had extended to her friends beyond the physical and technical curiosities she justified it with; she had managed to logic her smothered jealousy over friends' boyfriends and crushes on shiny-faced Ryan Phillippe, Freddie Prinze Jr., JTT, and James Van Der Beek. But during their sophomore year of college, Perene had burst through all Rosalie's intellectualization with a simple press of lips against lips.

Rosalie had been insatiable then; whatever study rooms and deserted labs they could find to kiss and touch each other were made somehow sacred. They ate most of their meals together and were permanent fixtures in each other's rooms, to the annoyance of their roommates. Rosalie had been ecstatic to discover the force that made knees weak and schoolwork a distant priority to the work of soft words and touches.

But that didn't mean she was ready to shout its glories to the world. Always reserved, Rosalie had rerouted her formidable intellect from its former job of obscuring her sexuality from herself to the no less damaging task of preventing anyone from knowing she and Perene were a couple. It was no one's business, she said again and again. Why would they want to subject themselves to the leers and glares of every gross frat boy and homophobe on campus?

But Perene had seen through her defenses a second time, and after months of arguing and oceans of tears, Perene had ended things. Only then did Rosalie realize her shame and discomfort had been forcing her hand, not reason. She felt numb with her own stupidity, wondering why her aptitude for academics didn't carry over into understanding her own emotions.

Since then, Rosalie had ventured out of the closet slowly. First, she told a counselor at the student health center, then a few trusted friends, then her parents. All had responded with soft, mellow encouragement, if not a whiff of surprise. Her coming out had been almost painless, save for the loss of Perene.

The following years had been good to her, bringing a string of amiable girls content to let her step out in her own time, so long as the closet door wasn't welded shut. Rosalie had come out inch by inch until all her social contacts knew. She still preferred to test the waters for a month or so with professional and academic contacts, when it was necessary at all, but she was less inhibited.

Though she knew it wouldn't change the past, she wanted Perene to know how far she'd come. But it seemed laughable to send her a message out of the blue, expressing pride in something Perene had done so far before her. So she said nothing, wondering if Perene thought of her in the same sad, fond way.

Rosalie was jerked from her thoughts when Alex returned, pulling the door open and walking toward the desk. "Sorry, I got caught up talking to Jorge for a bit, but I know what the problem is." She picked up her water glass and took a drink.

Rosalie wondered what Alex and Jorge might have in common, other than living in Ashhawk and having a distant association with Hearth. She wished she could find some commonality with Alex.

"What?" Rosalie asked.

"The nut that connects the pipes to the sink basin is broken."

"Is it hard to fix?"

"Not at all," Alex said. "I bet you've got a few spares in the shed out back."

Rosalie nodded. "Let me know if you need to get materials."

Alex nodded, finishing her water. "Shouldn't take too long," she said, setting her glass down. "I'll let you know what I find."

Rosalie watched as Alex turned and exited the lobby, heading around the building toward the storage shed.

As the day wore on, Rosalie wondered what Alex was doing. Rosalie imagined Alex's arms as she fixed Jorge's sink, strong and flexing in her black tank. Or perhaps she was rooting through the shed with her feet planted solidly on the ground. Wherever she was, Rosalie felt she needed water. She refilled Alex's glass and ventured into the heat.

She found Alex inside the maintenance shed, bent over an old toolbox, sorting through parts Rosalie didn't know the names of.

"Hey," Rosalie called, not wanting to startle Alex.

Alex stood, back creaking as she righted herself and ran her wrist over her upper lip. "Hey," Alex responded, breathing heavily.

"How's it going?"

"Okay." Alex bobbed her hand and placed her hands on her hips.

"It's hot out here," Rosalie said, looking at the way Alex's golden skin glinted in the sun.

"No shit," Alex said, as though to call attention to the fact that Rosalie had the luxury of working in the air-conditioned office while Alex endured the sun's cruelty. "I finished up with the sink." She gestured toward the guest rooms. She squinted in the harsh light, shielding her eyes with her hand. "I was trying to find a few tools to finish the pool tomorrow."

"Here," Rosalie said, feeling guilty as she held the water toward Alex.

Alex reached forward as she wiped her brow with her other hand. She drank the water in a long, graceful motion, throat pulsing as she swallowed, body seeming to surge with gratitude for the coolness and hydration. She finished with a small gasp, wiping her lip and bringing the cup down before extending it back to Rosalie. She crouched down again, frowning at a stack of paint cans.

Watching Alex sort through the shed, Rosalie wondered if Alex liked girls. Rosalie knew it wasn't so simple, but Alex's appearance gave conflicting clues: She wore comfortable clothing and practical shoes and kept her hair, face, and nails natural. Her posture was strong and unapologetic, but she had a feminine fluidity to her. Alex's presentation confused Rosalie, and her inexpressive face didn't help.

Pushing her curiosity aside, Rosalie realized Alex probably worked up an appetite.

"I was thinking of making lasagna for dinner. Do you want some?"

Alex looked up, stoic for a moment before she responded. "Sure. Let me know when."

Rosalie wrung her hands. "Whenever you're hungry," she said. "I need, like, five minutes."

"To make lasagna?"

"It's microwave," Rosalie admitted. "I don't know how to cook. But I figured you must be hungry at the end of the day..." She trailed off, embarrassed she had thought offering to microwave a lasagna was generous.

But Alex nodded. "Sounds good," she said, glancing back at her work. "I'll look around here for another ten minutes. If I don't find what I need, I'll go get it tonight."

Rosalie squeezed her hands to keep from fidgeting. "It'll be ready in ten."

Ten minutes later, Rosalie took two single-serving lasagnas out of the microwave. They looked plain in their cardboard dishes, the cheese crusting on the sides, hints of ruffled noodles poking out around the edges. Maybe there was something she could sprinkle on it to make it look more appealing. Parsley, maybe? Dried oregano? Did those things go with lasagna? Before she could contemplate it further, she heard the door open and the bells clang against the glass, announcing Alex's presence.

Rosalie poked her head out of the back room with a nervous smile on her face. "Hi," she said. "It's still too hot."

Alex nodded, looking around the lobby, catching Rosalie's eye as she did. Rosalie wondered what her eyes saw that Rosalie didn't. Was there an obvious electrical problem? An unstable shelf affixed to the wall? Black mold growing somewhere? Rosalie wanted to know.

"Do you want to eat in here?" Rosalie asked.

Alex's face stayed expressionless. "I'd like a break from the heat," she said, sighing a little bit.

Rosalie nodded, realizing eating in the lobby was their only temperature-controlled option unless she planned to invite Alex back to her room to eat at her rickety card table and sit on her folding chairs staring at Gran's ashes, which she didn't. Gran's room was too depressing to spend much time in.

"I have hard cider, if you want," Rosalie offered, her mind flashing to the two bottles she had left in her room.

Alex smirked, as though she had expected as much. "It's okay. I'm heading to the Peso after this. They've got good beer on tap."

Of course Alex had plans for after work. Who with, Rosalie didn't know, but it seemed fitting Alex would go to a bar and have a tall, frothing glass of something rather than sitting in Rosalie's sad lobby.

As she contemplated what Alex might do after work, Rosalie wondered where Alex would go to meet girls, if she was so inclined. Was there somewhere in town, or did she have to go to Albuquerque or Santa Fe? Was it safe to be out in a town like Ashhawk? She had no idea what it meant to be a lesbian in this part of the country.

But of course, she didn't want to assume anything based on Alex's appearance.

"Is the Peso any good?" Rosalie asked, setting the lasagna on the desk. She pulled an extra chair out from the back room, deciding she would give Alex the cushioned rolling chair she sat in all day.

Alex ventured around the counter. "It gets the job done."

Rosalie nodded as though she knew what Alex was talking about. She imagined the bars in New Mexico weren't places she'd want to go—filled with smoke, truckers, and rednecks. She'd rather sit in her room drinking cider and eating microwave lasagna. If only she had some company.

"Is that the only bar in town?" Rosalie asked.

Alex shook her head, eyeing the rolling chair Rosalie had offered her before sitting in it, occupying it as though it were strange and too large. Her knees fell open and her arms draped over the armrests, but she looked stiff and uncertain.

"I forgot forks," Rosalie said, darting up to retrieve them from the back room. When she returned, Alex was turning the chair from side to side, looking a little more comfortable.

"There's also the Hog on Galisteo Street. It's owned by the Stewarts. Do you know them?"

Rosalie shook her head, eyeing her lasagna. "I only know you and the housekeeper and the blond waitress at the diner."

"Shelley," Alex offered.

"Are bars the only social scene around here?" Rosalie asked, trying not to wince at the possibility.

"Pretty much, unless you go to church or AA or something."

Rosalie grimaced, nodding as she took a bite of her lasagna.

"You look disappointed," Alex said.

Rosalie shrugged. "It's different here than back home. It's hard not knowing anyone."

Alex nodded as though she now understood why Rosalie was always hovering around her. "If you want a great social scene with a nice blend of small town and urban culture, my brother's got a place an hour south of Albuquerque. He does these weekend events called 'salons.' Drinks, music, entertainment, and stuff. He does different themes every month. I usually drive down for the men's weekends."

Rosalie was confused. Even if Alex wasn't especially feminine, she was pretty sure Alex didn't think of herself as a man.

"Men's weekends?"

"Gay men from all over the country. I'm usually the only girl, but it's fun."

Rosalie perked up at the mention of anyone who wasn't straight. She was desperate to believe she wasn't the only lesbian in Ashhawk, but short of flat out asking Alex if she was Sapphically inclined, there was no way to know.

But she could drop hints about her own orientation and see how Alex reacted. She calculated how much she wanted to share; if she outed herself, maybe Alex would grow cold and distant. Or maybe she would start to open up over their shared experience. Rosalie figured if Alex enjoyed hanging out with gay men, she was probably okay with gay women.

Steeling herself, Rosalie took a risk. "I went to

Provincetown for Women's Week with my girlfriend once."

"Oh, yeah?" Alex's expression was unreadable.

Rosalie felt her pulse surge. "It was fun. Kind of overwhelming, but fun."

"How long have you two been together?"

Rosalie felt her body relax, coming down from the anxious high of outing herself. Alex was accepting.

"Oh. Uh...we broke up. It was a while ago. But I have someone I'm seeing in Philadelphia. We met about five months ago."

Rosalie realized she wasn't prepared for this conversation. She'd felt so awful after talking to Tara the night before. "We're in a weird place right now."

"I'm sorry to hear that," Alex said. Her tone was formal.

"Yeah," Rosalie said, retreating from further talk of her personal life.

Alex was hard to read; she wasn't irked by Rosalie talking about Tara, but she hadn't warmed up, either. Maybe she was being polite. Rosalie didn't want to make Alex feel uncomfortable.

"It's funny what inheriting a shitty hotel can do to a girl's life."

"I imagine."

Rosalie felt Alex studying her, scrutinizing her. She busied herself with her lasagna. She wondered if she'd been foolish to out herself so hastily to one of the only people helping her in this strange town.

"You're trying to sell this place, right?"

Rosalie wriggled, trying to shrug but not committing to it without guilt.

"I haven't met with any real estate agents yet. It's overwhelming just to run this place day to day. And I feel bad because I know it meant a lot to Gran."

Alex sat forward, as though she were about to confide something in Rosalie. Rosalie braced herself for it.

"I got to know your grandmother a little bit a few years back. She was a real nice lady. Took care of people in this town as best she could."

Rosalie nodded, jarred by the sudden closeness and subject change. People had spoken to her about Gran since she'd arrived in Ashhawk, but not like this.

Alex continued. "As much as she loved this hotel, she wouldn't want you to feel stuck here because of it. She'd want you to be happy."

Rosalie felt her throat tighten, not because of the way Alex was reminiscing about Gran, but because Rosalie knew what Alex was saying was true. Gran was gentle and kind to everyone. She hadn't pushed for Rosalie to come visit her over the last decade, probably because Rosalie had been insolent and whiny the last few summers she'd come to visit. Her teenage self had resented being sent away from her involvement in clubs and petty social drama and charades of crushes on boys. Gran had known Rosalie didn't love Ashhawk and didn't try to make her visit. Now Gran was gone, fifteen years of summers with her had been lost, and Rosalie had nothing to show for it but a few concert tickets and a Rollerblading scar on her left knee. Thinking of how poorly she'd treated Gran, she felt even guiltier about selling the inn.

"Yeah," Rosalie said, hoping she wouldn't get emotional in front of Alex. "I think you're right."

Alex leaned back, a trace of a smile on her face as she used her fork to carve out a large bite of her lasagna and bring it to her mouth.

Eager to change the subject, Rosalie waited until Alex finished chewing before she asked, "Have you always lived in Ashhawk?"

Alex swallowed. "I've bounced around a bit. Did some apprentice work in Albuquerque, spent six months here and there. But I always land back here."

Rosalie tried to phrase her next question so it didn't hold the judgment she knew she had. "What brings you back?"

Alex let out a chuckle, as though she was as confused as Rosalie. "Family, friends. The comfort of the familiar."

Rosalie nodded, as though she understood how such things could bind someone to a place as dismal as Ashhawk. She knew Gran had loved Ashhawk, but she couldn't understand what would draw someone as young and capable as Alex back time after time.

"There's lots of space here," Alex continued. "It's easier to figure out what matters when there aren't five hundred things happening at once."

Rosalie nodded as though she understood how the desert could help bring clarity when all it did was parch and overwhelm her.

"Where did you say you were from?" Alex asked.

"Philadelphia," Rosalie said, relieved to be on a safer topic. "I've been there since college."

Alex's eyebrows lifted, and Rosalie wondered if perhaps she shouldn't have brought up her college education again, especially after how it had irked Shelley the night before.

"What do you do in Philly?" Alex asked.

"I work for a reinsurance company."

Alex frowned.

"Insurance for insurance companies. Corporate

CYA," Rosalie explained.

"Sounds like a lot of paperwork and math," Alex said.

"It was," Rosalie said, thinking back to her clean, reliably climate-controlled office with its view of another building's side.

"*Was*," Alex echoed. "Did you leave?"

"No," Rosalie said, startled she'd spoken of her job in the past tense. "I'm on leave while I get things taken care of here."

"And then you'll go back," Alex said, finishing Rosalie's sentence.

"That's the plan," Rosalie said, weary hope dragging in her words.

"Hmm." Alex studied Rosalie. "Do you like the work?"

Rosalie shrugged. "It has good benefits."

Rosalie realized too late it was a snobby thing to say. Most people in Ashhawk didn't have benefits.

"But do you like it?"

Rosalie couldn't bring herself to shrug again. "It's not bad."

Alex raised her eyebrows. "You should figure out if you like it before you get rid of this place."

"I do like it," Rosalie said, backpedaling through the discomfort Alex had brought up. "I want to go back."

Alex bobbed her head and finished her last bite of lasagna before she leaned forward, as though to get up. "Then you better get those real estate agent appointments lined up."

Rosalie remained seated, disarmed by Alex's frank advice.

"Thanks for dinner," Alex said. "Where should I

put my plate?"

"Leave it," Rosalie said, swatting the air.

"Okay," Alex said, standing. "I'll be back in the morning to paint the pool."

"Okay," Rosalie said, sorry to see Alex go, yet relieved she wouldn't have to think about whether or not she actually wanted to sell the hotel. "See you tomorrow."

Alex gave Rosalie a familiar smile as she walked out from around the counter and left the lobby. Rosalie listened as Alex's truck roared awake and rattled out of the parking lot. She sat in the silence until she couldn't bear it any longer and got up, eager to see if the small gray cat had come back to find her.

Chapter Three

Recovery Suite

Alex was already at work in the empty pool when Rosalie got up the next morning. Rosalie walked over to the pool, more confident since their conversation the night before. Alex may not have gone out of her way to be friendly, but Rosalie no longer felt disliked.

Alex was wearing white painter's overalls, rolling bright blue rubberized paint over the curved side of the pool.

"Morning."

Alex turned around and looked up. "Morning," she said with a smile. Alex's smile was funny; half the time, it looked like she was determined not to let her tough exterior crack and was annoyed when something warranted a smile, and half the time, she looked relieved to have something to smile about.

A beat passed, and Rosalie was eager to fill it with conversation. "I took your advice."

"Oh, yeah?"

"I called a bunch of real estate agents last night."

"Good for you." Alex lifted her hand to shield her eyes from the sun and the glare off the bottom of the pool. "What did they say?"

"I'm meeting someone in a few hours."

"Good," Alex said.

Another beat passed, and this time, Rosalie felt like Alex was searching for something to say, too.

"I'd say you could help me paint for a bit if you're bored, but I wouldn't want you to get sweaty or covered in paint before your meeting."

Rosalie hesitated, considering Alex had invited her to hang around. But Alex was right; she didn't want to look or smell unprofessional for the real estate agent.

"Yeah, I should probably be in the office in case someone wants to check out."

"Of course." Alex looked back at the section of bright blue paint she was rolling over the faded blue with its white lightning bolts where she'd filled in cracks. "This should take me another hour."

Rosalie nodded, crossing her arms so she had something to do with them. "There's coffee and tea in the lobby, if you want."

"Thanks."

Knowing the conversation was done, Rosalie turned and headed back to the office to avoid hovering around the pool awkwardly.

Alex was a mystery. Stoic and strong, she was the perfect balance of masculine and feminine. Rosalie wondered how she had come to be that way. Had she been raised amongst brothers? Had the heat baked excess softness and vulnerability out of her? Or had she simply come into the world as Alex, hearty and unapologetic?

An hour later, Alex came into the lobby to get some water and tell Rosalie she'd be back in the late afternoon to do the second coat. Rosalie nodded, reminding Alex to give her an invoice for the work at some point.

When Tom, the real estate agent, showed up, he looked around the property distractedly as Rosalie greeted him. Rosalie had the sinking feeling he hadn't expected the property to look the way it did. She quickly launched into her dilemma—how she'd inherited the hotel, how she was keen to get back to her life in Philadelphia, and how much the property had meant to her grandmother.

After exhausting all her possible subject matters, the man cleared his throat.

"I'm not the best agent for this listing," he said.

"Can I ask why?"

He seemed impatient. "Honestly, this place isn't going to go anytime soon, and you're probably not going to sell it for market value."

Rosalie was disheartened.

"This town isn't exactly a prime location, sweetheart."

Rosalie stiffened at his condescension.

"Nothing in this town is selling, in case you couldn't see." The man gestured around as though they were surrounded by faded *For sale* signs.

"Yeah, I guess."

Rosalie had foolishly hoped the hotel would be different from the rest of Ashhawk. Its affiliation with Gran had made it seem separate to her.

When she saw the man take a breath to launch into what was likely going to be another condescending remark, she stuck her hand forward in an assertive closing gesture. "Thank you for your time."

He took her hand and shook aggressively before saying, "I drove all this way, so let me say you've either got to cut your losses or learn the business."

"Thank you for your time," Rosalie repeated,

hardening her voice to indicate his advice was unwelcome. Even if he'd been in the business for years, his attitude rendered his opinions useless to Rosalie.

"If you're interested in a distress sale, I know a few people," he said. "Give me a call."

"Thank you." Rosalie moved to the door to open it for him. He was the last person in the world she'd call to help her sell Gran's hotel.

As she watched Tom pull out of the parking lot, she wondered if contacting real estate agents herself was the right way to go.

When she'd first inherited the property, she'd asked Gran's lawyer if there was any way to let the bank handle the sale and give Rosalie the profits, minus whatever their cut was. But the lawyer had informed her—by some unlikely series of events involving a rather large life insurance policy on her late husband's part—Gran owned the building outright, and there was no mortgage for the bank to take over. This made things simple financially as Rosalie learned the ropes of running the place but gave her fewer options when it came to selling it.

After Alex came back and painted the second coat on the pool, she came into the lobby.

"How'd your meeting go?"

"Not good," Rosalie mumbled. She didn't want to go into too much detail. Her problems probably didn't seem so big to Alex. "It's gonna be hard to sell this place."

"Aren't you good with numbers?"

"Insurance numbers. I don't know anything about real estate."

"You know more than I do." Alex shrugged. Rosalie sensed a resistance to talking about selling the hotel further. "So do you want me to come back tomorrow and fill it up?"

"What?"

"The pool," Alex said slowly, pointing her thumb toward the parking lot. "I've got another small job in the morning, but I'm free all afternoon."

"Oh. Um..."

Rosalie was wary of putting more money into anything on the property since her meeting with the real estate agent. She knew it was pointless to fix the pool if she didn't intend to fill it, but having a functioning pool was one more thing she'd have to maintain. She knew she needed to replace the pool furniture, repaint the gate, and make sure the slide wasn't a liability before she made it available to patrons.

"I should probably get the slide inspected and stuff first," she hedged. "Insurance probably cares. Plus, I don't know if the filter's working."

A look of confusion passed over Alex's face. "I can look at the filter, if you want."

"I don't know anything about chemicals, either. Do you?"

Alex shook her head, studying Rosalie for a minute.

"I don't want to bite off more than I can chew," Rosalie admitted.

A frown passed over Alex's face, then smoothed, her expression growing somber. Rosalie wondered if she was as desperate for work as Shelley had been but didn't know what to say. She hadn't decided what else was a priority on the maintenance list.

"I guess I should give you an invoice." Alex asked for a piece of paper and jotted down the hours she'd worked. Without scrutinizing them, Rosalie cut her a check.

As she handed the check over, she realized how foolish her indecisiveness must look to Alex and that Alex wouldn't be around anymore if she didn't offer her more work.

"Actually, yeah, why don't you check on the filter and stuff tomorrow?"

"Sure thing."

Alex tucked the check in her pocket and breezed out of the lobby, leaving Rosalie alone with the unpleasant aftertaste of her meeting with the real estate agent.

Deciding the opinion of one misogynistic real estate agent wasn't enough to give up hope, Rosalie switched tactics. In addition to two other meetings she had with real estate agents the following day, she contacted a hotel management company in Albuquerque and arranged for a meeting with one of its representatives. Surely, there was someone who wanted to help her in exchange for a cut of the profits.

Just as Rosalie hung up with a pleasant older woman named Opal Thornbrock, Shelley wandered into the lobby. Rosalie looked up, surprised. She wasn't expecting Shelley.

"Hey," she said.

"Sorry I had to leave so quickly the other night. Bobby gets funny if he doesn't know where I am."

Rosalie tried to smile appreciatively, but it came out more as a grimace. She didn't think she'd like Bobby much.

"I'm free Wednesday night. Maybe we could grab some food?" Shelley's voice curved up with her eyebrows, even though it wasn't a question.

Rosalie warmed at the gesture. "I'd love to, but I

don't have anyone to cover the desk."

"Right. Duh," Shelley said with an anxious giggle. "Maybe I could get some food and bring it here?" Her voice lifted again.

Rosalie gave her a broad smile. "Sounds great. I've got more ginger ale."

Shelley smiled back, and they agreed to have dinner together later that week. Even if Shelley wasn't the most thrilling conversation partner, Rosalie was glad for the company.

When Alex's truck rumbled into the parking lot the following afternoon, Rosalie went out to meet her, trying not to make a funny face as she adjusted to the bright light and heat after sitting in the lobby for so long.

Alex greeted her, and they walked over to the pool area, slowing as they took it in. The pavement was cracked, the chairs bent and mismatched, the gate rusted and peeling. It looked pathetic, save for the fresh paint and new decorative tiles in the pool. Rosalie tried to remember the area as it had once been, when she went down the slide in continuous loops as a child while Gran watched her, beaming.

"This place used to be nice."

"It's seen better days," Alex agreed. "But it just needs some new furniture and paint."

Rosalie sighed. "What about the San Andreas fault?" She pointed to a jagged crack running across the pool deck.

"Eh, it's not too bad." Alex stepped closer to examine it. "You could get away with filling it rather than replacing the whole slab. It's not uneven enough for someone to trip on."

Rosalie stepped forward and examined the crack,

seeing Alex was right. Insurance would only care about it if it was significant enough to potentially injure someone.

"Do we have the stuff to fill it?"

"Yeah, there's some in the shed," Alex said, straightening up. "I'll go get it."

Rosalie nodded and examined the dilapidated furniture on the pool deck as she waited for Alex to return. When she did, she was carrying a package of sandpaper, too.

"It would make a big difference to repaint the fence," Alex said, holding up the sandpaper. "It should be sanded down first to take off some of the rust and chipped paint."

Rosalie nodded. For whatever reason, she had complete faith in Alex's vision for the pool area.

She glanced back toward the office, wanting to avoid its drab sterility for as long as she could. She knew she was a silly city girl in Alex's mind, but she wanted to be useful. "Can I help?"

"Sure." Alex smiled briefly. Rosalie felt welcome and needed.

For the next hour, Alex pumped some type of putty into the long crack along the deck while Rosalie cupped sandpaper up and down each rung of the metal fence surrounding it. It was hot, heading toward late afternoon, the sun beating down on them as they worked.

Rosalie felt her skin start to burn, the sweat leaking from her pores not doing enough to cool her. Her hands and feet were swollen from the heat, and sweat was making her eyes sting as it seeped out from under the scalding dark blanket of her hair. She knew she should take a break but didn't want to appear feeble in front of Alex. Latinas were supposed to be able to handle heat. Alex worked hours out in the hot sun every day and never wavered. If Alex could do it, Rosalie could, too.

Rosalie felt her arms grow shaky, but she pressed the sandpaper harder into the metal. She felt herself get woozy and decided she would take a break as soon as she'd finished the post she was working on. When things started to swim before her, she leaned forward onto the gate, wondering if she should sit down. Everything grew fuzzy, and she felt like she'd stood too fast. The slats wobbled before her. Everything turned gray.

She was sitting on the swings of a park with Tara like they had on their fourth date. Tara was looking at Rosalie with a pitying look. Rosalie wanted her to say something, but she didn't. Tara's feet dragged in the dust as they rocked back and forth, heavy with the lack of conversation. Rosalie looked down and saw Tara was making letters in the dust with her feet. Rosalie squinted closer, trying to see what Tara was spelling. As she did, she felt someone touching her face from behind, pressing something wet against her forehead. She blinked, wondering who was behind her before the whole scene faded to gray and Rosalie felt herself rising from what had clearly been a dream. She stayed in a hazy, gray space for some time as she felt a fierce prickling in her head, arms, and legs.

A voice was swimming into her consciousness. She resented it. She wanted to know what Tara had written on the ground.

"Rosalie...Rosalie, talk to me."

Someone was patting her arm, and Rosalie felt herself lying on something lumpy, her head at an odd angle.

"Rosalie, can you hear me?"

Rosalie recognized the voice as Alex's. She cracked her eyes, blinded by slivers of light struggling in through an old pair of blinds. She blinked hard and realized she was in the lobby. Why had she decided to take a nap in the lobby?

Hovering over her was Alex, a look of panic on her face.

"Can you hear me?"

Rosalie frowned, confused about what had happened. She moved to sit up, but Alex reached forward and pressed her shoulder into the couch. She felt her legs were at an odd angle and looked to see they were propped up on several pillows.

"Don't sit up," Alex said sternly. "You passed out."

Disoriented, Rosalie resisted Alex's hand, wanting to move and at least examine herself for injuries. Her head felt fuzzy, and her forehead felt wet. She lifted her hand and found a wet paper towel draped across it. She felt tingly all over.

"I passed out?" Rosalie asked, confused.

"I looked up just in time to see you sliding to the ground."

"What the *fuck*..."

"You must have gotten too hot," Alex said.

Rosalie lifted her hand to cover her eyes, embarrassed. She used her hands to map her head, feeling for any sore spots or lumps. She didn't find any.

"How long was I out?" she asked, confused about how Alex had managed to get her into the lobby, prop her feet up, and put a wet paper towel on her head without her registering any of it.

"A few minutes," Alex said, her voice slipping into a more soothing groove. She sounded almost maternal. "The paramedics are on their way."

"Oh, my god, I don't need the paramedics." Rosalie felt herself grow hotter with embarrassment.

"I want them to check you," Alex said. "Heatstroke is nothing to mess around with."

Rosalie sighed, knowing Alex wouldn't negotiate with her on this matter. Her body still felt hot and tingly, as though some of her blood vessels had fallen asleep and were slowly coming back online.

"Did you *carry* me in here?" Rosalie asked, wondering how Alex could have managed that while she was unconscious.

Alex shrugged. "Had to get you out of the heat."

Rosalie sighed and closed her eyes, strangely soothed by this protective and assertive version of Alex.

"I'm sorry," Rosalie mumbled, overcome with embarrassment.

"Next time you feel dizzy, you sit down right away. Don't try to be tough in this heat at this altitude when you're not used to it, okay?" Alex's voice was stern in a way Rosalie hadn't heard before.

"Okay."

It was quiet for a long minute. When Rosalie looked up, Alex was looking at her with a strange combination of fear and urgency.

"I'm okay," Rosalie said, willing herself to believe it. In truth, she was disoriented, confused by how she could be minding her own business in one place and wake up minutes later in another with no recollection of what had happened.

"I'll feel better after the paramedics check you."

Rosalie gave into the lumpy sympathy of the couch, realizing she was too heavy and uncomfortable to do more than lie where she was. She was still hot, her hands and feet swollen despite their tingling, the itchy prickle of sweat collecting under her arms and behind her knees.

"Can I have some water?" she asked, feeling her throat stick together.

Alex jumped up, filling a glass with water and crouching back down and holding it up to Rosalie's lips so she could drink. It was an awkward angle, and Rosalie knew she would spill if she tried to drink, so she took the cup from Alex and lifted her head a few inches. Alex watched her as though she might choke on the water.

"Does anywhere hurt?"

Rosalie swallowed and scanned her body, feeling some soreness in her left shoulder. She reached across to touch it, finding it tender but not mangled. "My shoulder is a little sore."

"You fell on it," Alex said. "Be sure to tell them that."

The silence felt heavy, and Rosalie felt anxiety seize her, racing with worst-case scenarios involving her fainting every time she had to go outside for more than five minutes. She knew she needed a distraction, but Alex wasn't as talkative as she would have liked. Figuring she could leverage her emergency against Alex's reticence, she said, "Tell me a story."

"A story?"

"Just take my mind off feeling so fuzzy."

"Do you feel like you're gonna pass out again?" Alex leaned in a few inches to examine Rosalie's face.

"I just want a distraction."

Alex settled onto the floor. Rosalie could tell she wasn't keen to tell a story, but she wouldn't refuse Rosalie right now.

"I don't know if I have any good stories," Alex said.

"Tell me about a vacation you took or something."

A beat passed before Alex said, "My family doesn't take vacations."

Rosalie felt guilty for calling attention to the differences between her situation and Alex's yet again.

"I did live on a Navajo reservation a few hours away when I was thirteen."

Intrigued, Rosalie tilted her head to look at Alex. She considered Alex's skin tone and long, narrow nose. Perhaps she was of Native American descent, or perhaps her skin was simply bronzed from the New Mexico sun.

"Are you Navajo?"

Alex gave a little shrug. "I'm something, obviously. My dad's white, but I don't know my mom's ancestry."

Rosalie nodded, glad she could relate to Alex on this small matter. Like Alex, her dad was white. Rosalie's mom was half Mexican, but she didn't feel she belonged in either culture. She looked too Mexican to be white, but she didn't speak Spanish, nor had she ever been to Mexico. She hadn't had a quinceañera and couldn't tell real Mexican food from Tex-Mex.

But she didn't say any of that to Alex. She just let Alex keep talking.

"We lived on the reservation for a few months. My dad went to help with a few construction projects. My mom had just left, so I went with him."

It was quiet for a moment, and Rosalie didn't

know if she should ask about Alex's mom. She figured she should play it safe.

"Was it fun?" she asked.

Alex did a funny little movement with her head and shoulder, and a shy smile crept over one side of her face as she glanced to the side. She was thinking about something but wasn't disclosing it to Rosalie.

"I learned a lot about construction and carpentry," Alex offered instead. "My dad gave me my first electric drill when we got back to town."

Rosalie mustered a smile, even though her face still felt tingly and hot.

"It was pretty cool living on the reservation. It's like a whole little society with its own rules and stuff. Once you got off the highway, it took an hour to get to the village."

Rosalie wanted to hear more, but the paramedics pulled into the parking lot, unloading and dashing into the lobby with a stretcher in a matter of seconds.

"Oh, my god," Rosalie said, covering her eyes again. "I don't need a stretcher."

"Let them decide," Alex said in a hushed voice. She stood and gave a few of the paramedics a sturdy handshake, explaining what had happened.

A concerned white man with a bloated face leaned over Rosalie. "Español?"

"English," Rosalie mumbled.

Unpacking a bag Rosalie couldn't see on the floor, the man lifted Rosalie's arm and slipped an inflatable cuff on it, pumping the cuff full as Rosalie felt it squeeze and her arm start to tingle. He stuck a thermometer in her mouth and waited until it beeped to start asking questions: her name, the date, who the president was.

"When was the last time you ate or drank?"

"I just had a glass of water. I had a slice of pizza a few hours ago."

"Are you taking any medications?"

"No."

"Is there any chance you could be pregnant?"

Rosalie tried to laugh, but it fell flat in her chest. "Definitely not."

"When was the first day of your last menstrual cycle?"

Surrounded by strange men and Alex, Rosalie was embarrassed. She didn't want anyone to think about her body's more private functions.

"Um...like a week ago," she muttered.

"How much do you weigh?"

Rosalie muttered a response, barely loud enough for the man to hear. She knew his questions were standard medical intake questions, but her answers felt too intimate to be sharing with a group of strange men and Alex.

Rosalie was still learning to live in a woman's body. As a teenager, she'd been acceptably thin and tan, her hips and breasts just the right size to avoid prolonged scrutiny, her stomach neither flat nor paunchy. But as she'd gotten older, she'd filled out more, wielding hips and breasts and a small belly that required some negotiation for certain outfits and activities. Looking in the mirror while she was clothed wasn't uncomfortable, but it wasn't comfortable, either. She was neutral on her clad shape, covering it in equally neutral beiges, pastels, and slimming black or gray. She didn't dislike her body, but she often dressed with the goal of pretending it barely existed. She would never volunteer information about her period or weight to Alex or anyone else in Ashhawk.

She was relieved when the paramedic changed the subject and asked her what had happened. He looked at her shoulder, pressing on certain parts and asking if it hurt. It was tender but not painful, and the man didn't seem concerned.

After asking Alex her version of the story and having Rosalie take a few shaky steps around the lobby, the paramedic said it was unlikely Rosalie had full-blown heatstroke; she had probably overheated while dehydrated at an unfamiliar altitude, causing her blood pressure to plummet. So long as Rosalie didn't feel like she was about to pass out again, she didn't need to go to the hospital. He advised her to stay indoors in a cool, calm environment and drink plenty of water and eat when she felt hungry. Still shaky but relieved, Rosalie thanked him and waved goodbye as the paramedics rolled the stretcher back out to the ambulance.

Alex turned back to Rosalie with a relieved look.

"I told you I didn't need to go to the hospital," Rosalie said over her embarrassment.

"I didn't realize you were a doctor," Alex deadpanned.

Rosalie paused for a minute, gauging to see if Alex was angry or simply mocking her, then gave her a shaky laugh. Alex's humor was dry, and Rosalie liked it.

Since she had taken a few steps around the lobby to prove she was okay, Rosalie stood again, heading toward the desk.

"What are you doing?" Alex asked.

"Getting back to work."

"No, you're not," Alex said as stern as ever. "The paramedics told you to rest and drink lots of water."

"I can rest in my desk chair, and there's water right there." Rosalie pointed to the cooler Alex had refilled. But even as she looked at her outstretched arm, she saw a slight tremble.

Alex shook her head, staring Rosalie down. She was so commanding, Rosalie bowed her head and shuffled toward the lobby door as though she were a dog Alex had reprimanded. Halfway to the door, she realized her phone and laptop were still on the desk and moved to collect them. She taped the sign with her cellphone number on the lobby door and locked it, feeling momentarily woozy as the heat from outside hit her. Alex put a hand on her shoulder when she saw Rosalie's reaction to the heat and watched her carefully for all forty steps it took to get to Rosalie's room.

"I should install a doorbell that rings in your room, so you don't have to be in there all the time," Alex said.

"Would that be hard?"

"It'd take me an hour. Two, tops," Alex said.

"Okay," Rosalie said, feeling light-headed with even the brief exposure to the heat.

She unlocked the door to her room and pushed it open. Alex boxed her way in, closing the door behind her, darting to the air conditioner to turn it on high.

"Lie down," Alex instructed.

Rosalie obeyed, not because she was keen to follow Alex's orders, but because her only other option for sitting was a folding chair at her card table. She was riddled with weakness and fatigue and was glad to have Alex watching over her.

The bed was hard and uncomfortable. Rosalie had never despised a mattress so much, but she was glad to have somewhere to lie down. As she did, she took in the room around her and considered what Alex might see. Everything was dingy and dated, with amber-colored light struggling to get in through the tired old curtains. Rosalie didn't know how the wallpaper and bedspread and art could have faded in such dim light, but they had. Perhaps most disconcertingly, Gran's ashes were sitting on the table in front of them, a morose centerpiece.

Rosalie's first night back in Ashhawk had been eerie and suffocating. The ashes themselves didn't bother her, but with only the contents of her carryon suitcase to alter the space, the remnants of Gran in the room dominated Rosalie's consciousness. She'd tried to remain detached and unemotional as she boxed up Gran's clothing and personal items, but it was chilling to be in a space that remained untouched after Gran's passing. Gran's lotions and jewelry and coffee mugs were exactly where they'd been the last time Gran touched them. Rosalie tried not to picture Gran getting up that morning a month ago, dressing and making coffee before her trip to the grocery store where she'd collapsed. Rosalie figured she should be grateful she didn't have to stay in a room where Gran had actually died.

She wasn't grieving Gran the way she'd expected to. It had been a long time since they'd talked. Like much of the town, Gran seemed like a faded memory, once vibrant. The natural way of the desert was for things to grow old, fade, and die. Rosalie wasn't bothered by it. But everything seemed so still without Gran around. The desert outside always loomed motionless, but now the inside of the hotel felt still, too. It was as though Gran's cheer had breathed life into the building and it was crumbling without her. The room felt heavy and stale, the pictures on the walls tired, the curtains sagging. Rosalie didn't like any of it. It reeked of death. Rosalie wondered if Alex could smell it.

Alex finished cranking up the air conditioner and looked around the little apartment.

"Do you need anything?" she asked.

Rosalie lay back, adjusting her pillow and exhaling in exhaustion. "I'm okay."

Alex looked around, anxious for something to do. When she spotted the sink, she stepped toward it, filling a cup with water and bringing it to Rosalie. Even though Rosalie was propped up against the headboard, Alex held the cup to Rosalie's lips.

"They said to drink tons of water," Alex said, lowering her voice as though she was speaking to a frightened child.

Rosalie sat still enough to drink from the cup while Alex held it. She was too tired to object to Alex's fretting.

As she finished the water and adjusted herself on the bed, she realized she wasn't going to get comfortable until she showered. She was so sticky with sweat, she felt like she hadn't showered in days.

"I want to take a shower," Rosalie mumbled.

Alex pursed her lips. "I don't know if that's a good idea."

"I feel so gross," Rosalie whined. "I'm all sweaty."

"The last thing you need is hot water," Alex said.

"I won't turn it too hot," she said, sitting up, daring Alex to stop her.

Alex bit her lip. "Keep the water cool and only stay in for a few minutes." She placed Rosalie's cup on the counter and sat in the chair at the card table.

Rosalie scooted off the bed, realizing Alex had

no intention of leaving her to shower and rest alone. While she appreciated the concern, she felt awkward.

"You're gonna listen to me shower?" she asked, frowning.

"I'm gonna listen to make sure you don't *pass out* in the shower," Alex said, daring Rosalie to tell her to leave.

Rosalie mumbled, "Okay," and slid off the bed, closing the bathroom door behind her.

She turned on the shower, making sure the water wasn't too hot before she stepped under the cool spray, feeling her body sigh in relief. Some of the swollen discomfort of excessive heat finally left her, and she felt her mind sharpen. She quickly sudsed her hair and body, feeling an odd urgency because Alex was in the other room worrying about her. When she was halfway done, a knock startled her.

She heard a muffled question through the door. "You okay in there?"

"Yeah, just rinsing," Rosalie called. It felt too intimate to be updating Alex on the status of her shower, but it must have been more frightening for Alex to see her pass out than for Rosalie to experience the aftermath of it. Like an earthquake, the worst had been over before she realized what was happening.

Rosalie finished and dried herself off, feeling her skin tighten with the forced coolness of the water. She rubbed cucumber-melon lotion on her skin and slipped into her pajamas, feeling them stick to the hastily applied lotion. She combed through her long hair and put some cream on her face before going back into the main room.

Alex was looking at something on her phone in the chair by the card table.

"Feeling okay?" Alex looked up.

"Much better," Rosalie said.

"Is there anyone you could call to come work the desk for you tonight?"

Rosalie picked up her phone, grateful Alex had reminded her she couldn't leave the office unattended for hours on end. She called Shelley, who was more than happy for her first shift in the front office.

Rosalie lay as comfortably as she could on the bed, watching Alex, hoping she would say something. Instead, Alex gestured toward the TV.

"Want to watch something?"

"Sure."

As Rosalie burrowed deeper into the bed, she felt her body go heavy and limp. She was hit by a wave of exhaustion that pinned her to the mattress.

Alex moved her chair so she could see the TV, positioning herself beside Rosalie's bedside table. She found the remote and turned the TV on. The sound blared on and the picture focused, and Rosalie saw *Jeopardy!* was on.

Rosalie felt herself grow heavier against the mattress. She'd watched *Jeopardy!* with Gran in this room as a child. It had been their afternoon tradition to watch together, in the lull between checkouts in the morning and check-ins in the evening. They would sit on the bed and play checkers during commercial breaks. Sometimes Gran would braid Rosalie's hair, cooing over how sleek and full it was, how easy to braid. Seeing *Jeopardy!* now highlighted Gran's absence.

"What do you want to watch?" Alex asked.

"This is fine, unless there's something you want to watch."

Alex pulled her chair beside the bed.

Given Alex's reluctance to initiate conversation, Rosalie figured she ought to try. Alex had proven herself reliable and good in a crisis, even if it had been a small one. After their conversation prior to the paramedics arriving, Rosalie knew Alex wasn't intentionally withdrawn. Opening up just didn't come naturally to her.

"Hey, before the paramedics came, you said your mom left." She made it sound like a question, an invitation to elaborate.

Alex nodded, working something out of her teeth with her tongue for a second. "She moved to Phoenix. Then Dallas. Last I heard, she was in New Orleans."

Rosalie wondered what it must be like to have such an absent mother. Marisol may have been distracted, but she always came home and kissed Rosalie on the forehead good night.

"I'm sorry." Rosalie wasn't sure if she was more sorry for Alex's plight or for having brought it up.

Alex shrugged. "We were never close. We don't have much in common."

Rosalie nodded, feeling like she understood, at least partially.

"Are you close with your mom?" Alex asked.

"We get along okay. We're different."

Alex was quiet, staring at Rosalie, urging her to continue.

"She's...energetic, I guess you could say. She's always trying new things and signing up for clubs and trips and committees."

It was quiet, and Rosalie kept talking just to fill the silence.

"Sometimes it felt like she was looking for excuses to not spend time with me and my dad." The admission embarrassed Rosalie, so she quickly covered. "But I think she just likes being busy."

"Are your parents still together?"

"Yeah."

The word sounded hedged.

"What's your dad like?"

"Quiet. Likes alone time. My mom said he's into owls right now."

"Owls?"

"Yeah. Like, learning about different types of owls and where they live and how they hunt."

"I saw lots in the mountains when I was living on the Navajo reservation. Took care of all the rodents. I don't think I saw a single rat or mouse the whole time I was living there."

Rosalie nodded, murmuring something like, "Cool."

Alex adjusted in her chair. "I'm gonna get some food. What do you want?"

Rosalie sighed, thinking food did sound pretty good.

"Grilled chicken," Rosalie said. "And sopapillas if they have it."

"This is Ashhawk," Alex said with a smirk. "You're not allowed to live here if you don't like sopapillas."

"Okay. My purse is over there."

Rosalie pointed to her purse on the table where it sat next to Gran's ashes.

Alex looked at the box, then back at Rosalie before she stood and swatted the air. "I got it." She handed Rosalie the TV remote and picked up her keys. "Back in a bit."

Rosalie waved, grateful for this unexpectedly

protective and generous side of Alex. When Alex closed the door, Rosalie settled into the quiet, ignoring the looming fatigue around her, not even trying to guess the answers before the contestants could respond. For a moment, she forgot Gran wasn't with her, forgot how tired and hungry she was, and forgot she was trapped in Ashhawk. She drifted near to sleep, exhausted.

Alex knocked and entered when Rosalie roused herself from sleep and invited her in. A large bag of takeout was dangling from Alex's index and middle finger. Rosalie hadn't moved from where she was lying in bed, overwhelmingly tired and ready for food. She realized she had done a number on herself and vowed to drink more water every day.

"Did I miss anything?" Alex asked with a smile.

"No," Rosalie said, sounding sleepy.

Alex set the bag of food on the card table, careful not to jostle the box of ashes and trying not to obscure the TV as she unpacked what looked like enough food for a family of four.

"What'd you get?" Rosalie asked.

"New Mexico's finest," Alex said with a grin. "If you're only gonna be here a little while, you've got to appreciate pine nuts and green chili while you can."

Rosalie gave Alex a tired smile and moved to sit up.

"Stay there," Alex said as she opened a few containers.

Rosalie didn't object, sinking back into the pillows. Alex took a few steps over to the small kitchen, finding plates and bowls and silverware. She plated a few things and brought over a dish steaming with fragrant Southwestern food. Rosalie had forgotten how good the food was in this part of the country when it was done right.

Rosalie couldn't think of anyone else in her life who would be so attentive to her in this situation. Even her own mother would have tired of waiting on her, leaving a twenty on the table for pizza and waving goodbye as she left to go bowling or to an art gallery opening or belly dance class with her friends.

"I haven't had someone bring me dinner in a while."

Halfway through her sentence, she realized Tara had brought her dinner a few weeks before she'd left for Ashhawk. She worried she'd never know if they had long-term potential.

"It's not like I made it," Alex said.

"Still. It's nice to not have to worry about it."

"Consider us even from the other night," Alex said with a fleeting smile, setting a fresh glass of water beside the bed for Rosalie.

Alex turned her chair so she could use the nightstand as a table while she ate and watched *Jeopardy!* As she was situating herself, she pointed to the door leading to the adjoining room.

"Do you ever go in the other room?"

Rosalie shook her head against the headboard. "It's set up for occupancy."

Alex pursed her lips, as though to hold in a comment about how unnecessary that was. The hotel wasn't even close to full. Rosalie could have used the adjoining room as an extension of her suite, giving her twice as much living space and more natural light in the daytime since the other room wasn't tucked back in the corner of the building.

"I don't have anything to put in there," Rosalie admitted. "Plus, I'm only here for a little bit."

"Right," Alex said, turning back to her food. She took a bite, humming in appreciation as she looked up at the TV. "Do you mind if we check the game?"

Rosalie felt foolish for not offering to let Alex pick what they watched.

"What channel?"

Alex instructed her where to tune and leaned forward, elbows on her knees in rapt attention.

Rosalie watched her, more interested in Alex than the cheering and shuffling and droning on the screen in front of them. Alex shifted in her seat, excited about whatever was happening. Rosalie had never seen her so invested in something. She knew Alex could focus on maintenance tasks for long periods of time, but she had never seen this kind of excitement from her.

Rosalie ate, quietly blowing through a silent O in her mouth when it got too spicy. Alex seemed to be able to tolerate the spiciness better than she, but Rosalie didn't want Alex to know that. She was supposed to be able to handle spicy food.

When Rosalie was half done with her meal, she asked what quarter they were in.

"Ninth innings," Alex said, trying not to laugh.

"Oh," Rosalie said, feeling embarrassment creep warm through her skin. "I didn't grow up watching sports."

"We can change the channel if you want." Alex looked up as though realizing she'd been ignoring Rosalie.

"It's okay," Rosalie said with a smile, spooning another bite. "I'm enjoying my food more than I'd enjoy any show."

Alex nodded and refocused on the game. She tensed a few times, fists clenched in front of her, flopping back in her chair when someone struck out or something. Rosalie tried to follow along, but it was hopeless. She knew less about sports than managing a hotel, and that was saying something.

After a few more minutes, Alex exhaled in relief as a commercial came on. She sat back and reached for her water. Rosalie realized she should have offered Alex a drink. "Do you want some hard cider?"

Alex contemplated for a second before saying, "Sure."

Rosalie knew hard cider wasn't Alex's first choice, but mostly, she wanted Alex to feel appreciated.

As Rosalie moved to get up, Alex sprang out of her chair. "I got it."

Alex stooped to open the little fridge. She took out a hard cider and popped the cap off, taking a swig. Rosalie saw a look of surprise cross her face at the taste.

"Pretty sweet," Alex said, examining the bottle.

"I know," Rosalie said apologetically. "I can get you some beer if you want."

Alex shook her head, and Rosalie knew she wouldn't be permitted to go out into the heat until the next day. Knowing she'd be shaky until she got more food into herself, Rosalie was okay with that.

"This is fine," Alex said, sitting back in her chair, legs spread out.

As Alex took a few more bites of her dinner, Rosalie looked at the clock. She was surprised to see how late it was. Given the dismal amount of natural light in the room, she hadn't realized the sun was setting. As much as she enjoyed having Alex around, she hoped the baseball game would be over soon so she could watch her favorite show.

It was her usual Wednesday night ritual; she'd

make herself dinner or order in, curl up on her couch, and watch in rapt attention as her favorite fictional firefighters battled flames, odds, and one another on *Light My Fire*. Aside from the terrible title, the show had been running for a few years, and Rosalie's interest hadn't waned. In recent months, her appreciation had only increased due to the addition of two drool-worthy female firefighters named Jill and Taryn.

"How long are innings?" Rosalie asked, trying not to sound anxious.

"You got something else you want to watch?"

Rosalie gave a small, noncommittal shrug. After all the kindness Alex had extended to her, Rosalie didn't want to deprive her of seeing the end of the baseball game.

"It's fine," she said.

"What do you want to watch?" Alex pressed.

Rosalie felt embarrassed for bringing it up. "You know that show *Light My Fire*?"

"Oh, yeah," Alex said.

"It's one of my guilty pleasures."

"Why guilty?"

Rosalie gave another shrug. Even if Alex had been neutral when she'd outed herself, she didn't want to divulge that she had a theory about Jill and Taryn being secretly in love. It seemed childish.

Alex looked at the clock, noting the show would be on in five minutes. She glanced anxiously back at the TV, tapping her feet on the carpeted floor and leaning forward on her knees again. Rosalie finished her dinner.

After an especially loud crack of a bat colliding with a ball, Alex sat up stiff and straight, fists clenched, and held there for a few seconds before she lifted her fists in a silent victory cheer.

"Did we win?"

Alex nodded. "Man, that was a great hit."

Rosalie looked at the TV, wondering how one type of hit could be better than another.

"Okay, let's catch up with the heroes on channel eleven," Alex said, nodding toward Rosalie's lap where the remote was lying.

Rosalie lifted it and changed the channel just in time to see the fadeout of the preceding show.

Rosalie tried not to let her body betray her excitement. Having Alex be privy to her enthusiasm over a TV show and two characters who weren't even written as lesbians felt risky. Her attempt to play it cool felt like suffocating herself.

Alex, on the other hand, remained calm and quiet in her chair, slouched back with her knees parted, arms crossed over her chest, save for when she reached for a sip of water or adjusted her back against the chair.

When Jill and Taryn appeared on screen, Rosalie held her breath. She was always waiting for their meaningful gazes, their subtle touches, the subtext that fueled her fascination. Tara hadn't understood when Rosalie insisted Jill and Taryn were secretly in love. She wondered if Alex saw it.

If Alex liked girls, maybe she would agree about Jill and Taryn. If she didn't, Rosalie would feel even more foolish around her. So she said nothing, keenly aware of Alex's presence as she muted her reactions to the happenings on screen.

Halfway through the show, Rosalie saw Alex's shoulders tense. She looked over and saw goose bumps running up and down Alex's arms as she held herself against shivers. Under the covers, Rosalie hadn't realized how frigid the room had become. She sat up, leaving the bed to turn down the AC.

Alex looked over at her warily. "Sure you're cool enough?"

Rosalie nodded. She found a sweatshirt in her suitcase and offered it to Alex, who eyed it for a moment.

"I'm pretty sweaty," Alex said.

"We have washers here."

Alex eyed it again before taking it. "Thanks," she said.

Rosalie crawled back into the bed as Alex fitted the sweatshirt over her head and pulled it down, relaxing as she adjusted from the chill.

When the show finished, Rosalie realized she'd forgotten about the stray cat for the second night in a row. She'd been so focused on calling real estate agents the night before, she hadn't thought about the cat until she walked from the office back to her room and saw it sitting on her doorstep. She'd greeted it, giving it a few loving strokes before opening a can of food.

"I need to feed the cat." Rosalie sat up and moved to where she'd stashed the cans she'd bought.

"Cat?"

"A stray. I've been feeding him the last few nights."

Alex stood and started cleaning up from the dinner she'd brought.

"You don't have to go." Rosalie realized her statement about feeding the cat could have been perceived as dismissive.

"I have to go check on my brother. You gonna be okay?"

"Yeah," Rosalie said, curious why Alex would have to check on her presumably adult brother. "I should call my dad and ask him about owls. I haven't talked to him since I got here."

Alex nodded. She took Rosalie's plate to the sink to wash, but Rosalie insisted on doing them herself. She also insisted Alex take the leftovers.

Alex packed up the extra food and hovered near the door. "I know you're only here for a little while, but if you want to come hang out with me and my friends sometime, you're totally welcome." She scratched her neck, looking sheepish for the first time since Rosalie had met her.

Rosalie smiled. "Thanks. I'll keep it in mind."

Alex gave a stiff nod, turning to leave. As she put her hand on the door, Rosalie realized she didn't know when she'd see Alex next.

"Will you be back in the morning?"

Alex looked back at her, and Rosalie realized she needed to give Alex a reason to return.

"I need help finishing the fence. And probably a few other things around here."

Alex smiled and gave another stiff nod. "Sure thing."

Chapter Four

Extended Stay

It had been a long day of fruitless meetings with real estate agents while Alex worked on the pool filter and painted the fence, insisting Rosalie only help for short intervals after she'd hydrated to Alex's satisfaction. Before Alex left, Rosalie reminded her about the doorbell and asked if Alex could do a general safety inspection of the property the next day. It seemed like something she should do, given that she was planning to call the insurance company to see if filling the pool would be worth the expense and maintenance.

Shelley came over an hour after Alex left. They were eating pizza in Rosalie's room and talking about the latest Beyoncé album when Shelley tilted her head and frowned. She lifted her finger from her ginger ale can to quiet Rosalie.

"Did you hear that?"

Rosalie strained to hear whatever Shelley was listening to. After a few seconds, she heard a scuffling, like tiny nails scratching into wood, followed by a squeak.

"It's coming from under the sink," Shelley said, her face shifting into a wince.

Hesitantly, Rosalie got up. She examined the

cabinet under the sink before gingerly opening the door. Immediately, the scuffling intensified, and Rosalie saw a small gray rodent flash over a box of baking soda. She squealed, slamming the door shut. Shelley shrieked as Rosalie jumped away from the cabinet.

"It's a mouse!"

Shelley was crouched on her chair, comically bunched up with her hands over her face. Rosalie didn't have the dramatic reaction Shelley had had, but she wasn't pleased. If there was one mouse in the hotel, there were probably more.

"Oh, my god, what are you gonna do?"

Rosalie shook her head, hands raised as though she wanted nothing to do with anything on the property.

"I can call Bobby if you want."

Rosalie considered but knew she didn't want Shelley's deadbeat boyfriend coming into her room and going through her cabinets. She wanted someone quick and efficient. She pulled out her phone, wondering if she should be ashamed to call Alex about something as trivial as a mouse.

Alex answered after the first ring. "Hello?"

"Hey," Rosalie said, knowing she didn't need to introduce herself. "How's it going?"

"Pretty good. Watching the game," Alex said.

"Are we winning?" Rosalie asked, wanting to make polite conversation before asking for help.

"Depends on who you're rooting for." Rosalie could hear the smirk in Alex's voice.

Rosalie let out a nervous attempt at a giggle before saying, "Um, I'm wondering if you know anything about mousetraps?" Her voice curled up at the end in the same way Shelley's did. She cringed, hoping she didn't sound ditzy.

"You got some little visitors?"

"One that I know of," Rosalie said, eyeing the cabinet.

"They sell traps at the grocery store. You still got about twenty minutes before they close," Alex said.

Rosalie knew the traps Alex was referring to. "The little wooden ones with the springs?" she asked, cringing further. She didn't know if she could stomach disposing of used traps with dismembered mice in their clutches.

"Those are the ones."

"Are there any other kinds?" Rosalie knew she sounded like a wimp, but dead rodents were almost worse than live ones.

"Not in town. Although...hold on."

Rosalie heard rustling and figured Alex was moving around. It was quiet for twenty seconds.

Shelley looked at her with an inquisitive expression, and Rosalie shrugged.

"I've got some nicer traps here, if you want. They're the plastic kind that keep everything contained. I can bring them over."

Rosalie exhaled in relief. Alex always had the best solutions to the many problems the hotel presented her.

"That would be awesome."

"Want me to come now?"

"Please."

"I'm on my way."

Alex hung up, and Rosalie lowered her phone.

"Who was that?" Shelley asked.

"Alex. She does maintenance and stuff for me. She knows more about this place than I do."

"Oh." Shelley seemed to retreat.

Rosalie gestured with her phone. "Do you know her?"

Shelley remained cool. "Yeah, I've seen her around."

"Did you guys go to school together?"

"No. She's, like, ten years older than me."

"Oh."

"Are you guys friends?"

Rosalie thought she detected a hint of disapproval, but she couldn't be sure.

"Kind of. She helped me when I passed out the other day. She's nice."

"I guess," Shelley said.

Rosalie frowned. Shelley was acting odd. "Is there something I should know about her?"

Shelley gave a shrug Rosalie knew was meant to intrigue her.

But Rosalie didn't want to play into Shelley's shift in demeanor, nor did she want any reason to distrust Alex. She turned her attention back to the cabinet. "She's coming to take care of the mouse. That's all I need to know about her right now."

Shelley took a sip of her ginger ale and looked away. Rosalie flipped on the TV, filling the awkward silence Shelley seemed intent on prolonging.

Five minutes later, Rosalie heard Alex's truck pull into the parking lot. A gentle knock sounded, and Rosalie got up to open the door. Alex grinned at Rosalie, stepping inside, then looking surprised to see Shelley.

"Hey, Shelley," she said, giving a polite nod.

"Hey." Shelley became as hard to read as Alex usually was.

It was quiet before Alex said, "Where's this mouse?"

Rosalie pointed to the cabinet.

Alex held up a small box and a jar of peanut butter. She unwrapped the box, producing a small plastic contraption big enough to conceal a mouse.

"What's the peanut butter for?" Shelley asked, frowning.

"Mice go crazy for it," Alex said with a wry grin. "Better than cheese in these things." She tapped the plastic mousetrap.

Rosalie retrieved a knife and watched as Alex put a small amount of peanut butter into the trap, then set it.

Rosalie studied Shelley, who in turn studied Alex. Shelley wasn't looking at Alex in disapproval, but she wasn't as appreciative as Rosalie would have expected her to be to someone volunteering to exterminate a mouse. Rosalie was perplexed by it.

Alex quickly opened the cabinet, sliding the trap inside. "Now you wait for the snap," she said, dusting off her hands.

"The snap?"

"You'll hear it go off when the mouse goes in for the peanut butter."

"I don't want to hear that!" Rosalie said, covering her mouth in horror.

Alex smirked, and Rosalie felt like a wimp. "It's either that or let the mouse invite all his buddies to come live with him."

"How do you know it's a him?" Rosalie asked, hoping to distract Alex from her squeamishness with humor.

"Yeah, how do you know it's a him?" Shelley

echoed.

Alex glanced between Rosalie and Shelley and let out a sigh. "Maybe it's a lady mouse, but either way, it's gonna be a dead mouse soon."

"Is the snap loud?"

Alex put her hands on her hips, amused by Rosalie's squeamishness. "It's pretty loud."

Rosalie groaned, anxiety rising as she anticipated the snap of the trap. "I can't be in here," Rosalie whined. "That's like in school when you know a fire drill is about to happen..."

Alex kept grinning. "Then you gotta find somewhere else to go."

"Let's go sit in the lobby," Rosalie said, glancing at Shelley. "I should be in there anyway."

Shelley nodded and got out of her chair, eager to get away from the impending snap of the mousetrap.

"Want to join us?" Rosalie asked Alex.

Alex glanced between Shelley and Rosalie. "I think I'm gonna get back to the game."

"Oh, right," Rosalie said. She hadn't put two and two together; Alex was missing some kind of sports game to assist her with her mouse problem. "Thanks so much."

Alex pointed to the cabinet. "After the trap goes off, a little red indicator will pop up on the top. It might tip over. Just reach in there and take the trap out and throw it in the garbage."

"Can I leave it in there as a warning to other mice?"

"I wouldn't recommend that," Alex said, amused. "It will start to smell and attract bugs after a day or two."

Rosalie groaned. "I hate mice so much."

"I should probably check around some of the other rooms for evidence of mice tomorrow," Alex said. "Too bad there aren't any owls we could entice to come live nearby."

Shelley frowned, confused as to why Alex was talking about owls.

"Owls are great rodent control," Rosalie explained. "My dad is, like, super into owls right now."

Shelley gave a skeptical and unimpressed nod, and Alex turned toward the door. "I'll let you guys get back to your pizza."

"Do you want a slice?" Rosalie offered.

"I'm good." Alex seemed eager to leave. "Good night."

"Good ni—" Rosalie called after her, the word getting cut in half by the door.

Rosalie was stunned.

"Geez, what's her deal?" Shelley said, pulling a face.

Rosalie shrugged, wondering if Alex's abrupt exit had something to do with Shelley. It was hard to believe the gentle, concerned person who had taken care of her the day before had just left in a rush after coming over so willingly. But perhaps Alex was mercurial.

Rosalie tried not to let Alex's exit faze her as she turned back to Shelley, gesturing toward the pizza box as she suggested they move to the lobby.

An hour after Shelley left, Rosalie busied herself on her computer in the lobby, telling herself she was doing work while checking Tara's Facebook page again and wondering if she should call as a way to avoid going back to her room to await the snap of the mousetrap. She had almost decided she should call when the door to the lobby opened. Expecting a disgruntled guest, she straightened up.

Instead, she saw Alex walking in with her long, confident stride. There was no evidence of anger or frustration on her face, as Rosalie had feared after her abrupt exit.

"Hey," Rosalie said, giving Alex an inquisitive smile.

"What are you doing in here so late?" Alex asked, folding her arms and leaning onto the counter.

"Just...some work." Rosalie nodded toward her computer.

Alex smirked, jerking her head in the direction of Rosalie's room. "So you're not avoiding Señor Raton back there?"

"*Señorita* Raton is offended by your insistence she's a man," Rosalie said, avoiding eye contact to prolong the joke.

Alex chuckled, then looked at Rosalie for a moment before she stood up from the counter. "Okay, this is ridiculous. Come on." She walked around the counter and grasped Rosalie's elbow.

"Heyyy, don't." Rosalie pretended to protest as she let Alex guide her toward the door. "I don't want to pick up a dead mouse."

"You won't even see it. It's inside the trap," Alex said, patience waning despite her smile.

"But what if there's blood or a little tail sticking out?" Rosalie objected.

"Oh, my god," Alex said, rolling her eyes. "Who let you run a hotel?"

"My dead grandma," Rosalie retorted.

Alex's smile fell. "I'm sorry."

"It's fine," Rosalie assured her, smiling to indicate she wasn't offended. "We weren't close anymore. And she *shouldn't* have left me this place. I don't know what she was thinking."

They reached Rosalie's room, and Rosalie unlocked it. She felt her body tense in anticipation of a loud snap or cries of a mouse in distress. Instead, she heard only the hum of her mini-fridge.

"How do we know if it's dead?" Rosalie whispered, as though speaking in full voice would trip the trap.

Alex crouched by the counter, opening the cabinet. Rosalie took a step back, bringing her hands up to her chin, prepared to suppress a squeal if the mouse flew out. Instead, she saw the trap had fallen onto its side as Alex had said it would.

Alex gave a satisfied smile. "*Señorita Raton ya murió.*"

Rosalie didn't want to embarrass herself by admitting she didn't know exactly what Alex had said. She was pretty sure it meant the mouse was dead, but she had no way of being certain.

"What do we do now?"

"Just take the trap out to the dumpster," Alex said with a casual motion of her hand.

Rosalie cringed. She didn't want to get any closer to the dead mouse, even if she couldn't see any blood or mouse guts.

Alex looked up at Rosalie expectantly, and Rosalie gave a little shake of her head.

Alex rolled her eyes and picked up the trap box, walking past Rosalie out to the dumpster. Rosalie stood where she was, still tense, until Alex returned, walking to the sink to wash her hands. Alex flicked the excess water off her hands and dried them on the thighs of her jeans.

"If you hadn't played the 'dead grandma' card,

I'd charge you for that." She cracked a smile, and Rosalie felt some of the tension leave her body. Even though Alex had feigned annoyance, Rosalie realized she'd come back solely to help her with the mouse.

"Can I get you a beer?" Rosalie offered.

During a moment of boredom earlier in the day, she'd jogged across the street to get a six-pack in case Alex saved her from any future fainting spells.

"It's the least you could do," Alex said, suppressing a smile.

Rosalie opened her fridge, taking out a cold beer and opening it for Alex.

Alex pointed toward the TV. "Any more hot firefighters we can watch?"

Rosalie felt her pulse quicken with a mixture of shame and excitement. "Not tonight," she said, glancing at the clock. She had no idea what Alex's political leanings were, but she took a risk. "*The Daily Show* will be on soon."

"Awesome." Alex pulled the chair out from where Rosalie had replaced it at the card table, dragging it back to where she'd sat the night before. "The new guy's not so bad, huh?"

Rosalie nodded and settled onto her bed, glancing over at Alex every few seconds as she found the remote and tuned the TV to Comedy Central.

Alex was quiet in a way Rosalie had only felt with her father. With most people, silence was heavy and apologetic, reeking of awkwardness and reluctance to be in the company of others. Rosalie had only been able to stand her father's quietness because she knew it was none of those things. But since his mother had died, Frank's quietness had grown painful and heavy, and Rosalie couldn't stand to be around it. She had frantically searched for conversation to drag him out of despair.

But Alex's silence was as familiar as her father's had once been. Rosalie felt grounded and protected by Alex's quietness.

She adjusted the pillows against the headboard, clasping her hands over her stomach, trying not to glance at Alex too many times while they watched. She wanted to remember which things Alex laughed at and which subjects might be safe for future conversations. Alex's responses were gentle, the tug of a smirk on her cheek, a silent chortle or shaking of her head. Rosalie catalogued each one, wondering if she would ever make Alex laugh in such a way.

As they said a quick good night, Rosalie asked Alex to come back the next afternoon to finish painting the fence around the pool and install the doorbell she'd suggested the day before.

❧❧❧❧

The next morning, Rosalie had a meeting at the hotel with Mrs. Thornbrock, the rep from the hotel management company in Albuquerque. Rosalie put on her best, most optimistic smile, but as the tour of the hotel went on, she felt herself growing more and more flustered. She tried not to fidget with her clothing or jewelry, but she couldn't help herself. By the time she led Mrs. Thornbrock back to the lobby, she was a nervous wreck.

"What do you think?" she asked, smiling too wide.

Mrs. Thornbrock gave a slow nod, studying the carpet of the lobby. "It's not the type of property we typically take on," she said. "It'd be one thing if it just needed a few repairs, but the location isn't ideal, either." Mrs. Thornbrock straightened up as she continued delivering bad news. "I don't think my supervisor will go for it."

Rosalie slumped, deciding she was done with the charade of cheerful hotel owner. She wasn't cheerful, and she didn't want to be a hotel owner. She let out a heavy sigh.

Mrs. Thornbrock reached forward to comfort Rosalie. "It's not all bad," she said. "It seems like you're at least able to stay afloat. In this town, that's nothing to sneeze at."

"I know," Rosalie sighed. "I just want to get back to Philadelphia in time to keep my job."

Mrs. Thornbrock pursed her lips. "How long did they give you?"

"Six weeks," Rosalie said, feeling her anxiety surge. "I've been here four. I wanted to sell the place, but no one's interested."

Mrs. Thornbrock's eyebrows lifted. "Sweetie, even if you had real estate agents beating down your door to represent this place, it would take you longer than six weeks to sell a piece of commercial property."

Rosalie felt her body getting pulled into the ground, as though the desert were trying to swallow her whole.

Mrs. Thornbrock gave Rosalie a sympathetic pout. "Don't worry. All things are temporary."

It was a petty, superficial consolation. As Rosalie thanked Mrs. Thornbrock for her time and walked her out, she felt her arms and legs grow heavy, her stomach churn, and something push up in her throat. When she shut the lobby door and slunk back to her desk, she let tears overtake her.

She'd managed to delude herself into thinking she'd be able to wash her hands of the inn in a matter of weeks. Sitting behind the counter now, she couldn't fool herself anymore. No one wanted to buy a mediocre hotel in a sad, depressed town like Ashhawk. The only way to get out now would be to pack up and go back to Philadelphia, pretending the hotel didn't exist, abandoning it and leaving it to the mercy of the desert heat and the desperation of drug addicts, down-on-their-luck townspeople, troublesome teens, and vagrants. As angry as she was at Gran for saddling her with Hearth, she knew she wouldn't be able to stomach the shame of leaving the hotel to crumble. What would she tell her parents? Tara? What would become of Susan and Alex and Shelley?

Rosalie folded her arms on the desk and cried into them. She was stuck in Ashhawk with no hope of escaping. She'd have to manage the hotel until she was as weary and blind as Susan.

The lobby door clanged open, and Rosalie jerked up, frantically wiping her face to hide any evidence of tears. She looked up to see Shelley untying her housekeeping apron.

"You okay?" Shelley tilted her head so her blond ponytail fell over her shoulder.

Rosalie sniffled, wiping under her eyes again. "Yeah," she forced out.

Shelley paused from removing her apron. "You're a terrible liar," she said quietly, as though she was sad for Rosalie.

Rosalie exhaled. "I know."

"What's going on?"

Despite her defenses, Rosalie appreciated Shelley's concern. "I won't be able to go back to

Philadelphia as soon as I was hoping."

Shelley pouted. "You miss your boyfriend, huh?"

Rosalie didn't respond, thinking how amusing she should find Shelley's assumption she was crying over a man. But it wasn't amusing. If anything, it made her feel even lonelier at the reminder that no one knew her in this strange place.

"I liked my old job," Rosalie mumbled. "And my apartment and having stuff to do besides sit behind this desk."

Shelley pouted. "I'm sorry, Rosalie," she said. "Is there anything I can do?"

Rosalie shook her head. A car pulled into the parking lot and honked.

"Shoot...Bobby's here," Shelley said, wincing apologetically.

"Go." Rosalie swatted the air with her hand. "I'll be fine."

The door opened again. Rosalie looked up, expecting to finally meet Bobby, but instead, she saw Alex breezing inside, sweaty from an afternoon of painting the fence around the pool. When Alex saw Rosalie's face, she slowed.

"What's going on?" she asked, glancing cautiously between Shelley and Rosalie.

Shelley didn't look at Alex as she said, "Rosalie's not going to be able to go back to Philadelphia."

"Dang," Alex said, keeping her voice low as she rested her arms on the counter.

Rosalie felt awkward, sitting in her chair while Alex and Shelley hovered over her.

"I'm fine. Just disappointed," she said, standing. She picked up her cup and walked around the counter to the water cooler, avoiding eye contact with Shelley

Lily R. Mason

and Alex.

The car horn sounded again outside. "I gotta go, but hang in there," Shelley said, picking her keys up off the counter. "Come by the diner tomorrow morning if you want."

"Okay," Rosalie said, filling her cup.

Shelley gave a few pitying looks at Rosalie before leaving, the door clanging behind her.

Alex adjusted her posture so she was facing Rosalie, one elbow on the counter.

"You really okay?"

Rosalie shrugged, bringing her cup to her lips. She took a long drink, wishing the water would take away the hot feeling in her face and throat.

When she lowered her glass, Alex remained quiet, waiting for Rosalie to speak.

"I was hoping to keep my job, but it doesn't look like that will happen. I'm stuck in Ashhawk."

Alex gave a slow nod. "Ashhawk isn't the worst place in the world."

Rosalie tried to agree with her. "It's not."

They stood quietly before Alex added, "It's also not the best."

Relieved to know Alex didn't harbor disproportionate affection for Ashhawk like Gran had, Rosalie agreed. "It's not."

"Used to be nicer," Alex said.

"I know," Rosalie said. "I used to come here as a kid."

The phone rang, and Rosalie answered it, trying not to sound annoyed.

"Hearth Inn, this is Rosalie speaking."

"Good afternoon, this is George Tackett calling from Shaylin Development. I was wondering if you've had a chance to speak to the late Mrs. Campbell's lawyer about the property I inquired about previously at 578 Cocheta Way."

"I haven't," Rosalie said, slumping and losing any air of professionalism. "I'm not aware she was the owner of any such property."

George tried to respond, but Rosalie was already setting the receiver down in its cradle, annoyed.

Alex stared at Rosalie for a quiet moment before saying, "Hey, want to come out to the bar tonight with me and my friends?"

Rosalie sighed, hand still on the phone as her grip tightened in frustration. Even if the bars in Ashhawk weren't particularly nice, she wanted to be anywhere but the lobby of Hearth.

"I wish I could." She sighed. "Shelley's busy tonight."

Alex pulled a face of regret and pushed back from the counter. "If you can get Susan to cover, you're welcome to join us at the Peso."

Rosalie paused. She'd never considered Susan might be able to cover the front desk. "Does Susan work the front desk?"

Alex gave a shrug. "Who do you think handled it last month until you got here?"

Rosalie contemplated before deciding it was worth a try. She was desperate to leave the property. "Let me give her a call," she said, lifting the phone.

Alex smiled and pushed back from the counter. "Come by if you can. If not, we'll probably be there tomorrow night, too."

Rosalie nodded, waving goodbye as Alex walked backward toward the door and left. She left a message for Susan but wasn't hopeful about hearing back from her.

Rosalie needed to talk to someone who knew her. She was hesitant to call Tara to ask for support but was too tired and distraught to think too hard about it.

"Hey," Tara answered after a few rings. She sounded as though she were walking down a busy street or had just finished a workout. Rosalie felt even farther away from her than she had previously.

"What are you up to?"

"Just getting home," Tara said. "What are you up to?" She sounded cheerful and active, which was discouraging to Rosalie, who was neither.

"Sitting in the lobby," Rosalie said, conveying her grimace verbally.

"How's Ass-hawk?"

Rosalie had called Ashhawk "Ass-hawk" several times via text when she complained about the heat and the depressed state of the town. Tara's participation in her joke made her smile.

"Still boring," Rosalie said. "Although I did have a little excitement a few days ago."

"What happened?"

"It was stupid. I overheated and passed out, and Alex called the paramedics and it turned into this big unnecessary thing."

"Oh, my god, are you okay?" Tara asked, momentarily panicked.

"I'm fine. I was dehydrated, plus the altitude and everything..."

"Did you hurt yourself?"

"I'm fine. Alex said I fell gracefully."

"Who's Alex?"

The question surprised Rosalie. Alex was the closest thing to a friend Rosalie had in Ashhawk, yet she hadn't mentioned her to Tara.

Because of the tenuous state of things, Rosalie opted to keep Alex as vague as possible. "Just someone helping out with maintenance and stuff."

"Is he nice?"

Rosalie knew she should correct Tara's assumption Alex was a man but decided it was better left undisturbed.

"Very," she said.

"Well, I'm glad you're okay."

"I'm fine," Rosalie reiterated.

This was how their phone conversations went—pleasant but not substantive, lacking in intimacy on Rosalie's account. Their unspoken agreement was to avoid talking about anything unpleasant.

There was a pause.

"Everything else okay?" Tara asked, sounding concerned.

"I guess."

Tara knew her well enough to know "I guess" meant "no."

"What's wrong?"

"I just don't want to *be* here," Rosalie mumbled. "I feel trapped. I got invited out for happy hour, but I can't go because I don't have anyone to work the desk tonight."

"That sucks."

There was a pause.

"But it's only for a little while, right?"

Rosalie let out a heavy sigh, feeling as though the ground beneath the hotel was somehow doubling gravity's effect on her. She knew on this matter, at least, she needed to be honest.

"I met with a few real estate agents this week, and

they all say it's a tough sell. I even talked to a hotel management company, and they didn't want to take it on."

"Is it that much of a shithole?"

Rosalie could picture her wrinkling her nose.

"It needs a lot of work."

Tara hummed in response, and there was a heavy silence. "So I guess you're not going to be coming back anytime soon."

Rosalie sighed again, wondering if her chair would hold her up as she grew heavier.

"That sucks," Tara said. Rosalie had the distinct feeling Tara was speaking into whatever room she was in rather than directly to Rosalie.

"It really does," Rosalie mumbled.

"I wish there was something I could do."

"Me too."

A part of her wanted to ask Tara to get on a plane and come keep her company for a few days and help her make decisions about which parts of the hotel to update first. But she knew such a request would only result in more tension. They weren't ready for that kind of partnership.

Rosalie knew that was her fault. She hadn't been willing to be as close to Tara as Tara wanted. Now she could feel Tara giving up on her.

Not wanting to subject herself to more discomfort, Rosalie constructed a lie. "A guest just walked in. I have to go."

"Okay," Tara said. "Call me any time."

Rosalie hummed in response, and they hung up without saying more than a quick goodbye.

Eager to forget their conversation, Rosalie heated up a frozen dinner in the back room while she tidied the front desk for the night. When her meal was ready, she locked the lobby and retrieved a can of cat food from her room before taking both meals out behind the hotel. She sat in the old chair she'd placed there, waiting for the cat, staring out at the desert before her, wondering if the desert would eventually suck the life from her like it did everything else in Ashhawk.

Chapter Five

Single Occupancy

After spilling her sorrows to the cat the evening before, Rosalie decided to console herself by buying a new mattress. The one Gran had left in her room was the most wretched surface Rosalie had ever slept on. If she had to forgo the comforts of home, she could at least ensure she slept well. She could even list the mattress as a business expense since it would remain on the property if she was ever freed from her captivity in Ashhawk.

After a day trip to Albuquerque to test mattresses while Susan covered the desk, Rosalie charged a mattress to the hotel and set up delivery for the next day. It was delivered midmorning, just when the sun was starting to get hot.

The drivers unloaded the mattress hastily, leaving it in its plastic wrapping against the wall in Rosalie's room. The drivers seemed eager to leave, saying they couldn't take the old mattress or even move it off the box spring: company policy. Rosalie rolled her eyes, thinking liability issues were often a ready scapegoat for unwillingness to help. She was glad Alex was on site reinforcing the banister of the stairs leading to the second story of the hotel. Alex would help her move the mattress, liability issues be damned.

Rosalie wandered around the building to find

Alex had finished the banister and was organizing the storage shed. She'd managed to tidy and organize it from the dangerous jumble Rosalie had waded through weeks before to find the fuse box.

"Looks good," Rosalie said, smiling to encourage Alex.

Alex looked up and gave only a gentle nod of acknowledgment.

"I just had a new mattress dropped off." Rosalie pointed her thumb back toward her room. "Can you help me move it? They wouldn't take the old one."

"Sure," Alex said, wiping her upper lip with her wrist. She followed Rosalie back toward Rosalie's room.

"How's it going?" Alex asked.

It was so unusual for Alex to initiate conversation, Rosalie was pleasantly taken aback.

"It's okay," she said with a halfhearted smile. "I keep getting weird calls about the Cocheta Way property. I called Gran's lawyer, and he didn't know anything about it. Maybe another Campbell owns it, and they've got the wrong number."

Rosalie opened her door and led Alex inside.

"Maybe," Alex said, looking around, gauging the best way to maneuver the old mattress out and put the new one in its place. She crouched beside the bed, sliding her hands under the edge of the old mattress.

"I'm gonna lift it and you hold the opposite edge in place until it's vertical. We'll walk it out together. Can you lift half?"

Rosalie may not have been as strong as Alex, but she was no weakling.

"Yeah."

"Okay," Alex said, a stiff smile crossing her face. "One, two, three."

Maintaining eye contact with Rosalie, she heaved the mattress up. Rosalie used her knees and hands to keep her edge from sliding off. When it was upright, Alex maneuvered to the bottom, sliding it across the box spring toward the door. Rosalie waited until the head end slid a little farther down before gripping it, helping Alex walk the mattress outside into the blinding light and parching heat.

Rosalie assumed they'd lean the mattress against the exterior wall, but Alex kept walking.

"Let's walk it around back."

Rosalie nodded, already feeling short of breath from the exertion. She struggled to keep up with Alex, but in a minute's time, they'd dropped the old, sagging mattress against the back stucco wall no one ever saw, save for Rosalie, the small gray cat, and the occasional coyote.

Wiping their hands, they walked back toward Rosalie's room to unwrap the new mattress and place it on the box spring. Rosalie was looking forward to her first comfortable night's sleep in weeks.

When they got back in Rosalie's room, Rosalie saw there was a stack of papers on the old box spring. Alex picked them up and handed them to Rosalie.

Rosalie frowned as she flipped a few pages. The top page was a piece of correspondence from George Tackett, the man who had called Rosalie several times since she'd taken over for Gran. The first paragraph of the letter begged Gran to reconsider her rejection of their offer.

The second page of the pile was another letter from the same company, this one less intelligible to Rosalie.

The third page, however, was the biggest shock

of all: the deed to a large plot of land in Ashhawk, New Mexico, seated at 578 Cocheta Way. It was signed to Estelle Campbell, dated two years earlier.

"Something interesting?"

Rosalie didn't answer as she frantically flipped through the rest of the pile. A half-dozen letters from Shaylin Development Inc., some legal correspondence, and what appeared to be the will of a man named Marvin Cobalt.

"I don't understand," Rosalie said, breathless.

"What?"

Alex sidled up to Rosalie to look at the papers as she matched Rosalie's frown. Then her face lifted, and she looked at Rosalie with a muted expression of surprise.

"Well," Alex said, as though it were almost comical. "You got yourself a nice chunk of land."

As the sole beneficiary of her grandmother's estate, Rosalie realized she owned even more property in Ashhawk than she'd thought.

"How did Gran's lawyer not know about this?" Rosalie asked, gaze flickering between the papers and Alex.

Alex moved closer, squinting at the documents.

"When did she buy the property?"

Rosalie flipped to the will. "She didn't," she said. "She inherited it from someone I've never heard of."

Alex bit her lip, frowning at the documents Rosalie was sifting through, trying to make sense of the discovery.

"Oh, Marvin," Alex said. "He must have left it to her."

Rosalie flipped to the deed and saw it was dated two years before. "Two years ago."

"And when did Estelle last make changes to her estate?"

Rosalie froze, realizing what Alex had already figured out. "Three years ago."

She stood staring at a tacky painting of a lake Gran had framed on the wall over her kitchenette. She couldn't believe she'd been saddled with another property.

Her resentment for Gran flared. Who left their grandchild two enormous responsibilities and no guidance? Was there a letter or note tucked somewhere in another mattress she had yet to lift? Had Gran given *any* thought to the consequences of the things she'd left Rosalie?

"So Estelle's lawyer didn't know about it," Alex said, reaching forward to smooth out the edge of one of the papers.

"Who the hell is Marvin Cobalt?"

Alex looked at Rosalie, serious and sad. "Her boyfriend, I guess you could say. He lived here with her for a few years before he died."

Rosalie was even more dumbfounded. Even though her grandfather had died when she was small— his life insurance had paid off the mortgage of Hearth— she couldn't picture Gran with anyone else.

"She had a *boyfriend*?" Rosalie asked, half disbelieving, half grossed out.

"Yeah," Alex said, her voice growing soft, as though she felt sorry Rosalie didn't know. "They were sweet together. He really loved her."

"Did you know him?" Rosalie asked.

"I saw him around."

Rosalie dropped the papers on the box spring, overwhelmed.

"Oh, my god," Rosalie growled, covering her face. "What the hell was she thinking, leaving me all this shit in the middle of nowhere?"

Alex took a step closer to Rosalie, resting her hand on Rosalie's back. "It's okay," she said. "You'll figure it out."

Rosalie drew her hands down, angrily gesturing toward the stack of papers on the box spring. "I can't even manage one property, let alone two."

"You're doing great," Alex assured.

Alex had previously been so stoic and detached, Rosalie was alarmed at how warm and calming she was now. It was as though she had taken off a brace or cast that confined her most of the time and was loose and relaxed in its absence. Rosalie turned into her, wanting to feel more of it.

"I can't even dispose of a dead mouse," she argued.

"That's why you have me."

"Hiring you is the only thing I've done right," Rosalie mumbled.

"It's a good start," Alex said, a gentle smirk creeping across her face.

It soothed Rosalie to see Alex so lighthearted.

"You don't have to make any decisions about the new property now," Alex said. "Or next week. Or next month. It can sit there for however long you want."

Rosalie nodded. Then she remembered something that had confused her when reviewing Gran's financial records.

"This explains why Gran was paying so much in property taxes..."

Alex hummed, giving a little bob of her head. "Do you want to go see it?"

Rosalie thought about the heat outside and the

endless dusty land spreading from one town to the next. She didn't want to own any more of it than she already did. Maybe if she pretended it didn't exist, she wouldn't have to be responsible for it.

"No." She let out a sigh and straightened up. "Help me get the new mattress on."

Alex nodded, zipping back into her usual demeanor. Rosalie cleared the pile of papers from the box spring, setting them on the table gingerly, as though another deed might spring out from the crinkled edges. She helped Alex take the plastic off the new mattress and heave it onto the box spring. It was taller than the old mattress, making the room feel smaller.

"Thanks," Rosalie said.

With the mattress on the bed and no urgent repairs to be made, Rosalie didn't know what to tell Alex. She'd justified most of the work she'd had Alex do recently because it was critical to the operation and safety of the hotel. But unless she planned to pay Alex out of her own pocket, it wasn't sustainable long term.

"I wish I could keep you here full time," she said quietly. "You're the only person helping me with any of this."

"I wanted to talk to you about that," Alex said, gaze falling to the floor as she scratched her ear. "Now's maybe not a good time, though."

Rosalie's eyebrows lifted, curious. "It's fine," she assured.

Alex raised a challenging eyebrow.

Rosalie lifted her eyebrows in response, impatient.

Alex's gaze drifted around the room. "A few years back, I was going through a rough time, and Estelle let me stay here in exchange for doing some repairs. I was wondering if—you know, if you don't need all the rooms for occupancy—if you might be open to a work-trade thing. I understand if now's not a good time. You've got a lot on your plate." She gestured toward the stack of papers they'd uncovered. "Just thought I'd ask."

Rosalie felt like she could fall to her knees in gratitude. "Oh, my god, that would be amazing."

"Yeah?"

"Can you move in yesterday?"

Alex smirked. "I was thinking, like, fifteen hours a week in exchange for staying here? And if you needed more help, you could pay me my hourly rate."

"Absolutely. I'll write up a contract right now if you want." Rosalie looked around for her laptop, feeling as though she'd had her first stroke of good luck in months.

Alex looked relieved and slightly less uncomfortable. "I don't need a contract if you don't. Your word is good."

"I'm happy to write something up if you'd feel more comfortable that way."

Alex refused, pushing her hand through the air. She looked around the drab room, eyes growing distant.

"Estelle was a real nice lady," she said, crossing her arms across her torso. "She took care of people in this town."

She seemed sad—as sad as Alex ever got—and Rosalie was curious.

"Was everything all right?" Rosalie asked.

Alex looked up, an expression of mild confusion on her face.

"When you lived here before. You said you were

going through a rough time."

"Oh. Yeah, yeah." Alex's gaze was traveling the room again. "Just one of those times."

Rosalie nodded, trying to convey sympathy without making Alex uncomfortable. She was curious, but Alex was a private person. "I'm sure Gran appreciated the help as much as I do."

Alex straightened up at the reminder of how useful her services were. "I hope so." She seemed keen to leave but didn't know how to end the conversation.

"Did you want to move in now?" Rosalie asked, trying to guess what Alex needed.

Alex let out a pent-up sigh. "That'd be great. As long as you don't need the room for occupancy."

Rosalie rolled her eyes over a creeping smile. "You know I never book up."

Alex smiled in admission. "I didn't want to assume."

Rosalie felt her body warm with relief. Alex would be nearby now whenever she needed help.

"Which room do you want?" Rosalie led the way out of her room.

"Whichever one's the cleanest," Alex said.

"I don't know if you've met Susan, but that might be a tall order."

Alex chuckled. "Fine, the one with the best view of the pool."

Rosalie almost reached out to shove Alex playfully. The pool was still empty. "You could live *in* the pool," she teased.

"As long as I get cable," Alex responded. "Maybe I could sleep on the mattress we just dumped out back."

Rosalie giggled and walked next to Alex the rest of the way to the office. Though the mysterious property on the other side of town was still on her mind, she felt better. Having Alex around more often was a good thing.

⚞⚞⚞⚞⚞

When Rosalie saw Tara was calling a few days later, she frowned. Usually, they scheduled their phone conversations, so an unplanned call couldn't be a good sign. She took a deep breath.

"Hey," she said, sounding unnecessarily cheerful.

"Hey," Tara replied.

Rosalie felt her discomfort rise as the line was silent for an excruciating five seconds. She was supposed to be able to have conversations with her girlfriend easily.

"So...I hate to do this over the phone, but I've been thinking."

Rosalie felt her stomach drop and her heart rate pick up. She knew what was coming. "Yeah?"

"Yeah..." Tara said, sounding apologetic. "I know we said we'd wait until you got back in town to figure stuff out, but I've had some time to think, and...I'd rather end things on a good note and not try to juggle long distance with all the other uncertainties."

Rosalie felt something settle heavy in her chest. She wasn't surprised. She wasn't even upset. There hadn't been a big enough spark between them to justify navigating long distance. It wasn't for lack of goodwill or affection. They just didn't spark.

"Are you there?"

Rosalie realized she hadn't responded. "Yeah." She straightened up, not wanting to sound too depressed by Tara's decision.

"Are you okay?" Tara asked.

"Yeah." Rosalie sounded as weary as the rest of Ashhawk.

"I'm sorry to do this over the phone," Tara repeated.

"It's okay. I figured you were gonna say that."

It was quiet.

"I wish I could see your face, so I'd know what you're thinking."

Rosalie smiled sadly. "It would have been nice to go to Zippy's one last time. I thought we'd get to do that, at least."

"Yeah..." Tara said, her voice drooping. "I was hoping that, too."

There was a pause, and Rosalie took a deep breath, letting it flow out, rendering her heavy again.

"I'm doing my best to sell this place and come back, but I don't know how long that will take."

"I bet it's so much work," Tara said.

Rosalie sighed again. Tara was a kind person. "It is a lot of work. But this way, I'll be able to focus on it without worrying you're sitting around waiting for me to get back."

Rosalie doubted Tara was waiting around for her to return; she'd seen more pictures of Tara out with friends posted to Facebook since she'd been in Ashhawk than in the entire time they'd been dating. Tara wasn't waiting for her. But saying as much was a nod to their mutual consideration for each other.

"I do want to see you when you get back," Tara offered.

"You'll see me," Rosalie assured her. "It's not like we're ending things in a big fight or something."

"Definitely not," Tara said. "I have nothing but

good feelings about you."

Rosalie felt herself grow heavier, sadness seeping in. Tara had been so refreshing from the string of anxiety-provoking relationships Rosalie had had before. Talking to her had been easy; they liked the same books and movies and food. They enjoyed time spent quietly together, cleansing themselves of the stress and noise of their work lives. Remembering all the easy sweetness they'd shared in months past made Rosalie sad for it.

"Yeah, me too," she said. She felt her throat tighten and her chest constrict, a warning tears were coming.

Her relationship with Tara could now be added to the death toll of the desert.

Panicking, Rosalie racked her brain for something to steer the conversation away from anything that would encourage tears. "Hey, is there any way you could send me some of my stuff? I thought I'd be here for two or three weeks, tops, so I didn't bring much."

"Definitely," Tara said. "I can send you the stuff you had at my place, and I'm happy to swing by your place tomorrow and grab anything else."

"Thanks," Rosalie said, grateful for Tara's willingness to help.

"Is there anything else I can do to make Ass-hawk less awful?"

"Can you send me some lesbians?" Rosalie asked, joking.

As soon as she said it, she felt guilty. She didn't want Tara to think she was too eager to move on. She just didn't want to be the only lesbian in Ashhawk, and since the jury was still out on Alex, she felt alone. "Not to, like, date. Just to combat the overwhelming heterosexuality of this place."

Tara gave a soft giggle. "They might be a little hard to ship, but I'll see if I can corral a few into a FedEx box."

Rosalie smiled. "You're a good friend, Tara."

"You're not so bad yourself."

Rosalie held the phone to her ear, thinking back on the way they'd related to each other the last few months. Just because it hadn't been passionate didn't mean it wasn't good. Rosalie knew the lack of traction wasn't Ashhawk's fault.

"This is the best breakup I've ever had."

"I know, right?" Tara said, sounding cheerful. "We're pretty awesome."

"We are."

Rosalie thought about saying something in the vein of wishing Tara well in finding a new girlfriend, but she refrained. It would probably have sounded condescending.

"I hope some lesbians show up in Ashhawk soon," Tara said, signaling it was time to wrap up the call. "I'll call you when I drop by your place tomorrow."

"Thank you."

The door of the lobby opened, bells clanging against the glass as Alex walked in, sweaty and flushed from the heat. When she saw Rosalie was on the phone, she walked over to the water cooler and filled a cup with cold water.

"You're welcome to take anything that isn't spoiled out of the fridge," Rosalie said to Tara, watching Alex.

"Will do. I better get going," Tara said.

Rosalie figured Tara didn't have anywhere to be but knew they both wanted to end the conversation—

and relationship—on a good note.

"Okay. Thanks for calling. And for everything else."

"No problem," Tara said. "Talk to you soon."

"Bye."

Rosalie hung up the phone, feeling a weight lift as she set the phone down. She looked up at Alex.

"What's up?" Rosalie asked, wishing Alex had walked in a few minutes later so she could collect herself.

"Came in to get some water and tell you I figured out why the sinks are breaking," Alex said.

"Oh, yeah?"

"Yeah." Alex took a few slow steps toward the counter. She held up a plastic ring that looked worn. "The threads on these nuts are crap. Whoever put them in didn't know a lot about plumbing." She chuckled, and Rosalie wished she knew what Alex found humorous.

"I'll reimburse you for whatever you need to fix them."

"Yeah. Wanted to keep you in the know," Alex said.

"I know nothing about plumbing, so keeping me 'in the know' might be a tall order."

Alex leaned over the counter, examining the ring as though she was going to explain the problem further but thought better of it. She looked down at Rosalie with a smug smile before it fell.

"Are you okay?"

Surprised, Rosalie said, "Yeah." It sounded more tentative than she meant it to.

"You seem a little shaken."

"Oh...um..." Rosalie stammered. She recalled how Alex had responded to her outing herself and decided it was safe to confide in her. "Tara and I broke up."

"Just now?"

"Yeah."

Alex's face shifted into one of concern. "Oh, shit."

"No, it's okay." Rosalie lifted her hand to pat the air to demonstrate that Alex's concern was unwarranted. "We weren't dating that long. It wasn't a surprise."

"Still," Alex said. "I'm sorry. Breakups are brutal."

"I'm doing okay with this one. We'll stay friends, but now that I'm staying here for longer than I expected..."

"It was a matter of time," Alex finished for her.

Rosalie nodded.

Alex clucked her tongue in sympathy. "Do you want to come to Home Depot to get some more sink nuts with me? Maybe you'd meet a new girlfriend there."

Rosalie giggled at the unexpected joke. She tilted her head and looked at Alex, wondering if she liked girls or had simply heard a joke about lesbians and Home Depot on TV.

Rosalie did want to go with Alex; a few hours away from the hotel in Alex's company sounded relaxing. Perhaps the contents of her car, her music selection, or the conversation between them would bring out clues as to whether or not she liked girls.

But Rosalie couldn't abandon the desk on such short notice. Home Depot was an hour away, and while a trip to the grocery store or diner was feasible without someone to cover the desk, such a lengthy excursion would be irresponsible.

Rosalie sighed, the weight of Ashhawk latching onto her shoulders. "I wish I could," she said. "You gotta give me more notice for outings."

Alex made a disappointed clucking noise and bobbed her head regretfully. "I'll give you advance notice next time something's gonna break."

Rosalie managed an appreciative smile at Alex's attempt at humor. "Please do."

As Alex left, she looked back at Rosalie over her shoulder, a look of pity and regret, reminding Rosalie she'd just been dumped. Rosalie felt heavy and stuck. A hunger overtook her. Perhaps it was the desire to batten her body against an upheaval of sadness or anger that prompted her to stick her weathered sign on the door and zip down the road to the diner for a meal and a chance to talk to Shelley. Or perhaps she couldn't stand to be in the lobby without Alex's company.

Chapter Six

Wake-up call

The diner was slightly shabby, but it gleamed in comparison to the buildings surrounding it. Shelley was there in her powder blue uniform, her perky hospitality dimmed by fatigue and what Rosalie assumed was bitterness at having worked in a diner for ten years.

Shelley greeted Rosalie with a wave and a broadening of her usually forced smile, pointing toward an empty booth and mouthing *Sit there* before directing her attention back to the customer she was serving. Rosalie slumped into the booth, scanning the sticky plastic menu for something comforting.

Shelley approached her booth after a few minutes, bending her knees a few times to relieve the pain of being on her feet for a long shift.

"What's up?" Shelley asked.

"What do you recommend for a girl who just got dumped?" Rosalie asked, gaze fixed on her menu.

"Rosalie, *no*..." Shelley cooed, bending deeper at the knees before slipping into the booth across from Rosalie. "I'm so sorry."

"It's fine," Rosalie said, giving a forced smile and wave of her hand. "We had basically fizzled out already. I knew it was coming."

"Who would fizzle on a girl like you?"

Rosalie gave her an appreciative but skeptical look. The compliment might have felt more genuine if Shelley had known her longer.

"Men are stupid," Shelley huffed, dismissing Rosalie's look. "Almost makes you want to swear them off."

"Almost," Rosalie said, amused.

"I'd recommend the breakup special."

"I don't see that on the menu."

"It's for our most exclusive customers." Shelley tapped the menu and tried to wink, but it came out forced.

"I see," Rosalie grinned. "What is it?"

"A barbecue pulled pork sandwich with a side of coleslaw and some fries, a chocolate milkshake, and a slice of every pie in the case."

Rosalie smiled appreciatively. "Sounds great. Only one slice of pie, though. Peach."

"You got it," Shelley said, patting the table before heaving herself up onto her aching feet again. "One breakup special on the way."

Rosalie smiled long enough to thank Shelley before looking out the window at the parking lot and main road. Across the street, she could see a strip mall with a liquor store, its gated doors and windows covered from top to bottom with tattered advertisements for cigarettes and beer and lottery games. Beside it was a payday loan office, its new blue awning standing out among the other awnings in the shopping complex, which had faded from dark greens and reds to sages and dusty pinks. A dollar store with the plastic front missing off the illuminated sign sat beside a dental office and a pawn shop. A vacant slot sat on the end, its mangled blinds dangling at an awkward angle. Trash gathered against the curb along the whole strip. It was the saddest strip mall Rosalie had ever seen.

Rosalie tried to picture what the town had once been. The awnings sharp and new, the signs with all their pieces, the parking lot without cracks in the pavement. It was hard to imagine anything had ever been new there.

As Rosalie's mind wandered, she felt a resigned contentedness settle in next to her in the booth. Somehow breaking up with Tara made her feel slightly less alone. There was no one who was supposed to be by her side, no one she was supposed to think of or talk to every night before bed. She was a lone ranger now, free to tell her worries to the land or to the cat— who seemed to be a permanent lurker on the property now—without feeling she ought to be confiding in her girlfriend, nurturing an intimacy that wasn't second nature to her. The space she had kept for Tara no longer needed to be protected, and she could fill it with whatever she liked.

Sooner than she expected, Shelley sidled up to her booth, sliding a plate of food toward her.

"I think you're putting off some kind of vibe," Shelley said with another wink.

"What?"

Shelley glanced over her shoulder. "The guy at the counter asked me about you. He wanted to know who you were."

Rosalie glanced at the bar, seeing a man a few years older than herself seated at the bar, focused on a slice of pie. He was wearing a wide-brimmed hat and a T-shirt with the sleeves cut off, leaving too much space under his armpits. Rosalie tried not to convey her distaste with her face.

"What do you think?" Shelley asked in a dramatic whisper. "He's cute, right? He's got a job at a shipping facility a few towns over."

Rosalie nodded, horrified that being employed was considered a selling point for a single guy in Ashhawk.

"I'm not really looking for a rebound," she said, buying herself time. If she was going to come out to Shelley, it wasn't going to be while Shelley was serving her a breakup meal.

"Of course." Shelley held up her hand in apology before reaching into her apron for a straw, twisting the end off and popping it into Rosalie's milkshake. "Sorry."

"It's fine." Rosalie smiled. "There are worse things than you looking out for me."

Shelley pointed to Rosalie's plate. "Can I get you anything else?"

"I'm good," Rosalie said, glancing at her plate. The sandwich did look delicious.

Shelley bobbed her head and turned away, smiling.

The man at the counter caught Rosalie's eye and gave her an uneven smile that made Rosalie's stomach twist. She looked out the window as she ate, mostly to avoid further eye contact.

Rosalie thought about Shelley and how she must endure attention from such unsavory men far more often than Rosalie ever would. Rosalie and Shelley would have never been friends in high school, Rosalie knew; Shelley was probably popular in that polished, vulnerable way, while Rosalie, though pretty, was too introverted to be popular. She'd preferred books and journals and calculus to pompoms and compacts and going to the prom.

But her life had taken a strange turn. The desert had conspired to bring Shelley and Rosalie together in a temporary friendship, filled with hotel mice and diner rats. It seemed like a cruel joke the universe had played on her. Or more accurately, a cruel joke Gran had played on her. Gran had left her not only one useless property, but a secret second property with even fewer instructions. Whatever Gran's intentions in willing it to her had been, they were lost on Rosalie. Rosalie had no idea what lay on the other property, probably another piece of shit building that would drain her, mentally and financially. All she wanted to do was go back to her life in Philadelphia, its predictable comfort compared to the harsh lifelessness of Ashhawk.

She was filled with a bitter anger at Gran even the sweetness of the chocolate shake couldn't mask. She stewed on her anger as she ate, feeling her legs grow restless and her lungs hungry for great gulps of air as if she had exerted herself in some way. She tried to finish her food but was too upset to put in the effort, instead leaving money on the table and dashing out of the diner as fast as she could.

Rosalie decided as long as she was shackled to Ashhawk, she wasn't going to be complacent about her fate. Perhaps if she could make enough improvements, she'd be granted a reprieve from her plight. She'd show Gran she could manage. She was going to strip the hotel of everything ugly, everything her grandmother had let fall into disrepair. Even if Alex hadn't asked to move into the hotel, Rosalie would have hired her full time to undo the damage Gran's lack of attention to maintenance had caused. She wouldn't even wait until Alex got back to alert her to the plan. She held her phone to her ear as she drove back to the hotel.

"What's up?" Alex said, her ease apparent.

"I want you full time," Rosalie said, hoping her anger didn't make her sound too harsh. "We're gonna overhaul the rooms and fix everything that looks like crap."

Rosalie felt a smile in Alex's voice as she spoke. "Okay. What prompted this?"

"I just…" Rosalie choked on her anger. "I'm tired of living in a dump."

"You and the rest of Ashhawk," Alex said. "Is there anything else I need to get?"

"I don't know."

Rosalie was fuming too furiously to think of practical steps. She had her list of potential repairs in the lobby. When Alex finished fixing the sinks, they'd go over it together and start crossing items off with a heavy black pen faster than things could break or fade or crumble around them.

❦❦❦❦

The next morning, Rosalie's anger had dulled from its furious rage. She supposed it was good since she didn't trust herself to make decisions while angry. She also didn't want to scare off Alex and set a bad tone for their work together overhauling Gran's dump.

As they pored over the list of repairs to be made, Rosalie felt herself losing her enthusiasm for renovation. Everything she wanted to do—replace the bathroom vanities, buy new mattresses, update the drapes and window coverings, install keycard door locks, replace the carpets, fix the sign out front, and repaint the exterior—was expensive.

Alex must have sensed her disappointment

because she started suggesting budget-friendly alternatives.

"I could make some nice vanities," she offered. "I can get a good deal on some beautiful wood."

Rosalie pictured the shabby bathroom counters in the rooms now, their cheap finishes making the hotel look dated and simple.

"Won't the water ruin the wood?"

"Only if I didn't seal it well," Alex said with a smirk, as though doing such a thing would be idiotic. "Don't worry, I'll give it a nice stain and finish."

Alex looked back at the list. Rosalie was aware she was trying to paint a bleak situation as rosy as she could.

"I can replace the exterior lights for cheap." Alex pointed to an item on the list. "And we could power-wash the exterior to get another year or two out of the paint."

Rosalie nodded, feeling defeated, wishing she hadn't set herself up for such disappointment with her lofty goal of overhauling the entire place in a week. She'd let her anger delude her, and now she felt foolish.

Alex left to buy lightbulbs that were less yellow and creepy than the current bulbs and rent a power washer, while Rosalie turned back to her computer to drown herself in the soothing numbers of the previous week's revenue management spreadsheets.

✿✿✿✿

A few hours later, Rosalie felt her pulse surge when she saw Tara was calling. She didn't know how it would be to talk since they had ended their relationship.

"Hey."

"Hi..." Tara sounded uncertain about something. "I just got to your apartment."

"Is everything okay?"

"Yeah," Tara said hesitantly. "But it looks like someone's been living here."

"*What*?"

"There are a few pairs of heels by the door and a bottle of color-safe shampoo in the shower. And there are clothes all over the bedroom floor."

Rosalie racked her brain for who could possibly be living in her apartment without breaking in. The only people who had the key were Tara and—

Oh.

"What's the brand of the shampoo?" Rosalie asked.

"The kind in the red tube," Tara said.

Rosalie let out a sigh, simultaneously relieved and frustrated. "My mom."

"Oh," Tara said. "Did she tell you she was staying here?"

"Why would she do that?" Rosalie asked sarcastically. Tara knew the strange dynamics of her relationship with her mother.

"Maybe she had a wild night out and didn't want to bother your dad coming in late," Tara suggested.

"And happened to have multiple pairs of shoes and her shampoo with her?" Rosalie said, doubtful.

"Yeah, probably not," Tara said. "Well, I'm here now. What do you want me to send?"

Rosalie pictured the contents of each drawer and closet, letting her mind surround her with the familiar textures of home—the couch upholstery, the paisley shower curtain, the worn softness of the carpet, the sheen of the wall in the living room in the late afternoon. She wanted all of it.

"Everything," Rosalie said, hedging sarcasm.

"I'll need to get more boxes, but whatever you need."

Rosalie was almost frustrated with Tara's cooperativeness. Why couldn't she mirror Rosalie's frustration?

"No, not everything," she said. "I don't need winter coats or kitchen gadgets."

"Okay. But, like, summer wardrobe, jewelry, shoes, books?"

Rosalie mentally scanned her beloved bookshelf, raked her hand over her jewelry rack, calculated her shoes wistfully. If she had to be stranded in Ashhawk, she wanted her nice things around her. If that made her petty or shallow, she didn't care. She was trying to get through each day with as few tears as possible.

"I can hire someone to box everything up."

"Don't be silly," Tara said. "Just reimburse me for the boxes and shipping and maybe throw in a pizza for while I work."

Rosalie was calmed by Tara's easy generosity. "I'll throw in two."

"I'll go get some boxes."

"There are probably some decent ones by the dumpster," Rosalie offered. "No use paying for new ones."

"Okay, I'll text if I have any questions. Stay by your phone."

"I will. Thanks so much, Tara."

"No problem. Bye."

"Bye."

Rosalie hung up, satisfied for the first time with how a phone conversation with Tara had gone. Maybe they were better suited as friends.

But she was unsettled that her mother was staying in her apartment without telling her. She was about to call Marisol when she thought better of it. She already felt like she was hanging by a tenuous thread, and talking to her mother wouldn't help. She could call the next day, and it would make no difference. Marisol rarely had time to talk to her anyway. She justified her lack of action further by thinking at least someone was looking after her place. She'd prepaid her rent for two months before she left, so it didn't matter if Marisol was there. She texted her mom that Tara was going to box up her stuff and said nothing more, instead researching shipping companies to pick up and deliver the remnants of her life in Philadelphia to Ashhawk.

The bells on the door sounded, and Rosalie looked up, relieved to see it was Alex. She felt her body exhale, forgetting the strangeness of her mother living in her apartment. She could start the next few hours over fresh if she wanted to.

"Hey," Alex said, breezing inside as an unselfconscious smile crept across her face.

"Hey," Rosalie said. She recognized it as her natural voice, the one that didn't conceal her tiredness or frustration for the sake of politeness as she did most of the time.

"What's up?" Alex gestured toward the desk before scratching her nose and letting her hand hang loose at her side.

"Just lots of people coming in and out."

Alex gave a distracted nod. "Seems like you could use a vacation."

"You have no idea," Rosalie grumbled. She hadn't had a day off since she'd arrived in Ashhawk five weeks prior. She felt charred at the ends, as though the desert would start to blow bits of her away at any moment.

"I know you usually don't want to do stuff when I invite you out, but I want you to come to Malcolm's place in a few weeks. It's one of his famous men's weekends. I promise it'll be fun."

"I don't mean to always turn you down," Rosalie said, cringing with guilt.

Alex nodded, her expression conveying she was still uncertain. "If you can get Shelley or Susan to cover for you, I think you'd have a good time."

Knowing Alex was looking out for her in a way no one else did, Rosalie decided she should seize the opportunity to get out of Ashhawk.

"What weekend was that?" she asked, opening her calendar.

"Last weekend of July," Alex said, grinning at Rosalie's apparent receptiveness to her invitation.

"I'll call Shelley right now," Rosalie said, reaching for her phone.

Alex rapped her knuckles against the counter in excitement.

"Maybe throw in an extra night here for her and Bobby to entice her."

Rosalie nodded and mouthed *Good idea* over the receiver. She knew Shelley was desperate to get some alone time with Bobby away from her drunk father.

Alex rapped on the counter two more times in quick succession, then stood back, signaling she was heading out to continue working on something.

❦ ❦ ❦ ❦

When Alex returned fifteen minutes later, she lifted her eyebrows. "What's the word?"

"Looks like you're gonna have to put up with me for two full days."

Alex's face jumped in a look of happy surprise. "Really?"

"Yep." Rosalie felt excitement flowing through her. She couldn't wait to get out of Ashhawk.

"Awesome." Alex leaned onto the counter as though she hadn't left. There was an easy familiarity to her posture. "So I had a thought," Alex said. "I know we've got a big list of expensive things to do, but I was wondering what you thought of taking down the wallpaper and repainting some of the rooms to update the color scheme. After I fix another godforsaken sink."

"The rooms need updating beyond the color scheme," Rosalie grumbled.

"But this'll do until you have money to overhaul the place," Alex said.

Rosalie chewed on the idea. There was no reason not to make the rooms look nicer, and Alex's labor was dirt cheap now that she was working in partial exchange for housing.

"Sure, paint away," Rosalie said.

"What color do you want?"

"Whatever you want. Do you need me to write a check for the paint place?"

"You trust me to pick the color of the rooms? What if I pick burnt orange?"

"You wouldn't."

Alex hesitated. "Come with me," she said, as though promising to make their outing fun.

"I'm chained to this desk." Rosalie gestured with open palms to the plane before her.

Alex gestured with her thumb over her shoulder. "I think Susan needs a few minutes off her feet."

Even if going to the paint store wasn't a barrel of laughs, it was more fun than sitting in the lobby. Alex went outside to call out to Susan, who was sitting in an old, rickety chair smoking a cigarette. Rosalie picked up her purse and shut down her laptop, making sure everything Susan might need was in place. Alex stepped back into the lobby to wait for Rosalie, and as Rosalie walked toward her, Rosalie's gaze fell to the carpet and its ugly, worn cattle brand pattern. She wondered what kind of carpet company would make a fabric so hideous.

"I *hate* this carpet," Rosalie mumbled. "It's so ugly."

Alex smirked and held the door open for Rosalie. "Yeah, I'm not sure why anyone thought it would be a good design choice."

"Gran made a lot of bad choices." Rosalie sighed. "Like leaving this place to me."

"You're doing fine," Alex said.

Rosalie shrugged, not willing to admit aloud she was at least doing a decent job of keeping operations going. Guests had plenty of complaints, but Rosalie always responded quickly, throwing in extra coupons for the local pizza place or tickets for an ice cream cone across the street. Rosalie could handle the comings and goings of the guests and the residents, provided Alex and Shelley and even Susan were around to help.

"Where's the paint store?" Rosalie asked, pointing to her car, indicating she would drive.

"Next town over," Alex said, curling around the car to get into the passenger's seat.

Rosalie adjusted her sunglasses as she climbed into the driver's seat and started the car.

As she pulled out of the parking lot, trying

to ignore the depressed buildings around her, Alex studied the interior of the car.

"Estelle did a nice job keeping this thing clean," Alex said.

"She didn't drive it much. I rarely do."

"Happens when you live at work, I guess."

Rosalie was all too aware of the benefits and drawbacks—mostly drawbacks—of living at work.

When they neared the next town, Alex directed Rosalie to the paint store. They pulled into the parking lot, and Rosalie noticed as Alex got out of the car she adopted a bravado Rosalie hadn't seen before. She wondered if this was a way of Alex indicating the paint store was her domain, an air of comfortable sovereignty. Her widened stance made Rosalie wonder again if she liked girls and if the people around her knew she liked girls. Was Rosalie being implicated by association? Would the men inside the paint shop assume she and Alex were a couple? Or was she taking her curiosity to ridiculous lengths during a simple errand to get paint?

Alex held the door for Rosalie and ushered her to the corner of the store where chips were stacked in ascending slots. She studied them, arms crossed over her chest. She was acutely aware of two men behind the counter, idly leaning against it, studying them. Rosalie wondered if they knew Alex.

Alex turned to Rosalie. "What do you think?"

Rosalie shrugged. "Looks like paint chips."

"Maybe we should take a few back and see if they look good with the current fixtures."

"Sure," Rosalie said, eager to get out of the store and away from the scrutiny of the men.

Alex gathered some paint chips and tapped them into a neat stack in her hand. She nodded toward the men as they left the shop, climbing back into Rosalie's car and speeding back toward Ashhawk.

"You okay?" Alex asked once they were back on the near-deserted highway.

"Yeah," Rosalie said, hoping it didn't sound clipped.

Rosalie contemplated the paint store and how familiar Alex seemed with it. Rosalie didn't have an equivalent domain. She withered in the lobby, pouted in her room, and cried behind the hotel with the small gray cat. She wanted somewhere she was queen.

Perhaps it was all in the attitude. If she could adopt any fraction of bravado, if she could fake authority, she would feel better.

When they got back to the hotel, Rosalie turned to Alex and said, "I want to fill the pool."

Alex looked surprised. "Did you check with your insurance?"

Rosalie nodded. Gran had been paying liability insurance to have a pool and slide for however long the pool had been empty, another sign of her mismanagement.

"It's dumb to have it sitting there like a tease for everyone who checks in. The website advertises a pool, so it should probably be functioning."

"Probably," Alex agreed. "Is the new website bringing in more reservations?"

"Some, yeah. Occupancy is up about twenty percent."

"That's *great*," Alex said, displaying rare excitement. "You should be proud."

Rosalie shrugged. It was hard to feel proud of anything lately.

"Want me to get the chemicals?"

"Sure. How do we fill the pool?"

"Put a hose in there and let it run. Probably overnight," Alex said.

Ten minutes later, Alex had helped Rosalie get a hose out of the shed and attach it to the poolside spigot. They draped the hose over the lip of the pool and turned it on. It sputtered and gagged for a few seconds, sending a few bursts of water into the overheated blue pit. Rosalie saw steam where it hit the plaster. Finally, the stream steadied, and they were left watching the paint at the bottom of the pool darken in spots where the water hit it. The pit seemed enormous, as though it would take weeks to fill.

Yet they both stood there watching. After a few minutes, Alex looked around. "As thrilling as this is, I should probably go get those chemicals."

Rosalie nodded, heading back into the lobby to coordinate the shipping of her possessions from Philadelphia.

☙☙☙☙

Rosalie managed to avoid calling her mother for several days. Her belongings were already loaded into a truck when Marisol finally returned her inquisitive text.

Sorry, was out of town w the girls. Had a great chat w T while we packed up ur things. OK if i stay in ur place 4 a few more days?

Rosalie felt her frustration mount. Her mother's cheerfulness was an effort to distract her. Rosalie knew she was being avoided.

Still, she didn't have the energy to confront her mother. Getting through each day as the unwilling owner of a crappy hotel took all her strength. Figuring out what Marisol was doing was a task for another day.

Sure. Rent is paid through the end of next month.

Her mother replied back with excessive kissy face emojis. *Great! Love you!!!*

⚜ ⚜ ⚜ ⚜

Rosalie surged with relief when she saw the delivery truck lumber into the parking lot, fatigued with desert dust and thousands of miles between its origin and Ashhawk. She was eager to see her belongings intact, to be reminded of who she was by the familiar feel of her pillowcase against her cheek, her favorite brush in her hair, the slap of her work shoes against the foreign concrete of Hearth. She thanked the driver and signed for the shipment after counting the boxes, wondering if there was any way to know if some of her precious pieces had been lost or damaged and if her signature was a resignation to living without those things.

The driver seemed unconcerned and unaware of what the shipment meant to Rosalie, doing little more than placing the boxes on the curb before yanking the door of the trailer down, latching it, and heaving himself back into the cab of the vehicle, settling back into its cushion as he journeyed on to deliver whatever else was wrapped in grouped packages in the truck. Rosalie watched him drive away, an odd, empty feeling settling into her. There was no comfort of home, no confirmation she'd be okay. No pieces of Tara or Marisol or her old office had fluttered out of the truck to alight on her. She was as alone and as unwilling to be stuck in Ashhawk as before.

Alex came out of the office, striding casually toward Rosalie. "Everything there?"

Rosalie surveyed the boxes, noting numbers one through fourteen, giving a vacant nod. "I think so."

"Need any help getting them inside?" Alex offered.

"I got it."

It wasn't so much a rejection of Alex's offer as a rote gesture of self-sufficiency. She was capable of lifting and carrying boxes a few yards into her little room. She felt she shouldn't depend on Alex to help her.

But as she picked up one of the boxes, finding it surprisingly heavy, Alex stooped over another box next to her, heaving it up with ease. "Let me help you," she said, following as Rosalie struggled toward her room. She didn't object as Alex helped her carry in the rest of the boxes, stacking them against the wall so they formed a barricade over the door leading to the adjoining room. Once all the boxes were stacked inside, making the room feel even smaller, Alex offered more help.

"Want me to hang out in the office while you unpack?" she said, faintly breathless from the lifting.

This time, Rosalie accepted without hesitation, yet without enthusiasm. Alex strolled back to the office, opening the door and entering the lobby without looking back.

Rosalie studied the boxes before her. They took up more space than she expected. She opened the first, finding her yoga mat, running shoes, jewelry box, and DVD collection stashed haphazardly inside. Tara would never have packed her things this way. She pictured her mother, mojito in hand, casually tossing things into boxes with little regard for organization or categorization. She sighed, taking the yoga mat out to stuff it under the bed, wondering where she was going to put all her belongings.

Before she could even get started, Alex knocked on the door with a flustered, apologetic look on her face.

"I'm sorry, but I need to go help my brother." Everything about Alex's body was tense and agitated, and Rosalie felt a shock of concern for her.

"Of course," she said, leaning forward. "Is he okay?"

Alex gave a frustrated sigh. "He's into some tricky stuff," she huffed, wiping her sweatless brow. "I gotta go."

Intrigued by Alex's vagueness, Rosalie nodded. "Yeah, no problem. Family first."

It was a phrase she'd heard many times but never understood. Marisol hadn't often put her first, and her father, though kind, was usually preoccupied with books or chess or calculus. But Rosalie willed it to be true; Rosalie wanted Alex to have a family that put one another first.

"Is this the brother with the place a few hours south?"

"*No*, no," Alex said, as though the mix-up were comical. "This is my little brother, Jason. He's...kind of a mess. That's why I didn't want to live with him anymore."

Rosalie nodded as though she understood. As always, there was more to Alex's story than Alex was telling.

"Sorry to run," Alex said, glancing around at the mess of boxes, clothes, and books. "I'll try to come back as soon as I can."

Rosalie felt guilty for being another one of Alex's burdens. "It's okay. If I need help, Shelley has the night off."

Alex bobbed her head. "Okay. Later." She swung out the door and into her truck, zooming toward whatever problem her younger brother had created.

Rosalie emptied the first box, flattening it, and dove into the second, grateful for the doorbell Alex had installed that enabled her to stay in her room without neglecting the guests. As she dug deeper into the contents of her Philadelphia life, she felt a sense of confusion swirling up through her. Seeing her makeup mirror and clothing and accessories unearthed after months of being buried under the sediment of forgetfulness that was Ashhawk, she felt even more hopeless. She had hoped having her things would make her feel better, more sure of her footing, more certain she was capable of managing the hotel. She knew it was silly—a pair of shoes didn't render her more capable of selling a piece of commercial property—but she had thought she'd feel better about being in Ashhawk once she was surrounded by familiar things. Instead, she felt more alone and sad. Her possessions didn't belong here any more than she did.

By the time she'd finished unpacking, Rosalie was in a fragile state. Seeing all the pieces of her disintegrated Philadelphia life brought her close to tears. Knowing a distraction would stave them off, Rosalie called Shelley. They'd been getting friendlier over the last few weeks, sharing beauty tips and talking about the hotel and the sorry state of Ashhawk. Shelley had taken Rosalie around to all the shops and made sure the owners knew Rosalie was a local now. If she had to be in Ashhawk, at least she had a friend.

After checking that Bobby didn't need her to watch the game with him, Shelley was all too happy to come over. She brought over some chips and soda, and Rosalie invited her to sit out back. It felt like the only place in the hotel they could have some privacy.

Rosalie studied Shelley's face, how she was always so put together, hair perfectly styled even after a long day of work.

"Where do you get your hair cut?" Rosalie asked.

She'd seen a few salons across town as she drove through but none that inspired confidence. She'd rather not sit in the cracked fluorescent lighting in a worn plastic chair while a girl with too much hairspray in her over-curled bangs snipped at her, snapping her gum and looking impatient.

"You need a trim?" Shelley asked.

Rosalie nodded.

"My cousin and I do each other's hair. She does a nice job, huh?" Shelley studied Rosalie for a minute. "Your hair's real simple. If you want, I could take a crack at it."

Rosalie tried not to laugh at the suggestion. She'd never let an amateur near her hair. Not since her mother had sat her on top of the dishwasher when she was five during her mother's cosmetology school phase.

But she'd never been in Ashhawk when she needed a haircut.

Rosalie chewed her lip and squeezed her hands together for a second before surprising even herself with a shrug. "Sure."

Shelley's eyes lit up. "Yeah?"

"Why not? If you mess up, I can find someone to fix it."

Shelley gave a rapid nod, gleeful at the prospect of cutting Rosalie's hair. Rosalie had her reservations but knew she couldn't back out now without damaging their budding friendship. Who did she have to look nice for, anyway?

Shelley draped a hotel sheet around Rosalie's shoulders and spritzed water through Rosalie's hair, tugging at it with a comb. Rosalie thought she would be babbling nervously through the whole thing, but Shelley was focused.

Rosalie felt a little dangerous, letting someone near her head with scissors. But it wasn't like she had people at work to impress or girls to look hot for. If Shelley messed up, it wouldn't really matter.

"I promise it'll look good," Rosalie heard right before the first snip. She felt her stomach give a little zip at the sound.

Shelley held a brush tip of wet hair before Rosalie's face. "This much?"

"Yeah," Rosalie said, soothed to see Shelley was trimming less than an inch off.

"Nothing feels quite like getting a haircut," Shelley said. "That little bit of lightness. You wouldn't think it makes a difference, but it does, you know?"

Rosalie held her head still as Shelley focused on the next snip.

"Long hair is easy," Shelley mused, running the comb through Rosalie's hair before snipping again. "I wouldn't be messing with your hair if it were shorter. You need a professional for short hair." She paused and made a few more snips and a few more tugs of the comb. "My friend has hair about to here," she gestured below her chin before disappearing behind Rosalie again. "She let some girl who didn't know what she was doing cut her hair once, and she looked *so dykey.* It was awful. She came over to my house and cried for, like, three hours."

Rosalie felt punched in the gut at Shelley's casual hatred. Her body froze, angry and fearful. She was helpless under the sheet, at the mercy of Shelley's shears. She feared they might plunge into her back if she did or said the wrong thing.

If she'd been a braver person, she would have swung the sheet off her like a matador's cape, plucked the scissors from Shelley's hand, and defended the honor of every lesbian who had ever been hurt by that word. But sitting in the late afternoon light, alone and at the mercy of the desert and the few people in its clutches who had been kind to her, Rosalie couldn't find any more bravery than it took to manage the hotel. She shriveled, shamed by her cowardice. The snipping of her locks behind her felt like the snipping of her clothing, exposing her so that she might be laughed at and ridiculed, the soft, lovely parts of her painted ugly and bad. She felt tears push up into her eyes, and she batted them away fiercely. For once, she was grateful for the desert heat that dried them before they could fall.

When Shelley finished, a satisfied and eager smile on her face, Rosalie could hardly face the mirror to look at the even line Shelley had managed to cut while snipping away at Rosalie's pride. She nodded and muttered a few vague compliments, fetching a ginger ale from the refrigerator before mumbling something about needing to check that Susan had finished sorting the towels. Shelley didn't seem to notice Rosalie's sullen state and flounced out to the parking lot as though she had been rid of the small weight that was Rosalie's hair trimmings.

Rosalie watched her trimmings stir and scuttle across the desert, scattered like small sacrifices to the land in exchange for her continued survival.

Somehow, the sacrifice felt too big.

Wanting to distract herself, Rosalie pulled out her phone. Though she knew Alex would be back soon, she texted her:

Next weekend cannot come soon enough.

Chapter Seven

Bed and Breakfast

R osalie hoisted herself up into the cab of Alex's truck. The bench had been reupholstered with a colorful Southwestern tapestry. She hadn't known what to expect from the inside of Alex's truck. She didn't think Alex would have beer cans and beef jerky wrappers littering the floor of her car, but the well-kept interior was a pleasant surprise.

She looked up, noticing a small dreamcatcher hanging from the rearview mirror. She didn't peg Alex as the superstitious type and didn't know what to make of it.

"Do you think those things work?" She nodded toward the dreamcatcher.

"Do you?" Alex volleyed back. It was half challenge, half curiosity.

Rosalie shrugged. "I haven't thought much about it."

Alex gave a contemplative nod as she started the car. "I got it when I was living on the Navajo reservation a few hours north. It's the real deal. Not like those souvenirs you find in Santa Fe."

Rosalie felt guilty for bringing up Alex's dreamcatcher when she knew nothing about it. Maybe she had offended Alex without meaning to.

As the truck jostled out of the parking lot, Rosalie

reached for something to hold on to, finding only the edge of the upholstered bench. Without a bucket seat to hold her, she felt exposed, as though she might fall out of her seat accidentally.

"Where are you taking me?" Rosalie asked, eager to change the subject.

Alex smiled. "A little corner of New Mexico called Corte del Cuervo," she said.

As she looked both ways before pulling onto the main road of Ashhawk, she caught Rosalie's eye. "You'll have a good time, I promise. There'll be lots of good people."

Alex was quiet as they drove, and Rosalie realized she couldn't imagine what her friends were like. Rosalie imagined Alex as a brooding loner. Perhaps Alex preferred to surround herself with books or knowledge or tasks, as she did at the inn. Or perhaps Alex had a large group of friends Rosalie was unaware of.

Alex kept her gaze fixed forward and steady, as though determined to bore a hole through the windshield. Sweeping through the rubble of rocks and sage and dust, Rosalie wanted to know why Alex was so serious. Rosalie found the vast dryness of the desert overwhelming, but Alex seemed calmer and even more contemplative than she did at Hearth.

Rosalie knew it was a stereotype, but she wondered if Alex's stoicism had come from her time on the Navajo reservation. Knowing little about any of the local Native cultures, she fell back on the Hollywood caricatures she'd seen. She felt bad about it; she knew the portrayal of Natives as serious and quiet might be unwarranted. Wanting to mask her ignorance as she corrected it, she said, "Tell me more about your time on the reservation."

Alex tilted her head to the side and adjusted the angle of her hands on the steering wheel. "It was a long time ago," she said.

Rosalie considered; Alex had been thirteen when she'd gone to live on the reservation, putting over twenty years between then and now. Rosalie wondered if the monotony of small-town life might have burned those memories brighter into Alex's memory than they might have in Rosalie's, or if time was an equal-opportunity eraser.

"I do remember this one ceremony," Alex said. "The Navajo believe when a baby is born, it takes a few months for it to fully descend from the Spirit World. After a month or two, people in the tribe start asking the new parents if their baby has laughed yet."

"Laughed?" Rosalie asked, wanting to make sure she'd heard right.

"The Navajo believe when a baby expresses joy in something found on earth, it has fully descended from the Spirit World and is ready to begin its lessons in generosity, which is a highly valued trait in Navajo culture."

"Huh."

"So it's a big deal when a baby laughs for the first time," Alex said. "Whoever makes the baby laugh throws a party, and the baby symbolically gives gifts to everyone as its first act of generosity. Everyone in the community comes to celebrate."

"What if a person didn't make them laugh, though? Like, what if it was a dog or a squirrel?"

"Whoever was closest to the baby throws the party."

Rosalie looked at the sweeping desert before them and wondered how old she'd been when she laughed for the first time and what had inspired it. She made a note to ask her mother—if her mother ever returned her calls.

"You look like her."

Rosalie started, looking over to see Alex glancing between her and the road. "Like Marisol?"

Alex's brow furrowed. "Who's Marisol?"

"My mom."

Alex's brow peaked farther, and Rosalie realized they hadn't been talking about Marisol. Her mind had wandered there.

"I meant Estelle."

"Oh." Rosalie was further perplexed by this statement. No one had ever said she looked like her grandmother. They had different skin, different hair, different eyes, and different smiles.

But her memory of her grandmother was hazy. Perhaps Alex saw them both more clearly.

"What was she like?"

Alex adjusted herself on the bench. "Sweet. But also no-nonsense. Calm, but also kind of..." She hitched her shoulders and a smile flashed across her mouth.

"Joyful," Rosalie said, memories of Gran's steady happiness coming back to her. Despite the weariness of the desert, something was perennially joyful about Gran.

"Yeah," Alex said. "She never lost her sense of wonder."

Rosalie smiled a thin-lipped smile, wondering if she had ever had a sense of wonder or joy. She certainly hadn't wondered at anything in Ashhawk since she'd arrived. She had assumed the rest of New Mexico was like Ashhawk, but as they drove farther and farther away from it, she realized she was wrong. Besides desert, there were mountains and valleys and cities Rosalie hadn't considered before.

Rosalie could tell when they neared their destination by the way Alex sat up straighter in her seat, gripping the steering wheel with more intention than she had along the long, lonely highway. Rosalie was glad Alex was driving; this weekend, she had no responsibilities for the first time in a long time.

Alex slowed and turned onto an unassuming dirt road with a thin metal gate framing it a few yards in. *Corte del Cuervo*, it said, with intertwined horseshoes resting between the words. Alex put the car in park, hopped down out of the cab, and pushed the gate open before motoring through. When she stopped the car again, Rosalie unbuckled herself, mumbling something about shutting the gate for Alex. But Alex was quick, and soon they were each pushing half of the gate closed behind the bed of the truck.

They drove up the smooth dirt road a quarter mile toward where it disappeared behind a hill. Rosalie grew nervous. Would they get cell reception here? Would there be hot water? Would she be forced to live in a "rustic" cabin with Alex for a night? She had imagined the hotel to be decorative and comfortable, not outdated.

"How long has your brother owned this place?"

"'Bout ten years. He and Logan have done good things with it." She glanced at Rosalie with a brief smile. "You'll like it."

Rosalie hummed, anxious as they crawled farther into the desert, leaving a wake of dust behind them.

The land was almost identical to Ashhawk's surroundings—vast and dusty, dotted with sage-colored shrubs and rocks. Though they drove for a full five minutes, the hill before them seemed to creep only a few inches closer. There was nothing to scale the surrounding earth formations with; the only objects were rocks and shrubs and clouds. Rosalie felt lost in it.

As they finally drove around the hill, a set of neat adobe buildings came into view. It was beautifully landscaped, with dramatic, transplanted cacti and abundant succulents surrounding the entrance. There were several large steel and glass sculptures Rosalie assumed were by local artists. Despite the heat and dryness, a fountain bubbled between what appeared to be the main building and block of guest rooms. The parking lot was laid with clean, even white gravel.

"It's *gorgeous*," Rosalie said quietly.

Alex smiled triumphantly and pulled into a parking space, and Rosalie's head swiveled back to keep her gaze on the sculptures and buildings. She hadn't seen anything so nice since she'd moved west.

Alex swung out of the cab, heaving Rosalie's bag up from the truck bed before Rosalie realized what she was doing. Rosalie hopped down from the cab, feet crunching on the sun-bleached gravel. She followed Alex toward the main building, thirsting after the fountain, realizing she needed water.

The heat only scorched her the few paces it took to enter the lobby, but once she was inside, the perfect amount of coolness wrapped her in its graces. The blinding sun from outside was dimmed by tasteful tapestries wrapped around the windows, air circulated the room from a wide-leafed fan, and the sound of running water soothed her as panpipe music warbled faintly from hidden speakers. There were overstuffed leather chairs in several formations around the lobby, an unlit stone fireplace, and a wine bar prepped for afternoon tasting.

Alex had brought her to heaven in the desert.

Alex set their bags down before striding around the counter and receiving what Rosalie assumed was her brother in a crushing hug. Rosalie watched with amusement; she had never seen Alex so enthusiastic about seeing someone or being somewhere. Rosalie supposed she had a special bond with her brother. It was nice, knowing that about Alex. It made her seem less distant.

"You must be Rosalie," Alex's brother greeted. He was shorter than Alex and at least five years older, his head shaved and his clean white shirt untucked without a tie. He wore pressed slacks and nice leather shoes. He looked relaxed, yet stylish.

"Hi," Rosalie said, extending her hand. "You must be Malcolm."

"What is this, a handshake?" Malcolm said, glancing at Alex in disapproval. "We hug here at Corte del Cuervo."

He drew Rosalie into a hug as crushing as the one he'd given Alex. He braced her shoulders with his hands, studying her.

"She's adorable," he said to Alex. "We'll have to be sure we don't handle her too rough this weekend."

Alex didn't get a chance to respond.

"Usually, I make my kid sister stay in the back near the maintenance shed in case I need her to fix something, but I can do better for you, bijou," he said, taking Rosalie's chin between his thumb and index finger before letting her go.

"You two take the suite," he said, flicking his

hand toward Alex. "No one sprang for it this weekend anyway."

Alex gave a nod and heaved up their bags again as Malcolm scurried behind the counter, producing a key attached to a miniature horseshoe with the number six hammered into it.

"Now, Rosalie, there's no cell reception here, so if you need to give anyone an emergency contact number, give them the front desk. We do have Wi-Fi, though. We're not complete barbarians." He winked. "You ladies get settled. Logan will be around with the bus in about an hour. Wine tasting starts at five, and you don't want to miss it. We have a *fantastic* selection we picked out on our latest trip to Napa. Rosalie, do you like wine?"

Rosalie nodded, relieved to be around people who drank something other than beer.

"Fabulous," Malcolm said. "See you soon."

Alex turned toward the door, and Rosalie followed.

Alex clearly liked her brother, but Rosalie was bewildered as to what they had in common. Malcolm was outgoing and cultured and effeminate, while Alex was quiet and content with her small-town surroundings. Rosalie wondered why Alex had wanted to bring her here in the first place, though she appreciated it.

Alex led the way to their suite, Rosalie trailing behind, feeling lame carrying nothing but her purse and the room key while Alex shouldered both their bags.

"I can carry my own stuff," she offered.

"I got it," Alex said. Rosalie could see sweat forming on her brow and knew she was sweating, too.

Their feet crunched in the sun-washed gravel for a few hundred yards until Alex stopped in front of an adobe cabin with the number six nailed to the wall by the door. The number was hammered metal, unlike any uniform hotel door number she'd ever seen.

"This place is fantastic," Rosalie said.

"I know," Alex said with a smirk. "You were worried I was gonna make you go camping or something, weren't you?"

Rosalie bit her lip over a smile, not wanting to admit she'd made such an assumption. "I didn't know what to expect."

Rosalie unlocked the door and opened it and almost cried with happiness.

Inside was a gorgeous lounge room with overstuffed chairs, a sofa, a table with a glass mosaic set into the top of a halved barrel. A glass credenza rested against the wall near the door, holding a sweating pitcher of cucumber water flanked by two glasses. Everything was clean and white and soft turquoise. It was light and airy and filled with the delightful chill of an almost-silent air conditioner. In comparison, Hearth looked like a homeless shelter.

Alex set down their bags, dropping her keys on the credenza with a delicate clink.

"Alex, this is *incredible*," Rosalie gushed. She walked over to the coffee table, running her fingers over the glass pattern set into it.

Through two separate doors, Rosalie saw a bathroom with a freestanding tub and detailed tile work against the wall and a bedroom with a clean, pillowy white king bed.

Rosalie eyed the bed, suddenly anxious. Did Alex expect them to share the bed? What exactly were Alex's intentions in bringing her here?

As if reading her thoughts, Alex said, "I'm fine

sleeping on the couch if you want to take the bedroom."

Rosalie nodded vaguely, trying to pretend she hadn't been so worked up about the matter.

In the corner of the room was a small bar, complete with sink. Alex washed her hands and poured two glasses of cucumber water. She brought one over to Rosalie before slumping down on the couch with the other.

"This is exactly what I want the Hearth to look like," Rosalie said quietly. She worried if she spoke louder, the scene before her would start to crumble.

"Hearth might look better with a midcentury modern tone, but you could do it," Alex said. "Hearth has good bones. The rest is just sweat and a good color palette."

Rosalie knew Alex had had something to do with transforming Corte del Cuervo from whatever it had been before.

"How long do you think it'd take?" Rosalie asked, coming to sit on the couch opposite Alex.

"Years," Alex said, smirking when she saw Rosalie's dismay. "But with the right team, you'd get it done."

Rosalie nodded, knowing the only person she had on her team was sitting beside her. She didn't have money to hire anyone else.

"The important part isn't the fancy tables or the snobby light fixtures," Alex said, pointing overhead where Rosalie saw a state-of-the-art chandelier made of white antlers, painted white horseshoes, and candle-shaped bulbs.

"What's the important part?"

Alex took a long sip of her water before smiling. "You'll see."

Rosalie took a long drink of her water. It was sweeter than Ashhawk water.

Rosalie went to freshen up in the bathroom, studying the tiles around the sink, the elegance of the bathtub, the fine thread count of the sheets on her bed. She asked Alex about the work she'd done, making note of how skilled Alex was; she could wire electrical systems, frame cottages, design built-in furniture, and restore almost any antique Malcolm collected. Rosalie felt lucky to have been unknowingly bestowed with a woman of such talent, but at the same time felt herself sink with the realization she wouldn't be able to use it to the degree Malcolm had. Her hotel was shabby, and she didn't have the money to facilitate any magic Alex might have been able to work.

≈≈≈≈≈

When they walked back to the lobby an hour later for wine tasting, Rosalie noticed the lot had many more cars parked in it than when they'd arrived. The shuttle she assumed Logan had driven was parked near Alex's truck. She was eager to see the clientele; would they all be like Malcolm, social and fabulous and preened? Would they ignore her because she was a girl and probably younger than them? Or would it be the lively, welcoming crowd Alex had promised?

Alex opened the door, and the merry sound of men drinking swelled into the late afternoon air. Peering inside, Rosalie saw the room was filled with every kind of man she could imagine—tall, short, fat, hairless, scruffy, tan, pale, old, and young. Most had wine glasses in their hands, the occasional clink sounding as they made conversation with one another.

Some greeted each other with handshakes, others with slaps on the back. There was a jovial energy to the room.

As they entered, several men turned to the door to see who had walked in. Their faces lit up.

"Alex!" they called. "Come here, girl!" Alex was drawn into hug after hug, and Rosalie warmed again to see her being so affectionate. There was a sweet, soft side to Alex in certain situations, like when someone was excited to see her or when Rosalie was hurt.

"And who do we have here?" a man in a flannel shirt asked.

"This is my friend Rosalie," Alex said, gesturing across her body with her hand.

"Can I get a friend like her?" another man piped up.

A few men laughed before someone asked Alex what she'd like to drink, and Malcolm swooped over to Rosalie, taking her by the hand and drawing her toward the bar.

"How do you feel about merlot?"

"Um...it's okay," Rosalie stammered.

"No," Malcolm said. "We don't serve any of that crap here." He stepped behind the bar, lifting a bottle with a flourish and pouring an ounce into a large, thin-rimmed glass. "Try this. Let's see if we can't refine your palate a bit, hmm?"

Rosalie forced a grin and lifted the glass to her nose, giving the obligatory sniff before tilting her glass up and her head back to sip. She smiled and nodded in what she hoped was a convincing signal of approval.

Malcolm seemed satisfied with her response, slapping a hand against the counter. "When you're done with that, we'll start you on something a little more robust," he said. "In the meantime, bring this to my stubborn little sister," he said, reaching below the bar and producing a sweating bottle of craft beer. "We stock it just for her."

Rosalie indicated she would deliver the drink and stood on her tiptoes to find Alex. She wasn't hard to find amid the clusters of men with her long curly hair drawn back. Her lean shoulders were prettier than any of the overworked muscles of the vainer men in the room.

No sooner had she handed Alex her beer, a man came up to Rosalie and began talking. She found herself swept up in conversation after conversation, her glass continually filled with tastings. Malcolm and Logan circled the room with bottle after bottle and plate after plate of crackers and nuts. The volume in the room grew louder as the guests became more uninhibited.

When she inquired about the history of the men's weekends as a way to continue a discussion she was having with a lawyer from Tucson, she learned Malcolm and Logan had designed the hotel to be a gay desert oasis that assembled several times a year. The rest of the year, the resort hosted conferences, retreats, and trainings for various corporations and businesses in nearby cities, which paid the bills, but the heart and pulse of the place had always been the men's weekends.

While at first Rosalie had been taken with the decorations and ambience, she came to realize—like Alex had said—it wasn't the decorations people came for. The company, camaraderie, and tradition of bringing gay men together to bond in the desert was the heart of the ranch.

As the wine tasting died down, Malcolm got everyone's attention and announced, "The wagon is ready!"

When Rosalie looked at the man next to her quizzically, he explained Malcolm and Logan always set up a traditional chuck wagon in the parking lot for their guests to eat dinner.

Outside, the sun was about to set, and the worst of the heat had abated. In the shade of the buildings, rows of picnic tables sat, linen cloths hanging limp save for an occasional breeze. A great chuck wagon smoked near Alex's truck, and the men formed a line, hands on wine glasses and in pockets, still conversing and laughing with gaiety, eager to eat.

Alex appeared at Rosalie's side.

"This is great," Rosalie said for the dozenth time. "I needed this."

Alex bobbed her head. "How do you think Susan's doing with the desk?"

"Don't talk about that," Rosalie whined, loose from the wine. "I'm on vacation."

"Sorry," Alex said. "You deserve a break, Ros'lie."

Rosalie couldn't quite tell, but she thought she'd heard Alex call her Rosie. Or maybe Alex had drunk too much and was slurring her words. Rosalie looked her up and down, noting her stance wasn't wavering, her eyes sharp and alert as ever. She didn't even have a bottle with her.

A couple of men linking arms walked past them and said something to Alex in Spanish. Alex nodded and smiled, responding with a short, rhythmic phrase Rosalie didn't understand.

Perhaps the alcohol had loosened her, perhaps the beautiful surroundings had relaxed her, perhaps the warmth of a carefree summer night had pried her open, but Rosalie felt the urge to get closer to Alex.

"I have a confession," she whispered, leaning toward Alex as they slow-stepped forward in the chuck wagon line.

"What?" Alex asked, leaning closer.

Rosalie flushed with momentary shame at what she was about to say. "I don't speak Spanish."

Alex stifled a laugh. "What?"

"I know, it's embarrassing," Rosalie mumbled. "I took Mandarin in high school because I didn't want my classmates to know."

"Why are we whispering about it?" Alex asked, smiling.

Rosalie shrugged, realizing Alex wasn't shocked. "It's embarrassing because everyone assumes I speak Spanish."

Alex tilted her head, admitting Rosalie had a point.

"You could take a class or get Rosetta Stone or something," Alex suggested.

Rosalie had toyed with those ideas, but the shame she always felt when she tried to pronounce foreign words she was supposed to know stopped her.

"It's not just that," Rosalie admitted. "I still wouldn't know where I'm from."

Alex gave a confused frown. "Aren't you from Philadelphia?"

"Yeah," Rosalie said, embarrassed she had tried to talk about anything as intangible as her identity crisis while tipsy. "Never mind," she said, swatting the air and then gesturing to her wine glass.

But Alex didn't let the subject go.

"You mean you don't feel spiritually connected to any place?" Alex offered.

"Yeah, I guess." Rosalie was relieved Alex understood so well.

"I get it." Alex took a step closer to Rosalie to reassure her. "That's why I always end up back in Ashhawk."

Rosalie nodded, trying not to judge Alex for being spiritually tied to such a depressing place. It wasn't like Alex had a choice. Rosalie was jealous Alex felt tied to somewhere, while Rosalie, with her vague ethnic appearance and relative lack of culture and language, only confused people, most of all herself. Rosalie wanted to feel like she fit in somewhere, like she belonged unequivocally to a place and community. She was starting to wonder if such a feeling was a myth.

Before she could get more bogged down by her spiritual vagrancy, they reached the front of the line. Alex helped Rosalie balance her plate with her wine glass as their plates were piled high with beans, meat, rice, and a handful of other fragrant, steaming dishes ladled through the thick chuck smoke. Once they'd been served, Alex gestured with her chin to follow several clusters of men who were making their way toward a bonfire in the center of the property.

The smoke from the fire was warm and heavy as it wafted up into the huge desert sky. Rosalie settled down on a tree stump meant to serve as a seat beside Alex, who had offered to carry their plates. Rosalie looked down at the thick ooze of beans seeping into the spiced rice, admiring the tenderness of the meat, sliced thin and steaming beside a tuft of salad. She thought of the meals she usually shared with the small gray cat. Though she missed her little companion, this meal was preferable to anything in Ashhawk.

"Did you grab any napkins?" Alex asked.

Rosalie shook her head, looking down at the beans as she scooped up a spoonful. Alex hitched herself up off her stump and went to find napkins. She returned moments later, body turned toward Rosalie, offering her a napkin. Rosalie accepted it with a tipsy hum of appreciation.

"Want me to refill your drink?" Alex pointed at Rosalie's empty glass.

Rosalie nodded eagerly. The only thing better than a good meal was a good meal with a great glass of wine. She didn't want to lose her buzz with the absorbing weight of her meal. She planned to try to stay in the doorway between buzzed and drunk for as long as she could maintain the balance.

Alex returned with a beer, a fresh glass of white wine, and a hunk of bread.

"Malcolm gets this fresh from a local pueblo. It's one of my favorite things about coming here." Alex ripped off a piece of bread and stuffed it in her mouth, chewing in big, circular bites. She ripped off a smaller piece and held it up to Rosalie's mouth.

Rosalie paused. She wasn't accustomed to being fed. In fact, she couldn't recall a single instance in her adult life where someone had done what Alex was doing. She kept her lips closed and looked at Alex's face.

Alex had a playful grin on her face, and Rosalie felt something stir in her stomach that had nothing to do with the beans or campfire smoke. She realized with a jolt Alex might be flirting with her.

Alex still hadn't said or done anything conclusively proving she liked girls, but there was a sense about her beyond appearance and associations. As Rosalie looked at the way Alex's gaze grazed her face, lingering on her lips as she held the bread up, Rosalie thought it was the strongest clue she'd had.

Rosalie hadn't considered Alex as a potential date. Not because Alex was different from the polished femmes Rosalie usually dated. Rosalie simply didn't waste her time wondering whether people liked her in that way unless she was certain they were inclined toward her gender in the first place.

Alex wasn't a bad catch. She was handy and caring and smart. She didn't entertain gossip or trivial chatter. She was employed and reliable and easy on the eyes.

But she was also unlike anyone else Rosalie knew or associated with.

Not wanting to stall in her reception of Alex's gesture, Rosalie smiled and opened her mouth, allowing Alex to place the fresh-baked bread in her mouth.

Rosalie chewed and hummed, taking a sip of her wine to wash down the bread before looking back at her plate.

She was probably imagining things. Alex was being friendly, and because she didn't talk as much as other people, Rosalie was likely reading too much into her playful gesture.

"So tell me about these guys." Rosalie gestured with her spoon to the men gathering around the campfire. "How'd they hear about this secret desert oasis?"

"Logan's a social media genius," Alex explained. "One celebrity tweet and they're booked for the season."

Rosalie nodded, wondering how she might find an affordable social media expert to help her put Hearth on the map if she ever managed to overhaul the place and make it something she was proud to promote.

But Alex was one step ahead of her. "I bet he'd help you out once we make a few more repairs to

Hearth."

"I can't afford him, I'm sure."

Alex shrugged. "I can come work here for a weekend or two. Make it a trade."

Rosalie took a bite and chewed on the idea. "Maybe," she said, swallowing.

"Sorry, no more talking about work," Alex said. "You're on vacation."

"Cheers."

Rosalie lifted her glass toward Alex's beer bottle.

Once most people had eaten their dinner, Rosalie heard a guitar strum a few chords. She looked behind her and saw musicians setting up to entertain the guests. Rosalie saw a mandolin, a fiddle, and several percussive devices. From the outfits, she knew the guests were about to be treated to some variety of musical fusion. It seemed exciting to her; she hadn't had a chance to see any of the cultural draws of the Southwest.

Within minutes of the band starting to play its quick, scraping music, men got up to dance. Some knew what they were doing; graceful arms found partners and feet moved quickly against the gravel in practiced samba or salsa or rumba steps Rosalie didn't know.

"You gonna dance?" Alex asked after a few minutes.

"I'm not drunk enough to willingly embarrass myself," Rosalie grumbled.

Alex smiled and took a sip of her beer, looking relieved.

They sat and watched the merry men move around them, content to watch rather than experience it firsthand.

Two glasses of wine later, the dancing had grown

frenetic as the sunlight had extinguished and the sparks of the fire darted about. Rosalie begrudgingly allowed a friendly older man to lead her in a dance, hoping his expertise would make her look less foolish. She laughed at her clumsy feet, grateful for the many glasses of wine she'd drunk.

Rosalie was passed from man to man, never having to do more than follow their lead. They seemed to take great pleasure in dancing with one of two women on the property. Rosalie felt as though she were an accessory or pet they were passing around to coo over. Men offered her more wine between songs, and soon all the men and songs and steps blurred together.

Finally, breathless, she plopped down on a stump to rest her feet and allow her dance partner to find another novice to tutor.

Rosalie teetered on her stump, leaning out of the way of the campfire smoke when it drifted her way. It was dark now, a fuchsia and gold sunset having faded around the edges of the resort. Rosalie was loose with wine and good company, glad to throw off the responsibility of Hearth for a weekend. But as she sat, she felt disoriented. Which way was her room? How would she get back there? Where was Alex?

Through her anxiety, she saw Alex's face across the campfire, flushed gold in the dancing light. Her gaze was boring into Rosalie, her shoulders hunched as she leaned her elbows on her knees, fingers tapping on the neck of a beer bottle. Rosalie was disarmed to find Alex staring at her, yet after a few seconds, she softened. How lucky was she to have someone like Alex, who knew Rosalie needed a break from the hotel and had orchestrated a weekend away for her benefit? She wasn't sure she'd ever had such a good friend. Even

Tara hadn't done anything so nice.

Rosalie felt all warm inside, like a perfectly toasted marshmallow pressed between two graham crackers. She grinned, feeling it spread lopsided across her face. Across the fire, Alex mirrored her smile, and despite all the noise and boisterousness around her, Rosalie felt peace. She was suspended in quiet joy. Maybe inheriting the hotel and being forced to move across the country wasn't the worst thing to ever happen to her.

Too quickly, a man stepped between Rosalie and the fire, chatting about something they'd conversed on earlier. Rosalie looked up, half engaged in the conversation, bringing her wine glass to her lips before she found herself being tugged to her feet, forced to dance again. She didn't mind. She liked dancing, and the night felt as limitless as the starry sky above.

As the campfire wore on and she consumed another glass of wine, Rosalie felt herself getting drowsy. When she decided to sit back down, she almost fell off her stump. The man next to her caught her, helping her right herself and giving her a watchful eye. He wasn't judging her for getting sloppy drunk; if anything, a gathering of gay men was the safest place for Rosalie to overindulge. She had been temporarily adopted by the flock; they were protecting her. She shook, muscles contracting, and realized she was cold. The heat that baked into the earth during the day had lifted, and the night chill of the desert was settling in. Rosalie had almost forgotten how cold the desert grew at night. Gran used to bring sweaters out behind the hotel where they roasted marshmallows, helping Rosalie into hers once the heat flew up into the sky to come back in the morning.

Wondering if she could get into her cabin to get a sweater, Rosalie shivered again. She didn't have the key. Where was Alex? She'd been there a minute ago. Rosalie looked around, realizing how disoriented she was.

Something scratchy draped over her shoulders. Someone had cloaked her in a colorful wool blanket. Looking over her shoulder, she saw Alex and felt her hand pressing against her back.

"You looked cold," Alex explained, lifting her beer bottle to her lips.

"I was. Thanks."

"No problem."

Alex took another sip and settled herself on the stump next to Rosalie.

"I used to do this with Gran," Rosalie said, hoping she wasn't slurring her words.

"You used to get drunk around a campfire with Estelle?"

"Nooo," Rosalie growled playfully. "She used to make a..." Rosalie gestured to the bonfire, the word on the tip of her tongue. "A *fire*, you know, behind the building, and we'd roast things on it and she'd tell stories. I was th' best s'more maker..." Rosalie trailed off, head tipping forward more than she intended.

Malcolm came around with another bottle of wine, topping off anyone's glass who raised it as he passed. Rosalie wasn't sure she should lift hers but found it was being filled before she decided.

"Malc," Alex said.

Rosalie looked over to see Alex giving her brother a warning look.

Malcolm feigned innocence. "She needs a vacation," he said, defensive.

"A vacation, not a blackout," Alex shot back.

Uncomfortable with Alex and Malcolm arguing over her, Rosalie tipped toward Alex. "I'm fine," she said. "Just a li'l tisspy—*tipsy*," she corrected.

"It's all in good fun," Malcolm agreed, daring to splash a few more sips into Rosalie's glass.

As soon as he moved on to the next person, Alex turned to Rosalie. "You don't have to drink that."

"I'll be fine," Rosalie said, trying to keep things light with a giggle.

Alex eyed her skeptically before looking back toward the campfire and the rowdy men singing and dancing around it. Rosalie felt herself sway to the side unintentionally. Maybe she was drunker than she thought, but she was able to right herself.

She took a few more sips and felt herself listing the other way, overcorrecting. She swerved dangerously close to Alex's shoulder, and Alex seemed wary. Alex refocused her attention on Rosalie.

"Can I have a sip?" she asked, gesturing to Rosalie's glass.

"Sure."

Rosalie handed Alex the glass with more fling than she intended, almost dowsing Alex's shirt in wine.

As Alex lifted the fingerprint-stained glass to her lips, Rosalie frowned.

"I thought you didn't like wine."

Alex said nothing, only took a long sip, pouring half the glass down her throat before lowering it.

"Are you stealing my wine 'cause you think I'm too drunk?" Rosalie said, half accusatory, half amused.

Alex said nothing, gaze boring into the fire before taking another sip.

"Allllexx," Rosalie drawled. "Are you stealing my

wine 'cause I'm drunk?"

Alex drained the glass, cringing as the last of the wine slid down her throat. She set the glass on the ground, securing the base with her foot so it wouldn't fall over. "Yep."

"I'm not gonna puke or anything."

"You better not," Alex said.

"I'm *fine.*"

As she spoke, she tilted too far forward and found her face smushed against Alex's muscular, tanned shoulder. She tasted salt and realized her mouth was slightly open. She'd accidentally licked Alex's shoulder. Embarrassed, she tried to sit up, feeling her head spin as she tipped too far back and was caught by one of her new friends whose name she couldn't remember.

Alex sighed, standing. "I think I need to get you to bed."

"But I'm having so much funnn," Rosalie whined.

"A little too much fun," Alex muttered. "C'mon, Rosie."

This time, Rosalie was almost certain she'd heard it. Alex pulled her to her feet off the stump as she slurred, "Di'joo jus' call me Rosie?"

"No," Alex said, draping Rosalie's arm over her shoulder, catching the blanket as it slid off.

"Thanks for the blanket," Rosalie slurred. "I was getting cold."

"That's why I brought it to you," Alex said, steering Rosalie toward their cabin.

"You're so nice," Rosalie pouted. "Why are you so nice to me?"

Alex let out a sad chuckle and let the crunching gravel and fading noise of the bonfire fill the silence. They walked a ways, the silence heightening the buzzing and spinning in Rosalie's head.

"Where are you taking me?" Rosalie asked as they neared the cabin.

"I'm putting you to bed."

"Oh." Rosalie sighed. "Thanks, bijou."

Alex leaned forward, laughing.

"Why are you laughing?" Rosalie asked, worried she'd said something embarrassing. "That's what Malcolm called me, and it sounded nice, and you're nice, so I called you bijou."

Alex chuckled at Rosalie's drunk reasoning, stopping as they came to their front door. "Bijou means dainty and feminine, Rosie."

Rosalie spun to point her finger at Alex's face, nearly poking her in the eye.

"You just called me Rosie."

Alex took Rosalie's finger in her fist, lowering it as she pushed the door open. "Maybe I did."

"No one calls me Rosie anymore," Rosalie mumbled as Alex ushered her inside with a soft hand at her back. "Not since I was a little kid. I used to hate it."

"Do you hate it now?"

Rosalie turned and looked Alex up and down while she decided if she liked Alex calling her Rosie. Alex closed the door and set the key on the glass credenza, slipping out of her shoes while Rosalie studied her.

"No," Rosalie decided.

Alex gave her a rare smile. Rosalie was so disarmed by it, she accidentally dropped the blanket she'd managed to hold as they walked from the fire to the cabin.

"Let's get you to bed, Rosie," Alex said, leaning

down to pick up the blanket.

"Okay, bijou."

Rosalie meant to giggle at the joke of calling Alex *bijou* again but found herself captivated by Alex's face. She was so near, so warm, and the taste of her salty shoulder lingered on Rosalie's lips.

Rosalie found herself tipping forward toward Alex's face and realized halfway there she intended to kiss Alex. On the mouth. With her mouth.

As her lips slid against Alex's, she leaned farther forward, relief and excitement flooding her body, overtaking the effect of the wine. She felt uncorked, as though she'd been desperate to kiss Alex for weeks. She was as surprised as Alex seemed to be. It was as though a giant beam of light pointed toward Alex, illuminating her for the sake of making Rosalie aware she should have been pursuing her all along.

Rosalie shuffled closer, hands coming up to Alex's head, fingers threading into her hair, as though she would tip Alex's head to be able to drink from her more deeply. She hummed and stretched up onto her toes, giddy to be kissing in such a way, realizing what a romantic setup this weekend had been.

Alex put her hands tentatively on Rosalie's waist, making Rosalie feel small and protected and desired. Her touch was so powerful, Rosalie fell farther forward, letting Alex support most of her weight.

When she needed air, she drew back for a minute, eager to see Alex's face. Alex was staring at Rosalie intensely.

"You're so pretty," Rosalie slurred.

Alex gave a lopsided smile, and Rosalie shivered with delight. She leaned forward again, tilting her chin up to kiss Alex with even more fervor.

Her mind slipped through the door behind her, drawing her toward the bed, urging her to pull Alex in that direction. She was getting dizzy on her feet.

Rosalie tightened her grip on Alex's head, then slid her hands down and wrapped her arms around Alex's neck. She deepened their kisses, sliding her tongue forward. As she did, she thought perhaps she should slow her tongue down so she didn't seem sloppy.

She pulled back. "Le's go'n th' bedroom," she said, trying to make her voice low and sultry. She reached for Alex's hand, fumbling before she found it. She tugged Alex toward the bedroom.

Alex's feet stayed rooted where they were.

"I'm gonna sleep on the couch, Rosalie," she said softly.

Rosalie glanced back, thrown off, then horrified. Had she misread Alex's cues?

"Do you not like girls?" Rosalie asked, panicked she might have forced herself on a straight girl.

Alex dropped Rosalie's hand and pulled her arm back toward her body, closing it around herself. "I *do* like girls."

She stood there, biting her lip, rocking up on her feet a few times while Rosalie's thoughts spun. Why couldn't Alex explain herself? Why was Rosalie always left guessing?

Alex kept her gaze fixed on the floor, and Rosalie understood.

Alex did like girls, but she didn't like Rosalie in that way.

"Oh. Okay," Rosalie said, shrinking into herself, reeling from the rejection and the wine. "Sorry."

She turned, shoulders hunching as she skulked into the bedroom, furiously embarrassed and wishing she hadn't drunk so much. Alex had been right to take her last glass of wine from her. She couldn't imagine what she might have done had she been more inebriated.

Rosalie closed the door before she realized her stuff was still out in the lounge area. She slipped back to get it and saw Alex making herself comfortable on the couch, then slid back into the bedroom and struggled out of her pants and shirt into her pajamas. She realized she'd intentionally packed her nicest pajamas because she knew Alex would see them. God, she was an idiot, wasn't she? She hadn't even realized she liked Alex, and now she'd drunkenly made a fool of herself and found out Alex only thought of her as a friend. The next day, she'd be cooped up in Alex's truck for hours while they drove back to Ashhawk. Her stomach churned thinking about it.

She washed her face, accidentally splashing water everywhere and poking herself in the eye. She brushed her teeth, feeling the toothbrush jab the back of her gums with her sloppy arm. She fell into the bed, hoping she wasn't so drunk she would snore. She pictured Alex out on the couch and buried herself under a pillow. Hazy images of the fire and Alex's stoic, pitying face tormented her as she struggled toward sleep.

In the morning, she woke with a splitting headache and a burning stomach. She knew the heat outside would be more unbearable than usual. She checked her phone, remembering shortly after digging it out of her bag there was no service. She didn't know the Wi-Fi password, so she showered and got dressed, avoiding checking on Alex as long as she could. She put on her favorite sundress—which she'd packed because she'd subconsciously wanted Alex to see it—and did her hair and makeup slowly. When she couldn't find anything else with which to procrastinate, she ventured into the lounge area of the suite, surprised to find it empty. Alex had folded her blanket and placed it on top of her pillow. Perhaps there was a breakfast event she wasn't aware of.

She dared to venture out into the morning sun, realizing as she did it was quite late. The sun was almost overhead, making the white gravel beneath her feet blinding. She put on her sunglasses but still had to squint. She walked toward the lobby, feeling every glass of wine in her dried and aching muscles crunch like the gravel under her feet.

Inside the lobby was a more subdued scene from the night before. It appeared many guests were resting or on a day excursion, and the few who lingered were sipping coffee and eating fruit and pastries slowly and with gentle conversation.

Malcolm walked over to Rosalie with his arm up as though he was going to draw her into a hug.

"Morning, bijou," he said. It looked like he was about to say something else when he got pulled away by another guest who needed his attention.

Logan came up to fill the void, handing Rosalie a glass of ice water and two aspirin. "Rough morning?" he asked.

"You could say that."

"If we can't let our hair down here, it's not worth coming," he said, shaking his head as though he had a great flowing mane rather than a short, neatly styled cut.

Rosalie hummed, downing the pills with cold water, trying not to wince at how the chill shocked her system and sharpened the pain between her eyes.

"Alex asked me to drive you home," Logan said, petting Rosalie's arm in a gesture of exaggerated affection. "Let me know when you want to leave."

Rosalie tried not to sputter into her water, choking on the ice and the realization that Alex had left without so much as an explanation or apology. The sting in her head warmed with the rest of her, her embarrassment igniting like a twig thrown into the bonfire the night before.

Alex wanted nothing to do with her anymore.

As Rosalie packed her belongings to slink back to Ashhawk, she realized how foolish her behavior the night before had been. There wasn't a worse person to kiss than Alex. Shelley, perhaps, though Shelley might have laughed it off as a drunken prank or party game. But Alex knew it wasn't a joke. Alex knew Rosalie had meant that kiss, and now they'd be forced to work together under a shroud of embarrassment and regret that was impossible to escape.

The ride back to Ashhawk seemed exponentially longer than the drive there. Logan tried to make polite conversation as he maneuvered the van onto the main road and sped toward Ashhawk, but Rosalie couldn't muster the energy to return the favor. She blamed her hangover and tipped her head back, feigning sleep for most of the drive.

Alex's truck was in the parking lot when Rosalie arrived. Rosalie slid out of the cab, relieved she could go hide in her room. She thanked Logan as profusely as her shame would allow, keeping her head down as she walked the few yards to her door. All she wanted was to be alone until Shelley had to leave for her diner shift.

She closed herself in her room, feeling her

eyes stop aching now that she wasn't blinded by the unforgiving desert sun. She dropped her bag, stepped out of her shoes, and cranked up her air conditioner. She poured herself a large cup of water and chugged it before flopping back on the bed. She stared up at the asbestos popcorn ceiling before flinging her arm over her eyes. She wanted to hide from everything. She'd been so desperate to get out of Ashhawk, yet she'd managed to mess up what was supposed to be a vacation.

It seemed the world didn't want her to rest because her phone pinged in her bag on the floor. Rosalie groaned, annoyed. She dragged herself up from the mattress, rummaging through her bag to unearth the phone. There were a few texts from her mom, a voicemail from the main office number, and a few dozen emails.

She avoided replying to her mother, instead checking the message, which was a brief narration of Shelley's quest for extra guest towels, culminating in the discovery of said towels and apology for calling her while she was out of town. Rosalie deleted the message and began scrolling through her inbox, deleting invitations to events in Philadelphia, a few Facebook notifications, and sale announcements from a handful of online retailers. Her finger hovered over an email from George Tackett from Shaylin Development from the previous afternoon. It seemed so long ago. The guilt and embarrassment Rosalie had endured since then had aged her.

This time, Rosalie didn't delete the message like she had before. She opened it, skimming George's message before clicking on the attached PDF of Shaylin Development Inc.'s offer for the Cocheta property. But before it could fully load, she changed her mind and pressed back to the home screen. She had too much on her plate to be able to process any business decisions.

Though she knew she would have little to say, Rosalie wished she could call Tara and talk. She was frustrated with herself, with Alex's inexpressiveness, and with having to be in New Mexico at all. Rosalie missed Tara's companionship, but she knew she couldn't call. It would ruin the placidness of their breakup. And Tara was the last person she should call to talk about Alex.

When it was time to drag herself into the lobby and relieve Shelley, Rosalie heaved herself up and slid back into her shoes, locking her door as she squinted against the light and heat. Shelley was sitting behind the desk flipping through a magazine, chewing gum. The only thing that would have made her look more ditzy would have been if she'd been twirling her hair. Still, she was reliable, and the guests liked her. Rosalie had been smart to hire such a pretty girl to work the desk.

Shelley looked up when she heard the bells on the door. She straightened, trying to hide the magazine. "Hey!" she said anxiously.

Rosalie lifted a hand to wave and indicate it was fine for Shelley to be reading a magazine.

"How was it?" Shelley asked, smiling.

Rosalie realized Shelley was one of the more cheerful people in Ashhawk. In comparison, she felt like an afternoon storm cloud.

"A disaster."

"Oh, no..."

Rosalie leaned against the counter, slumping. "I'm so hungover."

Shelley wrinkled her nose. "Hangovers are no fun."

Rosalie rolled her eyes as though to say *No kidding.*

"Do you want something for it?" Shelley asked. "I've got aspirin."

"I took some, thanks."

Rosalie leaned even farther against the counter, propping her head up with her hand.

"Is something else wrong?"

Rosalie sighed. "I did something dumb."

Shelley pouted. "Come sit and talk." She gestured with her chin toward the couch.

Rosalie hesitated. She couldn't tell Shelley about any of the things going wrong for her. Shelley had no idea Rosalie liked girls and no idea she and Alex had been with a bunch of gay men. Rosalie realized why Shelley was always cold toward Alex—Shelley must have known Alex liked girls and treated her accordingly. In a small town, the word would have gotten out. Rosalie knew it was too risky to say anything.

She took a few steps toward the couch as Shelley slipped into the back room, emerging with two cups, which she filled at the cooler.

Shelley settled into the couch beside Rosalie. "So what happened?"

"It wasn't a big deal," Rosalie lied. "Drunken nonsense."

"Did you hook up with someone?" Shelley asked in a hush.

Rosalie stumbled over the question. Was the color of her shame so specific that Shelley could see it?

"Was he married or something?"

"No."

"Did you forget to use a condom?" Shelley

asked, voice hushed. "'Cause there's this stuff at the pharmacy..."

"No," Rosalie said, grateful for Shelley's obliviousness. "There was no guy."

Realizing she was veering too quickly toward outing herself, Rosalie constructed a quick lie. "There were some real estate agents there, and I should have used the time to network, but I wanted to relax and take a vacation, you know?"

Shelley nodded, sipping her water. "Still don't have anyone interested?"

"Not yet."

Rosalie ran her fingers through the water accumulating on the outside of her glass. It felt good on her hands. She thought about the Cocheta property and the unopened proposal from George Tackett and wished she could talk to Shelley about that. But admitting she owned yet another piece of property in Ashhawk wouldn't endear her to Shelley or anyone else in town. Gran hadn't told people about the property for a reason, and Rosalie wasn't sure why yet.

Shelley gave a hum to indicate understanding and contemplation, but it sounded hollow.

Rosalie realized she should have asked about business matters first. "How were things here?"

"Totally fine," Shelley said. "I had to go on a little hunt for some clean towels. I guess Susan didn't move them from the laundry room to the storage closet."

"She's getting a little old," Rosalie hedged, trying not to sound like she was complaining. She wasn't sure what to do about Susan, other than relegating her to the desk as often as she could.

"Did you know she lives with a woman?" Shelley said, her voice hushed as though Susan's living arrangements were gossip.

Rosalie's hackles rose, remembering Shelley's casual use of the word *dyke* during her haircut.

"So?"

Shelley gave a shrug. "I thought I knew most people in town."

Rosalie tried not to squint at Shelley, to keep her voice from frosting. Shelley wasn't saying anything inherently negative, but Rosalie was wary.

"What's wrong with living with a woman?"

If Shelley was a bigot, she'd rather know outright than try to guess.

"Like, as a *couple*," Shelley said, almost in a whisper. "Like, they're gay together."

Rosalie wouldn't have suspected Susan shared her proclivities, but she didn't expect much from Susan.

What she did expect, at this point, was ignorance on Shelley's part.

"So?" Rosalie said, pressing her.

Shelley shrugged again, as though backing away once Rosalie indicated she wasn't interested in gossiping about her employees. "I just didn't know."

Rosalie heard a bit of steel in her voice as she said, "I don't care *what* my employees do on their own time."

Rosalie knew she sounded cold, calling attention to the power discrepancy between them while also dismissing the time she and Shelley had spent together socially as insignificant.

Shelley's gaze flickered to the side, uneasy with Rosalie's chilly demeanor.

A tense moment passed while Rosalie imagined that she was brave enough to tell Shelley she was gay, too, and if Shelley had a problem with it, she should find employment elsewhere. But such an order seemed harsh. Coming out to Shelley was a moot point anyway; Rosalie's Sapphic inclinations were theoretical for the moment since Alex wasn't interested and there didn't seem to be any other lesbians in Ashhawk. Aside from Susan and her partner, apparently.

A car horn sounded in the parking lot, and Shelley perked up like a trained animal, relieved to be released from the tense conversation with Rosalie.

"That's Bobby," she said apologetically. "Sorry I can't stay longer. Come by the diner later if you want."

Rosalie nodded, relieved to not have to lie about anything for the rest of the evening. She gave a lackluster wave and sighed into the empty lobby.

Chapter Eight

Communications Center

A few hours after Shelley left, Alex came in the lobby looking wary. Rosalie cowered, lowering her head so her face couldn't be seen from above the counter.

"Hey," Alex said, curling over the counter to try to get Rosalie's attention.

Rosalie burned with embarrassment. She wished Alex would leave her alone to pretend she'd never made a pass at Alex. It was bad enough they lived on the same property. Rosalie wondered if she could tack a to-do list on the shed every few days and let Alex do whatever maintenance projects interested her. It would be clean and easy, and Rosalie would spare herself being reminded every day what a fool she was.

But Alex seemed to have the opposite plan.

"I'm so sorry."

Rosalie kept her head down, pretending to study an insurance document she'd unearthed. "Don't worry about it," Rosalie mumbled.

In a way, Alex had done her a favor by disappearing. She hadn't had to sit through hours of awful silence in the cab of Alex's truck, sweltering with shame and exhausted by tension. Instead, the cool, tinted van Logan had driven her home in had shrouded her embarrassment enough to make it back to Ashhawk without collapsing in on herself.

There was a tense silence, and Rosalie wondered if she wished hard enough, Alex would hear her thoughts and leave her alone.

"Is there anything I can do?" Alex asked.

"The sink in room seventeen is leaking," Rosalie mumbled.

Alex paused, adjusting her arms against the counter. "Okay..."

There was no sense of sheepishness in Alex's voice. Rosalie wondered at it; did Alex understand how she'd messed with Rosalie's head? All these weeks Rosalie had wondered if Alex liked girls, only to be shepherded to a beautiful desert escape and learn Alex *did* like girls, but not her. It was the perfect seduction, only Alex had backed out at the last minute. After she got what she wanted—Rosalie coaxing her into bed—she'd refused, content with her unfulfilled conquest.

Was this a game Alex played? Rosalie had no idea where Alex went sometimes. She could easily drive to another town to seduce other girls. Maybe she followed through with them. Maybe she even brought them back to the hotel after Rosalie was asleep.

"I guess I'll be in room seventeen," Alex said, placing her hand on the counter for a second, as though to conclude the conversation with a pat.

Rosalie dared to look up at Alex for the first time. Damn her. She was so attractive in her black tank top, curly hair falling down her back.

Alex's behavior only confirmed their kiss had meant nothing to her.

Rosalie looked down at the desk again, and Alex exited, letting the lobby bells clang behind her.

Rosalie let out a breath she didn't realize she'd

been holding. She brought her hands to her face, exasperated with herself. She felt she was spinning out of control in a series of bad decisions. Since moving to Ashhawk, every choice she'd made was wrong. All her circumstances were beyond her control. From the way Rosalie was handling things, she thought Gran had to have been senile when she left the property to her. Only someone heading toward dementia would do such a thing.

Rosalie had always been a bit indecisive, but not as cripplingly so as she'd become in recent months. She'd thought as she neared thirty she'd become more self-assured, but her journey thus far had mostly involved wishing she was in her teens again, when Marisol and Frank helped her make good choices. She had good judgment, but only with smart people advising her. Now she had no one to advise her.

Desperate for some semblance of control, Rosalie turned to her computer. Within minutes, she had found multiple listings for online hotel management courses. She scrolled through them, eyes bugging out at the price tags. She wanted to get better at her job, but she didn't want to invest in something her heart wasn't in. The courses would be there if she needed them. Right now, what she needed was a drink. Or maybe a good meal.

She trudged around the building until she could hear shuffling inside the shed. Rather than face Alex directly, she simply called out, "I'm going to the diner," before whipping around and walking out. She heard Alex call back *Okay*. She didn't want to look back to see if Alex was watching her.

She zipped down the street, angry and desperate for some kind of relief. She debated swinging by a bar but didn't think it would be a good idea. She pulled into a spot at the nearly deserted diner and stalked inside, sliding into her usual booth without catching Shelley's eye.

Shelley came up to her immediately. "Hey," she said, trying to be perky through her fatigue. "Long time no see," she said with a wink.

Rosalie sighed. "You guys don't serve alcohol here, do you?"

Shelley scrunched up her nose apologetically. "Sorry."

"Damn." Rosalie picked up her menu and let the bottom edge slap against the table as she held it upright. As she did, she realized she probably sounded terrible to Shelley, who had an alcoholic dad and deadbeat boyfriend. "It's okay," she amended. "I'm fine without a drink."

"I can get you a chocolate milkshake?" Shelley said, voice curling up at the end of her non-question.

"Yeah. And a big basket of fries."

Rosalie ate quickly, then wished she had brought her laptop so she wouldn't be faced with either sitting idly at the diner or going back to Hearth, prickling with shame in Alex's presence. She pulled out her phone, hoping Tara or even Marisol would magically know she needed to talk and would call or at least text. But there was no magic in Ashhawk. Only flies and dirt and hippies and rednecks and mice.

As the food settled in her stomach, so did her desperation. She knew her extraction from Ashhawk would not be instantaneous. It would come bit by bit. First, she could divest herself of one thing, and then another, until she was free to return to whatever was left of her life in Philadelphia.

Whenever she'd been panicked or overwhelmed as a child, her father had told her to take tasks one at a time, in manageable chunks. *You don't read a book all at once,* he'd say. *You read it page by page.*

Rosalie could stomach one page of her life in Ashhawk at a time. Right now, all she had to process was sitting in the dumpy diner and digesting the food she'd eaten, and in a few minutes, paying her bill. She could manage those tasks.

And while she was at it, she could actually read the proposal from George Tackett. She didn't have to make a decision about it.

She pulled out her phone, waiting for the antiquated data roaming service to load the PDF. It took a full minute before it opened. Rosalie read it, trying not to let her jaw drop when she saw what Shaylin was willing to pay for the property. Soon the numbers were swimming on the page, and her heart raced with the pressure to make a decision. Before she even got through the first page, she clicked back and set down her phone. She wondered if anyone in the diner suspected she was the incompetent owner of such a big piece of the town as she sat there with her empty plate and glass.

She felt sick again. She shouldn't have read the email. It was too much, too big a decision for her aching head.

She bit the inside of her cheeks repeatedly as she paid her bill and drove back to the hotel, letting the dull ache of her flesh bear the punishment for her behavior the night before. She settled behind the desk, looking through the previous week's revenue reports. Even though revenue was up a surprising twenty percent, Rosalie didn't feel good about it. She couldn't feel good about anything.

When her phone rang and she saw it was Marisol calling, she wasn't sure if she should answer. Marisol had a way of dramatically brightening or ruining her day. Such was the power of mothers, Rosalie figured, which was precisely why she wasn't sure she ever wanted to be one.

Even though she knew it might be a mistake, her hope Marisol would be in one of her more maternal moods prompted her to answer the call.

"Rosalie, honey, how *are* you?" Marisol cooed into the phone.

Rosalie adored the sincerity and love she felt oozing from her mother when she had her attention.

"I'm okay. Sorry I didn't call you back right away. I was out of town for the weekend, and I didn't know I wouldn't have cell service."

"Where'd you go?"

"This little resort called Corte del Cuervo."

"By yourself?"

"No…I went with—a new friend."

"New *friend*?" Marisol said knowingly. "What's her name?"

Rosalie felt herself blush. "Alex," she said. "It's not like that. She's helping me fix up Hearth."

"Useful with her hands, huh? Lucky you," Marisol said with a giggle.

Rosalie flushed scarlet, never comfortable with her mother's casual references to her sex life. Marisol was often more enthusiastic about the fact that Rosalie liked girls than Rosalie was. Perhaps because it was one of the few interesting things about her, and Marisol wanted an interesting life.

"I wanted to ask you something."

"Yeah?"

"When did I first laugh?"

"First laugh?"

"Yeah."

"I don't know. A long time ago," her mother tittered.

"Do you know what I laughed at?"

"Probably your dad doing something silly."

"How old was I?"

"Like six or eight months. Why?"

Rosalie felt herself sink. "No reason."

"You thinking about having kids?" Marisol asked.

"No."

"You know I'll love you no matter what you decide," Marisol said. "Right now, Hearth is your baby, isn't it?"

Rosalie bristled. She didn't want any attachment to Hearth, much less the unbreakable sort that was motherhood.

Rosalie didn't doubt her mother was sincere in her apathy about grandchildren, but Marisol's tone indicated she wanted to wrap up the topic so she could get to whatever she wanted to talk about next.

Rosalie felt a rare swell of anger at Marisol. She'd wanted to learn something no one else could tell her, save for maybe her father. She wanted someone to shine light on who she was and why she never felt grounded anywhere. If she hadn't laughed until late in her infancy, perhaps there was a part of her spirit that hadn't wanted to descend from whatever celestial realm her ancestors were associated with. Perhaps she would always feel resentful of the earthly places she inhabited.

Or perhaps she was putting too much stock in a

belief held by a culture to which she didn't belong.

There was a pause that made Rosalie nervous. Marisol was usually bubbly, and a pause in conversation was never a good sign.

"How's Ahbie?" Rosalie asked.

"She's doing well," Marisol said, sounding more distracted by the minute. "Baby, I wanted to tell you... Your father and I have been talking."

Rosalie stiffened. Marisol and Frank rarely talked. It couldn't be a good sign if they were now.

"We've agreed I should move out."

Rosalie was stunned. She had often wondered why her parents were married, but she never expected them to separate. As she thought about her quiet, gentle father, she knew it hadn't been his idea. He would never have wanted Marisol to move out.

"You're *separating*?" Rosalie's voice squeaked in disbelief.

"We're trying it out for a bit, yeah," Marisol said, her voice dripping with concern for Rosalie. "That's why I've been staying at your place. But don't worry. Your father and I have always been good friends. That's not going to change."

Rosalie felt panic pushing up in her chest, and she had to fight not to blurt out that *everything* was going to change now.

"Everything will be fine, I promise. I bet you won't even notice the difference next time you're home," Marisol said, her voice too sweet and hopeful for Rosalie to believe it.

Luckily for Marisol, Rosalie was too upset to protest. She thought of her dad, completely alone, eating his overcooked vegetables and chicken in front of the TV, hoping Marisol would come home a little earlier than usual. Her heart ached for him. She had never in her life wanted to hang up on her mother, but in this moment, she did, if only so she could call her dad and make sure he was okay.

"And Dad is okay with this?" Rosalie managed to choke out.

"He's fine," Marisol said. "He's got a date this weekend with that cute librarian from the downtown library."

Rosalie felt like she was about to vomit. There was no way this was happening.

"He's *dating*?" Rosalie said, trying not to gag.

The idea of her dad dating anyone was incomprehensible. She couldn't even imagine Frank dating Marisol back when they'd met. Dating didn't seem like something he was capable of.

"He's always had a little crush on her," Marisol said so casually it hurt Rosalie. "I think it's sweet."

"Mom…" Rosalie objected, wanting her mother to stop delivering harsh news in rapid sequence. "How long have you guys been talking about this?"

"A few months," Marisol said, as though Rosalie had asked her how long they'd been planning a weekend trip up the coast. "It just felt right."

It was quiet, and Rosalie felt herself getting light-headed.

"You know I was never home anyway," Marisol said, as though to absolve herself of any guilt.

Rosalie couldn't even bring herself to sound bitter. Mostly, she was trying to make sure she got enough air.

She leaned her elbows on the desk to fortify herself. Marisol sounded so upbeat about giving up on her marriage. Rosalie needed to call her dad right away, which meant ending the conversation with her mother quickly.

Rosalie had spent years tamping down her anger at her mother, to the point she didn't even realize she was doing it. She'd tamped down until her ire was as tough and impenetrable as desert dirt. But now something was quaking below the surface, and Rosalie worried all her work would be undone; her anger would erupt, and her fury would become so permanent she'd never be able to speak to her mother in a civil tone again. She panicked, something harsh grating up in her throat on its way to lash out at Marisol.

Luckily, Alex opened the door of the lobby and strode in. Even more agitated, Rosalie grabbed onto the opportunity like a lifeline.

"I have to go. A guest just walked in."

"Okay. Don't worry, sweetheart. I promise everything's gonna be fine."

Rosalie didn't believe a word of it. "Okay. Bye."

"Love you, baby—" Rosalie heard as she lowered her phone and ended the call as quickly as she could.

Overwhelmed by the news that her parents were separating and disarmed by Alex's presence, Rosalie didn't lift her gaze to meet Alex's. She kept her eyes down and said, "Excuse me, I need to make a call."

"No problem," Alex said. Her voice was as smooth and calm as ever.

Rosalie twisted out of her seat and walked into the back room where the microwave and mini-fridge and extra towels were housed. She closed the door and called her dad, pacing the small space as her body surged with panic. This couldn't be happening. Her sweet, calm, lonely father didn't deserve to have Marisol ruin his life. Especially so soon after his mother had died.

She held the phone to her ear, desperate for Frank to answer and tell her Marisol was playing an elaborate and cruel joke on her.

But the call went to voicemail, and Rosalie thought she would burst into hysterical tears. She held herself together, zipping up long enough to leave a message.

"Hey, Dad." She gulped. "I, um..."

She paused, realizing she was talking to a soulless answering service about something as personal as her parents' thirty-two-year marriage. She didn't want to talk about something so precious with no response on the other end of the line.

"I have some questions about owls. Give me a call when you get this." She swallowed one last time. "Love you."

She hung up, wondering if the machine would ever be able to relay how her heart ached for her father, the last two words a concealed plea for reassurance Frank was okay.

Rosalie was as shaky as she'd been after she'd fainted weeks before. She wished she could teleport to her bed and roll herself in her comforter and never come out.

Rosalie pictured the rest of her life in Philadelphia: her parents' home, her office, Tara's apartment, her favorite sandwich place. She realized none of those places existed anymore. Her parents' home only housed Frank's belongings now; her own apartment was full of Marisol's things. She hadn't spoken more than five words to Tara in weeks, and she didn't have a job to go back to. Even her favorite sandwich place would probably be different.

Rosalie wondered when she'd ever feel like she

was home again.

Steeling herself to face Alex, she took a deep breath and opened the door. She hoped she didn't look visibly upset. The last few times Alex had seen her, she hadn't been at her best—drunk, hungover, and furiously ashamed—and didn't want such unflattering situations to become habit.

"Sorry," Rosalie managed.

"Everything okay?" Alex said.

Alex was leaning on the counter, tilted forward. Rosalie saw the intense way Alex was looking at her, the depth of her concern, and caved. Alex's silence invited confidences.

"My parents are splitting up."

Alex's face shifted back into a look of surprise and apprehension, but she didn't say anything.

Rosalie realized one of the things she liked most about Alex was how much space she afforded Rosalie. She never talked over Rosalie, never pushed her own agenda, never became distracted by her plans for after work. She never swept unpleasantries under the rug. She was always present, which both unnerved and soothed Rosalie. Rosalie had time to figure out what she wanted to say. She appreciated that more than ever now.

Rosalie felt something push up and clamp in her throat. Hot tears prickled in her eyes, and though she fought as hard as she could, she knew they would spill over. Her face scrunched and her shoulders locked and her stomach tensed.

Seeing Rosalie start to cry, Alex straightened up, striding around the desk. She stood before Rosalie for only a moment before wrapping her in a protective, nurturing, and unexpected hug. Rosalie felt herself give into Alex's arms, her shakiness leaving her body to be replaced by heaviness. Alex held her with her usual sturdiness. Rosalie relished it as long as she could before reminding herself this was the girl who had rejected her the night before. She stepped back, running her hands under her eyes to wipe away her tears. Alex stayed close, monitoring Rosalie for any subtle change.

"I'm worried about my dad."

Alex gave a serious nod and kept listening, hands lifted toward Rosalie without touching her.

Rosalie felt the need to keep rambling. "I don't want my parents to split up."

"Of course not," Alex said. Her voice was low and honeyed the way it had been at Corte del Cuervo.

Rosalie kept sniffling for a few minutes before Alex took charge. "Let's sit down," she said, anticipating Rosalie's heaviness would overtake her soon. She guided Rosalie by the elbow to the weary couch under the window.

Rosalie sat in the sagging center while Alex perched next to her, twisting so she was totally attuned to Rosalie.

"Maybe I'm being selfish, but I want their house to be there when I go back, you know? I don't have anything else to go back to."

Alex hummed to indicate she'd heard Rosalie but didn't have any comment of her own.

Rosalie felt her tears start to mount again and took several heaving breaths to fortify herself against them.

"C'mere." Alex drew Rosalie into her arms and nudged Rosalie's head onto her shoulder. She sat back, bringing Rosalie with her so they were leaning against the back of the couch.

"It's okay, Rosie," Alex cooed. "You're gonna be okay."

Even though Rosalie knew she should push away from Alex and deal with this herself, she didn't. As hard as it was to be pressed to Alex's warm, ripe skin knowing Alex didn't feel the same way about her, it would have been harder to reject the only tenderness she'd received in months, perhaps even years. Rosalie never wanted it to end. She wiped her nose so it wouldn't drip on Alex and let herself breathe into the space below Alex's collarbone.

"Ever since I came here, everything's falling apart," Rosalie mumbled.

"Not everything," Alex said. "Not the pool or the sinks."

Rosalie took an appreciative gulp of air, wishing she could laugh.

Disinhibited by her emotions, Rosalie figured now was her chance to apologize for her behavior at Corte del Cuervo.

"I'm sorry about last night. I don't usually drink like that."

"It's okay," Alex said with a little smile. "Happens to the best of us."

Rosalie sighed. Alex had probably never made inebriated advances on an uninterested girl.

"Sorry I made things awkward," Rosalie mumbled. "I'm not good at reading people, obviously."

"Obviously?"

Rosalie resented the question. It felt like Alex was fishing for a verbal acknowledgment of Rosalie's unreciprocated feelings for her.

"It's dumb," Rosalie said, scanning the ugly

carpet. "I thought you were into me."

It was quiet and still for a second before Alex said, "Probably because I am."

Rosalie's gaze darted up, searching Alex's face for any trace of sarcasm or mockery.

She found none.

"What?" Rosalie asked.

"I *am* into you," Alex said, slipping her hand onto Rosalie's knee.

Rosalie felt her skin tingle at the touch. "Then why did you—" Rosalie cut herself off, not wanting to relive Alex's rejection.

But Alex knew what Rosalie meant.

"Because you were *wasted.*"

Rosalie felt a wave of humiliation pass over her, followed by confusion. "But you left."

Alex froze, looking stricken. "Did Malcolm not tell you?"

"Tell me what?"

Alex's whole body drooped as she brought her hand to her face. "Oh, my god, I'm gonna kill him," she exhaled. "Malcolm was supposed to tell you Jason needed me to bail him out. I would have left you a message or a text, but I knew you didn't get service…"

Rosalie recalled Malcolm approaching her at breakfast and being distracted by another guest. Knowing Alex wasn't a good liar, nor did she have a reason to lie, Rosalie felt the weight of her shame lift instantaneously.

"Rosalie, I swear to god, I did not mean to ditch you. I was looking forward to having breakfast with you…and seeing what you remembered."

Rosalie recalled the events of the night before, the clear pictures of the hotel in the evening leading into blurrier, more emotional snapshots of Alex at the campfire, Alex leading her back to the room, Alex pressed flush against her while they kissed. That memory seemed the brightest, yet the most fleeting.

"Like when I kissed you?"

Alex's face lifted in a sheepish grin. "Yeah."

Rosalie felt a giddy warmth spread through her. "I do remember that."

Alex's smile spread even wider, and she looked suddenly very young. "Good."

Rosalie sat there radiating with happiness before she grew curious and concerned. "What do you mean Jason needed you to bail him out?"

Alex's gaze flitted around the room, and her smile wavered.

"Bail him out of *jail*?"

Alex sighed. "He's an idiot."

Rosalie sat stunned, not sure how to respond. But silence around Alex was okay. Silence didn't have to be tense.

"He gets in trouble a lot. More than usual lately."

"He's been arrested before?"

Alex gave a gruff nod. "I guess I'm an idiot for rushing to the rescue every time."

"No," Rosalie objected. Hearing Alex speak poorly of herself made Rosalie want to shake her. "He's your brother."

She thought about the intricacies of family and how, despite all the infuriating things her parents—mostly her mother—did, she still loved them.

"If I had a brother, I'd probably bail him out of jail, too."

Alex fidgeted with something at her knee for a minute.

"This is the last time," Alex said. "My dad gets real mad every time I do. It's hard because he's my kid brother, and after my mom left, I was kind of the mom substitute...I didn't know what I was doing, but I tried to take care of him."

Rosalie chewed her lip. "I'm sorry," she said quietly. "I wish I could help."

"It's not your problem."

"I know. But you've helped me with almost every problem I've had since I got here. It'd be nice to feel like I can return the favor once in a while."

Alex nodded and took a deep breath, letting it out. The tension was broken, the air cleared from their series of miscommunications. But there was still a heaviness hanging over them that had nothing to do with each other.

"We've had a banner weekend in terms of family drama, huh?" Rosalie offered.

Alex cracked a fatigued grin. "Yeah, this weekend didn't exactly go the way I hoped."

Rosalie paused, wondering if she dared to ask. "What were you hoping for?" She hoped she didn't sound too flirtatious, even if she meant to hint at it.

Alex's expression shifted from tired to sly. "Actually, for the most part, it did." Her gaze flickered to Rosalie's lips.

Rosalie felt her body accelerate.

Alex took a breath. "I was coming in here to see if you wanted to have dinner with me sometime this week. Like, you know...a date. But I figured I should wait until you were feeling better."

Rosalie resented her parents even more for deterring Alex from asking her out.

"Ask me," Rosalie said, feeling her body surge

and lighten, as though it might lift off the couch if she didn't ground herself.

Alex twisted her torso even closer to Rosalie with a confident smile. She placed her hand on Rosalie's knee again.

"Rosie, will you have dinner with me this week?"

Even though she knew it was coming, Rosalie felt a heavy flutter in her stomach. She let out a nervous giggle, eyes dancing all over the lobby as she fought the blush overtaking her face and chest.

"Yes," she said.

"I don't know if I believe you actually want to go," Alex teased.

Rosalie felt her face grow warmer, and she directed her smile toward Alex. "Yes."

"What was that?" Alex lifted a hand to cup her ear.

Rosalie swatted at Alex's arm, but Alex caught it and held Rosalie firm, wrapping her other arm around Rosalie and pulling her head back onto her shoulder. Rosalie pulled her legs up so she was completely curled into Alex, giggling.

"Yes, I will have dinner with you, *Alex*," she said through a laugh.

Alex gave her an extra squeeze for good measure. "Good."

Chapter Nine

First Date

S moothing down her hair and checking under her arms for deodorant stains, Rosalie braced herself against her nerves. Susan was covering the front desk, and Rosalie had more faith in her competence as a receptionist than as a housekeeper, so she knew her anxiety was about Alex. She couldn't remember the last time she had been so nervous to go out with a girl. Her first date with Tara had been a casual meet-up for a glass of wine after a few pleasant message exchanges on a dating website, so Rosalie hadn't worried about it too much. If they didn't mesh, she'd be out ten dollars and a few hours of her time. But if this date with Alex didn't go well, she'd be out much more.

She picked up her purse, taking one last look in the mirror to check that nothing was stuck to the back of her khaki skirt. Seeing nothing, she opened the door, squinting against the early evening light that shone directly in her face in an onslaught of blinding gold. The sky was painted vibrant colors, but Rosalie couldn't see it beyond the glare. She shielded her face as she turned toward Alex's room, wondering if she should knock or wait for Alex to come out.

Alex stepped out of her room before Rosalie had to make a decision, hitching her chin in greeting. "You look nice."

Rosalie looked down. She didn't look much different from her everyday office attire. "Thanks."

Alex strode toward Rosalie, then paused. What happened now?

"Do you want to drive?" Alex asked.

Rosalie looked at Alex's truck, thinking of its elevated cab and how nice their conversation had been the last time she'd been in it. She shook her head, wondering if Alex had been hoping she'd say no.

"Hop in," Alex said, unlocking the truck and climbing into the cab.

Rosalie climbed in as gracefully as she could, hoping she didn't flash Alex in the process. She wanted to keep a tiny bit of mystery about her until they'd been on a few more dates.

"There's this place the next town over I wanted to take you," Alex said. "They do these caravan things every first Saturday. It's fun."

Rosalie didn't know what Alex meant by caravan, but she went along with it. "Sounds good."

Alex turned the ignition until it rumbled and guided the truck out of the parking lot heading south.

They drove for a minute in silence, worry creeping up on Rosalie as she wondered if it would have been a good idea to come up with some conversation topics before the date. She and Alex had spent plenty of time together in peaceful quiet, but now that they were on an official date, things were different. When they hit a bump in the road, the dreamcatcher on the rearview mirror swung, reminding Rosalie of their conversation about Alex's time on the Navajo reservation.

"I asked my mom about my first laugh."

"Yeah?" Alex turned her head to smile at Rosalie, understanding the mental connection Rosalie had made.

"She didn't remember."

"Oh."

"That's typical for her."

Alex nodded. Rosalie hadn't been outright abandoned by her mother like Alex, but not all absences were physical. Rosalie and Alex understood having absent mothers.

"Maybe your dad knows. My dad remembered mine."

"Yeah?"

Alex gave a subtle nod and looked at the road, saying nothing.

"Are you gonna share?" Rosalie teased.

Alex smirked, adjusting her hands on the steering wheel. "I was three months old, and my parents took me out for dinner in my little carrier thing. The waitress was fawning all over me. Apparently, she did something I liked, and I laughed."

"Was she hot?"

"Probably." Alex chuckled.

"Figures."

Alex turned her head and gave Rosalie a neat, fleeting little wink.

Rosalie was relieved the tension was broken. She would have winked back if she didn't think she would look silly.

"So what's this thing you're taking me to?"

"A food truck caravan," Alex said. "All kinds of trendy Southwestern food. Sound okay?" Alex asked with a tinge of anxiety.

Rosalie pictured it like the food truck gatherings she'd passed in Philadelphia.

"Sounds great." Rosalie smiled. She wished she could reach over and smooth Alex's arm to assure her, but the cab was too big to do so without it seeming forced.

When they got to the caravan, it was already teeming with people. Alex walked beside Rosalie, hands to herself, sunglasses shielding her eyes from the evening sun. Rosalie took it all in—the bright colors and smells and the heat weeping off the vans and people crowded around them. It smelled delicious. For the first time, she felt like she was experiencing the Southwest outside of the dried-up corner she'd been banished to and the cultivated oasis that was Corte del Cuervo.

Alex elbowed her way through some lines, securing them each a plate of food. They found a section of curb in an area without too much traffic and sat. There was an air of frenzied competition around them; each truck boasted something more imaginative than the next. Rosalie devoured all of it, relishing her precious time away from Hearth with Alex.

This town was nicer than Ashhawk. It still felt quaint, but there was less dust and trash and peeling paint and other signs of disrepair. The area they were in seemed like it had been intentionally curated to represent what Rosalie would call Southwestern Boutique.

It was crowded and noisy, and their mouths were so busy scarfing down food they didn't talk much. Rosalie supposed it didn't matter; Alex was a woman of few words to begin with. Still, eating beside each other was different from eating with each other. Rosalie hoped the next part of their date would be more personal.

Once they'd finished their food, Alex took their plates and threw them away, snagging a few wet wipes for their hands.

"Want to take a walk?" she asked, rubbing a

towelette into the crook of her thumb before throwing it away.

"Sure."

As they left the noise of the food caravan behind, Rosalie felt herself relax. This was what a date was supposed to be: walking together, observing the sights, opening themselves up to whatever happened. Yet it felt a little empty.

Alex seemed to think so, too. She stepped closer, keeping her gaze ahead, and in a low voice said, "I would take your hand if you wanted me to. But I understand if you want to just walk like this. It's different here than in Philadelphia."

Rosalie digested Alex's words. She knew things were different here. The clash of Catholicism and Native American spirituality yielded conflicting attitudes about same-sex couples. Had they been in Ashhawk, Rosalie would have known for sure she wasn't ready to out herself. But since they were a few miles removed, she slipped her hand into Alex's, giving a momentary squeeze before sliding her hand back out. It was a promise for authenticity wherever she felt safe.

Alex smiled, understanding. "Let's go in here," she said, pointing at a shop.

Rosalie had seen dozens of similar shops with a combination of cheap tourist trinkets and authentic New Mexican wares: turquoise rings and necklaces, woven baskets, blankets and throws in colorful tribal patterns. Rosalie wasn't sure she knew the difference between the cheap trinkets and the real goods, other than how they were displayed. The clothing toward the back of the store was less flashy, more like the desert in its color schemes. Dusty oranges and blues and tans, hats without logos or names of cities emblazoned on the front. Alex gravitated back there, as well, and leaned over a lit case of jewelry.

Alex didn't wear jewelry. Rosalie figured it was a good thing; a ring or bracelet could catch in one of her tools and pull off a finger or hand in a split second. But Rosalie wondered if she would have if that hadn't been the case.

Not wanting to appear clingy or insecure, Rosalie turned to a rack of dresses with bold patterns on them. One in particular caught her eye: halfway between orange and red, like a violent sunset, with large, black shapes traced vertically over it in an indistinct tribal pattern. The material was a stretchy blend, something that would fit effortlessly over her curves, breathing in the heat her other clothes seemed to suffocate in. Its thin straps made it questionable to wear for work, but a cardigan could remedy that and protect against the air conditioner's chill. She looked at the price tag—twenty dollars. Not bad for a little piece of color and style.

"You should get it," Alex said, appearing over Rosalie's shoulder.

Rosalie tried not to startle; she hadn't noticed Alex had moved away from the jewelry case. "I don't know," Rosalie hedged.

"It's pretty. The color looks great with your skin."

Rosalie looked at her hand holding the soft material and saw it did make her skin look like it was glowing. "Where would I wear it?"

Alex's breath stopped for a second before she whispered, "Out on a date with me."

Rosalie's heart raced, and she bit down a smile. Alex had plans for more dates together, which made the prospect of whatever sentence she had to serve in Ashhawk almost bearable.

Rosalie took the dress off the rack, deciding

twenty dollars wasn't worth making a full pros and cons list in her head.

Alex grinned, hovering an appropriate distance away from her as Rosalie paid the cashier. She stuffed the bag and receipt into her purse and gestured with her head for Alex to follow her back out onto the sidewalk.

They walked up and down the streets of the town for a little while longer, finding few places open besides the bars. Alex strode casually with her hands in her pockets while Rosalie's hands shifted from her purse strap to her sides to her face.

Even though she was basking in a rare break from the stifling responsibility of Hearth, Rosalie couldn't help thinking about her parents. She didn't know much about their courtship, but she imagined they'd gone on dates like this, where her father, quiet and kind, accompanied Marisol all over Philadelphia, indulging whatever whimsy struck her. Rosalie thought of him sitting alone at home now, watching whatever National Geographic Channel program piqued his interest that day.

"What are you thinking about?" Alex asked, a weakening softness to her voice.

"My dad," Rosalie admitted. She was struck by the swiftness with which Alex had picked up on her shift in demeanor.

"Have you heard from him?"

"I got a weird email."

"What did it say?"

"I'd asked him about what kinds of owls are indigenous to this part of New Mexico, and he said desert owls are burrowing and I shouldn't worry because owls are crafty and find ways of thriving even in the harshest conditions. But I never said I was worried about desert owls."

They strode along quietly before Alex said, "Maybe he wasn't talking about owls."

Rosalie stopped in her tracks. Of course. Her father had been telling her he was okay in his own way. She gave Alex a shaky smile before she resumed walking. "Thank you."

Alex gave her a soft smile. "No problem."

The car ride back was quiet. Rosalie wished they'd had time to see a movie or walk around longer, but Susan had made it clear she needed to be home by ten. As they neared Hearth, the silence between her and Alex began to feel less easy.

"You're quiet," Rosalie said.

"Always," Alex said with a brief smirk.

"I like it. Except when I don't know how you're doing."

"Doesn't get much better than a night out with a pretty girl."

Rosalie smiled, her flush precluding her from speech.

Alex pulled into the parking lot, putting the truck in park. "I believe one should only speak if it improves on silence."

Rosalie nodded, studying Alex in the fading light mixed with the spooky glow of the exterior lights of Hearth.

Alex shut off the engine, leaving them encased in quiet.

Rosalie thought about all the quietness surrounding Alex and how she was learning to read when it was tense and when it was calm. It was calm now, Rosalie realized, and she leaned into it.

Rosalie stared into Alex's dark, serious eyes.

Unbuckling herself, she scooted toward her, asking with her eyes if she should continue.

Alex stared at her, leaning forward so Rosalie knew she was welcome.

Rosalie brought her hand up to Alex's cheek, kissing her soberly this time, drinking in the softness and taste of Alex without the muffling noise of the alcohol. She felt each nerve of her lips, each muscle moving beneath, each fraction of breath on her upper lip. Her heart rushed, and her ears prickled to hear the tiny smacks of wet against wet, the pull of fabric against fabric where their arms and chests pressed together. The kiss was slow and soft, full of everything their previous kiss had lacked.

When Rosalie pulled back to gauge Alex's face, Alex followed her forward before opening her eyes and giving Rosalie a soft, drunken smile.

"That improves on silence, too."

Rosalie grinned, heat spreading through her face and chest. She leaned forward again for a few more strokes of lips against lips before she pulled back and reached for her door handle. "Thank you."

"You're welcome," Alex said, eyes trained on Rosalie's face. She seemed to contemplate something but decided against it. "Good night."

"Good night," Rosalie replied.

Alex paused before opening her door and slipping out, giving Rosalie one last nod. Rosalie grinned like a fool as she got out of the cab and walked to her room.

Rosalie was giddy at the way Alex treated her. Had she been more zealous, she might have invited Alex back to her room with her.

But the silence of the night was perfect as it was.

Chapter Ten

Turndown Service

Rosalie pulled up to the bar, nerves tingling in her stomach. She never went to bars like this and certainly not with someone she was newly dating to meet her friends. She'd agreed to go because she wanted to know Alex better and because she felt guilty for always turning Alex down for such outings prior to their weekend in Corte del Cuervo. Perhaps getting to know a few locals would help her feel better about being stuck in Ashhawk. When Shelley had been available to cover the desk, Rosalie had jumped at the chance to leave the hotel.

Rosalie wondered if she was dressed too formally; her button-down shirt and khakis might make her look uptight in front of Alex's friends. But it was too late now. She switched off Gran's car, glancing at her purse in the passenger's seat. It looked too stuffy to bring into the bar. Surveying her surroundings and deciding it was safe, she took a twenty out of her wallet, stuffed it into her bra, and shoved her purse under her seat.

She got out of the car, wilting in the heat. She tried to look confident as she walked up to the bar, holding her head high and ignoring the men huddled beside the door smoking and speaking in rapid Spanish.

Inside, she found what would have been called a dive bar in Philadelphia but was simply a bar in

Ashhawk. The walls were so heavy with old photos, vintage signs, hats, mirrors, and ads for beer, they seemed to be curling in on Rosalie. It wasn't crowded, but it was the most populated place Rosalie had been to in Ashhawk. Mustached and bearded men of all ages cradled sweaty brown bottles and glasses in their hands, speaking both English and Spanish. There weren't many women, but they were there, frizzy hair and faded clothing making them blend into the dated scene. Several televisions hung in corners of the room, garnering fragmented attention from the people in it.

Rosalie spotted Alex at one end of the bar, hanging on the fringe of a group of men Rosalie would never have approached on her own. They were wearing jeans or basketball shorts and worn tees with grease stains on them. A few wore baseball caps. Two were sporting stubble on their cheeks, and all were drinking beer. Alex would have blended in with them, with her worn, straight-cut jeans and black muscle T, except Rosalie found her so attractive—her lean muscle and bronzed skin set her apart from the ruddy, sun-parched, deep-fried, stubble-covered bodies of her friends. Rosalie slipped up beside her, grateful to have Alex's protection as she navigated such foreign terrain.

Rosalie put her hand on Alex's arm, feeling how smooth and warm it was.

Alex turned, a smile blooming across her face, a private greeting for Rosalie. "Hey."

Alex's whole body turned, and Rosalie froze as she realized Alex was turning in to kiss her. She didn't know how to respond—was it safe for two women to kiss here? Had she not made it clear she wasn't ready to be out in Ashhawk?

Thankfully, Alex turned past her lips and past

her cheek, placing her lips near Rosalie's ear. "You look great, babe," she whispered.

Rosalie's body surged with Alex's compliment and the anxiety of having almost kissed in front of all these strange men. "Same." She giggled, giving a subtle glance down Alex's body.

Alex grinned and turned back to her friends. "Guys, this is Rosalie," she said, gesturing in Rosalie's direction with her beer.

Rosalie realized she shouldn't have been worried about Alex outing her. Alex was careful and polite in all exchanges.

"She just took over the Hearth Inn for Estelle. She's cool. She's also my boss, so don't give her any shit." Alex glanced back at Rosalie with a proud expression that would have included a wink if Alex had been more expressive.

Rosalie gave a little wave.

"What's up, Rosalie?" said a guy in an American Spirit T-shirt. A few others nodded, lifting their beers without moving to shake Rosalie's hand. Rosalie wasn't sure how to greet them in response.

"Sorry to hear about your grandma," one guy said, standing tall with his chest puffed out in a confident manner. "She was a real nice lady."

"Thanks, she was."

The bartender leaned toward their side of the bar, asking if he could refill anyone's drink.

"Rosalie wants a drink," Alex said, gesturing to Rosalie. "You can put it on my tab."

"You got ID?" the bartender asked, raising his eyebrows at Rosalie.

Rosalie looked at Alex and the boys in disbelief. Surely, she didn't look *that* young.

"She's with me," Alex said.

"Still need to see some ID."

"Um…it's in my car," Rosalie said. "I'll be right back."

Rosalie walked out to the car, already worried about what she would talk about when she returned. She leaned into her car, taking out her ID and tucking her purse back under the seat.

As she walked back into the bar, the presence of the men at the door made her feel too aware of her body. She felt where the fabric of her shirt pulled across her chest, where her khakis strained against her backside and thighs. She felt as unnatural here as a neon balloon drifting into the desert only to pop.

She thought she'd passed them without incident when she heard one of them mutter something that ended in, "Ay, mami."

Rosalie cringed. She knew she'd stick out here. She was a useless city girl in a town that didn't want her any more than she wanted it.

As she approached the end of the bar where Alex and her friends were clustered, she heard Alex speaking to the guy in the American Spirit shirt, fingers casually tapping her beer. "You'll have to ask Rosalie."

"Ask me what?"

"If you're single," the guy said.

Rosalie's gaze darted to Alex, trying to convey her panic without being too obvious. She wasn't ready to out herself in Ashhawk, but she also didn't want to make it seem like she was available to any of the guys in the bar.

Rosalie took comfort in Alex deferring to her to respond but wished she knew what to say without undermining their new romance. She decided to play it safe and not mention dating at all.

Rosalie gave a forced, pitiful laugh and said, "I'm pretty busy with the hotel right now, and I just went through a breakup, so..."

"Damn," the guy said, glancing at Alex as though to express mutual disappointment.

Rosalie gestured to the bartender, showing him her ID and receiving a beer she hadn't requested in response. She looked around and saw all the guys and Alex were drinking the same beer.

"Sure you're not looking for a rebound?" the guy said with a grin. It wasn't creepy or lecherous. Just misdirected.

"Sorry," Rosalie said with a conciliatory smile.

She shot Alex a smile she intended to be conspiratorial but conveyed some of her panic.

Alex took Rosalie's cue and turned toward the guy. "So how are things at the shop?"

"Good," the guy said, seeming bored with the topic. "My dad's letting me do more customizing work, which is fun."

Alex nodded and asked subsequent questions, from which Rosalie gathered the guy worked in some sort of auto body or mechanic shop. Rosalie tried to ask questions and participate in the conversation, but she was at a loss for questions and contributions. She hovered on the edge of the group, anchored only loosely by Alex, who kept a safe distance to protect Rosalie's secrets.

Rosalie learned several of the guys worked in a casino the next town over. One particularly burly man was a security guard. He seemed to be the most arrogant of the group, the most unconcerned with the poverty of the town. Another worked in construction in Albuquerque, commuting at ungodly hours. The rest were unemployed.

Rosalie finished her drink, feeling little relief from the alcohol or the looseness of everyone around her. She wondered if another drink or three might help but didn't want to venture close to getting drunk around Alex again. Rosalie wondered why she didn't know how to navigate conversation with these people. She realized it had as much to do with being around small-town folk as it had to do with being closeted.

Alex seemed aware of her discomfort, glancing at her often, seeming to encourage and apologize with her eyes. When Rosalie set her empty bottle on the bar, fidgeting with her sleeve for lack of something else to do with her hands, Alex drew closer.

"You want to split?"

Rosalie tried not to seem too eager as she nodded.

Alex bobbed her head in response, paid her tab, and turned to the guys. "We're gonna head out, but I'll catch you guys on Friday for the game." Alex tipped her chin up in a gesture of familiarity.

The guys hitched their chins up in response, raised a few sweaty bottles in farewell, and turned back to their conversations. Alex headed toward the door without getting too close to Rosalie.

When they were outside, Rosalie felt her body start to unravel, as though she was being released from a wrapping of rubber bands that had encircled her from head to toe.

"You okay?" Alex asked quietly.

"Yeah," Rosalie said, feeling guilty.

"It's probably not your scene," Alex said, as though she should have known as much.

"It's okay," Rosalie said, trying to escape her

lingering discomfort. "Do they know?"

"That we're dating? No," Alex said, keeping her voice low and smooth to comfort Rosalie.

Rosalie was uneasy with the certainty of Alex's answer.

Alex tilted her head, considering. "They might wonder since I never bring girls around. But I doubt Dan would have asked about you if he thought we were an item. They usually stay out of other people's business."

Rosalie nodded. Alex was probably right.

Rosalie wasn't so terrified of coming out in Ashhawk that she would go to great lengths to conceal herself, but she needed to have some sense of control in her life. She'd had her job, her apartment, Tara, her family, and pretty much everything else taken away from her in the last few months, and there had been nothing she could do to stop it. She was drowning in the desert, desperate to grasp anything that might steady her. Deciding when and how she came out here was the one thing she could control.

Alex hovered next to her truck, hands in her pockets, waiting for Rosalie to work through whatever knot of worry she had tied. She seemed to know Rosalie needed someone to change the subject for her. "Have you looked at the Cocheta property yet?"

Rosalie reeled at the reminder of that particular burden. She shook her head.

"Maybe we should check it out," Alex offered with an indifferent shrug. "You should at least know what it looks like."

Rosalie nodded. She'd been putting off a trip to the property. Some irrational part of her was worried she'd find something disturbing there; not a body or another rundown hotel, but some new information about Gran's life Rosalie realized she knew so little about. Visiting would only create more questions, she was sure.

But going with Alex was better than going without Alex. If she had to face something unknown, she would rather not be alone.

"Sure. Let's go."

Alex bobbed her head and gave a fleeting smile. "We can drop your car at Hearth on the way."

Rosalie nodded, turning to get into her car. Behind her, she felt Alex pause, waiting until she was seated in her car before climbing into the cab of her truck. Alex was watching her, noticing the worry that clung to her like static, trying to figure out a way to conduct it away from her. Yet Rosalie worried about the shock if she tried.

They left Rosalie's car at Hearth and drove to the other side of town. Rosalie held her breath as they approached the end of the road where her property was situated. They passed a few dilapidated houses, some abandoned, until the road turned to dirt and the buildings ended, as though the desert would eat anything daring to venture farther into its depths. It was impossible to tell where the edge of her property met the wildness of the desert. They were indistinguishable, save for some arbitrary legal line that said Rosalie had rights to some of the dust and rocks and shrubs and not the others. It was funny to think ownership mattered so much to people.

Alex pulled the car to the side of the dirt road and turned off the motor. She seemed to be moving slowly. Probably so as not to spook Rosalie.

To prove how little she needed soothing, Rosalie

unbuckled her seat belt and slid down from the cab quicker than usual, as though visiting her mysterious desert property was a task of no particular importance or hassle, like grocery shopping or going to the post office. Her feet crunched on the ground as she took a few steps away from the truck, her footsteps loud in the alarming silence of the desert. She stood straight, back to Alex, and surveyed the land with her hands on her hips. She owned this land. She was in control.

Yet as she stared out at it, she felt her confidence and certainty waiver, as though a breeze was blowing through, touching only her. The land before her was so vast, its sage greens and shades of brown and rust stretching as far as she could see, blending together in the hazy horizon of distant hills and rock formations. She didn't own all of it, she knew. Only a few square miles. But the ownership wasn't what made her falter.

Rosalie had the sensation she was about to be crushed. The sky above felt enormous, its bright blue with wispy clouds stretching so wide and thick she felt it would fall on her. There was too much dry, hot air being forced into her lungs, dragging with it the dust from the land. There was nothing to steady herself on, save for a few bony shrubs that would crumble under her weight and rocks that would jab into her weak and delicate skin.

The desert was inhospitable and threatening. She hated it. She hated the burden of owning any piece of it. There was no piece of Gran here. Rosalie realized she'd been hoping to find clues as to what she was supposed to do with the land. Instead, she found only dust and shrubs and a feeling of doom hovering over her and half the town.

Alex drew up cautiously beside her.

Rosalie tightened her stomach. "Looks like every other piece of desert," she said, pretending to be unfazed.

"Sure does," Alex said softly.

Rosalie folded her arms across her stomach in a gesture of feigned indifference.

"This particular piece is yours, though." Alex tipped her head to the side an inch. "That counts for something."

Rosalie gave a stiff shrug. "I guess."

She tried to take a few calming breaths but only felt the desert choke her more.

"Not a great spot for a date, though," Rosalie said, signaling she wanted to leave.

"Where do you want to go?"

Rosalie hesitated, unsure. What she wanted most of all was to hole up in her room, undisturbed by the heavy threat of the land before her. But that wouldn't have been fair to Alex. Hiding wasn't a date, and disappearing was the opposite of the apology Rosalie knew she needed to make for being so awkward around Alex's friends.

"Maybe get some sopapillas?"

"Where do you want to eat them?"

Rosalie shrugged.

"I'd say we can take them back to Hearth, but I know you like to get away."

"That sounds fine, actually," Rosalie said, relieved she wouldn't have to endure much more time spent around the strange people of Ashhawk.

They drove back to the hotel, picking up food on the way. Rosalie offered to pay, but Alex refused. "I like paying for my date's dinner once in a while."

Rosalie wasn't sure she should be comfortable

with such antiquated chivalry but decided ten dollars spent on takeout wasn't worth an argument. She'd put her foot down for bigger things.

Alex pulled her truck around behind the hotel, buying them some privacy from Shelley's curiosity without the expectation attached to being in one of their bedrooms. Rosalie changed into jeans and a cotton T-shirt, returning behind the building to find Alex had set up a makeshift picnic spread in her truck bed. Rosalie was relieved with the casual presentation. The desert was peaceful around them.

After they ate, Rosalie felt more guilty about her behavior in the bar. She hadn't even made an effort to get to know Alex's friends.

Rosalie watched Alex as she bagged up their plates and dropped them over the side of the truck, making a soft splash of plastic against the desert dirt. Alex stretched out and leaned back, grinning at Rosalie. Her posture wasn't sexual, but it invited intimacy. Rosalie felt like Alex was open to anything.

"Do you ever feel like you know someone but don't know a lot *about* them?" Rosalie asked.

Alex smiled. "Sure."

Rosalie bit her lip. "I feel that way about you."

Alex adjusted herself, her brow turning in a small expression of concern. "I'll tell you anything you want to know. 'Cept maybe my Social Security number and my complete browser history."

Rosalie smirked. "I have your Social Security number on file from previous years' tax documents."

Alex laughed. "True, true. And my browsing history isn't that interesting. So I guess anything is fair game."

Rosalie smiled and took a risk. "What's going on

with your brother?"

"As you could see, he's almost too gay to function outside Corte del Cuervo. Though the same could be said of me."

Rosalie's smile grew tense. "I meant your little brother. Jason, right?"

Alex's grin wavered. "Yeah. He's…well, he's an addict. That's about all there is to that."

Rosalie twisted her face into a look of compassion and pity for the pain Jason had caused his family. "Heroin?" She knew its use was widespread throughout the area.

"And meth. Whatever he can get his hands on."

Rosalie let out a heavy breath. She almost wished she hadn't asked because now she didn't know what to say. "That must be so hard," she said quietly.

Alex gave a slow nod, contemplating her nails for lack of anything else to do.

"That's why I was in such a hurry to move in here. I couldn't handle being around him all the time. When he isn't high as a kite, he's tweaking out."

Rosalie was desperate to relieve the tension, so she said, "And here I thought you just liked being around me."

Alex looked up appreciatively. "That definitely didn't hurt."

Rosalie gave another pitying smile. "I'm glad you moved in. But I'm sorry it's because your brother is sick."

Alex nodded, wrapping up the heavy conversation with a tense smile. "My turn."

Rosalie adjusted into a more relaxed position. "Shoot," she invited.

"When did you first know you liked girls?"

Rosalie bit her lip as one side lifted. She liked this topic among other queer women. There was a sisterhood to their shared experience.

"Well, I could tell you about the first time I kissed a girl and all that boring stuff," she started.

"Oh, please do." Alex grinned.

Rosalie sniffed a giggle. "But I think the first big clue was when I was thinking about God or whoever was running the universe."

Alex tilted her head. "I didn't know you were religious."

"I'm not," Rosalie said. "But when I was younger, I liked to entertain all the different theories about celestial power to see which ones felt real."

"Did you reach any conclusions?"

"When I was about ten, my dad gave me this book on paganism and other earth-based religions, and I remember reading something about Mother Earth and Father Sky or something like that and thinking that if two beings were actually running the universe, they were probably both female."

Alex chuckled. "What a good little lesbian you are."

"I know, right? My first clue wasn't thinking about how beautiful girls are or how much better I got along with them. I just thought women should be running the universe. And then that sent me into a panic about whether I'd ever get along well enough with a man to sustain a marriage and if he'd let me run things my way...And then I probably got distracted by whatever Christina Aguilera was doing that week and who in my friend group wasn't talking to whom because they'd cheated another girl out of a good sticker trade or something. You know, more important issues than who was running the universe."

"Oh, my god, you're precious," Alex said, a look of amused adoration on her face. "I don't know if I can handle how cute you were."

"I wasn't *that* cute," Rosalie argued. "I was kind of shy and awkward."

"So were we all at that age," Alex said with a shrug.

"My turn again." Rosalie thought for a minute about what she wanted to ask. She felt she'd dug a little too deep with her first question, so she opted for something lighter, but something she'd been curious about for a while. "Do you have girl friends?"

Alex shifted, adjusting herself against the wall of the truck bed. "That depends on what I should call you." She gave a coy smile.

Rosalie felt something shiver inside her, a nervous giggle coursing through her. She leaned forward and pressed her lips to Alex's cheek. She liked Alex a lot and didn't want to date anyone else. She supposed the word for that was *girlfriend*, but she wasn't ready for it. It seemed so permanent and serious.

Alex turned her head to the side and met Rosalie's lips, drawing a kiss out, as though it was sweet, juicy fruit. She let Rosalie's avoidance slide, and Rosalie was grateful for it.

Rosalie transferred so she was sitting next to Alex, leaning half against the wall of the truck bed and half against Alex. They kissed for a minute, slow and lazy in the warmth of the desert evening. Rosalie felt excitement stir in her belly, but it settled into happiness.

"I do have a few female friends," Alex said when she pulled back. "But I don't see them often."

"Why not?"

"We only get together every few weeks when one of the bars a few towns up has a gay girl night."

"There are other lesbians in New Mexico?" Rosalie asked, feigning surprise.

"It turns out there are." Alex grinned.

"Can I meet them?"

Alex squeezed Rosalie against her. "Of course. They'd love to get their hands on you." She kissed Rosalie again, gripping Rosalie's side in a tentative squeeze. Rosalie kissed back with an earnest flick of her tongue.

Their kiss escalated until Rosalie felt they were nearing clothing removal. As much as she liked Alex, she didn't want their first time to be in the back of a truck behind the hotel. It seemed both risky and trashy. She drew back, darting forward to give Alex a sealing peck on the nose.

Alex understood, drawing Rosalie closer to her so they could curl up together in the fading light.

"I want to take you somewhere tomorrow," Alex said against Rosalie's cheek.

Rosalie hummed into Alex's neck, willing to agree to almost anything to keep basking in the warm, protected feeling of being in Alex's arms.

❧❧❧❧

Alex greeted Rosalie with a peck on the cheek. "You look hot, babe," she said with a grin, body turning toward her truck in its usual spot in the parking lot.

"Thanks. Where are we going?"

Alex jingled her keys. "It's not super sexy, but I think you'll like it."

"Yeah?"

Alex nodded, scanning the parking lot. "I've got a contact at a carpet wholesaler a few towns over. They've got some remnants that go for real cheap. I thought we could take a look and see if there's something you like for the lobby."

Rosalie took a few steps toward Alex's truck. It hadn't been what she was expecting at all.

"We can get food and stuff while we're out, too," Alex offered. "So it's still a date."

"Pretty much anywhere is good as long as I get to leave the property."

Alex smiled, swung her door open, and hopped up into the cab of her truck, Rosalie not far behind. They fastened their seat belts, and Alex started the engine, pulling out of the parking lot heading down the lonely highway.

They drove past several large casinos. The buildings with their sprawling parking lots sprung up like money-hungry oases with little more than a gas station or drive-thru near them. Rosalie had been in a casino once or twice in her life and had little reason to go in one again. Still, she had a morbid curiosity; why were they the only establishments to flourish in the wasteland of the desert? They did nothing but sully the land and its people with booze, debt, and false hope of riches. Such corruption seemed like it should have no place in the vast, relatively untouched desert. Yet they were the only stable businesses around, save for the diner and she supposed, in a way, Hearth. It seemed unfair.

The carpet wholesaler was a large, stuffy warehouse full of ugly, industrial carpets. The remnant section was well-stocked, but most of the pieces were too small to cover the expanse of the lobby. The few large ones were hideous, and Rosalie was quickly discouraged.

Alex peeled back the corner on a roll of sage green carpet, cut just a few feet bigger than the lobby.

"What about this?"

Rosalie examined it. It wasn't the first color she would have been drawn to, but maybe that was a good thing since she had no design expertise.

"Will it go with the rest of the lobby?" She couldn't picture it with the dark wood paneling, worn plaid furniture, and the heavy counter.

"No, but you were planning to redo all that anyway, right?"

Rosalie grew even more hesitant.

"We could take off all the ugly paneling and get covers for the furniture. I can restain the counter."

"How long would that take?"

"A week. Week and a half," Alex said with a shrug.

Rosalie felt her resistance peak, and she backed away from the carpet remnants. "That's a big project..."

"Yeah, but this isn't too expensive." Alex tapped the carpet with her foot. "Sheet rock and molding is the biggest expense, plus my time, which you've already budgeted for."

Rosalie nodded distractedly, feeling like Alex was more invested in the hotel's beautification than she was. It was Alex's job, after all, but as the owner, Rosalie needed to be on board before any paneling was removed or carpet torn up.

"Is this not what you had in mind?" Alex gestured toward the stack of carpets.

"I don't know what I had in mind," Rosalie admitted.

In a flash, she realized—she hadn't had anything

in mind because she had hoped she would secretly magic the hotel out of existence. If the hotel didn't exist, neither would the ugly carpet or the horrible paneling or her dark, depressing little room with its dated art and yellowed wallpaper.

"Maybe we should go get dinner," Alex said, as though she wasn't fazed by Rosalie's reluctance to pick out a carpet.

"Yeah, I'm kind of hungry."

"Want to eat somewhere here?"

Rosalie thought the town was no sadder or happier than Ashhawk, its handful of restaurants far below the quality she was used to in Philadelphia. If they were going to go to a restaurant, at least she wanted to know the food was decent and there weren't any bugs.

"I'm kind of in the mood for pulled pork at the diner," she admitted, thinking of the nice meal Shelley had recommended the day Tara broke up with her. Since Shelley was working the desk, they didn't risk her seeing her with Alex and suspecting they were dating.

"Sounds good." Alex turned away from the carpets and drew near to Rosalie so they could walk beside each other out of the warehouse. She waved to her contact on their way out, calling out they'd be back another time.

They drove back to Ashhawk quietly. Rosalie felt uneasy, but she wasn't able to put her finger on why. Alex hadn't done anything wrong; the trip to the carpet warehouse had been a sweet gesture. But Rosalie couldn't shake her uneasiness. They slid into a cool, plastic booth at the diner and ordered before Alex made note of Rosalie's discomfort.

"You seem distracted," she said. It wasn't

accusatory or resentful, just curious.

"Thinking about Hearth. Renovating is going to suck."

"But you've got me."

Alex's smile faded when Rosalie didn't respond.

"I don't know what I'm doing," Rosalie admitted. "One day, I was minding my business in Philadelphia, and the next, I was the owner of a crappy hotel in—" She bit her tongue before she could say anything harsh about Alex's hometown. "In Ashhawk."

Alex gave a slow nod. "Yeah, that's a big change."

It was quiet while Alex chewed on Rosalie's preoccupation.

"You could always pull a *Desert Hearts*," she said with a chuckle.

"What?"

"It's an old lesbian movie. The main character moves to Nevada for six weeks to establish residency so she can get a quick divorce. The state pretty much made a business of helping women get out of their marriages."

"Does New Mexico have the same residency laws?"

"No," Alex said, amused expression fading as she took a sip of her water. "But that's no reason not to fill your hotel with eligible divorcees."

Rosalie gave Alex a raised eyebrow and continued eating.

After a quiet meal, Alex drove them back to the hotel. Rosalie felt so bogged down and overwhelmed, she felt like she was hardly in the same room as Alex, which made her feel guilty. She liked Alex and wanted to spend time with her. She just couldn't get it together today.

Maybe it was guilt fueling the suggestion

they watch a movie in Alex's room. She would have suggested they park out back again, but the expanse of the desert sky only added to her uneasiness. She followed Alex into her room, looking around at the drab, dated decor. Alex's sparse belongings were stacked and stored neatly in the simple furniture. She hadn't been in here since Alex moved in.

Eager for any distraction, Rosalie decided to throw herself into the physical. They'd known each other for a while now, and it was probably time they had sex anyway. Maybe a physical release would trigger an emotional one. This way, she could show Alex her apprehension wasn't about her.

She kissed Alex and pulled her toward the bed. Alex followed eagerly, keeping her lips affixed to Rosalie's face and neck as best she could. Rosalie pulled Alex by the shirt until they stumbled over the end of the bed, landing propped halfway up, with Alex trying not to let all her weight fall on Rosalie. The bed still had one of the crappy old mattresses, but it wouldn't matter for Rosalie's intentions. All they needed was a clean, supportive surface.

Alex was never one for idle conversation, and now was no exception. Alex didn't fill her mouth with words or eager giggles. Alex kept her eyes shut, leaning forward as though Rosalie were a spring she was drinking from after days in the desert. There was a desperate gratitude to the way her hands cupped Rosalie's neck and waist, yet there was something tentative, too. She was worried about handling Rosalie too roughly, and it showed.

Rather than tell her it was okay to be excited, Rosalie let her hands drift down over the seat of Alex's pants, gripping and pulling her fully onto the bed. Alex inhaled sharply and surged forward in response. They maneuvered up the mattress as Rosalie pulled Alex's tank up and off. Alex opened her eyes for the moment her mouth was free, smiling down at Rosalie before pushing forward again.

Alex's mouth was the busiest part of her body and the best thing Rosalie had felt in a long time. Alex's ponytail fell over her shoulder and tickled Rosalie's neck and cheeks.

As they undressed, Rosalie focused on how Alex's mouth felt: graceful, wet, intent on exploring her skin as thoroughly as possible. Alex's tongue sent shivers down Rosalie's back, making her wriggle out of the last of her clothes. It wasn't until she was naked and panting under an equally naked and panting Alex she felt overwhelmed.

She hadn't done this in a long time. She'd had a fair amount of sex with Tara and other girls she'd dated, but it hadn't been as alive as this, as unchoreographed and fresh and wanting. The volume of their breath was alarming against the sheets; it was as though all other sounds in the world had been vacuumed up, leaving only their mouths and lungs to fill the void.

Alex's mouth continued along Rosalie's neck and breasts as her hips fell against Rosalie's, securing her against the mattress. Rosalie should have felt eager, but Alex's weight felt as oppressive as the desert heat outside. She was trapped under Alex's body, Alex's mouth slowly sucking her foundation out from under her. She panted harder, trying to get her bearings.

Alex slid her hand up to cup between Rosalie's legs.

Rosalie panicked. This was not how she remembered sex feeling. Sex felt good and relieving. It shouldn't feel like she might choke or drown.

Alex slid her fingers through Rosalie, and Rosalie felt her head grow fuzzy, the confusing combination of fear and pleasure swirling through her, robbing her of her ability to speak or communicate. Her hands went stiff on Alex's back, and she stopped moving, save for her heavy breathing. Alex touched her for a few moments before she slipped her lips off Rosalie's breast, speaking for the first time since they'd entered her room.

"You okay?"

Rosalie gave a quick nod. She didn't understand why she'd seized up. She felt trapped.

"You sure?" Alex panted, squinting down at Rosalie.

Rosalie couldn't bring herself to nod again immediately, but she did.

"We can stop if you want."

Rosalie shut her eyes tight and shook her head.

It was only when Alex continued touching her she realized she wished she was anywhere but in Alex's bed.

Sleeping with Alex meant she was committing to staying in New Mexico longer than she intended to. Taking off her clothes and allowing Alex to touch her meant she was laying down roots in Ashhawk. She resented Alex for tricking her into bed as a way to anchor her to the hotel.

Alex was chaining her to a crumbling hotel, and Rosalie was desperate to get out.

But she couldn't make up an excuse to get out of having sex now. Not with Alex's fingers inside her and their clothes strewn across the room. Better to finish it off, she thought, and develop a plan for getting out of

New Mexico once she was alone with her thoughts in Gran's room later.

She mumbled something about wanting it harder as Alex hovered tentatively over her. Alex paused before obliging, her hand and fingers moving with mechanical reliability into Rosalie. Rosalie felt a modest surge toward release and figured it was good enough. She wasn't ready to make a full concession to Alex or Ashhawk or anything in her life. She tensed her whole body, trying to imitate some form of Kegel so Alex would find her faked climax believable. She let out a great gust of air.

She exaggerated her panting for a minute with her eyes closed, hoping Alex had bought her performance. When she dared to open her eyes, Alex was looking down at her with an unreadable expression. She wasn't angry or upset, but she wasn't pleased, either.

"Give me a second." Rosalie sighed.

Alex studied Rosalie for a second before she lifted her torso off Rosalie a few inches.

"You know...I'm good, actually," Alex said. Her tone was neutral, and Rosalie wondered what she meant.

"You sure?" Rosalie asked, concerned her hesitation had been obvious to Alex. "I'm pretty good with my mouth."

Alex gave Rosalie a muted smile, indicating that was the last thing she would agree to at the moment. "I'm sure."

She sat up all the way, looking around for her shirt. She stood to pick up some of her clothing. While Rosalie might have previously taken the opportunity to admire Alex's body, instead she felt acutely aware of her own nakedness, spread out on the uncomfortable mattress, on display for Alex to see.

She wasn't sure what to make of Alex's rejection. Clearly, Alex had picked up on something, but her reasons for stopping were unclear.

"Did I do something you didn't like?" Rosalie asked.

Alex didn't make eye contact as she pulled her shirt over her bare breasts. "No. Did I?"

Rosalie had only enough resolve to gently shake her head. Alex hadn't done anything specific she didn't like.

Alex pulled on her underwear and pants, not looking Rosalie in the eye. "I'm gonna go check on the vanities out back," she said, moving toward the door.

Without ceremony, Alex left Rosalie alone in dreadful silence.

Feeling an urgent need to cover herself, Rosalie scrambled to put on her clothes. She knew she'd done something wrong but couldn't clear her head long enough to figure out what it was and how to make up for it. She could have communicated something to Alex, but what could she say that wouldn't sound preposterous? Alex had never been anything but careful and kind with Rosalie.

She didn't bother putting on her shoes as she closed the door to Alex's room and slunk to her own, finding the small gray cat on her mat meowing at the door.

Normally, she would have greeted the cat with some kind, high-pitched words, but tonight her shame had pressed all the sweetness out of her. She opened the door, blocking the opening with her foot so the cat couldn't come in, and closed it behind her. She slipped out of her clothes again, feeling they contained too much of her evening with Alex. She showered and put on pajamas. Only then did she retrieve a can of cat food and peel off the lid, setting it on the doormat. The cat tried to slip around her arm into the room, but Rosalie held firm. She heard the cat meow a few times before it gave up and ate the food.

For the rest of the night, Rosalie tried to distract herself with mindless TV. There were reruns of *Light My Fire* playing, but even that couldn't dull the shame and embarrassment of her behavior. She knew she'd done something wrong. Sometime between dinner and Alex's fingers sliding into her, something had changed. She wished she knew what it was. When the stinging dryness of her tired eyes overwhelmed her shame, she turned off the TV and curled into herself, hoping sleep would find her soon.

As she tried to sleep, she heard a noise outside. At first, she thought it was the small gray cat again, but she realized it was farther away. The baby coyotes were calling louder than usual, their voices sounding scratchier and more like the cat's.

Wondering if the cat was still outside, Rosalie opened the door and stepped out into the night's chill.

At the end of the corridor, Rosalie saw Alex sitting in a chair, slouching with a beer in her hand. Rosalie was certain Alex saw her step out of her room. She was the only moving thing in sight. Yet Alex didn't look toward her, letting her gaze bore out into the still, black night. Rosalie felt something crush in on itself in her chest, so aching and heavy she slunk back into her room, convinced she'd ruined the only good thing about Ashhawk.

Chapter Eleven

Poor Hospitality

T he next morning, Rosalie woke heavy with guilt and dread. It took more strength than usual to pry herself off her mattress and into the shower. She dressed, taking little joy in her coffee, trying not to think of the empty day before her. When she went outside, she saw Alex's truck in the same spot it had been the night before, a painful reminder of everything that had gone wrong. She wished she could take it all back, everything from the carpet warehouse to the disaster in Alex's bed. But it was real.

As she made desperate phone calls to real estate agents, she saw Alex walk through the parking lot a few times as she went from room to room, making repairs. She saw Alex speaking politely to a few guests but could see something heavy resting on Alex, too. She felt bad about it; she'd obviously hurt Alex. But short of a meaningless blanket apology, Rosalie didn't know what she could say.

The desert had never seemed as harsh as it did today.

Until Rosalie got an unexpected phone call.

"Hearth Inn, this is Rosalie."

"Is this Miss Rosalie Campbell?" a scratchy female voice asked.

"It is."

"Oh, good!" the woman said, as though she was delighted. "My name's Coral Hatfield. I'm a corporate real estate agent from All Nite Inn. Are you familiar with our brand?"

Rosalie had seen a handful of All Nite Inns along the highway in the last few months. They were budget hotels catering to truckers and prostitutes.

"Yeah."

"I heard you had a property you're interested in selling. Is it still available?"

Rosalie was stunned. "Uh, yeah."

"Great," Coral said. Her voice was forcefully cheerful. "Do you want to set up a meeting?"

"Absolutely."

"Fantastic," Coral said.

They set up a meeting for a few days later, and Rosalie hung up with a confusing mix of emotions. She was thrilled a real estate agent would even take a meeting with her, but the crescendo of guilt she felt about Alex was growing deafening. She'd messed things up, she knew. But if there was still hope for getting out of Ashhawk without too much of a loss, maybe it was better if they didn't get in any deeper. Maybe her mistake had been for a reason.

They went about avoiding each other for the rest of the day. Rosalie almost thought they'd silently agreed to forget what had happened when Alex walked into the lobby around seven, heavy and anxious. She didn't make eye contact like she usually did.

"I have something to show you," Alex said, hovering above the counter.

Rosalie looked up, not sure if she should shut her laptop or if she'd be coming back to it in a minute.

"Should I lock up?"

"Sure," Alex said.

Rosalie closed her computer, taking her keys and phone with her, putting the sign on the glass door of the lobby before locking it behind her.

Rather than leading Rosalie to the room she'd been working on, Alex took her behind the building. In the same spot where Alex had parked her truck a few days before, the same spot where Rosalie had met the small gray cat, the same spot where Rosalie had roasted marshmallows as a kid was a brand-new fire pit with a ring of beautiful sanded wooden stumps around it. It wasn't glamorous by Philadelphia standards, but for Ashhawk, it was luxurious. Alex had taken great care to construct it for Rosalie.

"Oh, wow," Rosalie said.

Alex cracked a sheepish smile as she leaned over, plucking something from behind one of the stumps. She produced a sweaty brown bottle and offered it to Rosalie. Rosalie reached for it, grateful, before Alex bent over again to pick one up for herself.

Rosalie wasn't sure what Alex had intended, though she was grateful Alex had made a gesture at all. She watched as Alex used the bottle opener on her keys before offering to open Rosalie's.

Rosalie shivered as she stood there waiting for direction from Alex. Rosalie wasn't sure how she was supposed to respond. Alex took a seat, leaning forward on her elbows as she looked into the fire pit. There was wood but no flame.

"I figured I'd wait to light it." Alex nodded toward the perfect ring of brick.

Rosalie nodded, still standing stock-still outside the ring of stumps. It would have been silly to light the fire, as the sun was still up and it was still almost too hot to be outside. Only the coolness of the beer in her hand made it tolerable.

Alex looked up at her. "Are you gonna sit?"

Rosalie lurched forward, feeling foolish for thinking her feet were stuck outside the ring.

"This is nice," she said.

Alex let a smile grace her face for a second, looking up from under her brow at Rosalie before focusing back on the fire pit and the beer in her hands.

Rosalie perched herself on a stump next to Alex, knees pinned together.

"I used to roast marshmallows out here with Gran when I was little," Rosalie said.

"I know," Alex said. "I figured you'd like it fixed up for company."

"I don't have company," Rosalie said on reflex.

As she said it, she regretted it. Alex's gaze bored into the brick, and she hoped she hadn't offended. She could have added *Except you*, but the lump in her throat rose too quickly, and she took a swig of beer to combat it. "It's nice," she managed. "Thank you."

Alex gave a stiff nod, leaning farther forward on her elbows. Rosalie sat straight, knees and head turned toward Alex, unsure what to do or say next.

"I'm sorry about last night," Alex said. "I shouldn't have pushed you the way I did."

"You didn't push me," Rosalie said, surprised Alex was taking any blame. "I don't know what happened."

"But I went along with it, even though I knew you were uncomfortable."

Rosalie realized how transparent she'd been and felt ashamed. "I wasn't uncomfortable with *you*," she offered.

"That's good to hear," Alex said, still looking nervous.

It was quiet, and Rosalie knew she owed Alex whatever explanation she could muster. "I'm not sure what I'm supposed to do with this place."

"What do you want to do?"

Rosalie shifted forward, admiring the gaps in the brick as they formed a perfect circle. "I don't know. I'm not sure I'm cut out to be a hotel manager."

Alex gave a slow nod and took a sip of her beer. "It's a big job."

"It is."

"What makes you most nervous?"

Rosalie thought back to the office: the once-unorganized files, the slowly increasing revenue, the sorry state of the custodial staff. The whole endeavor was overwhelming.

"Nothing in particular. Just all of it."

Alex tapped her bottle with her fingers and nodded, gazing at where a fire should have been crackling. It was silent for a long minute, and Rosalie wondered what she was contemplating.

Rosalie didn't want to think about the hotel. It made her anxiety spike. She'd been presented with a new out, and she had to tell Alex about it. She dreaded the reaction she'd get.

"I have a real estate agent interested. She's coming to see the property on Thursday."

Alex's gaze fell to the ground, and she picked at the label on her beer bottle. "You still want to sell?" Alex asked, her voice as close to hurt as Rosalie had ever heard.

Rosalie felt guilty. "Can you blame me?"

Alex shook her head, but bitterness was clouding

her body, making her shoulders stiff and the little tugs of her fingers on the beer label more aggressive.

It was quiet for a long moment. Alex always thought every word through before letting it pass over her lips. Rosalie appreciated this; every word she received was incubated and thorough, never hitting anywhere but its desired mark.

Still, she knew whatever came next had the potential to knock her over.

Rather than speak, Alex swiveled her body so she was facing Rosalie, sitting up straighter, keeping her knees slightly spread. She looked at Rosalie at this new angle and reached forward, her fingers relaxed and gentle, tucking a strand of hair behind Rosalie's ear.

Rosalie felt herself flush at the tiny touch. Alex's work-roughened hands were intentional and gentle. Alex let a trace of a smile pass over her face, letting it fade into a look of pity. Rosalie wondered what that pity was for.

"I don't know anything about business, Rosie," she said.

Rosalie felt her stomach tense with the delight of being called Rosie. Few people called her that; she *let* few people call her that. Usually, she felt small and childish, but when Alex said it, she felt sheltered from any threatening dust cloud or desert storm.

Alex continued, "But I know at a certain point, no real estate agent or lawyer or hotel management expert has the answers for you. You may be new to this, but you can do it. I know you can. You have to trust your gut." She brought the hand with her beer bottle closer to her stomach, sitting up straighter to indicate how solid and reliable her gut was.

She held Rosalie's gaze steady, as serious as

Rosalie had ever seen her. Rosalie felt they could have been discussing something as grave as the fate of the town, until she felt they were discussing something much more sacred. For the first time, she saw a yearning in Alex's face, mirroring what she felt in her chest whenever she had called Alex to come fix something or help with a new project or ask which store in town had the best yogurt. There was something uncertain in Alex, too, and Rosalie had been given the power to fortify it.

Alex parted her lips, gaze flickering down to Rosalie's mouth for a second before she let her question pass through them.

"Do you trust yourself, Rosie?"

Rosalie was paralyzed, unable to move, speak, nod, or lean forward and press her face to Alex's. Alex had given her a rare opening into her stoic psyche. She knew she couldn't ruin it.

Yet the question itself sealed her fate. Under the intensity of Alex's gaze, she couldn't lie. She felt air escape her chest in a wounded puncture as she shook her head.

"No." She shrank back, disappointed and afraid of Alex's response.

Alex deflated, too, gaze falling to her beer. She glanced back at the remaining pack of beer, heaving herself up from the stump. "I'm sorry to hear that."

Alex walked away without saying anything more.

Rosalie sat in front of the unlit fire for a long time. She studied the dry land before her, looking for signs of life. The small gray cat came for dinner, and Rosalie heaved herself up to retrieve its food. A creeping sense of dread flooded through her when she saw Alex's truck in the parking lot. She'd hurt Alex's feelings. She needed to make sure she hadn't completely alienated her.

She went to Alex's room, feeling sheepish and obligated. When she knocked, Alex invited her in. Alex was lying on the bed, hand behind her head as she watched a baseball game. After glancing at Rosalie, she focused back on the screen.

There was a tense silence as the game made ambient noise in the background.

"How's the game?" Rosalie asked.

"We're up by four runs."

Rosalie looked around, debating sitting in one of the chairs. Taking a risk, she sat. "How's Toby doing?" she asked, parroting a question she'd heard one of Alex's friends ask.

"He's not pitching today," Alex said, her voice flat.

It was quiet again, and Rosalie feigned interest in the TV. The silence, once so normal around Alex, was excruciating.

As though knowing how uncomfortable Rosalie was, Alex spoke up. "Did you need anything?"

Rosalie squirmed, realizing Alex didn't want her there. But she'd come in with a purpose. "Just checking to make sure we're okay."

Another pause.

"Are we good?"

"Depends on what 'we' are," Alex said.

"What do you mean?"

Rosalie wanted Alex to turn her head and look at her, but Alex's gaze was fixed stubbornly on the television.

"If you're asking as someone I'm dating, no, we're not good. But if you're asking as my boss, yeah, we're good."

Rosalie felt her shoulders start to hunch up under her discomfort. She knew Alex wasn't trying to be difficult on purpose, but she hated the way Alex was making her feel.

"What about as your friend?" Rosalie asked.

Alex tipped her head to the side to look at her with contempt. "I don't want to be friends, Rosalie."

Rosalie fidgeted. She wished she knew how to fix this without sacrificing her hope of someday getting out of Ashhawk.

"Friends take care of each other and hang out. We've always done those things. What's the difference between that and what we are?" Rosalie asked.

Alex looked at Rosalie with an expression of blank incredulity. Rosalie panicked, realizing she'd said exactly the wrong thing.

"Are you joking?"

"No..." Rosalie said, feeling even worse.

Alex looked back at the TV, a look of sullen resignation on her face. "I guess there's no difference then."

Rosalie sat still, tuned to Alex, wishing she would call her *Rosie*. But Alex said nothing, staring at the TV as though Rosalie wasn't there.

Dejected and angry at herself, Rosalie got up and left the room, closing the door quietly behind her. She shuffled to her room, barely acknowledging the cat as she made her way inside.

⚜ ⚜ ⚜ ⚜

Rosalie didn't see Alex the next day. She would have thought she'd left, had her truck not been in the parking lot for most of the day. She felt they were doing some sort of passive-aggressive dance by the next day, when she still hadn't seen Alex.

Finally, Alex came into the lobby after Rosalie had eaten lunch. Her shoulders were more hunched than usual, hands jammed in her pockets.

"Hi," Rosalie said, steeling herself against any barbs or pouting from Alex.

"Hey," Alex said, gaze flickering around the lobby in a desperate attempt to look anywhere but at Rosalie. "I just finished up with the paint in room fourteen."

"Great," Rosalie said. "Thank you." She was relieved to be able to step into the easy roles of employer and employee, but it pained her that they had come to this.

"I'm gonna head down to Malcolm's for a few days," Alex said, scratching her cheek. "He's got an infrared sauna he wants me to install."

Rosalie bit her lip and nodded, hoping Alex's trip was coincidental and not because Alex couldn't stand to be around her.

"Okay. Say hi to him for me."

Alex bobbed her head. It was stiff and forced. She reached into her pocket and took out a square of paper. "I'll be back Tuesday. If anything breaks, call this guy." She set the paper gingerly on the counter, then shoved her hand back in her pocket. She bit her lip, eyes still looking everywhere but at Rosalie. "Good luck with the real estate agent tomorrow." Then she turned and slunk out of the lobby.

Rosalie felt a puncture in her chest. She'd never seen Alex so tense and uncomfortable around her. She knew she'd hurt Alex deeply, but Alex was too tough to let it show in traditional ways. It almost made Rosalie want to run after her. But she had nothing to say yet.

Rosalie's phone rang just then, and she was surprised to see it was her father calling. He was a man of few words, so phone conversations didn't suit him most of the time. Rosalie worried something awful had happened.

"Is everything okay?"

"Everything's fine," her father said.

He had a way of speaking on the phone that was different from the way he spoke in person. Even more measured and slow, as though speaking too quickly would cause the words to jumble together as they soared through the air between cell towers.

"Oh, good. How are you?"

"I'm good," Frank said. "Been having...lots of time to myself...reading books..." His words were slow, but Rosalie heard a smile through them. Frank was content. "How are you?"

The question caused Rosalie to droop. She never masked the truth with her father.

"I've been better," she said. "Managing a hotel is no joke."

"It's certainly not," Frank agreed. "You are a strong...brave young woman."

Rosalie wasn't sure how to respond to the abrupt compliment. She knew it was sincere. But she felt anything but strong and brave.

"Have you been learning a lot about New Mexico?"

"A little bit," Rosalie said, feeling guilty she hadn't done her daughterly duty of sending information back to him. "I don't have a lot of time to get to know the place. I'm always fixing something or helping a guest or managing our new website."

"It's a big job..."

There was a drop-off at the end of his drawn-out

sentence, and Rosalie felt obligated to give him at least one tidbit of information.

"I did learn something the other week," she said. "In Navajo tribes, a baby's first laugh is a big deal. There's a whole ceremony around it. Whoever made the baby laugh throws a party, and the baby symbolically gives gifts to everyone who attends as part of their lifelong education in generosity."

Frank hummed, a pleased, descending note that made Rosalie think of how he'd read to her at bedtime as a child. "I remember the first time you laughed."

A gentle chuckle pushed through his voice, and Rosalie's chest lifted with hope. He remembered her first laugh.

"You were so small...still looking a bit crumpled in your carrier. Gran had just arrived from Ashhawk to meet you."

"How old was I?"

"Let's see...she couldn't get away right after you were born...you were probably three months old."

Rosalie held her breath.

"Gran leaned over your carrier, expecting you to be asleep, but you weren't...You were looking right up at her. She was so delighted to meet you, she started giggling. You started laughing, which made her laugh more. It was the sweetest thing I'd ever seen...my mother and my daughter getting along so well right away."

Rosalie was speechless, imagining a younger Gran stooped over her carrier, giggling in her Gran giggle. Rosalie could hear that giggle now, a funny, girlish laugh that carried delicately through a room.

Maybe she was connected to Gran in a way she didn't understand. Maybe there was something between them that had existed before she'd been born. Maybe their connection was the reason Gran had left her the hotel. Even if she never got any proof, she wanted to believe, in whatever mutated way, leaving her the hotel had been Gran's attempt at a lesson in generosity. She felt guilty for not being grateful for it.

Rosalie tried to postpone her thoughts of Gran and laughter and generosity long enough to update her father on her life and make sure he was okay.

"I have an appointment with a real estate agent tomorrow," Rosalie offered.

"Oh?"

"Yeah. She's a rep from All Nite Inn."

"I'm surprised," Frank said. He wasn't disappointed or judgmental. "I thought you'd enjoy the challenge of taking over Hearth. But I understand. You can't run a business if your heart's not in it."

Rosalie felt a small pang in her chest, a resonance her father had identified. Her heart was ambivalent about so much of her life. She realized, of the many things she missed about Philadelphia, her father was chief. His unconditional concern and care for her, his content with her quiet presence made her feel needed. Rosalie wondered if perhaps he needed her more than ever now, with all the transition of Marisol moving out.

"I'll be back in Philadelphia soon. Then we can spend more time together."

Frank let out a gentle, contented sigh, as though to soothe Rosalie. "I'm doing fine, sweetheart. As long as you're happy, I'm fine."

Rosalie pictured her father sitting on the couch with a book and realized he *was* fine. Frank was a student of places and animals, a lover of knowledge. The reason he was so content despite the absence of

Marisol and the death of his mother was because he was content with knowledge over people, with one exception: Rosalie. Rosalie had always felt like his most important person. Whether things worked out with the librarian or not, Frank would be okay. He only wanted his daughter to be happy.

❧ ❧ ❧ ❧

Rosalie lay awake that night, staring into the darkness above her as it pressed heavy onto her eyes. The popcorn ceiling above her was probably raining down particles of asbestos even though the fan overhead was motionless.

Listening to the coyotes outside, Rosalie thought of Gran. Had Gran had sleepless nights like this? Had she found managing the hotel as overwhelming as Rosalie did? Did her boyfriend, Marvin Cobalt, make things easier for her? Rosalie supposed having someone to love would make living in Ashhawk easier.

Rosalie thought of the property on the other side of town. Maybe keeping it a secret had been Gran's way of holding on to a piece of Marvin that she could see and touch. The desert dust held a piece of him that hadn't been bound to his physical body. Though Rosalie had never met Marvin, she imagined he was tied to the land, peaceful as he contemplated its stillness, allowing it to teach him the generosity that had prompted him to will it to Gran, who had passed that generosity on to Rosalie.

Rosalie knew Gran hadn't meant to pluck her from her life and happiness in Philadelphia. Gran had wanted to give Rosalie a piece of her heart, a little piece of the desert. With it came the truckers and coyotes and the poverty of the small town that had contained most of Gran's life on earth. She had given Rosalie all she had. Rosalie knew she ought to be grateful for it.

Rosalie thought she remembered Gran well—the crinkling lines under her eyes, the elegant sweep of her hair over her ears up into its tidy bun, the gentle voice slightly cracked like desert dirt. Gran had always seemed so calm and elegant. Rosalie wondered if those things were real, or if she'd dreamed them up to obscure a woman as weathered and weather-beaten as the rest of the town.

Knowing she wouldn't sleep anytime soon, Rosalie got up to sit out back and look at the night sky as she tried to channel Gran. She didn't believe she'd actually be able to converse with her spirit as she might a living person, but perhaps a pearl of understanding would seed itself in her mind in the clarity of night, bringing her peace or wisdom as she learned to run the hotel.

But as she pulled on her robe, she saw where she'd flung her swimsuit over the rack in her bathroom and decided to take a swim instead. The pool was doing little more than sitting there, save for the occasional evening when a family came through town and the kids wanted to go down the slide. Rosalie had only been in the pool twice and only because she felt obligated.

She put on her suit and wrapped her robe around her, slipping into a pair of flip-flops she hadn't worn in a long time. She closed her door behind her and shuffled across the parking lot, noticing the empty spot where Alex usually parked her truck. The space felt huge and accusatory, a punishment for Rosalie's indecisive cruelty.

The exterior lights extended over the pool area, but the underwater lights were off. Rosalie looked down into the black waters and worried she might sink into the depths, never to be heard from again.

She draped her robe over a chair, feeling the chilly night air nip around her hips and buttocks, sending flares of goose bumps over her arms. She slid into the water, finding it comfortably warm for an unheated pool. Alex had been right; the relentless sun of New Mexico had a few perks.

Rosalie slid forward into the water, feeling it swirl around her, its chill seeping into the secret places the shower never reached between her legs and under her arms and at the backs of her knees. She took a few strokes forward, trying not to make noise lest she wake any guests or call attention to herself at this hour.

When she came to the middle of the pool, she slid under the water long enough to wet her hair, then twisted and rolled onto her back, surfacing face first, her breasts and hips and thighs and feet following as she leveled in slow motion. She kept her head tilted back, aligning her spine so she wouldn't have to use her hands to stay afloat. She vaguely recalled swim classes with her mother as a child, the red of her mother's bikini present in her peripheral vision as she struggled to stay afloat, the muffled sound of her mother's voice encouraging her to relax as Rosalie panicked, certain she would drown.

Rosalie looked up at the sky, almost as black as the water beneath her. She turned herself so she was floating away from the exterior lights of the hotel, seeing only the sky.

As the pinpricks of stars popped out of the thick wool blanket of the night, Rosalie knew this sky wasn't visible anywhere else in the world. Ashhawk's sky was bigger, its stars brighter than the stars of Philadelphia.

The sky was always alive here, while it struggled for air and color everywhere else. Rosalie lay there, suspended between the two darknesses and felt a seed of peace plant itself in her. After a few minutes of contemplating suns billions of miles away, Rosalie slipped out of the pool and tiptoed back to her room, quickly falling into a deep, rejuvenating sleep.

༄ ༄ ༄ ༄

The inside of the casino glittered and flashed with garish enthusiasm. It was unnervingly noisy compared to the desert surrounding it. Even the highway, with its swiftly passing trucks, seemed calm in comparison to the cacophony within.

Rosalie had passed this casino a handful of times but never gone in. Seated on a nearby reservation, it was the source of much local debt and woe. Yet it was thriving; at two o'clock on a Monday, half the seats at the slot machines were full, and the tables, busy by night, were never deserted.

Rosalie had questioned why the corporate real estate agent from All Nite Inn wanted to meet in a casino but figured it made sense. After a quick walk-through appraisal of the property the week before, Coral had given Rosalie a swift nod and told her to expect an offer within the week. Meeting to finalize the sale of an Ashhawk institution to a large corporation should be done discreetly, in a place where Rosalie was less likely to attract attention or be overheard by locals. A business transaction in the restaurant was one of the less concerning happenings in the casino.

Rosalie held the pen in her hand, looking down at the documents one last time before she signed anything. Beside her, Coral Hatfield flicked her tongue over her lipstick-flaked lips and ran her hands over her pasty arms, brushing off the Freon chill of the air conditioning. With her faux snakeskin purse, she looked like a fleshy, corpulent lizard poised to seize a fly from a cactus.

Rosalie thought back to Hearth, with its peeling paint and dated décor. Once she signed the documents in front of her, All Nite Inn would begin to take it over, plastering its surfaces with corporate-approved shades of white and beige and blue, ripping up its carpets and replacing them with industrial blandness. The sign above the parking lot would be replaced with a glowing plastic sign that held none of the life or care Gran had poured into the business for forty years.

Perhaps more disturbing was that Coral and her associates had no concern for Susan or Shelley or Alex. They would be dismissed, thrown back into the unrelenting desert to fend for themselves.

Rosalie found it hard to breathe. Something was twisting in her gut, and she wanted to double over or wriggle out of her seat to get it to stop twisting. She put her free hand to her forehead, wondering if she was coming down with something. She took a deep breath.

And then, clarity: Something was stopping her from signing.

The real estate agent had no personal investment in Gran's property. If the hotel couldn't profit to the corporation's standards, it would be sold, converted, or razed, and nothing would remain of Gran's legacy.

"I'm sorry," Rosalie said, releasing her breath in a giant exhale. "I need a few more days to think about this."

Coral's tongue flicked out over her lips, and her brow furrowed in discontent, impatient. "Is there something making you hesitate?"

"Yeah, I'm—" Rosalie kept her hand on her clammy forehead, hoping it would steady her. "It's been a lot of adjustment since I lost Gran," she said, fudging the truth.

"Of course," Coral said, donning a saccharine tone and leaning forward to put her hand near Rosalie's arm. "You poor thing. You must be all torn up about it."

Rosalie gave a faint nod, glad she had bought herself time.

Coral's plump, weathered hand flattened on the table over the contract Rosalie had been about to sign. "I'm just trying to help take a few things off your plate, you know."

"I know." Rosalie scooted back in her chair a few inches. "But I need a few more days."

The woman gave a stiff nod. "Fine," she said. "Give me a call when you're ready, and I'll bring the papers over. But I have to be honest with you: you're not going to get a better offer. With the state the property's in, you'll be lucky to sell it at all."

"I know," Rosalie said, already rising and collecting her purse. She couldn't believe how quickly Coral had gone from concerned to predatory. She knew she'd made the right decision, even if she had no idea what she was going to do now. "Thanks anyway."

She turned, never so eager to leave a room.

She rushed out to the parking lot, climbing into Gran's Oldsmobile and cranking the engine. The air conditioner blasted on, accosting her with hot air. Rosalie felt herself surge with an urgency she couldn't place. Putting the car into gear, she pulled out of the parking lot. She was almost back to the hotel when she turned around, heading for the other side of town.

By the time she pulled up to the Cocheta property, the sun was low in the sky, casting long, ashen shadows over the desert. The cacti and tumbleweeds loomed long where they stood, the distant hills glowing purple in stillness. Rosalie stopped the car and got out, looking over the land, searching for something. A breeze graced her face, and she wondered if it could carry a message from her to Gran or vice versa. Looking over the land that was seemingly barren but secretly alive, she understood why the Native people believed in spirits the way they did. The earth breathed of its own accord, creating magic in its stillness.

The land hadn't changed in generations. Perhaps that was what bound people to it. Most of the ancestors of Ashhawk had been driven out of their land, forced to relocate time and time again. Generations of displacement after displacement should have made the space feel fraught with tension and pain. Yet it was peaceful, grounding, and reassuring.

It was ironic, Rosalie knew, that she'd been so desperate to flee this place. Had she been born in a different time and place, her anguish might have been converse: pain at being forced off her land, her people tortured and killed. Instead, she'd been displaced *into* the desert. She wondered if that had been a mistake after all. Perhaps she was meant to be here.

She inhaled the dry, cooling desert air and felt her body calm from its previous frenzy. She stared at the land, watching the shadows lengthen until the sun was halfway behind the horizon. Knowing the last of the heat would start to lift soon, she got in her car and drove back to the hotel.

She had made a decision she never dreamed she'd

make. She was going to stay.

❧❧❧❧

Rosalie had almost fallen asleep that night when she heard the distant calls of the coyotes. The pups' cries had deepened, their yipping turned to earnest howls in the distant hills. A panicked thought seized her: What if the small gray cat was attacked by one of the coyotes? The cat may have been quick and able to blend in with the desert, but coyotes were skilled hunters. What if the cat died because she'd been too cruel to allow it to come inside? What if she never saw the cat again? What if her one reliably comforting thing was gone?

Rosalie sprang out of bed and ran to the door, flinging it open. An empty tin of food and little dish of water sat on the doorstep, half drunk. Rosalie took a few steps out, feeling the nighttime chill of the desert send flares of goose bumps over her skin. She scanned the parking lot and glanced under the chairs in front of the rooms for the small ball of fur. She saw nothing but a few beer cans she'd need to pick up in the morning and the empty space where Alex's truck usually was.

Rosalie felt awful for rejecting so much of the beauty around her. She'd been a terrible steward of the land and a begrudging servant to the people of the town. She wanted to be better than she'd been, to show she deserved the good fortune she'd been given. And above all, she wanted to apologize to Alex.

Not seeing the cat anywhere, she went back inside and climbed in bed, feeling heavy. As she tried to fall asleep, her heart howled like the coyotes in the distance.

Chapter Twelve

Honesty Bar

Early the next morning, Rosalie went to find the small gray cat. She was frantic to see him—if he was a him—and know he was okay. When she saw the faithful creature creep up to the building, she walked out to meet him with grateful urgency. Rather than tentatively stroke him or talk to him first, she scooped him up, feeling him purr immediately.

"I'm glad you're safe," she mumbled. "I was so worried about you."

The cat purred louder, as though to reassure her.

"Do you want to come live with me?"

Even though she knew it was silly, she was hoping for some sort of affirmation or response. The cat purred on as she opened the door and carried him inside, holding him to her chest as she walked to the cupboard to get a can of food for him. She set him down beside her bed and slid down to sit next to him while he ate.

"You need a name, don't you?" Rosalie asked, hand draping down his back and extending over his tail.

She thought of her happiest memories in the desert. Most were with Alex. Sturdy, quiet Alex, who had built her a fireplace to relive her favorite desert moments from her childhood. Those summer nights with Gran had been dearer than she knew. She thought of how the smoke had rested heavy and hot in her lungs. Yet there was a comfort to it, a feeling of being somewhere open and full of possibility, of perpetual summer, of light.

"Smoke. That's what I'm gonna call you."

The cat ate on, unresponsive to Rosalie's chatter. Rosalie admired him, noting his fur was exceptionally soft.

Once Smoke had finished, he turned around a few times and climbed decidedly into Rosalie's lap, settling down and starting up his motor. Rosalie smiled, grateful for his forgiveness.

Rosalie heard Alex's truck pull into the parking lot, making her feel guilty. Repairing things with Alex seemed almost as overwhelming as repairing the hotel. Rosalie decided to deal with other matters first: She needed to make Gran's room her own, to start laying down roots here. She would own and manage the hotel no matter what happened with Alex, and she needed to take ownership now.

Rosalie texted Shelley to see if she could cover the desk for a few hours. She hardly waited for Shelley to pull into the parking lot before getting in Gran's car and speeding out of Ashhawk. She drove until she got to the closest Target. Filled with excitement and a rare willingness to spend some money, she headed toward the home décor section.

Two hours later, Rosalie loaded her purchases into the trunk of Gran's car. She'd done well—a new area rug, new sheets and a duvet, a new lamp, new window treatments, new dishes, new art, and an order of larger furniture to be delivered later that week. New life for her suite. She spent the next few hours clearing out Gran's remaining possessions, packing them into boxes to take to the local church to be divvied up for the neediest residents of Ashhawk. She put up the new curtains and an under-cabinet rack for wine glasses. She took down Gran's old art and put up bold new prints. Her suite was still small, but it no longer felt sad and stale.

Rosalie unlocked the door leading to the adjoining room, yanking open the curtains to let the light stream in as she pushed the bed far against the wall, making space in the middle of the room for the furniture and bookshelves that would be delivered in a few days' time. Her tiny suite wasn't space enough for the life she wanted to live in Ashhawk. She deserved a living room where she could relax, read, and enjoy Alex's company. If Alex's company was to be had, of course.

She removed Gran's ashes from the card table and brought the table into her new living room with the chairs. She took down the heavy drapes from around the window, leaving only the blinds for privacy. The fresh paint Alex had applied a few weeks earlier made the room seem brighter and more stylish. Rosalie adorned the table with a cloth, matching dishes and metal cutlery, napkins, and a candle.

Rosalie didn't know where her burst of energy had come from, but she had a sneaking suspicion it was the desert's first gift to her as its newest long-term guest. No one owned the desert; the desert simply permitted him or her to live there for a few decades. Rosalie hoped her tenure would be a good one.

Rosalie gathered some old desert brushwood and put it by the fireplace Alex had built, then walked across the street to buy beer. Back in her room, she steeled herself to use Gran's kitchenette to make food that wasn't microwaved. She boiled water for spaghetti and heated sauce and managed to defrost some meatballs without incident, then slipped into the dress Alex had persuaded her to buy on their first date. She felt too loud in it. She was so used to neutral button-downs and dress pants; bright colors and patterns made her feel like a visitor in her own body. But perhaps she could get used to it.

As a final touch, she dabbed a hint of perfume behind her ears, hoping it wasn't too overwhelming.

There was nothing left to do but find Alex.

Rosalie felt her heart pound, her hands shaky, as she walked the short corridor from her room to Alex's. She paused, wondering if there might be a better time to do this. But she'd wasted enough time already. If she had any chance for Alex's forgiveness, it was now.

She raised her hand, taking a shaky breath before she knocked. She heard the muffled TV inside, then shuffling before the door opened.

Alex's face was blank and defensive when she saw Rosalie on her doorstep.

"Hi," Rosalie forced out.

"Hi," Alex said, the word tougher than usual, though probably normal if she were speaking to anyone else.

"I...um...was hoping you'd join me for dinner?" Rosalie asked, her words curling up at the end with her uncertainty.

"For dinner," Alex echoed, as though challenging Rosalie to say what she meant.

"To talk," Rosalie elaborated. She tried to find some foundation to speak from.

Alex leaned against the door frame, giving no indication she would be agreeable to dinner or conversation.

"I made spaghetti and meatballs," Rosalie said, feeling her throat clutch around the words. "And a fire in the fireplace for after, if you want."

Alex pursed her lips, studying Rosalie, noticing the dress she was wearing. She dropped her arms. "What do you want to talk about?" Her voice was softer and more forgiving.

"About...about us. About being more than friends."

Alex chewed on the thought for a minute before she loosened. "Okay."

She turned back into her room and shut off her TV, grabbing her keys and closing her door behind her. Rosalie led the way back to her room, wishing Alex would say something to soothe her frazzled nerves.

Rather than open the door to her room, Rosalie opened the door to the adjoining room. When she revealed the semi-romantic spread she'd laid out on Gran's card table, Alex stopped in her tracks.

"This is nice," she said, as though it pained her to admit.

"I'm trying to be nicer."

Rosalie ventured back into her room to get a beer out of the fridge for Alex, filling her wine glass perhaps more than she should have to calm her nerves.

Alex took a seat, glancing up at Rosalie. She kept her knees spread but made an effort to straighten her posture.

With no more to do, Rosalie sat, draping her napkin over her lap.

"That dress looks good on you," Alex said, shifting

in her seat.

"Thanks." Rosalie tried not to fidget as she searched for the words she should have planned ahead of time. When Alex made no move to start eating or drinking, Rosalie knew she had to start the conversation.

"I owe you a big apology. I got overwhelmed with everything here, and I took it out on you, which wasn't fair or cool," she said, trying not to sound frustrated with herself.

Alex's forehead curved in acknowledgment as she studied the food before her. She nodded. "Apology accepted."

"I...um...I was hoping you'd go on a date with me," Rosalie said, feeling her insides ratchet up with the speed of a cicada call.

Alex gestured to her plate, as though to say, *What do you call this?*

"No, a *real* date. To a restaurant or the movies or something. I want...I want to be better about defining things."

Alex bit her lip. "I mean...yeah, I'd like that. But if you're gonna be skipping town soon, I'd rather keep our relationship professional."

Rosalie nodded, glad Alex had said more than three words. She was even more glad she had an immediate response. "I know," Rosalie said. "That's why I was so noncommittal before."

She paused, picking up her fork and rolling some spaghetti on it to give herself something to do. She didn't raise it to her mouth. "I met with someone who wants to buy Hearth yesterday."

Rosalie saw Alex's face fall.

Rosalie took a breath and kept talking. "The

whole time, I had this...I don't know, this pain in my stomach. I couldn't make myself sign anything. All I could think of was: This shitty hotel is *mine*. I can do whatever I want with it. I could make it a roaring success, or I could fail miserably, but either way, it'll be because I did something. I won't get anything like this again. I thought about what you said about trusting my gut. So I did."

Alex stared at Rosalie hopefully.

"When I think about going back to Philadelphia, I get the same icky feeling. As much as I talk about hating Ashhawk, a little piece of it is mine. I don't want to throw it away because it's a lot of work. And I don't have much to go back to anyway. So...I'm gonna give running this hotel everything I've got."

Alex froze in disbelief. "Are you serious?"

Rosalie was finally able to crack a nervous smile. "Yeah. I even signed up for a hotel management course online."

Alex stayed stunned and still before she sat forward. "Wow," she said, blinking a few times. "I'm surprised."

"Happy surprised?" Rosalie asked, hopeful.

"Yeah," Alex said, finally letting a hint of a smile creep over her face. "Definitely happy surprised."

Rosalie felt her stomach settle enough to lift a bite of spaghetti into her mouth. Alex watched her as she did, and Rosalie felt as though Alex expected to say something more.

"So is this a date?" Alex asked, grinning as her gaze flickered down to the meal Rosalie had prepared.

Rosalie tried not to smile too hard as she chewed. Once she swallowed, she said, "If you want it to be."

Alex rolled her eyes, a glint of frustration tingeing

her smile, as though she'd been waiting for Rosalie to orchestrate a date since they'd met.

Rosalie felt her body warm as her agitation turned from anxiety to excitement.

"You're actually staying in Ashhawk?" Alex said.

Rosalie nodded again, her smile spreading as she thought of getting into a routine with grocery shopping and eating at the local restaurants and curling up with Alex in their spare time. Her idea of small-town life no longer felt confined. It felt calm.

Alex drew her napkin out of her lap and stood. "C'mere."

Caught off guard, Rosalie remained in her chair until Alex was standing over her expectantly.

Alex reached for Rosalie's hand to draw her up, putting her other hand around Rosalie's waist. Bringing her face perilously close to Rosalie's, she gave Rosalie a deep stare that begged Rosalie not to change her mind. Rosalie stared back, assuring Alex she wasn't going to.

Alex drew Rosalie into a kiss Rosalie had craved since that weekend at Corte del Cuervo, a kiss undiluted by alcohol or confusion or miscommunication or hesitation. It was potent, and Rosalie was glad Alex held on to her waist so she didn't sway too far.

Chapter Thirteen

Amenities

At seven o'clock, there was a knock on Rosalie's door. Opening it, she found Alex on her doorstep wearing a pressed collared shirt open a few buttons at the top and a nice pair of slacks. Her hair had been brushed—Rosalie could tell because the curls were extra poufy—and Rosalie smelled something halfway between perfume and cologne.

Rosalie felt underdressed in her jeans and plain shirt. She looked down and mumbled something before she asked if she could have a few minutes to change.

"No, you look great," Alex said.

"But you look so nice..."

Alex shrugged. "I figured you wouldn't want me in my sweaty work clothes."

Rosalie bit her lip over a small smile. She'd only ever been around Alex in her sweaty work clothes, and she didn't mind it one bit. Alex's sweat never seemed dirty to her, only clean and honest with a hint of something like sage.

"If you want to change, you can, but you look great," Alex said.

Rosalie looked down and held up a finger, deciding on a compromise. She went over to her closet and put on a skirt. She looked a little nicer, but not like she was trying too hard.

When they climbed into the comfortable cab of Alex's truck a few minutes later, Rosalie asked, "So where are we going?"

Alex started the engine. "I was thinking we could go check out this place in Santa Fe."

"Santa Fe?" Rosalie had expected they would go to a restaurant nearby, not drive forty-five minutes away for a meal.

"Have you been?"

"No," Rosalie said, wondering why Gran had never taken her to Santa Fe before remembering Gran hadn't had someone like Shelley to help her run the hotel.

"It's nice," Alex said. "Great restaurants and art. A pretty decent Shakespeare Festival, too. Maybe we could check that out sometime."

Rosalie studied Alex, noticing the agitated way her hands gripped the steering wheel. Alex was nervous in a way Rosalie hadn't seen before. For the first time, Alex was trying too hard. When it came to helping Rosalie around the hotel and caring for her when she was ill or upset, Alex was sure of herself, and her words and body language were natural. But she was thinking everything through too hard tonight.

Rosalie thought she knew what was happening, but she wanted to be sure. "Do you have a favorite Shakespeare play?"

Alex shifted her hands on the steering wheel so she could scratch her eye. "*Romeo and Juliet* was pretty good."

Rosalie thought about asking Alex if she'd actually seen the play or any production beyond the movie with Leonardo DiCaprio but didn't want to insult her or make her more anxious.

"I kind of like *Midsummer Night's Dream*," Rosalie said. "The movie wasn't so good. I don't think Stanley Tucci was the best Puck."

Alex took a stiff breath. "Yeah, probably not."

Rosalie eyed her with a smile. "Did you see the movie?"

"Nah," Alex said with a nervous smile.

"We can check out the festival if you want, but I'd be just as happy staying in and watching *Light My Fire*."

Alex seemed relieved, glancing over at Rosalie.

Rosalie let the conversation settle in the hum of the truck motor as she watched the beautiful desert creep past them as they drove toward Santa Fe.

She recalled when they'd watched *Light My Fire* together, when Rosalie had been shaky and fatigued and Alex had gone to such trouble to make sure she was fed and hydrated. She'd stifled her enthusiasm about the female firefighters then, but now she knew Alex liked girls, so she decided to let Alex in a little more.

"I have a theory," Rosalie said.

Alex glanced at her and waited for her to speak.

"I think Jill and Taryn are in love."

"Jill and Taryn on *Light My Fire*?"

"Uh-huh."

"Isn't Jill dating that guy from the other station?"

"Yeah. But the way she looks at Taryn... I mean, it's obvious, right?"

Alex glanced back and forth between Rosalie and the road a few times before she said, "I think you deserve lesbians who don't hide in subtext."

Rosalie tried to laugh the comment off, but she couldn't help but wonder if it was Alex's way of coaxing her to be a little less afraid of coming out in Ashhawk.

"Maybe," Rosalie said.

Alex glanced at her, seeming to understand she'd hit a nerve. "It's fun to think about, though."

Rosalie gave her an appreciative smile.

When they arrived in Santa Fe, Alex had calmed a little bit, but she still seemed as though her confidence had been shaken. When she pulled into a parking spot and turned off the car, she immediately jumped down and ran around to open Rosalie's door for her. Rosalie was surprised but smiled and took Alex's hand as she slid down. She'd never been courted so formally. Rosalie wondered where Alex had learned that—from her father? Her friends? TV?

Alex offered Rosalie her arm to walk into the restaurant, and Rosalie wasn't sure how she felt about it. On the one hand, they were in a liberal town and Rosalie wasn't concerned with what other people might think. But it felt rigid and inorganic for them. They were so at ease when they were sitting around a campfire or sanding a vanity or talking about paint. Doing something so formal felt awkward. But Rosalie took Alex's arm, knowing it meant more to Alex to escort her than it meant to her to be escorted.

The restaurant Alex had picked was the nicest one Rosalie had been to in a long time. In contrast with the adobe exterior, the inside was a beautiful balance of high-end finishes and industrial materials. Metal and warm wood and rich fabrics were combined in an unlikely but chic palette. Once they were seated, Rosalie thought back to Corte del Cuervo and wondered if Alex appreciated the design the way she did.

"The interior design here is amazing," Rosalie said under her breath.

Alex looked around, considering with a muted expression. "Yeah, it's nice."

"Kind of reminds me of Corte del Cuervo."

"I guess," Alex said.

Even though Alex was usually quiet, her anxiety had rendered her difficult to engage in conversation.

"I didn't do any of the design work," Alex said. "Malcolm and Logan did all that. I just made it happen."

"Well, between the three of you, you did an amazing job."

Alex shifted in her chair, looking at the menu.

Rosalie studied the way Alex was hunched over. She felt a subtle rocking and realized Alex was bouncing her leg, unknowingly shifting the table with every motion. Alex felt uncomfortable with something, and Rosalie was pretty sure it wasn't her. Without any more information, all Rosalie could do was guess what was bothering Alex.

"Is everything okay with Jason?" she asked. Alex hadn't gotten a call from him in a while, which could have been good or bad.

"What? Oh, yeah, yeah," Alex said. "I mean, he's still using, but what else is new."

Rosalie nodded slowly, studying Alex as Alex studied the menu with her brow furrowed. "Something else on your mind?"

Alex looked up, as though realizing Rosalie could tell she was on edge.

"Just you," she said with a smile intended to be reassuring but came across as nervous. She looked down at her menu, frowning again. She lifted her finger and pointed at something.

"Something look good?" Rosalie asked.

"I don't know what this is," Alex grumbled. She

sounded half annoyed, half embarrassed.

Rosalie leaned forward to see where Alex was pointing on her menu and realized the dishes served at the restaurant were not dishes served anywhere in Ashhawk.

Rosalie recalled their conversation about Shakespeare in the car and realized why Alex was so nervous. She felt something grow bigger in her chest, and an adoring smile swept over her face. She reached forward and took Alex's hand.

"Hey," she said, keeping her voice low.

Alex looked up, still bouncing her leg under the table.

"We don't have to go to fancy restaurants or Shakespeare festivals if you're not into that stuff."

Alex gave a timid shrug. "I want to do stuff you like."

"I would be happy eating spaghetti off paper plates in your truck in an empty parking lot."

Alex looked skeptical. "Really?"

"Maybe not for every date. But you don't have to bring me to places like this if it's not your scene. I like sitting around the campfire with you eating diner food."

Alex let out a short, relieved sigh. "Okay." She glanced down at her menu. "I just assumed dating was different in Philadelphia."

"So I'm a city mouse and you're a country mouse?"

Alex gave a playful frown. "I know how you feel about mice."

Rosalie's smile widened. She finally recognized the girl she liked sitting across from her.

"Can we get out of here and find a diner?" Rosalie said, already leaning forward as though she was prepared to get out of her chair.

"Can we get some ice cream afterward?" Alex asked with a wink.

"All the ice cream you want."

Alex drove them to a diner, and they slid into a booth. After ordering and chatting with their server for a minute, there was quiet. They both looked around, studying the sad little diner. It wasn't so different from the one in Ashhawk; flies slid through the air in the same dejected way people slid in and out of booths and chairs, waitresses looked as though they were wilting on their feet, and the same film covered the plastic-covered menus. Rosalie turned away from it, looking out the window, hoping to find something to occupy her mind instead of the ceaseless rumination about her properties in Ashhawk.

She thought back to her meeting with the real estate agent and the proposal from George Tackett still sitting in her inbox. She knew she wasn't going to sell Hearth, but she didn't have anyone advising her about the Cocheta property. She sat in silence, toes and fingers tapping randomly to distract from the passing of awkward, silent moments, painfully aware she was being unintentionally rude to Alex.

"Sorry if I'm quiet."

"I like quiet," Alex said with a forgiving smile.

"I know. I just feel like I should be talking to you because I like you."

Alex's smile stayed constant. "I like you even when you're quiet."

"Thanks," Rosalie said, still flustered. "I like you when you're quiet, too. Which, I guess you're always quiet, so all the time."

"Sometimes I'm too quiet," Alex said. "People

get uncomfortable."

"Only because they want to know what you're thinking. Your face doesn't betray much. I didn't even know you liked girls for the first month we hung out."

Alex nodded. "I could say the same for you."

"I thought I mentioned my girlfriend, like, the second time we spoke to each other."

"Yeah, but your face doesn't betray much."

"Really?"

Rosalie had never considered her face to be inexpressive.

"I have no idea what you're thinking about tonight."

"Oh. Well…um…besides you, mostly the Cocheta property and my five-year plan for renovating Hearth."

Alex gave a slow nod, smile fading and gaze falling to the table.

"Part of me wants to run away to Corte del Cuervo and avoid dealing with it, but I'm trying not to be that way. I've got developers beating down my door, and I want to do the right thing, you know? I want to make Gran proud."

Alex looked back up at Rosalie, adjusting in her seat. Rosalie realized Alex was uncomfortable with something. She felt her anxiety rise, hoping she hadn't insulted Alex or said something careless.

Alex cleared her throat. "I was wondering. Um… you know I love working with you. But…could we make our dates a business-free zone? I just…you know, I want to make sure there's more to our relationship than Hearth."

Rosalie surged with guilt, relieved Alex had voiced a request for once. It was a good one, too. Rosalie should have anticipated it.

"Yeah, definitely. Sorry. It's just…it's this big project I've taken on, and it's hard not to feel like I'm completely in over my head. You're the person I'm around most, so I talk your ear off about it. Sorry."

Alex's smile returned, graceful on her face. "It's okay." She reached across the table, caressing Rosalie's hand. "I'm excited for all the projects we've planned. Proud too. This is a big deal."

Rosalie exhaled, feeling Alex's hand tingle in her own. She was acutely aware they were in public and anyone might see them holding hands across the table. But she didn't pull away.

"I do want to talk about business stuff when we're not out on dates," Alex said, drawing her hand back. "I'm totally on board with whatever projects you decide to tackle first. I'm your righthand girl."

Rosalie nodded, feeling something in her stomach soften. Alex's reassurance reminded her she wasn't in this alone. She had Alex, she had Shelley, and somewhere, she knew, she had Gran. If those three people could put faith in her, perhaps it was time she trusted her gut once again. Her most immediate task was to make sure Alex didn't feel as though she was only part of a business arrangement.

"Yeah, we should make dates a business-free zone," Rosalie said, brushing her hair from her face with her free hand. "I'll try not to be so preoccupied."

Alex smiled, and her shoulders shifted with a gentle, silent laugh. "You'll always be preoccupied with something, Rosie," she said, folding her elbows on the table. "But it's okay."

Always subdued when Alex called her Rosie, Rosalie returned Alex's smile. She was happy to be out with Alex but still lost as to what to talk about if she couldn't talk about Hearth.

She held Alex's gaze, willing herself not to retreat into her worries or discomfort. Rosalie stopped breathing, wondering what would happen when they had to find commonalities besides Hearth.

What if they didn't have any?

Frozen for a moment, Alex seemed to surge forward with a thought. "Did you know I smoked for ten years?"

Rosalie lifted her eyebrows, trying not to wrinkle any part of her face in disgust. She hated the smell of cigarettes, hated the lingering staleness that hung in the rooms where guests had disregarded the no-smoking policy, hated the clouds of dust that mushroomed whenever she emptied an ashtray. Mostly, she hated the cloud of toughness and melancholy she always felt around smokers as they huddled in doorways, outcasts from whatever was happening inside.

"I know, it's gross," Alex said. "That's why I quit."

Rosalie's face must have betrayed her. She tried to apologize by engaging in polite conversation. "Do you miss it?"

"Like crazy," Alex said. "Nicotine addiction is no joke."

Rosalie bit her lip and nodded. "That's what I hear."

"But that wasn't the worst part of quitting," Alex said. "The worst part was I didn't have that connection to people anymore. There's this understanding amongst smokers that sometimes you're the one with the lighter or extra butt, and sometimes you're the one asking. It's easy to strike up a conversation with people when you're all standing outside smoking. I met some cool people."

Rosalie had never considered the social aspect of smoking. She had thought of them as people exiled by their own intentional disregard for their health.

"It was easier to feel seen," Alex said.

Rosalie frowned. "What do you mean?"

Alex shifted in her seat, leaning forward a little more on her elbows. "I had a lot of honest conversations in doorways and back alleys when I was a smoker. Smokers tend to reveal themselves on their cigarette break. It's an escape from pretending to have all your shit together for a few minutes. You can be real when you're publicly catering to a vice like that."

Rosalie slowly nodded as she let her frown shift out of place.

"That's all anyone wants," Alex said. "To feel seen."

In any other conversation, Rosalie would have asked for clarification. But hearing Alex speak candidly about something she had thought unilaterally pointless and despicable, she understood what Alex meant.

Whatever she and Alex had or didn't have in common, they both wanted to be cared for and seen.

Rosalie reached across the table and extracted Alex's hands from where they were folded under her elbows. She pulled them toward her and held them in her own.

Without saying anything, she looked Alex in the eye. For the first time, she didn't feel a hint of unease or uncertainty as she stared at Alex dead on. She squeezed and gave a little nod.

I see you.

Alex's face spread in a slow, peaceful grin. She gave a little nod back.

I see you, too.

Through all their obligations and defenses, despite family members who didn't understand or care for them, in the most unlikely of places, they had noticed each other. They'd seen through the haze of Rosalie's resistance, Alex's reticence, and the desert dust. If that wasn't miraculous, Rosalie didn't know what was.

Their food arrived, and they were forcibly shaken from their connection. Rosalie didn't worry—now she understood how to meet Alex, to care for her as she felt cared for, and she could pick up the connection any time.

They lifted their forks and began to eat.

"I have an idea," Alex said, shifting forward and putting her elbows on the table. "Tonight, we'll relax and have fun and not talk about business. Then sometime this week, we can have a brainstorm session and talk about every worry in that head of yours."

"*Every* worry?" Rosalie asked, playfully raising her eyebrows.

Alex smirked. "We can start with the Cocheta property. One thing at a time."

Rosalie leaned forward, picking up her spoon with her free hand. "Sounds good," she said. There was something satisfying about having a plan. Alex understood that about her.

"So what are you doing tomorrow?" Rosalie gave an impish smile to mock her own anxious desire to talk about the future of Hearth and to convey how much she loved spending time with Alex.

"I gotta drive back to Corte del Cuervo to help Malcolm install an electric fireplace."

Rosalie pouted, thinking of the desert oasis she loved so much.

"You can come. It's just a day trip," Alex said, sliding her hand toward Rosalie again to let her know she wanted Rosalie around her as much as possible.

Rosalie let out a heavy sigh. "Shelley can't cover the desk tomorrow."

Rosalie's thoughts drifted to Shelley, sitting behind the desk, unaware she was facilitating Rosalie's date night with Alex. Rosalie felt a spike of anxiety at the thought of Shelley finding out. But they were far from Ashhawk, and Shelley was probably too wrapped up in other matters to be curious about why Alex and Rosalie were both gone on the same night.

Alex gave a little pout back. "I'll have Malcolm pick out a nice bottle of wine to bring back for you."

Rosalie leaned forward, loving how simple and understandable Alex's affection was. For a girl with an inexpressive face, Rosalie had an easier time understanding how Alex felt about her than anyone she'd ever dated.

Rosalie looked into Alex's eyes, wondering at how she had managed to attract someone as reserved and independent as Alex. Her curiosity about who had been so fortunate as to receive Alex's affection in the past gnawed at her. But she didn't want to bring up Alex's ex-girlfriends. What she wanted more than names and dates and circumstances of past lovers was to know Alex better, to feel their connection deepen.

And perhaps a few clues about what she could expect if she told anyone in Ashhawk they were dating.

"Can I ask you something?"

Alex nodded, as though she was happy Rosalie was taking advantage of their closeness.

"What was it like coming out here?"

Alex's smile dulled. Rosalie worried she'd stirred

up old hurt, but Alex gave a halfhearted shrug.

"Mixed bag," Alex said. "Nothing that scarred me for life. Just high school kids being jerks. Mostly, people looked the other way. It probably woulda been worse if it wasn't so obvious."

"What do you mean?"

"I never grew out of my tomboy phase. I dress comfortable and like to play with tools. I'm kind of a walking stereotype, so they already suspected. That made it easier."

Rosalie nodded, wondering what a younger version of Alex looked like and how she behaved. She felt a specific, protective tenderness toward Alex, imagining her closeted.

"Were you scared to come out?" Rosalie asked.

"Were you?"

Rosalie thought of Perene and realized how silly the question was. *Everyone* was afraid when they came out. She'd been so afraid she'd lost the first girl she ever loved.

"How old were you?"

"Sixteen."

Rosalie tried not to cringe, imagining how hard it must have been to endure high school out of the closet in a small town. Rosalie wished Alex would say more to distract her from what she was now imagining had been a difficult teenage life that Alex had little control over.

"How did you come out?"

Alex sighed. "I got caught with my hand in the cookie jar, I guess you could say."

Now Rosalie couldn't stop herself from expressing concern. "Whose cookie jar?"

"Shelley's cousin."

Rosalie finally understood the tension between Shelley and Alex. Shelley must have felt Alex had tainted or tampered with her family in some way, and even though it had been decades, that wrong hadn't been forgotten. Rosalie grew even more afraid of what Shelley might think when she came out.

As she thought of Shelley and how Ashhawk often yielded certain ways of thinking, Rosalie realized she was now part of Alex's story. She wanted to give Alex as much control over her own story as possible. That was more important than soothing her fears about the disapproval she might receive.

"Do you want me to tell Shelley?" Rosalie asked.

"That I banged her cousin? I'm sure she already knows."

"No, about us."

"If you want to. But I'm not going to tell you to come out here if you're not ready."

Rosalie nodded. Telling Shelley meant telling the whole town. In Philadelphia, she could pick and choose who knew she liked girls, but in Ashhawk, everyone knew everyone's business.

At the end of their meal, Alex drove them back to Hearth. Shutting off the engine of her truck, Alex slid out of the cab, not bothering to open Rosalie's door for her, which made Rosalie feel better. She didn't need such traditional courtship. Courtship was different from romance. Courtship was rules and customs and stiff gestures. Romance could light up the night sky.

Rosalie wondered if their night was over, but Alex hovered in the parking lot, hands stuffed in her pockets. "I have an idea," she said. "Unless you're super tired."

"I can stay up a little longer."

Rosalie hoped she didn't sound too flirtatious or suggestive. As much as she loved Alex's company, she didn't want to attempt having sex again. They were still learning how to dance together; she didn't need to be dipped before their footing was in sync.

"Meet me out back in twenty minutes," Alex said, taking a few steps backward toward her truck.

Curious, Rosalie watched Alex get back into her truck and pull out of the parking lot. Rosalie went into her room to feed Smoke and check that her eyeliner hadn't rubbed off onto her upper eyelids in an unflattering way. She checked her email and wished there was some way to document her evening. She didn't keep a journal or a blog or photograph things for posterity; that would be too indulgent for her taste. But she wished there was a way to break a piece of their night off and keep it like prized turquoise.

When she walked out back, she saw Alex had parked her truck behind the hotel facing away from the building again. She had set up a projector with an extension cord running toward the maintenance shed. She had a glass of wine and a bottle of beer waiting beside the fireplace she'd built. The paused opening credits of a movie were glowing on the stucco wall at the back of Rosalie's room.

"I thought we could watch *Desert Hearts*," Alex said with a grin.

Rosalie beamed, climbing into the bed of the truck. The last evening they'd spent together in Alex's truck had been so peaceful and happy. She situated herself resting against the back of the cab on top of several blankets and pillows Alex had laid out.

As the movie began and Alex adjusted the sound so they could hear over the night sounds of the desert and the rustling of their legs in the blankets, Rosalie felt stiff with anticipation. She knew Alex wouldn't try to push anything sexually; the propriety of them watching a movie behind the hotel wasn't the issue. She was unsure she'd be able to lie comfortably in the truck bed, at its slight angle, with only the meager padding to position her body against. How close would they lie? Would they stay parallel to each other, maintaining a safe distance after their unfortunate first attempt at having sex? She waited for Alex's cue.

They watched the first few minutes of the movie, the opening credits faded against the stucco wall, the projected image less saturated than a television monitor counterpart. It was still clear, though, almost crisper. Rosalie enjoyed the novelty of watching a movie outside, with the crickets chirping and the faint calls of the coyotes in the distance, the spontaneity of the night air brushing over her face.

Rosalie could see Alex glancing over at her, anxious with her far arm behind her head. Rosalie wondered what she was observing or wanting to ask.

"You can come here if you're cold," Alex offered. "I promise to keep my hands to myself."

Rosalie gave a nervous, appreciative giggle. She wasn't shivering, but the space between her and Alex seemed cold. She scooted closer, limbs making a muted racket in the truck bed as she moved closer, pulling her pillow along with her. Alex threaded her arm under Rosalie's neck, supporting her, hand resting near Rosalie's elbow. There was nothing forward about it. Rosalie felt protected and safe. She snuggled an inch closer, keeping her gaze on the screen but her attention on the warmth pressing against her, the lean muscle she rested on. Alex was strong and supportive. Rosalie wondered if the weight of her head would start to pinch Alex's arm until it tingled, but as the movie wore on, Alex didn't indicate discomfort.

Soon Rosalie relaxed into Alex as she would a warm bath. Alex drew blankets over them, first making sure Rosalie's legs and hips were covered before covering herself. As she lay back, she pressed a soft kiss into Rosalie's hair. Rosalie closed her eyes and took a deep, contented breath, savoring all the sweetness and care she felt seeping off Alex's body. She had never been around someone so attentive and selfless. She felt impossibly lucky.

Rosalie tried not to squirm too much during the surprisingly graphic sex scene. She coped with her arousal by commenting that the scene was unexpected, given the film had been made in the eighties. Alex nodded and gave a vague, calm response, not seeming as fazed or aroused by the scene as she held Rosalie. She kissed Rosalie's hair again, and Rosalie felt something stir in the bowl of her belly, a fluttering of excitement.

When the film ended, Alex didn't move to switch off the projector or the laptop hooked up to it. Instead, she let her Windows desktop fill the rectangle of light broadcast against the wall. She acted as though the movie hadn't ended, and Rosalie was glad for it. She was so comfortable, she didn't want to move.

After five minutes of listening to the coyotes and crickets, Alex said in the gentlest whisper, "My arm's asleep."

Rosalie startled up to free Alex's arm, guilty her head was so heavy.

"It's okay," Alex said. "I just need to reconfigure our layout here."

Rosalie took the cue to lie down again, this time

facing Alex.

Alex massaged her arm before letting it rest between them. Illuminated by the gentle green light of the projector, Alex smiled. "You look so pretty tonight," she murmured, as though speaking normally would disrupt the nightlife of the desert.

Rosalie swallowed, never sure how to respond. "Thank you."

Alex extended her hand to Rosalie's waist and let it rest there, sturdy and soft, cradling her curve, admiring it without sight. Rosalie felt smaller and more feminine than she felt with the attention of eyes.

Rosalie couldn't believe Alex had given her a second chance, that they were actually spending such peaceful and natural time together, that the desert hadn't robbed her of something as tender as this budding thing between them. Rosalie wanted to protect it the same way she wanted to protect Smoke and the wonderful stillness in her body. She would work hard to allow Alex to feel seen the way Alex saw her.

Rosalie reached forward, grazing Alex's ear with her fingertips before lifting her face to meet Alex's. Their kiss was soft and slow, the biggest motions the gentle slip of their lips against each other, the quick lick of tongue against tongue. Rosalie felt Alex melt toward her, almost thirsting for whatever kisses Rosalie would give her. Rosalie knew she didn't have endless kisses; their kisses wouldn't lead to nakedness. She wanted to stay in the stillness that was her piece of Ashhawk. She felt Alex's kisses stiffen, jaw more measured as Alex's hands grew shakier against Rosalie's head and waist. She knew further probing of her tongue would lead to confusion, so she placed a row of kisses against Alex's jaw before shifting onto her back, directing her gaze to the stars.

Alex followed her attention, looking up. Rosalie wondered what stories were strung from those stars, stories of animals and warriors, gods and kings, lovers and fools. Stories from people who had loved this land before she had. Stories she didn't know yet because she hadn't taken time to look at them.

Feeling the warmth in her hands and feet, the gentleness of Alex at her side, and the courage of her own heart, she knew she had time to look now. She had all the time in the world.

Chapter Fourteen

Room Service

Rosalie didn't know what to make of George Tackett. He was the cleanest-cut person she'd met since moving to New Mexico, his hair slicked and his collar pressed precisely. Perhaps Rosalie was still peeved about the interactions she'd had with the male real estate agents she'd contacted who called her *sweetheart* and made her feel incompetent. But George was polite and formal, his smile professional, the handshake of his soft hands firm but unthreatening.

She'd agreed to take a meeting with him at Alex's urging. Alex had stressed that Rosalie needed to know her options for the Cocheta property and that she was under no obligation to make any decisions.

"Good afternoon, Miss Campbell," George said, standing and greeting her as she approached his table. After her panic in the casino, she'd asked to meet George at a McDonald's a few towns over. It wasn't the most professional place to meet, but outside of Ashhawk, she didn't have many options unless she wanted to drive all the way to Albuquerque. Part of her resented George for taking her away from her hotel when she was on such a high learning to run it.

Rosalie greeted him as curtly as she could without being rude, sliding into the hard plastic booth across from him.

"Can I get you anything?" George offered, gesturing toward the counter.

Rosalie shook her head. She didn't want to take anything from George, lest it indebt her to him in any way, even though the smell of French fries was making her mouth water.

"Thank you for meeting with me." George sat and arranged some files on the laminate table. "I know you're busy."

Rosalie nodded in agreement. So far, she liked George. He knew she was not here to mess around.

"So shall we jump right into it?" he asked pleasantly, opening a file.

"I have one question first."

"Absolutely," George said. A smile played on his lips, as though he was encouraged by Rosalie's participation after having been rebuffed so many times over the phone.

"Why are you so interested in *this* particular piece of property? There are plenty of small towns with open pieces of land."

"Ah, yes," George said, shifting in his seat as though settling into a clear story. "Our client finds the zoning codes in Ashhawk more attractive than others for their particular business."

"And what business is that?"

George hesitated. "I'm not at liberty to say who the client is by name, but they're in the industry of consumer goods distribution."

"What kind of goods?"

"The facility they're interested in building on your property would primarily be a book distribution center."

"Like Amazon?"

"I'm not at liberty to name our client, but that's the type of company interested in the land."

"Huh."

Rosalie hadn't expected someone would want to buy the land to build a distribution center for books. She loved books. Ashhawk could certainly use a few more, though she knew the books inside the warehouse wouldn't make it out to the actual town.

"Would you like to go over the proposal?" George held an open file a few inches off the table.

Hoping she could stomach it today, Rosalie nodded.

George turned the file so it was facing right side up for Rosalie and set it flat in front of her.

As Rosalie oriented herself to the figures on the page, she realized she wouldn't be able to determine whether or not this was a good offer. She'd need to consult a lawyer.

Still, the figures in front of her weren't small.

Rosalie bit her lip and furrowed her brow, scanning the document as though she understood all the real estate jargon and acronyms with which she'd been presented. She let out a few deep hums to feign engagement with the strange piece of paper. Once she'd looked for what she thought was a reasonable amount of time, she looked up with a halfhearted smile.

"I'll need to consult my real estate agent about these figures," she said.

"Of course. Feel free to take that copy."

Rosalie nodded, looking down at the file but feeling like she shouldn't close it yet.

"How long do I have to decide?"

George gave a regretful smile. "Our client is hoping to begin construction of the new warehouse early next summer, so within the next few weeks would be ideal," he said.

A few weeks wasn't much time at all, Rosalie knew. In her selfish urgency to divest herself of her properties before she'd decided to stay, she'd thought only of how she might benefit from the sale of her land. But if a company like Amazon were to construct a distribution center in Ashhawk, the town would change completely.

"Who would build the distribution center?" Rosalie asked.

"A reputable local construction company."

"And who would work there once it was built?"

George gave a more relaxed smile now. "Our client has an excellent reputation for helping struggling communities rebuild once the company has a presence in town."

"So there would be jobs for the locals."

"I can't guarantee anything, as I only work for Shaylin, but generally, companies like our client bring in a few key people to work in the offices and hire locals to work in the warehouses and as middle managers."

Rosalie bit her lip, trying not to look too excited about the possibility of reinvigorating sad little Ashhawk.

"Is there anything else I can clarify to help you make your decision?"

Rosalie thought the only thing she was left wondering about was why Gran hadn't sold the property before she died. Maybe there was a reason Rosalie was missing. Or maybe it was up to Rosalie to make this decision without wondering about a dead woman's motivations for sitting on a valuable piece of land. Rosalie was on her own.

She thanked George and rose, shaking his hand and promising to be in touch soon.

≈≈≈≈

For a few weeks, things had continued as blissfully as Rosalie had hoped. She and Alex had spent an entire day pulling the dark wood paneling off the walls of the lobby, hurling the shards into a dumpster before pulling up the ugly cattle-brand carpet, throwing it in, too. Alex showed Rosalie how to install sheetrock, but when Rosalie proved relatively inept, Alex had redirected her to laying colorful tiles over the dingy bricks of the long-dormant fireplace on the far wall of the lobby. Once the walls were finished and painted, they'd restained the counter and desk and laid down fresh carpet. It looked like an entirely different space, with room for social gatherings, meals, and entertainment. Rosalie no longer dreaded spending time there. On cooler nights, Rosalie lit a fire in the fireplace, giving life to the hearth of Hearth Inn. It wasn't the same Hearth Inn Gran had left her; it was her own. As the dust and rust and decay were slowly swept away under Alex's supervision, Rosalie grew more and more proud of her little hotel.

Alex repainted most of the rooms, save for the ones with long-term or residential guests. One afternoon, she even made a little bed for Smoke so he knew he had a permanent home at Hearth. The outside of the building was power-washed and the pool area revitalized. Bit by bit, everything was starting to look nice.

Their dates were simple and fun. They went bowling a few towns down, went back to the food truck caravan, and took a trip to Santa Fe to look at some local art while Rosalie tasted wine. They even tried cooking together, which was mostly disastrous, save for a batch of cookies Alex's grandmother had taught her to make.

One night, after going to a comedy show in Albuquerque, Alex pulled into the parking lot at Hearth. The night seemed potent and still, and Rosalie knew what was coming.

They kissed in Alex's truck as they usually did. It was a relatively private space without too much expectation. But they both wanted more. Rosalie knew it was up to her to initiate.

Rosalie drew their kisses out, hoping they might magically transport to a bed without having to talk about what was happening. But after twenty minutes of sloppy, desperate kisses, Rosalie knew she had to say something.

"Do you want to go back to your room?" she whispered against Alex's neck.

Alex kept her face nestled in Rosalie's hair. "It's up to you," she breathed.

Rosalie kissed and tongued Alex's neck, listening to the way Alex sighed in delight and desire.

Rosalie was certain of what she wanted with Alex and certain Alex wasn't trying to chain her to anything. If anything, she wanted some reassurance Alex wouldn't decide to move out of the hotel and leave her stranded in the desert. She knew it was silly—Alex didn't have anything or anyone calling her away. But Rosalie craved security, even when it was unnecessary.

Lifting her lips from Alex's skin, she mumbled, "Let's go to mine."

Alex hummed, a low, husky sound of pleasure

and surprise. She hadn't expected to be invited to Rosalie's room. They hadn't spent any time in there since they'd started dating, mostly because the living room Rosalie had put together was more spacious and they didn't have to dance around the bed as though it wasn't there, tempting them to fall onto it.

Rosalie pulled back, a quick apology in her eyes for the lack of contact as she fumbled for the door handle, finding it and swinging the door out before sliding down to the pavement without breaking eye contact.

Follow me, her eyes said. Keeping her gaze on Rosalie, Alex did.

Rosalie hastily unlocked her door, sorry she hadn't picked up her clothes but glad the room no longer resembled an old woman's apartment. The new bedspread, art, and curtains all looked like something a young woman would buy for herself.

"Check out the upgrades." Alex grinned when she tore her gaze from Rosalie.

Rosalie tossed her keys onto the counter and toed off her shoes, falling back into Alex's orbit. It was a surrender, a promise not to withdraw or change her mind once her clothes came off. She knew she could withstand being naked around Alex this time. Her focus wasn't on her own body; finally, she'd let her curiosity and awe of Alex's body usurp her hesitations about displaying her own. She wanted to see Alex's muscles move, the fluid motion of her limbs, the sheen brighten on her skin as they lay together.

After long minutes standing kissing by the door, Rosalie realized Alex wasn't going to take the lead. Lowering her arms from where they wrapped around Alex's shoulders, Rosalie stepped back, grasping the hem of her shirt, and lifted it over her head, letting her hair cascade over her shoulders. She smiled, a flutter of shyness coursing through her, quelling when she saw Alex's pleased smile.

Though Rosalie often wished Alex would say something, Rosalie had learned to read Alex's eyes instead. Alex's gaze ghosted over Rosalie's torso, alighting on her breasts for a second before landing back on Rosalie's eyes, a deeper expression of content solidifying there. Alex appreciated Rosalie baring herself first. Heart beating faster, her hands drifted to the button of her pants.

Alex wasn't going to undress her. Not because she didn't want Rosalie to be naked—the look in Alex's eyes said everything but—but because Alex wanted Rosalie to be certain, to make her own choices about when and how she was revealed. Rosalie had never had to do that before. She fumbled a bit, but she was certain.

Once she had undone and removed her pants, she reached forward for Alex's face. Alex couldn't contain her grin as their lips pressed together. Alex loved seeing Rosalie undress herself. Rosalie made note of that—perhaps if she could ever overcome the worst of her self-consciousness, she'd be able to give Alex even more of a show. But in the moment, all she had to do was undress.

Eager to feel skin against skin, Rosalie lowered her hands to the hem of Alex's shirt.

"Can I take off your shirt?" Rosalie knew the answer, but she liked asking.

"Please," Alex hummed. There was no weakness in her voice, only relish.

Rosalie lifted the hem but stopped short of

tugging it over Alex's breasts. She let her hands rest on Alex's stomach, warm and dense with muscle. She ran her hands over and around Alex's sides, enjoying the softness of the skin over the firm core. After a minute, during which Alex smiled into their kisses, Rosalie lifted and tugged the shirt higher, maneuvering it up and off.

The outline of the tank top Alex always wore was burned into her skin, the paleness underneath almost alarming. Rosalie adored it; in her panic last time, she hadn't noticed this beautiful secret.

Alex sighed as she looked down at Rosalie's chest. Again, she said nothing, but Rosalie knew she was hungry.

Rosalie reached behind her back, fumbling with the clasp of her own bra before it sprung open. She held the bra to her chest, teasing, before she reached for Alex's hand and encouraged her to peel each strap off her shoulders. Once Alex had removed the garment and Rosalie stood topless in front of her, Alex let out a shaky breath. It was the first sign of wavering Rosalie had seen, though not in resolve or enjoyment. Alex was wavering in her restraint. Rosalie could now feel her holding herself back. She understood why; Alex needed as much reassurance as Rosalie could provide.

Cupping Alex's cheek as Rosalie pressed her body into Alex's, Rosalie felt Alex quiver. Their skin felt so good together.

Removing Alex's bra, Rosalie took a moment to appreciate Alex's breasts. They were small and triangular and fit perfectly with Alex's body. She leaned forward, her mouth open and eager to brush each nipple with her tongue. Alex put her hand on Rosalie's back and sighed, shifting her legs as her arousal grew.

They shed the rest of their clothing and crawled softly onto the bed. Alex was gentle, her movements slow and cautious. Her hand threaded delicately in Rosalie's hair, and Rosalie wished she would grip it, committing with her whole body. But Alex was tentative and sweet. She had never seemed so feminine. They lay against the pillows kissing for long minutes before Rosalie decided to go first. Alex was waiting for her; she wouldn't disappoint.

As Rosalie dipped her fingers into the space between Alex's legs, breath flew from her mouth. The softness and liquid she found there were an oasis, a place unchanged by desert heat and sun. This small, protected part of Alex endeared her even more to Rosalie; the strength of Alex's body contained this little space of tenderness and vulnerability. Rosalie adored every inch of it with her fingers, caressing it. She had never found something so precious.

Alex panted and whined under Rosalie, and Rosalie realized she'd never seen Alex like this. When they'd had sex before, she'd been so focused on her own fear, she hadn't realized Alex wasn't experiencing pleasure. Now she was. Seeing Alex's strong, lithe body open before her, wanting for her touch, made Rosalie feel powerful. She stroked gently, thoroughly, watching Alex's eyes open and close as she rode through each feeling and sigh. Rosalie was captivated. Her dainty fingers that did little more than type or fret were rendering a strong woman putty against her sheets. She felt that power flow up her arm and into her chest.

As confidence flowed through Rosalie, she nuzzled into Alex's neck. She whispered, "Do you want me to use my mouth?"

Alex trembled with even greater force as she

nodded.

Rosalie felt power surge lower within her, nestling between her legs. She slid down Alex's body, lavishing both her nipples and the undercurve of each breast with her tongue, lathing Alex's stomach with her mouth, dipping into her bellybutton as Alex's muscles quivered. Rosalie settled between Alex's legs and licked at the creases of her thighs, kissing each hip bone, running her free hand over the soft skin of her inner thighs. She breathed heavy and hot against Alex's sex, watching her fingers pulse through her, breathing in the tang of Alex.

She withdrew her fingers, Alex's hips trying not to squirm with anticipation. Rosalie smiled when Alex lifted her head to see what Rosalie was doing. Rosalie had driven her to impatience. But Alex surrendered to Rosalie's control, dropping her head back against the pillow and letting out a breathy whine.

Rosalie leaned in, opening her mouth, pressing forward so slowly the warmth of her breath preceded her, and the moment her mouth met Alex was blurred with its anticipation. When the realization that they had connected hit, Alex's legs jerked, and her breath came out in a sharp gasp that sounded almost like an expletive. Rosalie caressed the wet flesh with her lips before sliding her tongue forward, licking slowly up Alex's center.

Alex's hand came down on Rosalie's head, anchoring herself as her feet slid near Rosalie's shoulders. Rosalie tried not to smile too hard and change the softness of her mouth. She was content to let her power flow from her lips into Alex.

It took only minutes before Alex was tensing beneath her. Rosalie sped up her tongue but didn't sharpen it, letting the natural suction of her mouth draw Alex higher. Alex gasped and panted, running her free hand through her own hair and through the sheets, eager for something to hold on to. Soon Alex's breath grew strained, turning instead to high-pitched whines and silent openings of her mouth. When her hand drifted restlessly near her hip, Rosalie reached up and clasped their hands together, helping secure Alex to the bed, buckling her in for the final push.

Alex clung to Rosalie's hand. Rosalie kept her mouth fastened to Alex, her movements steady, and pressed a bit firmer into her.

After a minute of increased tenseness in Alex's body, Rosalie felt her clench and pulse and lock, her legs rigid around Rosalie's head and back. It lasted for long moments, Rosalie's tongue steady as Alex careened through her release. At last, Alex broke through, her legs jerking, shivering away from Rosalie, her hand pushing Rosalie's head away, her breathing rapid.

Alex seemed fragile and overwhelmed. Licking satisfaction from her lips, Rosalie pressed a kiss to Alex's inner thigh, wiping off some of the wetness on her chin. Looking up, she saw Alex's brow set in desperate relief, eyes closed as she trembled against the pillow.

When Alex didn't open her eyes, Rosalie slid up to help bring her back down. Letting go of Alex's hand, she hovered over her, brushing tendrils of hair off her sweaty forehead. Alex looked small and precious.

When Alex opened her eyes, she gave Rosalie a shaky smile.

Rosalie let out a pleased giggle, hooking hair over Alex's ear to help soothe her. Alex's gaze bored into Rosalie, pleading for something.

Rosalie had never found anything more intimate than kissing one set of lips after another. Most of her lovers hadn't let her, though.

"Can I kiss you?"

Without answering, Alex threaded her hand into Rosalie's hair and drew her down, crashing their mouths together, smearing her own wetness against her face. Rosalie relished her enthusiasm, loving how eager Alex was to taste herself.

They kissed until their momentum slowed. Rosalie lifted her head to take a breath.

"Want me to go down on you?" Alex hummed as she nuzzled into Rosalie's neck. Rosalie felt her arousal mount.

But when she thought of what it would entail, she knew she wanted something different. She wanted to consume rather than be consumed. "Not yet," she said delicately. "I want to keep kissing you."

Alex grinned. "Fine by me."

Rosalie smiled down, moving her hair over her shoulder so it wouldn't get in the way of attaching her lips to Alex's.

As their kiss deepened, Rosalie settled herself into a straddle on Alex's leg. She felt her wetness spread against Alex's thigh, rocking into the right amount of pressure.

Rosalie felt power surge between her legs as she anchored Alex to the bed. She had never felt so sexy and alive, never so comfortable in her own skin. Alex was staring up at her, mouth parted as Rosalie undulated and rocked. She felt pleased moans vibrating through her chest and throat, but they weren't contrived. If anything, she tried to quiet herself in case the walls were thinner than she thought.

Alex's hands drifted over Rosalie's body in an unusual and delightful way. They seemed to rest most on the parts of Rosalie's body she was most uncertain about, the undercurve of her buttocks, the bowl of her belly, the pads of her hips. Alex seemed to only want to touch those places that wobbled and bunched. But Alex's hands were strong and gentle, pressing adoration into all of Rosalie's curves and dips.

After a few minutes, Rosalie felt herself ratcheting up. Alex's hands rested on her waist, encouraging her without steering her. Rosalie took one of Alex's hands in her own, guiding it between her legs, resting her fingers there to provide something for her to rut against. She gasped at the feeling, leaning forward a few inches, feeling her breathing grow shaky. She knew it wouldn't take much longer. She picked up her rocking until she was panting and clenching.

"Oh, my god," Alex whispered.

Rosalie's eyes flew open, concerned she'd done something to ruin the mood or make Alex uncomfortable.

But Alex was staring up at her, riveted.

Rosalie let out a breathy, relieved smile. She was encouraged; Alex was rarely content to sit back and watch while other people worked. But perhaps it was different in bed. Alex bit her lip and kept watching as Rosalie rode her.

Rosalie looked down, taking in Alex's breasts and navel, following to where her fingers tucked against her thigh, pressing into Rosalie's center. Alex was still and appreciative, her skin glistening and warm, her hair spread over the pillows. Alex's hand gripped her waist, fingers brushing over her flushed skin.

Rosalie felt herself peaking and closed her eyes as

she pressed down onto Alex's fingers harder. Alex slid her hand from Rosalie's waist up to cup her breast and gently toy with her nipple. Rosalie felt the final surge start in her body and rocked even more desperately.

"Babe," Alex said.

Rosalie opened her eyes.

Alex simply tilted her chin, and Rosalie understood. She leaned forward, rolling on the fulcrum of Alex's fingers, pushing herself over the edge. Their mouths came crashing together as Rosalie came, her rocking coming to a halt as she seized, then jerked a few times, breaking their kiss to gasp and let out a squeak while her hands flew up to grab at Alex's shoulder and head. Alex slid her free hand around Rosalie's back, pressing her closer, holding her steady.

Rosalie had never felt so protected and embraced during orgasm. Perhaps that was why it lasted longer than usual; she burst through it for long moments, gasping for breath, jerking her hips a few times, pressing closer to Alex.

At last, she was released from the clutches of her climax and came panting down, a string of breathy expletives landing against Alex's neck. Rosalie felt Alex smiling against her cheek. After a few moments, she was able to draw back enough to see Alex smiling up at her. Rosalie fell into that smile, giving Alex a sloppy, grateful kiss that lasted until she needed to catch her breath. She drew back, pulling errant strands of hair out from between their lips.

Alex studied her, removing her hand from between Rosalie's legs, wiping her fingers on the sheets before cradling the small of Rosalie's waist again.

"I was not expecting that," Alex said with a smile.

Rosalie giggled, relieved. Alex had liked her

unexpected assertiveness. She had no idea where it had come from, but judging by the smile on Alex's face and the ripples still coursing through her own body, it was a welcome surprise.

"Me either," Rosalie admitted.

"Do you not usually finish?"

"I do," Rosalie said, realizing she hadn't been clear. "But I'm not usually so...active."

Alex lifted her eyebrow over a wicked smile. "I don't mind."

Rosalie loved the playful look on Alex's face. This was the hidden part she'd hoped to find in Alex when they'd first met, a part that was smiling and carefree, unabashedly girlish and light. She wanted to encourage it.

"Are you a secret pillow princess?" she asked, teasing.

Alex chuckled and made a halfhearted attempt to roll Rosalie onto the mattress. "You wish."

"Maybe I *do* wish," Rosalie said, holding firm with her hands against the pillows.

Alex kept grinning and reached up to draw Rosalie's head down to meet her lips again, lulling in their playfulness before rolling Rosalie over onto her back with force. "I can totally top."

Rosalie giggled, surrendering as Alex gave Rosalie more sweet, gentle kisses to help her come down. They rested in the warm quiet, bodies still humming with satisfaction. Rosalie tangled her arms around Alex's neck, and the sheets rustled as they tried to get closer and closer to each other, the softness of their flesh the sweetest sensation of all.

At last, they were resting in the sheets, quiet and warm. Alex shifted onto her stomach, propping her head on her arms, while Rosalie lay on her side, staring down Alex's body, admiring the slope of her back as she lay on her stomach. She ran her hand down it, feeling how strong and warm Alex was.

"I'm so happy I'm here," Rosalie mumbled absentmindedly.

"I'll take 'Things I never thought I'd hear Rosalie Campbell say about Ashhawk' for six hundred," Alex said with a soft smile.

"I meant with you, silly."

"I know." Alex puckered her lips, and Rosalie shifted forward to meet them. They kissed for a moment before settling back into the pillows.

"I really, really like you, Rosie," Alex crooned.

In another life, Rosalie would have asked *why* Alex liked her, why she was so willing to bare herself after Rosalie had behaved so badly in previous weeks. Another, quieter part rejoiced in the affirmation she was lovable.

Yet the only thing Rosalie felt the urge to do was to return the compliment as genuinely as she could.

"I really, really like you, too."

Chapter Fifteen

Pillow Sweets

Alex rolled toward Rosalie in the early morning light of Rosalie's room. Stirring, Rosalie grinned, sliding closer to Alex, meeting her kisses with a closed mouth before apologetically excusing herself to pee and brush her teeth. After washing her face and taking a large drink of water, she offered Alex a spare toothbrush. They settled back into the bed, smiling at each other. In the light, Rosalie felt even more clear-headed about her relationship with Alex.

What she wasn't clear on, she realized, was Alex's past.

"I don't know anything about the other people you've dated," she said, twirling a strand of Alex's hair that had flown free from her ponytail against the pillowcase, tucking it over her ear.

"What do you want to know?"

"Who was the last person?"

"Her name was Yvonne. We were together for five years."

Rosalie was surprised. Five years was a long time, and Alex had never mentioned her.

"She moved to Chicago four years ago," Alex explained. "I haven't dated anyone since."

Rosalie was stunned, and it must have shown on her face. She couldn't fathom how someone as great as Alex wouldn't be coveted by every lesbian in New Mexico. "Why?"

Alex gave a calm, slow smile. "I feel the same way about girls as I do about speaking."

Rosalie thought back to one of their first dates and how Alex had said she felt people should only speak if it improved on silence. Rosalie tried to connect the sentiment to dating, but Alex beat her to it.

"Only be with someone if it improves on being single." Alex's brown eyes sparkled as they bored into Rosalie, explaining how highly she regarded her.

Rosalie melted into the bed, a puddle under Alex's flattery. She thought back to the relationships she'd been in and how so few of them truly improved on being single. They hadn't been bad, but she would have been as satisfied with her life without the presence of the other person.

But Alex was different. Rosalie's life was exponentially better with Alex in it. Alex's quietness, her laughter, her generosity, and her affection made Rosalie's life better.

"You make my life better, too," Rosalie murmured. "So much better."

Alex grinned and rolled toward Rosalie, pressing her back into the bed, a smother of welcome adoration.

"I never got to meet your girl friends," Rosalie said when Alex pulled back. She recalled their previous conversation about Alex's friends and how she'd avoided discussing their status as mates. She decided to make it up to Alex. "Aside from myself, of course."

Alex quirked an eyebrow.

"Your girlfriend," Rosalie clarified. "I want you to call me your girlfriend."

Alex shifted, tightening her arm around Rosalie's

back. "Okay, girlfriend." She leaned in for a kiss. "I'd love for you to meet my friends who are female."

Rosalie felt something shimmer and fan out inside her, a giggle of joy coursing through her. She pressed her lips to Alex's, thanking her for her patience.

"When did you know you liked girls?" Rosalie asked, smoothing her hand over Alex's hair. "I mean, I know you came out when you were sixteen, but when did you *know*?"

Alex smiled, lazy against the pillow. "Remember how I told you I lived on a Navajo reservation when I was thirteen?"

Rosalie nodded.

"There was this girl there..." Alex trailed off, and Rosalie let her lie in the quiet as she collected her thoughts.

"Her name was Alison. At least that's what I called her because she didn't tell me her Navajo name when we first met. We got close. Maybe too close."

"Too close?"

"Her dad figured out something was happening."

"And..."

"He was concerned, but he didn't tell my dad or anything."

Rosalie realized things could have gone badly for Alex under the circumstances. She didn't know how any of the local Native cultures felt about homosexuality.

"How is that usually received by the Navajo?"

"It depends how Catholicized they are," Alex said. "Very few tribes practice pure Native spirituality anymore. But Native Americans are the last people to try to regulate and monitor other people's rights. So unless you're two-spirit, they look the other way and let you do your thing."

"Two-spirit?" Rosalie had heard the term once before but hadn't known what it meant.

"Some Native American cultures believe some people are born with the wisdom of both male and female souls. They're revered in Navajo culture, like priests or healers."

Rosalie hummed and nodded.

"I thought maybe I was two-spirit for a while. I figured since Alison was so girly, I must be two-spirit if I felt that way about her. I'd only ever seen girls and boys together. So I thought maybe the male part of me was connecting with her femaleness. But I don't feel like I'm half man. I may not like dresses and heels, but I'm a girl."

Rosalie leaned forward to kiss Alex and run her hand over Alex's hip.

Naked in bed like this, Alex seemed strikingly feminine, as though her clothes and hobbies were intended to throw everyone off. Rosalie loved the delicate balance of Alex's femininity.

Alex met Rosalie's lips appreciatively, smiling as Rosalie pulled away.

"I guess when you feel something for a girl for the first time like that and you've never been around someone who isn't straight, you try to make sense of it as best you can," Alex said. "I needed something to make sense."

It was silent, and Alex stared at the sheets intently.

"You loved her, didn't you?"

Alex looked at Rosalie with a soft smile. "In that crazy, thirteen-year-old way, yeah."

"Back before you know what can happen," Rosalie said with a sigh. "That's the best way." She stroked Alex's arm and remembered how she'd felt about Perene.

Alex nodded faintly against the pillow. "When you don't know what getting hurt feels like, you can love as big as the sky."

Rosalie breathed with Alex. "Do you think we ever get it back?"

Alex shifted, twisting her torso closer to Rosalie. Her face was serious. "I hope so."

It was quiet, and Rosalie felt overwhelmed by the intensity of Alex's gaze. Alex was saying so much with those three words: that she wanted to be able to love that big again, that she wanted to forget their mutual ability to hurt, that she wanted to give Rosalie the sky.

Rosalie scrunched her body closer to Alex's, wiggling as though there was space between them she wanted to extinguish. Maybe if she burrowed close enough, she'd blend into Alex to the point where she could hear her thoughts. She pressed as close as she could, closing her eyes and breathing, listening as best she could.

"You know what's unfortunate?" Alex asked a few minutes later.

"What?"

"At some point, we're gonna have to get out of bed and run this hotel."

Rosalie whined, only to have it cut off by Alex's mouth. She didn't want to leave the room, let alone the bed and the endless combustion she felt was possible in its sheets.

"Can it not be today?"

"Call Shelley," Alex mumbled.

Rosalie reached blindly behind her for her phone, feeling for it on the bedside table without removing her face from where it ghosted in front of Alex's.

Shelley answered right away, more than happy for the extra hours. Rosalie had barely hung up before she was smothering Alex with kisses again.

"Remind me to give Shelley a big Christmas bonus," Rosalie hummed.

Alex hummed in agreement, already drawn back into Rosalie's lips.

Rosalie met her, only mildly distracted by her worry about what would happen when Shelley found out why she'd been spending so much time with Alex lately.

Chapter Sixteen

Housekeeping

R osalie slid into the lobby, hoping Shelley wouldn't look up from where she was perched proudly behind the desk. But of course, Shelley was an excellent desk clerk, and her head snapped up as soon as the door opened. She gave Rosalie a strange look. Rosalie was wearing nothing more than a bathrobe, her hair piled on top of her head until she could comb the sex knots out of it.

"Morning," Rosalie said, as though nothing were unusual.

"Morning," Shelley responded, tracking Rosalie as she walked around the counter and opened a file cabinet.

"Just getting some files," Rosalie said cheerily. Her voice was forced and dared Shelley to ask questions.

Shelley responded with an uncertain smile. As Rosalie walked out, she said, "Let me know if you need anything."

Rosalie pretended she hadn't heard, hoping Shelley wouldn't let her curiosity linger too long. Rosalie paid her to sit at the desk, not to wonder what Rosalie was up to.

Still, she was glad Shelley hadn't asked any questions or noticed Alex going into her room the night before. Her relationship with Alex was so new and tender, she didn't want to expose it to anything outdoors that might weaken or crack it in the harsh light and heat.

But at the same time, there was a seed of guilt and worry in her that echoed everything that had happened with Perene. Her refusal to be open, her insistence on keeping their relationship secret, had cost her the thing she held most dear. She felt stuck between two difficult things—losing her safety and losing her heart. She couldn't decide which was more valuable.

Luckily, that was a problem that could be put off for another day or week or year. There was another that couldn't.

She opened the door to her suite and was greeted by Alex, leaning back in her chair in the lounge room of Rosalie's suite. The late morning sun streamed through the blinds, making it feel airier. Alex was wearing a pair of boxers and a black tank top with no bra.

Rosalie set the files down on the table and slid her chair closer. She plopped into it, feeling a few sore spots in her legs from where she'd exerted herself. It was a good sore, one she knew wouldn't linger once her body got used to regular sex.

"This meeting of the managerial staff of Hearth Inn is officially called to order," Rosalie said, thumbing through some papers.

"Managerial staff?"

"As the director of maintenance, you are a manager."

"How many people am I managing?"

"Yourself."

"I see. And how's my managerial performance so far?"

"Excellent."

"Good. I've been working on managing myself."
Alex took a sip of her coffee and grinned, balancing her
ankle over her knee. "I haven't been in a lot of business
meetings, but this is my favorite so far."

Rosalie glanced up with a smirk. She knew it was
laughable to have a business meeting in bathrobes and
underwear, but one of the perks of being her own boss
was being able to do such things.

"Will you be able to focus?" Rosalie teased.

"Depends how tightly that belt is tied."

Rosalie waggled her eyebrows at Alex and
started to draw one side of her robe out to expose a
breast before tugging it tighter across her chest and
looking back down at the papers. Alex huffed in mock
exasperation and leaned forward, examining the papers
upside down.

"So what's going on?" Alex said.

Rosalie picked up the deed to the Cocheta property
along with the proposal George Tackett had given her.

"Shaylin Development wants to buy the land
from me to build a distribution center."

"And they're willing to pay market value?"

"Yep. And they intend to hire local guys to do
the construction."

Alex gave Rosalie a look.

"And girls," Rosalie added quickly. "But not you
because you're spoken for."

"Damn right, I'm spoken for." Alex grinned.

Rosalie lifted out of her chair enough to kiss Alex
briefly on the lips.

Alex smiled at her, then let her gaze fall back to
the papers. "And once the distribution center is built,
what happens?"

"There will be more trucks coming in and out of

town. Standard distribution center stuff."

"Truckers who might need a place to stay."

"Probably. And they'll hire locals to work in the warehouse."

Alex nodded slowly, trying to piece together Rosalie's dilemma.

"You'd also have a truckload of cash from the sale to put into renovating this place."

"Indeed I would."

Alex hunched forward, squinting at the papers. "Explain the problem because I'm not seeing one."

"That's the *thing*," Rosalie said, glad someone else was as confused as she was. "I know it would be good for the town and for Hearth and for me. But maybe there's a reason Gran didn't want to sell. Maybe she doesn't want a big corporation to come in and change everything."

Alex chewed her lip, brow knitting as she tried to consider Rosalie's point. "It could have something to do with Marvin," Alex offered. "Maybe she felt like selling it would make his death more permanent."

Rosalie hadn't considered that. Knowing how deeply Gran loved, it was possible she had clung to the empty property like a beloved photograph or sweater.

"Maybe."

There was a pause.

"I'm using Gran as an excuse not to make a decision, aren't I?"

Alex only bit her lip in agreement.

Rosalie sighed. "It's a really big decision."

Alex gave a gentle bob of her head. "Is there a reason you feel like you have to decide whether or not to sell right now?"

"George Tackett only gave me another week to

consider their offer."

"Ah," Alex said.

"It's not much time when you consider how many meetings I need to have with my director of maintenance."

Alex looked confused for a moment, then realized Rosalie meant she would rather spend her time having sex than try to make a decision about the Cocheta property.

"The director of maintenance does like to have 'meetings,'" she said with feigned commiseration for Rosalie's imaginary frustration. "But she's also invested in making sure you have all the support you need to run this place."

Rosalie relaxed back in her chair. Alex always calmed her.

"And the good news is you do have a week to decide," Alex pointed out. "I'm sure you'll know what you want to do by then."

"I hope so."

Rosalie thought about the faces she'd come to be familiar with during her time in Ashhawk—the other waitresses at the diner, the clerks at the convenience store across the street, the checkers at the quaint family-owned grocery store a few blocks over, the residential guests of the hotel. She thought of the welcoming committee who had brought casseroles during her first week. In her initial insistence that her stay in Ashhawk was temporary, she'd snubbed their invitations to become part of the fabric of the town. Now she was part of it, and she had a chance to make an impact on the well-being of the town in a way she never expected.

Alex shifted in her seat. "You seem anxious,

Rosie."

"I am."

Alex gave a pout, as though she wished Rosalie wasn't so hesitant around her.

"I was nervous you'd think I was leaning in the wrong direction."

"Why would I think that?"

Rosalie gave a timid shrug. "I'm not from here. I shouldn't get to make decisions about a town you've lived in your whole life."

Alex looked at Rosalie tenderly. It was the opposite look Rosalie had expected.

As always, Alex was quiet and calm, giving her space to talk through her thoughts.

Rosalie took a breath. "People might hate me for letting a big warehouse be built in such a beautiful place. They probably already hate me for having one of the only viable businesses in town. And if the warehouse ends up being terrible, it'll be my fault."

Alex nodded pensively. "Maybe. But for the most part, people will be excited about the possibility of more jobs and traffic through town. Those are good things. They know that."

Rosalie bit her lip and nodded, still not convinced her inclination to sell the property was the right choice.

"I'm not a businesswoman," Alex said, a phrase she repeated often when they discussed the hotel. "So talk to the people you need to talk to."

Rosalie nodded quicker, calming at the thought. "I have an appointment with a lawyer my dad helped me find to go over the proposal and make sure it's sound. And a consultation with a commercial real estate broker."

"Good," Alex said. "That'll be good information."

She paused, studying Rosalie for a moment longer. "What does your gut say, Rosie?"

Rosalie exhaled and closed her eyes, dropping into her discomfort full force like cannonballing into a pool. She held her eyes closed long enough to check how her hands and feet and legs and stomach felt about holding on to the property. She didn't feel anything. Then she imagined selling it. Immediately, her stomach unclenched, and a warmth coursed up from her hips. "Take the deal."

Alex smiled, a soft, early morning sun smile. "Good." She reached across the table and squeezed Rosalie's hand, sitting quietly for a long moment before she said, "I think Estelle would be proud."

Rosalie smiled and shrugged. Perhaps Gran would have been proud of it or perhaps she wouldn't. Gran had left her the property because she trusted Rosalie to do the best thing with it. That had been her final lesson in generosity.

⚜⚜⚜⚜

When she could pry herself out of bed with Alex, Rosalie found managing the hotel to be exponentially easier. Grumpy guests hardly fazed her, expense reports practically drafted themselves, and the list of immediate repairs she and Alex had put together didn't feel as overwhelming.

The only thing lurking in her mind as unpleasant was the inevitable conversation she knew she'd have to have with Shelley. Now that her heart was in Hearth for the foreseeable future, she knew she didn't have space in it for anyone who might make her feel uncomfortable about dating a woman. Guests would come and go, but her staff had to be the family she didn't have nearby.

Rosalie maintained a calm composure as she approached the desk. Shelley's hair was perfect as always, her sad, vaguely bored expression directed at the computer Rosalie would soon replace.

Rosalie loved the new lobby. It felt lively and fresh and set the tone for what she hoped was a successful remodel of each room in the building. The physical labor she had been doing with Alex to renovate the property was a welcome distraction from her looming deadline for a decision about the Cocheta property. She still had a few days to decide.

In the meantime, Rosalie was invigorated by the changes slowly occurring in the building around her. If Shelley wasn't inclined toward similar change, Rosalie knew she'd have to find someone else.

"Hey, Shelley?"

Shelley looked up, trying to seem alert. "Yeah?"

"I know you and Alex don't get along," Rosalie hedged.

"We get along fine," Shelley said, her voice creeping toward defensiveness.

Rosalie let the denial pass. "Maybe I'm imagining a little tension there," she said, giving a gentle shrug to convey she wasn't accusing Shelley of anything. "It's fine. You don't have to be best friends."

Shelley pursed her lips and nodded for lack of a better response.

"Anyway…She and I have been dating for a little while now. I wanted you to hear it from me."

Rosalie waited for a reaction. She got little; Shelley's hands stiffened where they hovered over the keyboard, and she blinked a few times. After a few seconds, Rosalie knew that was all the reaction she was going to get.

"I want everyone here to be comfortable since it's just the four of us. She's going to be doing more management stuff as we keep going with the remodel."

Shelley gave a slow nod, as though she had a lot to process before she would speak.

"You're doing a great job, and the guests like you. I like spending time with you. But if you're uncomfortable working here because of me and Alex, I'd be happy to give you a glowing recommendation somewhere else."

Shelley's perfectly tweezed eyebrows lifted almost imperceptibly.

"You're a great employee, but I understand if personal differences are a deal breaker."

Shelley nodded, not wanting to incriminate herself further or commit to staying or leaving.

Rosalie patted the counter. "Anyway," she said, smiling. "I'm happy to answer questions, if you have any. Well, most questions."

Shelley nodded quicker now, relieved the conversation was ending.

Rosalie left the office with her head held high, thinking Perene would have been so proud of her.

But more importantly, she was proud of herself.

She went immediately to Alex's room, wanting to reward herself with a kiss and the comfort of Alex's arms. Of course Alex wasn't there; she was busy ripping out a bathroom sink to replace it with one of the new vanities they'd designed together. Rosalie marched into the room, smile widening as Alex looked up at her, safety goggles strapped over her face. Rosalie walked up to her, pulled the goggles off, and planted a big, wet kiss on her mouth. Alex's eyebrows lifted, and her arms wrapped around Rosalie's waist as Rosalie drew her closer, smiling with her whole body, wanting to wrap herself farther into Alex than their clothing and daytime obligations would allow. When she pulled away, she was beaming.

"Hello to you, too." Alex grinned.

"I came out to Shelley."

Alex's eyebrows arched.

"She didn't say much," Rosalie explained. "I said I hoped she still wanted to work here, but I understood if she wanted to leave."

"Really?" Alex asked, surprised.

Rosalie nodded. "This is our *home*. I want everyone who works here to be cool with us."

Alex glanced back at the vanity for a moment as her smile spread. She tightened her grip on Rosalie's waist. "Have I told you today how great you are?"

"Yeah, but I wouldn't object to hearing it again."

Rather than speak, Alex hunched forward to kiss Rosalie again, staggering a few steps forward so Rosalie almost lost her balance. Alex gave her another, more smacking and playful kiss before placing a few smaller kisses on her chin and cheeks.

"You're pretty great," Alex said. She helped Rosalie stand upright.

Rosalie darted forward to leave one last kiss on Alex's cheek. "Do you want sopapillas for dinner?"

"Always," Alex said.

As Rosalie left the room, Alex watched her go, halfheartedly reaching for the drill she'd set down moments before.

"Hey," she called after Rosalie.

Rosalie stopped walking and lifted her eyebrow.

"I love you," Alex said.

She said it simply, as a fact or compliment or encouragement. There was no anxiety or pretense. It simply existed as true, as an expression of the generosity flowing through her as effortlessly as laughter.

Rosalie flushed, a burst of comfort pulling her mouth into a smile. Her feet took her back to Alex, and she threaded herself into her, wanting to wear her like a coat.

"I love you, too," she hummed, eyes dancing between Alex's eyes and lips.

❧❧❧❧

Rosalie and Shelley avoided each other as much as they could for the next few days. Shelley showed up on time and worked as hard as she ever did, the smart knot of her apron secured around her waist, hair drawn back in an almost severe ponytail. Rosalie danced around her, wondering if this was how Shelley handled distaste for someone, or if she simply needed time to process. Either way, Rosalie was uneasy.

But it was easy to stomach Shelley's behavior when she had Alex's bed to fall into as often as she did. She had never been so glad to be naked with someone. She continued ravishing Alex night and day, eager to consume rather than be consumed.

After a few days, Shelley came into the lobby at the end of her housekeeping shift, head bent as she removed her apron. Rosalie thought she would come and go silently, but after hanging her apron in the back room, Shelley stood awkwardly to the side of the counter. Rosalie looked up.

Shelley wrung her hands and blurted, "I kissed a girl once."

Amused by Shelley's strange admission, Rosalie raised her eyebrows.

"Bobby wanted me to," Shelley said, rolling her eyes.

Rosalie dared to respond. "How was it?"

Shelley let out a nervous, gasping giggle. "Pretty good."

Rosalie gave a subtle bob of her head, as though thanking Shelley for whatever odd declaration she was trying to make.

"I don't want you to think I'm grossed out by it or anything."

"I don't think that."

Rosalie hadn't assumed Shelley was grossed out by girls kissing. She just knew Shelley was uncomfortable with Alex. Shelley's superficial Sapphic experiment for the viewing pleasure of her boyfriend had little to do with tolerance, but Rosalie decided to give Shelley the benefit of the doubt. Shelley seemed flustered enough.

"I like working here, and I love working with you," Shelley said, as though she were apologizing. "And if Alex makes you happy, that's cool."

Rosalie relaxed in her chair, understanding now that Shelley was pledging her allegiance to Hearth and to being a good employee despite whatever bad blood there was between her and Alex.

"How did you guys, like, start dating?" Shelley asked, inching forward to continue their conversation now that Rosalie was receptive.

"We were friends for the first few months," Rosalie explained. "I had a girlfriend back in Philadelphia when we met."

Shelley looked surprised. "Alex isn't your first?"

Rosalie shook her head gently.

"But I thought you had a boyfriend when you first got here."

"I was in a relationship but not with a boy."

Shelley's eyebrows crept up her forehead. "Wow. I guess I assumed..."

"That Alex converted me?" Rosalie said, lifting an eyebrow playfully to challenge whatever assumptions Shelley had about Alex. "Actually, I made the first move on her."

"Huh..." Shelley said, looking utterly confounded. "Well, you never can judge a book by its cover."

Rosalie studied Shelley's apologetic and confused stance and made a quick decision. She was getting better at those—quick decisions—even though they still made her uneasy. But if she could bank on anything, it was Shelley's work ethic.

"Changing topics," Rosalie said, shifting in her seat. "I need a director of housekeeping and hospitality." Her smug grin widened in anticipation of Shelley's reaction.

"Are you serious?" Shelley asked, her body lurching forward a few inches.

Rosalie nodded. "Are you interested?"

"Fuck yes," Shelley said. Her hand flew to her mouth. "I mean, *heck yes.*"

Rosalie's grin split as she laughed. "You can curse when there aren't any guests in here."

"What do I need to do to apply?" Shelley asked, trying to restrain her enthusiasm.

"You don't need to apply. The job is yours if you want it."

Shelley gaped at her. "Are you fucking with me?"

"I thought I made it clear I was fucking Alex," Rosalie said, mostly as a joke, but also to test Shelley's tolerance.

Shelley let out a great, gawping laugh she tried to choke back with her hand like she had her expletive.

"Oh, my god, you're bad," Shelley said, body relaxing from her tense apology. Finally, Rosalie recognized polite, polished Shelley before her.

"We can talk salary and benefits in an official contract meeting," she said. It wouldn't be difficult to draft a job description and write out a contract that would hold up in the unlikely event Shelley didn't work out. But Rosalie knew Shelley's work ethic well enough to know that it would.

"I'd want you to take at least one course online," Rosalie said, pointing vaguely to her computer. "I'm taking some hotel management classes, and they've got some for hospitality managers. The hotel will pay for it, of course."

Shelley was beaming, nodding as though she would agree to almost anything Rosalie suggested. "Oh, my god, this is *amazing*," she said, dipping at the knees and lifting her voice as though her stomach muscles had tensed at the last word.

Rosalie loved giving good news.

"I actually had an idea," Shelley said, whispering as though her idea were either unstable or clever.

Rosalie raised her eyebrows to invite Shelley to continue.

"I know we're never going to have the facilities to offer, like, room service or anything," Shelley said. "But what about, like, taking pre-orders for breakfast from the diner the night before and having it delivered hot the next morning? And we could charge a delivery fee or something?"

Rosalie's eyebrows danced up again, pleased

with Shelley's industry. Rosalie knew the lack of room service and decent breakfast were bothersome to some of the guests who came in for a night or two. The idea of collaborating with the diner had never occurred to her.

"That's a great idea," Rosalie said, giving soft little bobs of her head to show she was processing it. "I'll definitely look into it."

Shelley looked pleased with herself, clasping her hands together. "So does this mean I can quit the diner?"

"You'll have to," Rosalie said, knowing Shelley wanted to hear that more than ever. "Your new position is full time."

Shelley gave a little pump to the air, her voice still muted, as though her boss at the diner might hear if she expressed too much joy in no longer having to work there after ten years.

Shelley fidgeted before extending her arms forward awkwardly. "Can I have a hug?" she asked, as though Rosalie might reject her.

Surprised by Shelley's affection, Rosalie stood, stepping tentatively into Shelley's embrace. She gave her a gentle squeeze, so as to not awaken any residual fears that lesbianism was contagious or that she was some sort of letch. Shelley squeezed tighter than she did but stepped back quickly, not out of discomfort, but because she was having trouble keeping her body still in her excitement.

❧ ❧ ❧ ❧

The casino wasn't the most romantic place for a date, but it was nicer than the diner without the pretension of something more upscale. Rosalie hadn't been to the casino since her meeting with Coral. They were seated toward the back of the restaurant that opened onto the floor, tucked away from the worst of the zipping and clanking and pinging of thousands of machines promising riches, delivering few.

Despite all the distraction, it was easy to fix her attention on Alex. They sat and skimmed the menu, ordering a drink while deciding on their entrees. Once their drinks arrived, Alex leaned forward.

"Cheers," she said, holding her beer forward for Rosalie to clink.

"Cheers." Rosalie met the bottle with her wine glass.

"To the sale of the Cocheta property."

"Amen."

They took a sip of their drinks, beaming.

"Thanks for holding my hand through it."

"Psh, I could do it in my sleep."

"You two ready to order?" a server asked in a pinched voice.

Rosalie and Alex glanced down at their menus.

"What sounds good, babe?" Alex asked.

Rosalie glanced up at the waiter, unsure how he would respond to Alex's verbal affection. The waiter only smiled professionally at Rosalie, and the little swell of anxiety she felt quelled.

They ordered and settled deeper into their seats.

"I know we're not supposed to talk about business on dates, but I just want to say: I'm excited for the coming months," Alex said with an unabashed smile. "It's been a long time since I've worked for someone who wasn't on a shoestring budget."

"Don't go getting too crazy," Rosalie teased. "I

only have a few hundred thousand dollars to spend."

Alex laughed. "You realize that makes you a Rockefeller by Ashhawk standards."

"So will you let me pay for dinner?" Rosalie asked, gaze boring into Alex.

Alex glanced down at the table, biting down her smile. "Fine," she said. "Feels kind of weird, though."

"You've never had a girl buy you dinner?" Rosalie asked, surprised.

Alex shook her head.

Rosalie raised her eyebrows in objection. "Clearly, you haven't been having dinner with the right girls."

Alex shrugged. "I'm pretty happy with this one," she said. "I think I'll stick with her."

Rosalie leaned forward, almost close enough to kiss Alex.

"Good."

Chapter Seventeen

Check-in

W hat are we gonna do if it rains?" Rosalie asked Alex. They were in bed together in Rosalie's room, and Rosalie's voice was shriveled with worry.

"We'll have the party in the lobby."

"But what if there's too many people?"

"Yesterday, you were worried no one would come," Alex said, smirking as she ran her hand down Rosalie's arm to her waist, resting it there.

"I know."

"What's your ideal size crowd for this thing? I'm not clear."

Rosalie pouted in the not-serious way she did when Alex teased her for worrying about something she couldn't control.

Alex drew Rosalie closer, kissing the top of her head, squeezing extra hard, as though to wring out all the worry.

"Shelley may not know accounting or what feminism really means, but she knows people and she knows this town. People will come."

Rosalie breathed into the sun-bronzed skin of Alex's chest. "I hope so."

"They will," Alex said. "If only to get a look at the new town lesbian."

Rosalie groaned into Alex's chest. In the months since she'd sold the Cocheta property and come out to Shelley, she'd noticed a few people looking at her longer than usual. But no one said anything hurtful, and no one leered or glared like she'd worried they would. The looks she got now weren't much different from the ones she'd gotten when she first moved to town.

"If it rains, we can put the construction canopy over the grill and people will sit under the awning and in the lobby. It'll be fine."

Rosalie exhaled, letting Alex coax her worry out of her.

"And afterward, we'll come back here and snuggle," Alex added.

"Naked?"

"God willing."

Rosalie let out a quiet chuckle that shook her shoulders and brought her even tighter against Alex. "Okay."

The next morning was sunny and bright, the air seeming lighter than its usual choking dryness. Rosalie did her opening routine, reviewing the comings and goings of guests from the day before, checking incoming reservations, making note of which rooms were ready for cleaning. She looked over the breakfast spread on the counter Alex had built near the watercooler as she set to work on a module of her current hotel management course. She distracted herself long enough with that to forget she was hosting a barbecue that night. Shelley had suggested it as a way to bring the town together in celebration of the groundbreaking at the Cocheta property. It was an eve of change for Ashhawk, one that Rosalie hoped would be positive and endear her to a few townsfolk.

Shelley had put the barbecue together, getting deals on meat from the local market, ordering a few kegs and some cases of wine, even hiring a band to play. Alex suggested getting a fire pit to place in the middle of the cleared parking lot.

"Just like Corte del Cuervo." Rosalie had grinned.

Alex turned to her and winked, that sly, fleeting wink that still made Rosalie's stomach flutter.

They'd been back to Malcolm's a few times for more private weekends together, during which they barely left their room, aside from meals, sunsets, and a private wine tasting with Malcolm and Logan. Rosalie was careful not to drink too much. It was one of her favorite places in the world, made even more dear by Alex's presence.

But these days, Hearth wasn't so bad, either. Shelley had stepped into her role of director of hospitality such that Rosalie, with her newly gleaned knowledge of hotel management, only had to worry about the business end of the operation, while Shelley handled housekeeping and customer service. With Alex heading up maintenance, Susan covering the desk half the time, and a handful of hourly hires for housekeeping and the occasional maintenance job Alex couldn't do alone, the hotel was operating smoothly and on a balanced budget. They'd even booked up for the first time in years recently. It was almost unrecognizable from the place Rosalie had arrived at shortly after Gran's death.

The party was supposed to start at six o'clock, and by quarter til, Rosalie was so worried Alex had to take her into her room and run her hands up and down Rosalie's arms and back. Right as Rosalie was preparing to say something to protest Alex's stubborn certainty the party would be a hit, they heard a car door shut outside.

Rosalie pulled back from Alex's embrace, a hopeful expression on her face.

She heard voices outside, then someone asking, "Where's Miss Rosalie?"

Alex grinned.

"*Miss Rosalie*," Rosalie mocked. "That makes me feel like a stuffy church lady."

"It's a respect thing," Alex said, leaning forward to kiss Rosalie on the forehead before giving her a gentle swat on the butt. "You better get out there, babe."

Rosalie opened the door, smiling as she greeted Bobby and a handful of his friends who'd shown up with an extra case of beer.

"'Eyyy, there she is," Bobby said, loping toward Rosalie. "The hostess with the mostest." He gave her a wide, goofy smile and held out some potato salad.

"Hey, Bobby," Rosalie greeted. She'd grown to like Bobby in certain situations. He wasn't the controlling jerk she'd imagined, though he wasn't the prime cut she would have picked for Shelley if she'd been given a chance, either. But he was benign, and he made Shelley happy.

"Me and my boys are stoked for tomorrow," Bobby said, mashing a fist into the open palm of his other hand. "Making money, getting paid." He grinned.

A few dozen local men had been hired to help with the construction, improving the town's employment rate even before the warehouse was completed.

As Bobby spoke, another car parked on the street, this time with a family Rosalie had seen around town getting out and making their way toward the parking lot. Rosalie smiled and waved, and the kids pointed to the pool, asking if they could dip their feet in.

Slowly, the parking lot filled with people drinking, eating, and buzzing with excitement about the construction starting in the morning. By the time the sun went down and Alex lit the bonfire and the band started up, Rosalie was glowing with the success.

People had come to her party. And it hadn't been because they wanted to gawk at the town lesbians or take the free food or criticize the new sign or patio furniture or retouched exterior. They'd come because Rosalie had thrown a party for the community, and they'd accepted her as part of it.

Rosalie felt tipsy with joy as she was drawn into conversation with dozens of people she'd only seen in passing until now. Local business owners wanted to pick her brain, women wanted to know who did her hair and nails (Shelley, of course), and kids wanted to ask if they could play in the pool even if they weren't staying there.

The night spun on, Rosalie feeling warm even as the sun descended and left them with only the orange glow of the bonfire, the new sign above, and the exterior lights. Shelley was giddy with the party's success, cornering Rosalie at one point, rolling out her plan for a series of movie nights and community events Hearth could host over the coming months.

Gradually, people left, the families with young kids, then the older couples, then the young folks, until it was just a handful of Shelley and Bobby's friends sitting in the lobby around the fireplace, talking in warm voices as they finished cups of beer and soda. As Rosalie emerged from the back room where she had placed the leftover drinks, she saw Shelley and Bobby nestled together on the couch, surrounded by friends.

Rosalie felt Alex's hand on her waist before she felt her breath near her ear. She smiled and turned her head just enough to plant a kiss on Alex's cheek. Alex returned the gesture as she brought her body flush with Rosalie's, pressing the invisible layers of barbecue smoke on their clothes together as they observed the scene before them. Bobby had his arm around Shelley, his hand soft on her shoulder.

"They're sweet together," Rosalie said, quiet so only Alex could hear.

Alex said nothing, which Rosalie understood as a silent agreement.

Seeing her domain so in harmony with the town, Rosalie dared to hope everything would fall into place for the people she cared about.

"Do you think he'll propose?"

"Yeah," Alex said. "Once he's got a little money. He's crazy in love with her."

Rosalie nodded, glad Alex had faith in Bobby.

"I want her to be happy," Rosalie said.

Alex nodded and pressed her lips into Rosalie's hair. "You 'bout ready for bed?"

Rosalie looked at her watch and saw it was well past midnight.

"Everything's brought in," Alex said.

Rosalie nodded and called out to Shelley and Bobby that they were turning in and to make sure the fire was out before they left. They gave mellow, cheerful waves as Rosalie and Alex turned toward the door, Alex's arm around Rosalie's waist.

For the first time since arriving in Ashhawk, not even a little part of Rosalie wanted Alex to move her arm.

᪄᪄᪄᪄

Rosalie woke the next morning with a calm stillness that felt foreign to her. Alex was missing from her bed, but Rosalie didn't panic. Sometimes, Alex got up to start projects early so she wouldn't have to work during the hottest part of the day. Rosalie looked at the ceiling for a few minutes, letting the most pleasant parts of the previous night play out on the smooth, now asbestos-free ceiling. She smiled, feeling her body warm with happiness.

Everything was settled, save for the dirt being turned and moved across town as construction began. She looked around, wondering what she ought to do that day. During one of their weekly business meetings that now occurred fully clothed because they included Shelley, Alex had gently urged Rosalie to schedule regular days off, and today was one of those days. Rosalie didn't know what to do with herself yet, other than perhaps read and paint her nails and go for a swim.

As she sat up and looked around the room, her gaze fell on the box of Gran's ashes. With a gut certainty that was still new but unmistakable to her, she knew what she wanted to do.

After she showered and dressed and fed Smoke, she opened her door and was surprised to find Alex sitting in one of the new chairs beside her doorway, cup of coffee in hand.

"G'morning, beautiful." Alex grinned up at her.

Rosalie felt a smile overtake her as Alex stood and extended the cup toward Rosalie.

"Thanks." Rosalie took it, savoring the aroma.

Alex slid her hand into her back pocket. "It's your day off."

"Yeah."

"Anything you want to do?"

Rosalie took a sip of coffee. "Yeah, actually." She handed her coffee back to Alex and stepped inside to retrieve the box of Gran's ashes, holding them in front of her rather than saying anything.

Alex pursed her lips and nodded, her expression more somber. "Where do you want to do it?"

"I don't know," Rosalie said, frowning. "I thought about doing it at the Cocheta property, but I kind of missed my opportunity."

"Estelle wouldn't want to lay under a big distribution center for all eternity anyway."

"Maybe I should sprinkle them out back. She loved this place." But even as she said it, Rosalie wasn't sure.

Alex frowned in thought and nodded. "I have a place you might like. Hop in my truck."

Rosalie glanced back at her room, then climbed into the cab of Alex's truck and clung to the seat as it jostled out of the parking lot. Alex turned in the opposite direction of the Cocheta property and drove through the heart of town.

Rosalie took in the fading signs, the drooping roofs, the abandoned businesses. The semi-ghost town was still a sorry sight, and the early morning light made it even more eerie. Rosalie knew Gran had hated to see her town fall on such hard times.

But Rosalie also knew things would start to change soon. Not all at once; there would never be a morning when she woke and was greeted with a shiny, bustling town. There would always be a thin layer of dust and fatigue over Ashhawk. But slowly, signs would be replaced, buildings would be repainted, and business would pick up. A few more families would be able to pay their bills. Fewer things would be broken and sad. A few more people would have hope. Rosalie was happy for that.

Alex drove to the edge of town, not stopping as they headed into the vast, open desert. Rosalie settled into her seat, oddly content to be a passenger on a trip to a mystery destination.

Alex glanced down at the bench next to her. "Move closer."

Rosalie pulled at the lap belt that was tucked into the groove of the seat. She quickly unbuckled and shifted into the center seat, feeling her side press into Alex's. She buckled herself in and felt a flurry of warmth. She studied the side of Alex's face for a moment before she took a deep breath and lay her head on Alex's shoulder.

Alex lifted a hand off the steering wheel to caress the side of Rosalie's face. Rosalie burrowed deeper into Alex's side, the ashes in her lap heavier than their weight.

They drove for twenty minutes, listening to the faint sound of Alex's radio crackling before Alex turned off the highway onto a barely distinguishable dirt road. Rosalie would have missed it even if she'd been looking for it. The tires bucked and the cab of the truck rocked, and Rosalie had to lift her head so she didn't hit Alex in the jaw as they bounced through the dusty desert. They drove for five minutes before the road curved up and around a hill, climbing higher. After a few minutes, Alex slowed the truck, putting it in park. She turned off the ignition and gestured for Rosalie to follow her as she slid out of the cab.

Rosalie climbed out, eager to be on solid land. Alex took her by the hand, offering to hold the box of ashes as she led her up an incline of rock and dust, a few perilous steps around the side of a boulder, until they crested the hill. She helped pull Rosalie up, a calm determination on her face. Rosalie accepted the help, wishing she'd worn something other than sandals.

When Rosalie was securely standing at the top of the rock, Alex gestured out behind her. Rosalie turned and was met with the most majestic view she'd ever seen: the desert stretched out before her, wild and hearty and tinged with gold in the morning light. Rosalie could hear the murmurings of desert life— lizards and birds and insects going about their daily routines. In the distance, to the right, she could see a pueblo, a few tendrils of smoke curling up from the adobe buildings, their forms blending into the earth as though they could never be separated. In the distance to the left, she could see Ashhawk, so faded and small it was unremarkable.

As she took in the land before her, its ashen greens and golden browns and rusty yellows, she felt the urge to plant herself on that rock so she might hold on to the feeling of awe and peace she felt overwhelm her.

"I thought it might be a good place," Alex said quietly, as though speaking too loud could disturb the desert stretching out in front of them.

Rosalie nodded, turning her head to take in the vast land. She could turn in a complete circle and only see a few signs of human presence. It was beautiful.

After a few minutes, Rosalie decided to sit. Here in the morning, time was elongated. Hearth was in

Shelley's capable hands, and there was nothing she needed to do more than sit with Alex and admire the view. She sat down, tugging Alex with her, and hung her legs off the edge of the rock. It was a steep drop-off—not a complete ninety-degree angle, but it was still unsettling. But sitting next to Alex was anchor enough for her.

Rosalie took in the view, breathing in the hearty peace of the desert. She felt something flow through her body, something good and calm and nourishing. She breathed it in, wishing she could hold the feeling forever.

Marveling at it, Rosalie recognized what it was: gratitude. A sense of overwhelming awe for everything life had given her. She had a home, she had a loving partner, she had ambition, and she had hope.

She had finally learned what Gran had wanted to teach her. Gran's first lesson to her had been generosity; her final lesson had been gratitude. Rosalie felt her chest swell with it.

She closed her eyes and thought about Ashhawk. She thought of its sad, down-on-their-luck residents and her hope the warehouse would help them. She hoped Gran would approve of her choice.

As though providing an answer, she felt a gentle breeze on her face. She wondered if Alex had turned her head to look at her and she was simply feeling her breath, but it wasn't as warm as Alex would have been. There was something present there with her, and Rosalie bent her ear to it. Whether it was a spirit or angel or simply a thought borne of Rosalie's own heart didn't matter. Rosalie opened her eyes.

She took a breath, feeling the decision settle in her belly. It was good and right and warm. She took a few moments for herself before she said, "Gran wants to stay here."

"Yeah?" Alex said, the same peace Rosalie felt echoing in her voice.

"Yeah."

Alex held the box out toward Rosalie, and Rosalie took it.

For the first time, Rosalie opened the box. She wasn't sure what she would find, but it certainly wasn't a neat plastic bag filled with gray lumps.

The ashes weren't fine and silty like she'd expected. They were coarse in places, a few chunks of bone discernible through the bag. The ashes clumped together like the clay earth all around them.

Hesitantly, Rosalie opened the bag, taking it out of the box. She dipped her hand in the ashes, feeling the grit against her skin, lodging under her nails. She took a handful and held it out over the ledge. She let it fall like sand, a few flecks sticking to her shins and feet as they fell. She sprinkled handful after handful with growing certainty that this was what Gran would have wanted.

Alex didn't comment when her jeans became flecked with ash. She watched Rosalie somberly, stoically, following the bits of ash as they fell, the chunks of bone as they hopped and rolled down into the valley below.

Finally, Rosalie took the bag by the corners, tipping the rest of Gran out into the desert. She set the bag and empty box aside, tilting her head to rest on Alex's shoulder, letting her ash-covered hands rest in her lap. She was sad, but she was also peaceful. Alex kissed her hair before returning her gaze to the goldening land before them, reaching over to take one of Rosalie's ashy hands in her own.

"You ready to go back?"

"I want to sit here for a bit."

Alex turned her attention back to the land sprawled before them. It was quiet for a moment before Rosalie took a deep breath and let it out in a calm, satisfied sigh.

"You know how I told you on our first night at Corte del Cuervo that I didn't know where I was from?"

"Yeah."

Rosalie took another slow, peaceful breath. "I know now."

"Yeah?"

"Yeah."

Alex turned her head to look at Rosalie, but Rosalie kept her gaze set on the desert with its forgiving vastness. She stared out at it, giving Alex's hand a squeeze.

Alex smiled and turned her attention toward the landscape before them.

About the Author

Lily R. Mason started writing fan fiction for Louisa May Alcott's Little Women when she was eight years old. Since then, she's written everything from plays to poetry to trauma treatment protocols to novels to grant applications; the only written art to stump her to date is Twitter.

Lily has written books in a variety of genres, including her debut coming-of-age novel, Taking the Long Way, and its follow-up domestic drama, Me and You and Daisies. She explored multiple realities in Wherever the Dandelion Falls, and immersed herself in months of research for her historical fiction YA novel, Lilies of the Bowery, which was named one of the top five Lesbian YA Books of 2015 by AfterEllen. She was a featured presenter at ClexaCon 2017 where she gave a lecture on the difference between smut, sex, and love scenes in fiction.

Lily is a mental health provider, personal assistant, and author. She has BA in Psychology and an MS in Counseling and currently practices therapy in San Francisco's Bay Area. She's passionate about music education, cheese, and positive LGBT representation in media.

Other books by Sapphire Authors

Add Romance and Mix – ISBN – 978-1-948232-06-7

Briley Anderson hasn't been in a serious relationship for the past two years. The pain of her last breakup has made her weary of giving her heart away again. She spends her days flipping houses and her down-time baking treats for her neighbors. Falling in love wasn't in her plans, but then again, neither was her next-door neighbor.

Leah Daniels is a divorced mother of two and a grandmother at the age of forty-nine. Love was the last thing she was looking for, especially with a woman sixteen years her junior. All she was hoping for was a quiet neighborhood to raise her fifteen-year old son.

What she hadn't expected was the unavoidable draw she felt toward Briley.

Through laughter, heartache, love, and fear it's up to Briley and Leah to figure out if what they've created is strong enough to make a relationship last and if taking the chance on love is really worth the risk.

Reclaiming Yancy – ISBN – 978-1-948232-04-3

Her bossy best friend Roxie criticizes her risky behavior, and warns that she'd better shape up before something serious happens. Her socialite mother loves when she dresses properly, but laments that the clothes hang off her strong yet unhealthily lean body.

Colorado rancher Yancy Delaney is a woman grieving past losses, escaping her past by running from any commitment—except to her beloved horses and her work at Valley View, the rural medical organization her family founded.

Enter Dr. Genevieve Lambert, the hot new medical director of Valley View's rural clinics, where Yancy is Board Director. They immediately feel the sparks of attraction, but Gen wants no part of Yancy's seduction game or her reputation for casual one-nighters. And Yancy's missteps and risk-taking may finally be catching up with her, resulting in an injury to herself and a path of broken hearts left in her dust.

Gen and Yancy embark on a journey of romance fraught with rocky rides. Can they overcome their tough trails and find true love?

Highland Dew – ISBN – 978-1-948232-11-1

Bryce Andrews, west coast sales director for Global Distillers and Distribution, is tired of the corporate hamster wheel. She needs a change.

A craft whisky trade show offers her inspiration and a chance to revisit Scotland and the majestic scenery of the Speyside region—best known for the "Whisky Trail." Bryce and her coworker, Reggie Ballard, need to find a wholly original whisky for their international distribution division by visiting a number of small distillers.

A blind curve, a dangling sign, and weed-choked

driveway draw Bryce directly into a truly unique opportunity. She discovers a struggling family, a shuttered distillery, and a spitfire of a daughter called home to care for her confused father.

Fiona McDougall—the only child and heir to the MacDougall & Son legacy, had her career teaching in Edinburgh curtailed by fate...or serendipity.

When the stars finally align, the two women work together to resurrect a dream for themselves and the family business—if they can weather the storms of unscrupulous business practices in the competitive whisky market.

www.ingramcontent.com/pod-product-compliance
Lightning Source LLC
Chambersburg PA
CBHW020356260626
47156CB00007B/2137